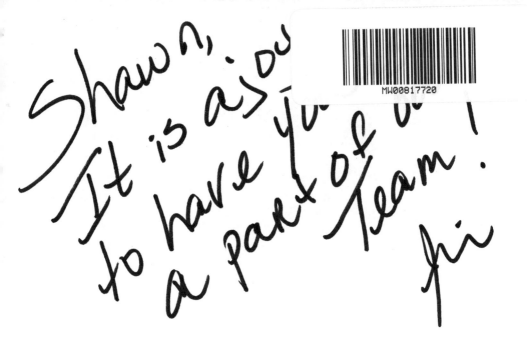

Shawn,
It is a joy
to have you
a part of our
Team!
Jim

ONCE YOU'VE TOUCHED THE HEART

ONCE YOU'VE TOUCHED THE HEART
By Iris Bolling

Siri Enterprises
Publishing Division

ISBN 978-0-9801066-0-2

Once You've Touched The Heart

Cover and book design by: *Judith R.E. Wansley*

Edited by: *Battinto Batts, Batts Communications*

Published by:
Siri Enterprises
Richmond, Virginia 23222

Website: *www.irisbolling.com*

Acknowledgements

To my Heavenly Father, Thank You.
To Raymond, thank you for putting up with me all these years. The best is yet to come.
To my mother, Evelyn, don't think you can really retire now; you have more research ahead of you.
To Turk, much love for you, big brother.
To LaFonde Harris and Gemma Mejias, thank you for being my sounding boards and I pray my telephone calls will never go unanswered.
To Valerie Johnson, Tanya Thompson and Rosaline Terry, do not ever learn restraint, stay real....
To Judith Wansley, Justin Wansley, Sakeitha Horton, Shannon Pilgrim and Sonya Marie, your generosity will never be forgotten.
To Linda Gordon, thank you for simply taking the time.
To the "HU" boys, Devin, Jarrell, Scott, and of course, Chris, you guys are the epitome of awesomeness.

To all of my readers, your wait is over. JD and Tracy have finally arrived. Thank you for your patience. Enjoy their story and the beginning of a saga of love, politics and intrigue that will lead to the White House...on Pennsylvania Avenue.

This book is dedicated to my son, Chris. Regardless of what life brings you, always believe in yourself.

Prologue

We all go through life wondering if the old saying is true, "God has a plan for everyone. He made that special someone just for you. All you have to do is be patient and wait for him to reveal that one person to you." We have no idea who that person may be, or if that person exists. Nevertheless, we go through life trying to find that someone to fulfill our meaning for life.

We go out with men and women who we know are not right for us. Like the guy who comes up to you in a club and says, "If your left thigh was Thanksgiving and your right thigh was Christmas, can I visit you in between the holidays?" You laugh, but end up dancing with the fool anyway. Yes, you are desperate. But you are also tired of being alone. Everyone around you seems to be going out and having a good time while you are sitting in the dorm room with a book on a Friday night. So which do you choose? Well, Tracy Alexandria Washington chose the book. The fool could spend the holidays by himself.

Tracy, the youngest of four children, was a quiet girl who spent most of her time in libraries. Any library would do; it didn't matter, as long as there were endless books. She could get lost in them forever. Books were a comfort and escape from the day-to-day drama in her life. As long as a library was open, Tracy had a safe haven.

Home was empty these days for her. None of the love and laughter that surrounded her as a child existed under the roof she once shared with her parents, two sisters and brother. Within the short time span of one summer, she lost her oldest sister Valerie to a husband; her brother Turk to the street life; her sister Joan died and her father—well, he just disappeared. Now, only Tracy and her mother, Lena, lived together; or more like existed under the same roof together. It seemed Tracy was always doing something to upset her mother, so she stayed away as much as possible.

Tracy never really knew what happened to her sister Joan and did not see her sister Valerie too often, but her brother Turk would come by to check on her. Turk spent time teaching her things, like dancing, shooting pool or hitting three pointers on the basketball court. He gave Tracy the love and guidance she believed her father would have given, if he were home.

For some reason Lena blamed Tracy for her dad leaving and acted as if she hated the sight of her. Tracy was young and didn't understand. For a while she tried everything she could to make her mom love her again, but it didn't work. By the time Tracy reached high school, she simply gave up. She put all her time into studying to earn scholarships for college. Turk said he would help her if she did well in school. Tracy never asked how, but Turk always had money to do things. Therefore, if he said she could go to college, she believed him.

Tracy graduated from high school with honors and received scholarships, but not enough to attend Harmon University. But, true to his word, Turk was there in her time of need. You see, Harmon was a private university where, not all, but most girls went with the hope of meeting the next basketball player heading to the NBA, or maybe the next NFL prospect anticipating a signing bonus. Tracy, on the other hand, wanted to go there because it was away from home and it had an excellent five-year MBA program. The tuition was extremely high, but the biggest obstacle was the up-front cash needed to get in. Her scholarship money would not post to her account until later in the semester. Tracy had no idea where the money she needed was going to come from. But Harmon University was where she wanted to go. She didn't know why, but in her heart she knew that was the only school for her.

Jeffrey Daniel Harrison, better known to all as JD, was an assistant district attorney with the city of Richmond, which had one of the highest per capita murder rates in the country. Most of the murders were gang related. The city was where he wanted to be. JD wanted to help clean up the city that his father lost his life protecting. His father died at the hands of a 14-year-old gang member. Now JD was responsible for the family his father left behind. Even though they were financially stable, it was up to him to keep the family united. His father would say to him, "No matter what, make sure you always take care of your family."

James and Martha Harrison raised their children in a very loving environment. They would get their children up on Sunday mornings, have breakfast, and then head off to Sunday school and church. Afterwards, family and friends would come over for dinner. Both parents, or at the very least one parent, would be at every game JD had or at every recital Ashley, his little sister, performed. His parents had a strong sense of family and community values, and they showed it. As a police officer James Harrison was looked upon as the authority figure to the fatherless boys in the neighborhood. He tried to intervene whenever he saw one of the boys going in what one may call "the wrong direction." Martha Harrison always had food on the table for the hungry and a pleasant word for anyone in need. JD and Ashley were raised to help others less fortunate than themselves. It was just a way of life for them. JD understood this and accepted the responsibility of looking out for others at a very young age. When his little sister would get into fights in school, usually for taking up for someone else, he would go to the school and argue her case until the principal simply got tired and gave in. Afterwards, he would go home and try to argue Ashley's case with his mom; but that was a lost cause. Martha Harrison did not care who Ashley was taking up for, fighting was not the way to do it.

JD always had many friends. For some reason people always liked him; but none more than "the boys," his friends Calvin, Brian and Douglas. They had been with him through the high school basketball championships, the football games and many other escapades that probably should never be mentioned. Calvin graduated from law school along with JD. He was the one voice of reason; he would get the boys to think about their actions before they got into trouble. Brian, who joined the FBI after college, was the protector. If you wanted a piece of the boys you had to go through him first. Douglas was the oldest and the one with the business mind. He started a promotional company after high school and now owned one of the most exclusive clubs in the city. JD could turn to any one of them in any situation and he knew they would have his back. To them, he was the one each of them looked up to for answers to just about every question. If you asked them, each would say, "That boy is going to run the country one day." Whether it was business, law or women, they were there for each other.

Women: now that was one area where JD never seemed to have a problem. They seemed to come out of the woodwork for him. He never allowed any one woman to get too close. He had career plans to move up in the district attorney's office. His focus was to eliminate or at the very least reduce gang activity in the city. It was the only way he knew to honor his dad's life. There was no time for the drama women brought with them. Whenever his current girlfriend began with the drama, he would let her go. In a nice way, of course, but she had to go.

Presently, JD's problem was convincing the admissions counselor that his little sister was Harmon University material. Her grades were fine, as were her S.A.T. scores. However, the extracurricular activities that had landed her on the suspension list in high school more than once was not quite what Harmon University was looking for in a potential student. But Ashley had her heart set on Harmon, since some of her friends were going there. She begged JD to get her in. He was usually firm with women, but when it came to his little sister he could not say no. Fortunately for her, the admission counselor was a female. He worked his magic and got Ashley in at the last minute. Little did JD know, it was more his destiny for Ashley to be at Harmon than it was hers.

Chapter 1

On the day Tracy was scheduled to leave for Harmon she did not have the money needed for the initial payment. But Turk told her to pack her things, so she did, and he drove her to Harmon University. Knowing she was going to school strictly on financial aid and scholarships, Tracy prayed when the *campus by sea*, as it was referred to in Tidewater, came into view, she would be allowed to register, (no up front cash, no entrance).

Well, Tracy's prayers were answered. Turk made the initial cash payment; made sure she had a room assignment and gave her cash to open a bank account. She was so overwhelmed that something good was happening in her life, she never asked where the money came from. Turk had given her a chance to make something of herself. She remembered his words to her, "I got you out. Make me proud baby girl and stay out." Turk turned to leave and for some reason, Tracy had a feeling they may not see each other for a while. She ran over and hugged him, "Thank you, Turk. I won't disappoint you."

He grabbed her around her neck and ruffled her hair. "Bye Sugie." He smiled and then walked away.

When Tracy moved her things into her assigned dorm room, her roommate had already moved in. While she was arranging her clothes, someone knocked on the door. She opened the door and there were two girls standing there.

"Hey, is Ashley here?" one asked.

"No, I'm not sure who Ashley is," Tracy said with a smile, "but she's not here."

"Well, tell her Cynthia and Rosaline came by."

"Okay," Tracy said and closed the door. "Oh, I hope my roommate is not like them." One had been drop-dead gorgeous, like Vanessa

Williams, face, hair, body, the works. The other one was pretty too, just in a different way. She was shorter, with a short stylish haircut, chestnut brown skin, and very shapely.

Tracy knew coming to Harmon that she was not going to fit in with the "in" crowd. The girls on this campus were the cream of the crop. There were very few who could not be on any page of a fashion magazine or in somebody's video. In Tracy's mind she did not fit in that group. *Oh well, that's not why I'm here,* Tracy thought as she continued to set up her room.

Tracy had crawled under her bed to run the cable cord to the 27" flat panel television Turk brought, so the cord would not be seen by visitors, when the door opened.

"Hey, you must be Tracy."

Tracy hit her head as she was trying to get out from under the bed."Hi," Tracy replied, smiling as she beat the dust off her jeans. "Yeah, I'm Tracy."

"I'm Ashley. I guess we are roommates."

"Looks that way."

Ashley sat on the bed. "Do you need some help with your things?" she asked Tracy.

"No, this is it."

Ashley giggled. "I think I brought everything from my room at home and some more. My brother said he was not bringing one more thing up to this room. Did I leave you enough space for your things?"

"I'm good," Tracy replied. She was not used to talking this much to anyone. "Two girls came by looking for you earlier."

Ashley sucked in her lip. "That would be Cynthia and Rosaline."

"Yeah, that's who it was."

"I was kind of hoping they wouldn't find me this soon. Oh, well, I'll deal with them later; I'm late for registration."

Tracy looked at her watch. "Me too."

"Come on." Ashley grabbed her hand. "Let's go."

Ashley talked the whole time they were walking, while Tracy listened and answered whenever she had to. Ashley seemed different from her friends. Just like the other girls, Ashley had the kind of beauty that you would see in the center of *Jet* magazine. Her skin tone was peanut butter brown. She had silky, shoulder length hair. Her figure was one men dream of, standing five feet eight inches and 130 pounds or so, with long legs that had a graceful and confident stride. This girl could wear anything, or nothing at all, and it would still look good on her. She had the look of a fly girl—the ones that are so cute they can't be touched—but without the attitude. Ashley smiled and had a pleasant comment for everyone she encountered. It was easy to be around Ashley and Tracy liked her immediately, although she felt insignificant standing next to this girl.

Ashley's two friends came into the hall where late registration was being held. Ashley introduced them to Tracy. When Tracy said hello, Cynthia looked at her as if she were nonexistent. "Whatever," she said, then turned her back and continued talking to Ashley. The other one, Rosaline, said, "Girl, pay her no mind, and it's nice to meet you."

Tracy took a step back to allow them space to talk. The two were telling Ashley about people on campus.

"Look, I'll have to catch you guys later. Right now I have to register for these classes," Ashley said as she turned back to Tracy.

"I'm sorry. Cynthia is just like that. Come on; let's get this English class straight."

The only English class still open was one being instructed by a Professor Wood. Ashley asked the girl helping with registration, "Why is this class so empty?"

The girl replied, "Professor Wood is really good, but does not take any nonsense from his students. If you take his class you will work and learn or you will not pass."

Ashley turned to Tracy. "I ain't scared of him... Are you?"

"The correct phrase would be," Tracy replied, "'I am not scared of him,' and no, I ain't *scarrrrred* of him either, bring him on..."

Ashley laughed as they registered for the class. "I sure hope you are good at English, 'cause I can't fail a class my first semester."

Tracy smiled. "I got your back."

That's how it was throughout their time at Harmon: Ashley had Tracy's back and Tracy had Ashley's back. Not even Ashley's friends were able to penetrate the bond the two of them developed during their time at Harmon. As for Ashley's friends, Tracy liked both of them, but she did not fit into Cynthia's idea of a Harmon girl. To Cynthia, Tracy was from the wrong side of the tracks and did not belong. She referred to Tracy often as "the wannabe from the projects." Tracy's family did not come from money and no one was involved in politics, law, medicine or any other influential career. In addition to that, Tracy was not fly girl material; she did not act, look or dress the part.

Tracy was not hard on the eyes by any stretch of the imagination. She was 5 foot 6, 125 pounds, with a smooth paper bag brown complexion, and very curvy, but no one would ever know it. Tracy's entire wardrobe consisted of jeans, big white tee shirts and Nike Air Force One sneakers. She had all the right equipment, but just did not know how to display it. She was what the guys would dub "what if." What if she dressed differently? Or, what if she got her hair styled? But those surface issues did not faze Tracy. Her goal was to get a degree in business administration, start her own business by the age of 21 and be on her way to Oprah-rich by 30. She did not have time to be concerned with makeup, clothes, partying or men. Her objective was making enough money to never have to go home to live again. Her objective was about to change. She was about to meet Ashley's brother, JD.

JD was on his way to being a major player in politics, whether he wanted to be or not. Every other week he was in the news for one case or another. Whenever he was out partying, there was always a beautiful woman at his side. But what available woman wouldn't be? JD was 6 foot 4 and 240 pounds of pure chocolate with thighs as solid as a horse's back. The man's body would make any pair of jeans look good and a tailored suit even better. His face was handsome, with deep brown eyes that seemed to make love to you every time they looked your way, dimples deep enough to stick your tongue in and lips so thick you could suck on them for days.

Currently JD was seeing Vanessa, a local model looking to make it big or to marry someone who had made it. The relationship wasn't serious. JD was concentrating on his career.

His passion was making people lives a little easier, especially neighborhood kids. His goal was to eliminate gangs and to give kids a chance to make something of their lives. He didn't care what, just something, but he wanted it to be their choice. He believed gangs took that choice away from kids at a very early age, and before they knew any better, it was too late to change. The only way to escape was to be put behind bars or in a grave.

When JD solved gang-related cases it made everyone look good. The DA's office up to the governor's office, Republicans and Democrats, they all noticed. Both political parties wanted to claim him as one of their own. Unfortunately for the political powerhouses, JD was his own man and could not be swayed. People respected him because of that. Some politicians wished they had that trait, and police officers loved a DA who could not be influenced.

As for JD's street credibility, that came on the heels of his cases. The word on the street was simple. If you made a deal with Harrison, he stuck by it, no surprises. There were no head games. If he got your case, before he went into court, he had you. The man hated to lose. He was fair. He would tell you what he had, and say, "You can deal now or we can deal in court, your choice." Of course a few dumb brothers tried him and ended up with forty to life. They learned the hard way that JD Harrison was the real deal in court and he took no prisoners.

At this point in his life, JD had no idea what was about to happen to him. He had not met nor ever heard of Tracy Washington. But from the moment they met, their life was on a collision course going full speed. Neither of them saw it coming until it happened.

Chapter 2

Jeffrey was 24 years old and Tracy was 19 when they first met. It was spring break, sophomore year at Harmon University, and Ashley had plans for the entire week. If you live on campus, the freedom is hard to give up when you go home. It was no different for Ashley. Realizing her party time would be seriously limited at her mom's house, she begged JD to let her spend the time at his house. Remembering those days, and not being able to say no to his little sister, JD convinced their mom to let Ashley spend her break with him. Ashley invited Tracy to join her. Since the library on campus was closed during the break, Tracy did not have to work, so she accepted.

Since their father's death, JD had been more than just a brother; he was also a father figure to Ashley. He gave her a key to his condo to make sure she knew he was always available to her. With keys in hand and Tracy at her side, it was good-bye to the campus, at least for one week.

The ride to Richmond was about an hour. As always, Ashley talked about JD. She talked about him so much, Tracy felt she already knew him. JD and Ashley had the type of relationship Tracy wished she had with her brother. She knew without a doubt that Turk loved her and would always be there when she needed him. But she didn't get to see him that often. He would show up whenever things were crazy at home just to reassure her that things would be alright.

When she won awards at school, he was the only one from her family there. But he never stayed. When things happened with Ashley, the entire family showed up. Her mom, brother, the uncles, aunts and cousins, all made an appearance. Tracy longed to have that, but was thankful for what she did have with Turk.

"Wait until you see JD's condo," Ashley said, ending Tracy's thoughts. "He has everything in there."

"Why do they call apartments 'condos'?" Tracy asked.   "Whether you are paying rent or mortgage, you still connected to someone else's home. In my book, that's an apartment."

The question was answered as they entered the condo. JD's home was 2,400 square feet of luxury. Tracy swore her whole house in Norfolk could fit inside. The three-bedroom condo was tastefully furnished with every comfort imaginable, from the 52-inch plasma television hanging opposite the fireplace to the double-door master suite at the end of the hallway. It was impressive.

Ashley went into the bedroom and dropped her bags on the floor. "A whole week of freedom and parties. Oh, don't let me forget to call my mom every day and go to church on Sunday. It's your job to make sure I do that, or JD will never forgive me for the blessing out he will get."

Tracy put her bag in the room and dropped her books on the dresser. "Okay, what's the plan for the week?"

"Well, JD normally works late and goes out after work with his friend Calvin. Then on the weekend, he is usually with the flavor of the week. So first we are going by my house to keep Mama satisfied and tonight we are going to the club with Cynthia."

"Hold up, you expect me to hang with you, Cynthia and Rosaline? I don't think so."

"Oh, come on, Tracy. You said you would help me with this week. You know I need this break. And besides, it wouldn't hurt you to get out a little."

"You know Cynthia will dog me out all week. Why would you make me deal with that?"

"You don't have to talk to Cynthia. You can hang with Rosaline and me."

"Like that has ever stopped her before. Ashley, Cynthia doesn't like me very much. I am not in the mood to be put down the whole week. Besides, I have some studying I need to do."

"Okay, Tracy, I tell you what. If you go out with us tonight, I will make sure you have a good time, and if you don't, I won't make you go out with us again."

"You know, I could have easily stayed in a hotel near campus this week and would not have to deal with your uppity friend."

"I know you could have, but you love me like a sister and would not subject me to another spring break at home with my mom. I love her. However, I need to get busy and have some fun this week. Come on, Tracy, do this for me," Ashley pleaded.

"I got you covered," Tracy reluctantly replied.

"Good. On Sunday we will have dinner at my mom's house," Ashley said with a smile.

"Girl, if she cooks some corn pudding, I am there."

"I heard that, Mama can throw down." Ashley cleared her throat, "Umm, Thursday, David is having a little get-together at his house and I think I may drop in."

"Ashley, tell me you are not talking about David Holt."

"The one and only."

"The man has a girlfriend and is old."

"Old! David is older, not old, and he's not married."

"Ashley, he is committed to somebody."

"Okay, I understand that. I am just going to see how he's doing."

"You need to let that one go."

"I know. But I can't just yet," she replied sadly.

"I'm sorry, Ashley. I wish things were different." Tracy consoled her friend.

After a minute of silence, Ashley smiled. "Well, don't worry about me. I know how to go out and have fun with other people. Now what's your excuse?"

This was not a subject Tracy wanted to get into again. "I have to study."

"Tracy, you have to learn how to live. Loosen up, you know; have some fun. Maybe get a man." Ashley smirked.

"Yeah, right, like somebody is going to look at me."

Ashley did not understand what Tracy saw in the mirror when she looked in, but Ashley saw a pretty girl. Tracy had those eyes that pull you in, and when she smiled her whole face would light up. She knew arguing with Tracy about her looks was a moot point. *I'll fix that later*, Ashley thought.

"Well, I am young, sexy as hell and hungry. Let's go to the kitchen and raid the refrigerator."

Tracy smiled. "A refrigerator full of food—a college student's best friend." The two laughed.

For the past two years, Ashley had shared the adventures of JD and his women with Tracy, so not much would surprise her about him—or so she thought. The two girls were in the kitchen preparing dinner. Tracy put steaks on the George Foreman grill and sautéed green peppers and onions. Ashley baked potatoes in the microwave and threw together a salad. Within a matter of minutes they were seated at the breakfast bar throwing down. When the door to the condo opened, Ashley hopped up, ran and jumped in her brother's arms full speed.

"Hey, big brother, what's up?" JD had no choice but to catch her before they both fell.

Tracy sat there motionless. A GOD of a man walked through the door in a suit and tie. He was a tall, dark brother with a body that was built for riding. JD was fine.... In her wildest dreams, Tracy could never imagine a man like this existed. She tried to close her mouth, but couldn't, not before he noticed.

"Don't worry," JD smiled. "She hasn't gone crazy. She always acts like that when she comes home."

Tracy began to laugh, not at what he said, but at the fact that this man actually spoke to her. He dropped Ashley to the floor and walked towards her. He put out his hand. "Hi, I'm Ashley's brother Jeffrey, and you must be Tracy."

Oh God, he said her name—talk girl, talk.... "Yes, I am, it's nice to meet you," Tracy replied.

Ashley looked at Tracy as if surprised by what she said or maybe how she said it. Either way, Tracy had no idea why Ashley looked at her that way, so Tracy gave her one of those "what" looks. Ashley went into the kitchen behind JD.

"What have you guys been cooking? It smells good in here."

"We fixed some for you. Grab a plate and a Heineken," Ashley smiled with pride.

JD did just that; sat, bowed his head to say grace, and then began to eat. JD and Ashley talked non-stop for what seemed like hours. Tracy sat there, listened and remembered how much she missed her talks with Turk.

Later that evening, after visiting her mom, Ashley and Tracy were dressing to go out. JD and his boy Calvin Johnson were in the living room watching a basketball game on television. Ashley walked out of the bedroom with a red body-hugging dress on, looking too grown for JD. Calvin, who was sitting on the couch with his back to the bedrooms, saw JD's expression and turned just as Ashley walked into the room. Calvin watched Ashley walk from the bedroom, through the living room and into the kitchen without blinking.

He turned to JD. "Man, you can't let her go out looking like that. I love her like a little sister and my mind is wandering. What the hell you think the dogs gonna do?"

JD could not say anything. This was his baby sister, who wore jeans and cut-off tops most of the time. Now she was in the dress every dog liked to see.

"Ashley, where are you going tonight?" JD asked as inconspicuously as possible.

"To Jazzy's with Cynthia and Rosaline," she replied. "What about you guys? Are you staying in?"

Not anymore, JD thought. "We'll be out and about," he replied.

He did not want to be the bad guy and tell her she couldn't go out. That's the whole reason she didn't want to stay home this weekend. After all, she was nineteen about to turn twenty and should be able to go out and have fun. But did she have to dress like that?

Before he could finish his thought, Tracy walked out of the bedroom and took the same path as Ashley. JD's first thought was, *Who in the hell was this woman coming out of one of his bedrooms and why wasn't he in there with her?* Tracy was wearing Ashley's little black dress, which would have been short on Ashley, but fell just above the knees on Tracy. Tracy was thicker than Ashley and the dress showed every curve in her body, and man, did she have a body. Her bare legs were very shapely and smooth in the three-inch black strapped sandals. With her hair pinned up she looked more sophisticated than Ashley. Tracy walked past the guys into the kitchen. The dress revealed a bare back and the full curve of her behind.

Damn, JD thought as he watched Tracy's every move.

"Ashley," Tracy called out, oblivious to the reactions of JD or Calvin, "I think this dress is too tight. Do I really have to go?"

Ashley grabbed Tracy's arm and stopped her in front of JD. "JD, please tell her she looks fine in this dress," she begged.

Ashley turned Tracy around as if modeling the dress. JD looked at Calvin, then back to Tracy.

That had to be a trick question, he thought. "Hmm yeah, you do look good in that dress," he responded, nodding his head in approval.

"Do another turn for me. I, I haven't decided yet." Calvin held a thoughtful gaze. "Yep, yep I agree you look good in that dress." He beamed the response.

"Thank you, Calvin," Ashley sighed, giving Tracy an exasperated look.

Tracy smiled shyly. "That was nice of you," she said, then walked out of the room embarrassed.

JD hit Calvin on the head. "Man, that's a teenager," he said as if scolding him.

"Okay, let's go, before you wimp out on me," Ashley said, pushing Tracy towards the door.

"Hold on Ashley," Tracy begged, feeling uncomfortable about the dress. "I need to get a jacket."

"Yes, Lord, please put a jacket over that dress," JD pleaded quietly.

Tracy went in the room and put on a blazer. "Okay," she sighed, "we can go now."

Calvin and JD tried to refocus on the game after the girls left. They both sat there for a moment. "Teenagers; jail bait." They both laughed.

Knowing what he prowled for in the clubs, there was no way JD was going to let these two out of his sight tonight. "Calvin, we are going to Jazzy's."

"I'm with you. But you realize Jazzy's is an underage club. I will have to wear a disguise; I have a reputation to protect."

That Sunday, as promised, JD, Ashley and Tracy went to church and then to Mama Harrison's house for dinner. Sunday dinner at Martha's house was always lively and crowded. The whole Harrison family and friends gathered for dinner, including their minister, Pastor Smith, and his wife. Tracy wasn't used to crowds and this one was a bit much for her. Therefore, she spent most of the day in the kitchen. With that many people coming and going there were always dishes to wash. Ashley was visiting with family in the den and JD was out back playing a pick-up game of basketball with his cousins. When Martha came into the kitchen with Pastor Smith, she saw Tracy washing dishes.

"Child, why are you still in here? Why don't you come out and meet some of the family?" Martha encouraged.

"I thought I would try to knock out some of these dishes so you won't have too many to clean later," Tracy replied.

"Well, thank you, honey, but you are a guest. You don't have to work."

"Oh, I don't mind helping. You want me to get that for you?" she asked, referring to the bowl Martha had in her hand.

"No, I can get this. Will you get those glasses the boys left on the table?" she asked, pointing to the patio.

"Yes ma'am," Tracy replied.

"My, my," Pastor Smith said, "a teenager with manners; you don't see that too often."

"Yes, she's a sweet girl," Martha replied. "That's Ashley's roommate from college. Kind of a quiet girl."

Just as Tracy went out the back door a basketball came straight at her. "Heads up!" someone yelled. Tracy caught the ball, bounced it a few times and made a jump shot from where she stood.

"Whoa!" the group yelled.

"I think the idea is to put the ball through the hoop, like that," she teased. Tracy picked up the glasses and went back into the house.

JD hit one of his cousins on the back of his head. "Another shot like that and I'm putting her on the team."

Tracy was finishing the glasses while Martha was talking to Pastor Smith. JD came in from the game and grabbed a bottle of water from the refrigerator.

"Had enough, son?" Pastor Smith teased.

"Yeah, I think I am done for the night."

"Exercise is good for the soul," Pastor Smith replied laughing. "It keeps you young."

JD's Uncle Joe, who was always loud and had to let everyone in the state know he was there, entered the kitchen. "Hey, what y'all doing up in here?"

The loud voice frightened Tracy. She froze. The glass she was holding fell to the floor and shattered. JD noticed her reaction to Uncle Joe—or was it his voice?

"I'm, I'm sorry," she stammered.

"What's wrong with you, gal!" Uncle Joe yelled.

"Joe," Martha said with a scowl, "stop scaring the girl. Honey, it's okay, it's just a glass. I have too many glasses anyway." She laughed.

Tracy still had not moved. It appeared to JD she was holding her breath as if waiting for something else to happen.

"What do you need, Uncle Joe?" JD asked.

"A piece of that cake," he grinned. As Joe stepped towards the table, Tracy stepped backward, but there was nowhere to go; her back was to the sink.

JD picked up the cake. "Here you go, Uncle Joe. Take this with you and I'll bring some plates."

"Alright now, that's what I'm talking 'bout," Uncle Joe replied as he left the kitchen happy.

JD, Martha and Pastor Smith looked at each other. Once Uncle Joe was out of the kitchen, Tracy seemed to relax. She bent down and started picking up the shattered glass.

"Mrs. Harrison, I am so sorry about this. I will replace it tomorrow."

JD got the broom and dustpan out of the closet.

"I'll take that," Tracy said, taking the broom out of his hands. "I have a tendency to be a little clumsy," she smiled weakly.

"JD, why don't you take some plates out to Joe before he comes back in here," Martha suggested.

JD handed Tracy the dustpan. "You alright, Tracy?" he asked.
"Yeah," she replied, shrugging her shoulder, "just a little clumsy."

JD picked up the plates and left the kitchen.

At JD's house later that night, he couldn't sleep. It was about two in the morning and as always when he was involved in a case he had sleepless nights. Tonight was no different. He had lost two cases and did not want this one to be the third. His mind was distracted not only by the prep work he had to do in the morning, but by the nagging feeling that he was missing something with the case. He hated losing and knew this would be another loss if he took the case to court in its present state. JD got out of bed and headed to the kitchen. He noticed a light was on in there. He walked around the counter and saw Tracy sitting at the table reading and eating a slice of cake.

"Why are you up this late?" he asked with a frown.

Tracy jerked her head up from the book and began to get up. "I'm sorry. I didn't mean to wake you," she said.

"No, sit down. You don't have to leave and you didn't wake me." He smiled; it seemed he had unnerved her.   "What are you reading?"

"*Quantitative Measures,*" she answered.

"For one of your classes?"

"No, I have to take it next semester."

JD frowned with a look of confusion and then smiled. "You're reading a book for a class you're taking next semester?"

She blushed. "I've finished my books for this semester."

"Okay." JD laughed.

Tracy got up to put her glass in the sink and was about to scrape the rest of her cake into the trash. "Hey, hold up. Let me have that."

She looked at him. "What, the cake?"

"Yeah, that's good cake," he exclaimed.

She smiled and handed the cake to him. He stepped towards her and reached into the drawer to get a fork, then sat at the other end of the table. Tracy began to pick up her books to leave.

"Stay and talk to me a minute," he said. Not giving her a chance to refuse, he continued. "I see you have form—who taught you to play ball?" He pointed to the chair for her to sit; she did.

"My brother," she replied.

"Are you that good or was that just a lucky shot?"

"I got game," she boasted with a smile.

JD noticed her eyes sparkled when she smiled. He laughed. "Oh, you do?"

"A little," she replied.

"Do you play at school?"

"No."

"With a jumper like that, why not?"

She put her head to the side. "Practice would interfere with school."

"Oh, so you're an intellectual?" JD asked, nodding as he continued to eat the cake.

"No, well, maybe." She thought about it. "I am guided more by intellect than emotions."

"Humm, really. That would mean you are very rational." He took a bite of cake. "You know, it seemed like Uncle Joe scared you tonight."

Tracy pulled her legs up into the chair, wrapped her arms around them, and laid her chin on her knees as JD talked. "Your reaction did not appear to be very rational. Uncle Joe is loud and usually wrong, but he's innocent enough. He wouldn't hurt a fly."

"No one is completely innocent. Everyone has a propensity for violence given the right circumstances," Tracy replied sharply.

JD's eyebrows went up and his eyes widened, surprised by her answer. "So you believe people have a natural inclination to be violent. They actually prefer to be that way?" he asked.

"I think people are given free will. If they can do things and get away with it, they will. And yes, I do believe most people have the inclination to do bad versus good."

Before JD could respond, Ashley walked in and pulled up a chair. "What are you two doing up?" *Why would a person so young think the worst of people,* JD thought.   "Hey! Just talking," JD replied.

"You got anymore of that cake?" Ashley asked.

"In the refrigerator," Tracy replied.

Ashley got up to get a slice of cake. "So what y'all talking about?"

"The propensity for violence," JD answered.

"Whew, so deep so late at night," Ashley said with a sigh as she sat down with her cake.

"Tracy was telling me she believes people would choose to be bad versus good," JD explained.

"I agree to a certain extent," Ashley responded as she put a fork full of cake into her mouth.

"Really," JD replied puzzled, "why?"

"Well, it's easier. Being good is hard work. Hell, you should know that, JD."

"Oh really, why?" JD asked as he smiled at his sister.

"Haven't there been times when you would prefer to break the law rather than uphold it?"

"No."

"Of course there are," Tracy commented.

"You think so?" JD curiously asked.

"Sure, you may not want to admit it. But if given the right circumstance you would consider it, simply because it's easier," Tracy responded.

"I believe the justice system is our check and balance to deter people from doing wrong. Don't you believe in the justice system?"

"Tracy doesn't trust or believe in too many people, and definitely not the justice system," Ashley offered.

Hmm, Tracy thought, *a man who doesn't run away from a serious conversation.* "The justice system is as good as the people in it," she said. "If you have a corrupt judge, is justice being served?"

"Valid argument, but I choose to believe that a corrupt judge or anyone else in the system that is corrupt would eventually be brought to justice. I believe in our justice system."

Ashley sat there and looked from JD to Tracy. She had never heard Tracy talk this much to anyone but her. *And JD seems to be into this debate. Hmm, interesting,* she thought.

"As you should," Tracy said, "because you represent that system. But, unless you truly possess an uncompromising disposition, which is very unusual, you will have the propensity to be corrupt."

"Well, Tracy you lose on that one," Ashley said with cake in her mouth and pointing her fork at Tracy. "JD is the most uncompromising person on earth. He has his sense of right and wrong that doesn't waver. That's why he pisses so many people off."

Feeling a need to change the subject, as engaging as it was, JD smiled and hit Ashley on the nose. "What are you doing up so early, Squirt?"

Ashley laughed. "No one has called me that since I left home. I got up looking for this one," she answered, pointing to Tracy.

Tracy smiled.

"She was keeping me company," JD explained with a smile.

"What's wrong? Can't sleep?"

"Nope, my propensity for violence was keeping me awake," he said while smiling at Tracy.

Ashley laughed and Tracy smiled. JD liked that smile.

"A big case?" Ashley asked.

"Yeah, I have to prep the case tomorrow and we're not ready. I feel like we are missing something," JD replied with a sigh.

"You know," Ashley said with a devilish grin, "Tracy is really good with research and organization if you need some help."

"Really?" JD asked with a questioning expression.

"Yep," Ashley replied.

A little more relaxed now, Tracy stood up. "Well, now that Ashley has volunteered me for work I guess I should go to bed and get some rest."

Ashley smiled. "I'm always glad to find something for you to do besides reading."

"I like reading," Tracy replied.

"Bring your cases home," Ashley laughed. "She'll have all of them read and memorized by morning."

"I'll be happy to help with your case if you need it," Tracy said to JD.

"Thank you. I might take you up on that."

"Good night," Tracy said and left the room.

"Ashley," JD asked, "what's the deal with her?"

"She's good people; actually, the best."

"I'm sure she is," JD responded, "but where's she from, what's her story?"

"I don't know."

"Does she have family around here?"

"Just a brother who I know of. She doesn't deal with anyone else in her family."

"Why not?"

"I don't know. But I don't think things were good at home," Ashley added.

"Why you say that?"

"Cuz she never goes home."

"Where does she go during the summer?"

"Well, last summer she rented an efficiency and worked near campus."

"What about the holidays?"

"Same thing."

"That sounds like a lonely life."

"I know. But she is really a very sweet person, once you get to know her. And the girl is deep. I mean, she is like some type of freaking genius or something."

A few days later, after he had turned his case files over to Tracy and Ashley, JD came home to find Ashley, Cynthia and Rosaline on his balcony dancing and laughing. He smiled at the scene, but didn't interrupt. He was a little thankful to have a few minutes to himself. He had stayed the night with a friend and did not get much sleep. Turning towards his bedroom he heard singing coming from his office. Walking towards the sound, he looked inside and the vision made him smile. Tracy was inside the office lying on her stomach with a laptop in front of her. Her feet were up in the air swinging back and forth. She had on a pair of jeans, a white tee shirt and a pair of sneakers. Her hair was in a ponytail and she had on earphones. It was good to see her like this. The Uncle Joe incident and the information Ashley shared about Tracy disturbed him. Here she looked like a typical college student with no concerns or worries in life. It seemed like she was in her own world really enjoying herself.

"Got you," she gleefully said. "You were trying to evade me, but I got you." She was talking to her computer. "Now let's see if you work."

JD stepped back so she would not see him as she went to his computer and started keying.

"Okay, transfer." She spoke to the computer. The computer responded to her command and she smiled. *Damn, she was beautiful;*

her face lit up when she smiled, he thought. She was wide-eyed with excitement, for whatever she just did to his computer worked.

"Yes, victorious." She jumped up. "Thank you, thank you, thank you."

JD could not contain himself any longer. He started laughing and stepped into the room. "What on earth are you doing?"

Tracy stood there smiling at him. *She should smile all the time,* he thought.

She removed her headphones, turned the music off.; put her hands on her hips. "Well, Jeffrey, your office and computer are now ready for you."

"Really? You seem rather pleased with what you have accomplished."

"Oh, it's good." She replied excitedly. "We switched some things around so your flow will be a little smoother."

"Is that important?"

"Heck yeah, if you are trying to work with time frames, a smooth operation is always important. We put your case files on your computer. Now you have electronic and paper files." Tracy walked over and grabbed him by the arm. "Now your files can communicate with each other."

"OK?" he said, not knowing why she was excited by that.

She stepped back, crossed her arms in front of her and sighed. "You don't get it do you?"

JD leaned back in his chair. "No, not really. Do you care to explain?"

"Okay," she said and leaned across the desk in front of him. "Try to keep up; this is going to go fast." She explained, "Every file you have with one of three common elements will appear at the same time.

As she explained the adjustments, he could see her eyes were lit up with excitement. Her smile was so contagious; he couldn't help but smile back. *A man could get lost in those eyes,* he thought. Forcing himself to look away, he turned to the computer. "Well, let's see what I have missed."

Tracy stood up, suddenly feeling uncomfortable. "Well, my job is done here. I've conquered," she boasted proudly while picking up her laptop and other items. "Now I must depart and leave you to your work."

He smiled at her as she was leaving the room. "Thank you, Squirt Two."

"You're welcome, Jeffrey," she replied and walked out of the room. He started to tell her to call him JD, but changed his mind. *That's a beautiful young woman; intelligent, too.* He shook his head. *No,' girl.' She's a young girl,* he repeated to himself, *very young girl. Clear your mind.* JD turned back to the computer and started to open one file, when a name popped out at him. "That must be wrong, they can't be related." He opened the file and read for a moment. Stunned with his findings, he picked up the phone to call Calvin.

About two hours later, Tracy, Ashley and Rosaline were cooking while Cynthia was sitting at the table in the kitchen talking. JD and Calvin came out of the office smiling. JD walked over, picked Tracy up, hugged her and kissed her on the cheek.

"Thank you, Squirt Two," he said, smiling as he set her down.

He and Calvin left the condo. Ashley and Rosaline were smiling at Tracy as Cynthia exclaimed, "What the hell just happened here? Did JD just walk past me to kiss her?"

"Yeah, that's what he did," Ashley answered laughing.

"Bust your bubble," Rosaline joined in.

Tracy stood there with her head down, afraid to move; she thought her knees would buckle beneath her.

"Well, like I was saying, Cynthia, the probability of you ever getting that man is slim to none." Tracy continued with the conversation they were previously having. She turned toward the stove and kept on cooking. Tracy's back was to Cynthia and Rosaline, but Ashley could see the blush that came over her.

In court that Friday, JD not only received the conviction on the case, but also secured two additional arrest warrants, thanks to Tracy. That Saturday JD and Calvin took the girls out to celebrate their victory and the girls' last night of freedom before heading back to campus.

At the club the music was pumping, and everyone including Tracy seemed to be having a good time. They took turns dancing with each other, but whenever JD and Tracy danced, Cynthia would give attitude. She had this thing for JD and hated the idea of Tracy getting his attention. Everyone else liked watching the two on the dance floor; they had great chemistry.

JD enjoyed being with Tracy. She was different from Ashley's other friends. After a few days he could see what Ashley saw; Tracy was special.

"Gentleman's choice," the deejay announced. "We gonna slow it down for a minute or two. Men, pick your poison."

The deejay played old school Luther, "Anyone Who Had a Heart." Tracy turned to walk off the dance floor but JD put his hands around her waist, pulled her close and began to dance in a slow rhythm.

"You are full of surprises, Squirt Two. Who taught you to dance like that?" JD smiled.

"My brother," Tracy answered bragging.

"Umm, I should have known. Did your brother teach you everything?"

"Just about," she responded, feeling very uncomfortable being this close to him. Well, not uncomfortable, that was not the word. But something was feeling a little strange to her. Okay, strange was not the word either. Hell, she wasn't sure what the word was, but her body was feeling different with him holding her like this.

"Tracy, where did you go?"

"Hmm, I'm sorry, what did you say?"

"Your brother would be proud to know how well you turned out."

"Maybe," she replied smiling.

The music played on as JD pulled her a little closer. *Why did he do that?* she thought. A knot began developing in the pit of her stomach and her breath became ragged as they continued to dance.

"Thank you, Tracy," he said as he looked into her eyes. "I don't believe I would have won that case without the information you pulled out."

"You've already thanked me for that," she replied with a twinkling smile.

She has seductive eyes, JD thought. Suddenly, the temptation to kiss her was so overwhelming he actually tilted his head towards her lips. He stopped. *She is nineteen and Ashley's best friend. Back up, damn it, back up,* he ordered himself.

"Let's get some fresh air," he suggested to break the mood. He took Tracy out of the main area of the club to a glass-enclosed veranda.

"Thanks, it was getting a little hot in there," she sighed.

"Yeah, it was."

"Wow, look at that," she beamed. JD looked through the window where she gazed at the view of the city skyline. That's funny. He saw that view every day and never thought twice about it. Seeing it now, here with her, made it seem special. It was an amazing view, especially at night.

"I get to see that every day," he stated as he came to stand behind her. "That's my office right there."

"Really?" she turned and smiled in awe. "It must be nice to see that every day."

There was that twinkle in her eyes again. God, he wanted to kiss her. Instead, he shook his head and stepped back. "Yeah, it's kind of nice."

For a moment Tracy thought JD was going to kiss her. She turned back to the window, disappointed. "Is something wrong?" she asked, confused by his actions.

Something was drawing JD towards her. He put his hands in his pockets and stood a step behind her. "No." He inhaled. "I find myself in an awkward situation."

She turned toward him and asked, "What situation is that?"

Unintentionally he seductively replied, "You."

Her smile faded as she innocently parted her lips and glazed at him. His mind was telling him to get away from this girl, but his body wasn't complying. He wanted to be close to her. Unable to resist the twinkle in her eyes or the need to taste her lips, JD gently kissed her lips.

Startled, Tracy stepped back with a look of confusion. She had no idea how to respond. His lips felt so soothing to her. She had to feel that again. Stepping closer to him, she placed her hands on his chest, tiptoed up and returned the kiss. Enjoying the sweetness of her touch, JD ran his tongue across her smooth lips. He felt the slight shiver that raced through her body. He parted her lips with his tongue to taste more of her. The moment their tongues met it felt as a jolt of lightning had struck the very soul of them. For JD it felt as if the weight of the world he carried on his shoulders became lighter, bearable.

Taking his hands from his pockets, he placed them around her waist to pull her closer, deepening the kiss. He could feel her hands pressed against his chest, as the kiss went much deeper than he intended. His mind reeled; *her kiss is so sweet, so innocent.* Then his senses returned. He suddenly pulled away and held her at arm's length. "I should not have done that."

Tracy wasn't listening. She never felt anything like that in her life.

"We better go back inside." Taking her hand, he turned to reenter the club.

"Wait," she said, pulling back. "What did I do wrong?"

Wrong? he thought. That was the conflict for him it felt so right. But he knew it was wrong. "You didn't do anything wrong. I did." He sighed heavily. "I should have never brought you out here."

Tracy did not understand the problem. "I came willingly, Jeffrey."

"Yes, you did. But I should have known better."

"I'm a little confused here." She sighed heavily.

He squeezed her hand. "Tracy," he began, trying to find the right words to explain what he was thinking, "you're Ashley's best friend and as much as I would like to, I can't forget how young you are. I made a mistake. I should not have kissed you."

It felt as if the pit of her stomach began to twist up. Tracy pulled her hand from his. JD could see the shell that had disappeared for a few days return almost instantly. Tracy clasped her hands behind her back. "I'm sorry you feel that way. Shall we go back inside?" It was as if the past few moments had not happened and they were only acquaintances having a general conversation. JD stepped aside as she walked past. He wanted to say something, but thought better of it.

"Hey," Ashley said as they approached the table, "you two finish dancing for the night?"

"I think so," Tracy replied as she looked away.

Just then Vanessa, JD's most recent lover, walked up. He was actually relieved to see her. He needed a little distance between him and Tracy.

"JD, are you enjoying yourself?" Vanessa asked sarcastically.

He glanced at Tracy. *I did the right thing,* he told himself. He took Vanessa's hand. "Come dance with me," he said with a smile and walked away. That was the last Tracy saw of him for the rest of the night.

JD came in around four in the morning. When he walked through the door, the telephone rang. "Yes, Vanessa," he answered angrily. "It's four in the morning. I don't want or need the drama again."

"You do realize she is a teenager and you are a grown ass man. Isn't that contributing to the delinquency of a minor or something?" Vanessa questioned with a warning.

"I'm a district attorney and you presume to tell me the law. By the way, she's nineteen, over the age of consent, if there was anything to consent too!"

"JD, I'm not trying to tell you the law. But you fail to see what it looks like. I don't care how old she is. She is too young for you to be involved with. What is it you always say to me—it's the appearance of it."

"Don't talk to me about appearances. Nothing is happening here, Vanessa. For goodness sakes, you're jealous of a nineteen-year-old girl," JD yelled into the phone.

"She may be, but I'm not blind," Vanessa replied curtly. "I know what I saw. And you are lying to me and yourself if you say I'm wrong."

"I'm done, Vanessa. I'm not dealing with this anymore tonight." He hung up the telephone and went to bed.

JD did not notice the balcony door was cracked. Tracy sat there with her book in her lap. She overheard his side of the conversation. *I'm just a teenage girl to him,* she thought. She dropped her head down. *What in the hell would make me think it was anything else? Stupid; stupid; stupid. You set yourself up for that.* She laughed to herself. She really liked being around JD and thought maybe.... "But it will not happen again," she said to herself.

In bed, JD lay awake wondering how in the hell he could convince Vanessa nothing was there with this girl when he wasn't sure himself. Something stirred in him every time he was around Tracy. She was young, but that wasn't really the problem. There was only a five-year difference in their age. With the career he planned, the appearance of him with someone so young could be damaging. Vanessa was right and he knew it. Besides, he did not have time for drama or issues in his life. Dealing with someone so young would bring drama. From that night, in his mind, Tracy Washington was off limits.

The next day Ashley and Tracy were loading up the car to return to Harmon as JD and Calvin helped. Other than the normal niceties, Tracy was very quiet.

"You two have everything?" JD asked.

"Sure do," Ashley replied.

Ashley jumped on JD's back as if taking a piggyback ride, kissed him on the cheek and hugged him. "Thanks, big brother, for letting us stay with you. I'm going to miss you."

He pulled her around his waist and carried her with one arm at his side.

"Don't you drop me," Ashley screamed while laughing.

"I will miss you too, Squirt," he smiled and put her on her feet by the driver's door.

As he opened the door for Ashley he glanced at Tracy. "It was good having you over, Tracy. You take care."

"Thank you. You take care, too," she replied as she got into the car.

He could see the shield was up full force. As they pulled off, JD felt so much was unsaid with her. He wondered if he should have talked with her about last night.

"You did the right thing," Calvin commented.

JD turned to him. "What?"

"You are not ready for her," he replied. "Let it go."

JD put his hands in his pocket and did just that, let it go.

Chapter 3
Six Years Later

JD and Calvin were raising stars in the DA's office. They worked well together and the friendship was now a successful partnership. JD had become an expert on gang prosecutions. He was usually given the lead on major cases and he always selected Calvin as his point man. On occasion he was asked to assist with cases with other ADA's across the state.

Personally, JD was still uncommitted to anyone. His latest conquest was Carolyn Roth, the daughter of John Roth, a U.S. senator representing the Commonwealth of Virginia. The family had the kind of connection that could win presidential elections without much effort, if they wanted to. Senator Roth was a straight-to-the-point type of man, just like JD; that's why the two got along. Even with JD's reputation with the ladies, the senator did not mind JD seeing Carolyn. What the senator did not know was that Carolyn was wide open. Whatever it took to get the man she wanted, at that moment, was what she would do. And she definitely wanted JD. Carolyn actually believed JD was her ticket to the governor's mansion, if not the White House itself. He was young, not bad on the eyes, intelligent, well liked and respected by both major political parties. More importantly, JD was a straight-up freak in bed. He could go for hours and match her stamina without breaking a sweat.

JD went into the office on a spring day in April not expecting to accomplish much. Nor did he expect a life-changing event. He had recently been asked to handle a few federal cases. His success against small gangs made him a perfect candidate to handle the prosecution of larger gangs that were causing mayhem in the not-so-prominent neighborhoods of the city. He was asked to prosecute certain gangs under the Racketeer Influenced and Corrupt Organizations (RICO) statute. This was a big deal for the DA's office and for Gavin W.

Roberts, the district attorney. To have someone from his staff assigned to this type of case meant major publicity for the office and, more importantly, for him. Gavin made sure JD had all the personnel and tools he needed to be successful. Gavin knew how JD operated; he would not take a case to court until he believed he could guarantee a win. This case was exactly what Gavin needed to gain a new level of popularity that would get him to the governor's mansion.

JD could care less about the popularity aspect of this case or where Gavin wanted to go politically. His concern was the children in the neighborhood. Gangs were recruiting at the age of ten or eleven. JD believed all children should have what his father had given to him and his sister: a childhood.

"Good morning, Mrs. Langston, how are you today?" JD smiled as he entered the office.

Mrs. Langston was the receptionist for the DA's office. She was a wise elderly woman with a knack for dealing with people. She loved JD and treated him as if he was one of her children.

"Hello, Mr. Harrison. I am well, how about you?"

"Hanging in," he replied.

"Here are your messages, and just so you know, Mr. Roberts is on the prowl for you."

JD hung his head. "Why? What could he possibly want to know this early in the case?"

Mrs. Langston hunched her shoulders. "Who knows?"

"Thanks for the heads up," JD said as he started to walk away. He stopped and turned back to her. Before he could say a word she handed him a sandwich bag containing oatmeal raisin cookies. JD took the bag and put it in his suit pocket, looked around to see if anyone was looking.

"This is our secret," he said.

"I won't say a word." She smiled.

JD returned the smile and headed to his office.

Mrs. Langston shook her head. "My Lord, if I was twenty years younger."

Calvin met JD at his office door and handed him a file. "Here we go again. Are you ready?" he said with a touch of excitement.

"As ready as ever," JD replied. "Did we investigate everyone from the top down?"

"Yes, and from what I can tell we are looking at a major player and three small ones. But we could clear several unsolved murders and indict on at least one kingpin charge and that's just for starters."

"Okay, let's see what we have," JD said as he took his seat behind his desk.

Calvin sat in the chair directly in front of the desk. Before JD had opened the file, Brian, one of his boys from high school and a federal agent, came in.

"JD, what's up, man? Thanks for the recommendation."

"Hey, B, nothing to it. They said get who you need on this case, so I opted for the best."

They shook hands and Brian hit Calvin on the shoulder. "Hey, Cal, how's it going?"

"Hey, B," Calvin replied.

"This is going to be a big one," Brian commented as he took a seat.

"Yes, it is, that's why I need you at the beginning of this case," JD replied.

"Okay, I'm here and I see you have the file. I ran an investigation on everyone, but did an in-depth on Albert Day. He is the brains behind this group."

JD opened the file. "Okay, give me the run down"

Calvin started, "From what I read, we have a thug with a conscience. He sets his people up well. Gives them forty percent of the take and makes them work towards cleaning up by starting legit businesses under another name. Some of those who followed his lead have a good small business being run by a relative and in that relative's name."

"So we can't touch the legit stuff," JD interjected.

"Right," Calvin acknowledged, "but everything else is open season."

"Give me a ball park." From the summary JD was getting, he formed a certain curiosity for this man. This man was looking out for the community and his people. He was putting his people's future before profit. JD had to respect that. He continued to read the file as Calvin summarized. Calvin was quoting figures when something in the file caught JD's attention. In reading the family bio on Day he noticed the name of his little sister.

Brian, who is very observant, caught the look on JD's face. "What is it, JD?"

Calvin stopped talking and looked up.

"I know that name from somewhere," JD replied.

"What name?" Calvin asked.

"Tracy Washington."

"Day's little sister?" Brian asked.

"Yeah, where in the hell do I know that name from?" JD wondered.

"One of your many conquests," Calvin joked.

JD laughed. "I don't think so, but maybe. There have been many, you know."

"Yes, we know. I'm still trying to catch up," Calvin replied.

Brian laughed at Calvin. "Like you could."

JD laughed along, all the while knowing this name meant something to him; he just did not know what. The conversation turned back to the file. By the end of the meeting the three had developed a strategy to start the case. Calvin and Brian left, after all agreed to meet at their hangout spot, Maxi's, after work.

Later in the day JD was in Gavin's office giving him an update on the case when it came to him. Tracy Washington was Ashley's roommate. JD stopped mid-sentence and told Gavin he wanted to dig a little deeper before he went on. Gavin did not make much of it. He knew JD was a perfectionist and probably wanted to make sure of events prior to conferring with him.

"Alright, JD, get back with me when you are ready. Is this one we can win?"

JD's mind was on Ashley now. "I'll get back to you on that one, Gavin."

JD left the room with no idea what he was supposed to get back to Gavin on. He took out his cell and called Brian. "B, man I need to see you, where are you?"

JD met Brian in the parking deck. "B, I know the sister and I pray I'm wrong."

"Man, don't tell me Calvin was right," Brian laughed.

"No, man." JD hit Brian on the shoulder. "Tracy Washington is Ashley's roommate."

"Your sister Ashley?"

"Yes! When you ran the investigation on Day did you come across anything on the sister?" JD asked, hoping to get something to eliminate Tracy.

"No. There was no communication between them. There was communication between Day, the older sister and his mom, but nothing with the little sister. In fact, there was no communication between the little sister and the rest of the family. From what I got, she left for college and never looked back."

"Did anything indicate what college she attended or when?" JD asked desperately.

"Nothing on where, just that she disappeared at that time."

JD shook his head and shoved his hands in his pockets. His mind was racing. He remembered Tracy not keeping in touch with her family and her having a brother. That was too much to be just a coincidence. "Tracy and Ashley have a business together," he said. "We need to make sure there is no connection between Day and that business before we go any further."

Brian had known JD and Calvin since high school and could read both of them like a book. At that moment he knew JD needed other possibilities to this scenario. "Could it be another Tracy Washington?" he asked.

"I hope so," JD replied wishfully as he slide into Brian's black Suburban. JD called Ashley's cell. There was no answer. He called the office, and Monica, the receptionist answered. "Hello, Next Level."

"Hi, Monica, it's JD. Is Ashley in?"

"Yes, JD, she is on another line. Would you like to hold?"

"No, thanks, Monica. Is Tracy in?"

"Yes, she is. Would you like to speak with her?"

"Yes, thank you." JD held the line.

"Tracy Washington, may I help you?"

"Hi, Tracy, this is Jeffrey."

Tracy knew who he was the moment he said hi. She had not seen or really talked to him since graduation, but she knew it was Jeffrey. The churning inside her stomach told her so.

Talk, girl...talk, Tracy coaxed herself. "Hi, Jeffrey, how have you been?" *Stupid, stupid, stupid, you were supposed to say something provocative, not how you been....* Tracy rolled her eyes at herself.

"I'm fine, thanks for asking," he replied.

"What can I do for you?" Tracy asked. *Okay that was a little better; weak but better,* Tracy thought.

"Tracy."

"Say my name, say my name," went through her mind. She laughed to herself.

"I need to talk to you without Ashley around, is that possible?"

She thought for a moment, because in her mind, that conversation was going a little different. *Oh, something like, I can't live without you in my life any longer, be my lady. Oh, if only for one night....*

"Tracy?" JD called out when she did not reply.

"I'm sorry, Jeffrey. Is everything alright?"

"Yes, things are fine, but I need to talk to you alone."

"Okay, it sounds serious." When Jeffrey did not respond, Tracy continued. "You can park in the back and come in the door on the right, it leads into my office. I'll unlock it so you can just walk in."

"Thanks, I'll be there in a few minutes."

"Okay, see you then."

"What's the plan?" Brian asked as JD closed his phone.

"No plan, just straight questions and hopefully some straight answers."

Tracy was in her office wondering what Jeffrey wanted to talk about. She looked at the calendar; it wasn't Ashley's birthday. Maybe it was something about his mom. Either way it did not matter why he was coming—he was coming. She checked herself out in the mirror. Looking nice mattered to her now. One man mattered.

Ashley had taken a lot of time to teach Tracy how to dress and how to carry herself. Tracy had the "it factor," that certain something every man looks for in a woman, but she was clueless to it. Tracy looked at her reflection in the mirror. The black sleeveless mock turtleneck dress she wore was fitting in the right places; black three-inch heels, sheer stockings and a red blazer, which was on the back of her chair. She was presentable, she thought. Her hair was worn straight, falling right at her shoulders.

The change in Tracy's appearance was not by choice. Ashley came out of her room one Saturday morning, turned to Tracy, who was in the kitchen, and threatened, "If I see you in a ponytail one more day I'm going to strangle you with it. Come on, you're going with me today."

"Going with you where?" Tracy asked.

"To see Penne."

"Who is Penne?"

"My hairstylist."

At first sight Penne screamed, "Girl, you need help, quick, somebody call 911." Penne got hold of Tracy and she was changed forever. Sensing Tracy was a little uncomfortable, Penne did not go overboard, as he had a tendency to do. However, he knew the girl had serious "what if" potential. He closed his eyes, put his free spirit back into his inner box and went to work on Tracy. He did a perm, a cut, a wrap, and then used a flatiron to bump her hair out. When Ashley saw the results, she turned to Penne and said, "Girrrrrl, what a little perm and a flat iron can do...." She gave Penne a high five. Penne responded, "Girl, a sista got the gift and I had to use it." They both fell out laughing. Tracy looked in the mirror and could not believe it was her. She actually looked okay; no, more than okay, she looked good. From that day on Tracy took a little more time getting dressed in the morning. With a new wardrobe she discovered a new person. Tracy had a little more pep in her step when she went out the door now. She knew the new her was working. She started getting all kinds of attention from men. But at the moment, that little confidence was all going out of the window, because he was walking through the door.

"Tracy?" Jeffrey said as he looked around the opened door.

"Hi, Jeffrey." Tracy extended her hand and he hesitated for a moment.

"Hello, Squirt Two, it's been a while." JD smiled.

"Yes, it has been," she responded with a smile.

"You've changed a little," JD said, but her smile still had the same effect on him.

"I hope that's a good thing," she replied nervously.

Brian stepped in the door behind JD. Noticing him, Tracy spoke. "Hello, I'm Tracy Washington," and she extended her hand.

"Hi, Brian Thompson," he replied in a deep voice and shook her hand.

"It's nice to meet you, Mr. Thompson."

"Oh, Brian, please," Brian replied pleasantly.

JD glared at Brian.

"Excuse me for a moment," Tracy said as she left the room.

Both men watched as she walked across the room and out. They stared at the closed door for a moment. "DAMN," they both breathed simultaneously.

"Man, what is wrong with you, you didn't introduce us. That was rude, and you didn't say she was a dime," Brian stated.

A dime, she's a whole damn dollar bill, JD thought, but before he could respond to Brian, Tracy came back in the room.

"I'm sorry. I wanted to make sure we were not disturbed. You sounded so serious on the phone. Please have a seat," Tracy said and pointed to the two chairs in front of her desk. "How may I help you?"

JD and Brian looked at each other as Tracy watched them. Neither of them wanted to approach the subject with her now. However, JD had to, for Ashley.

Tracy spoke first. "Jeffrey, you have never been a man who had to search for words. Come on, it can't be that bad," she teased.

Tracy had eyes that looked all the way into a man's soul, combined with an electrifying smile—a man could lose his mind. JD remembered the feeling well. Today her smile brought back those feelings he had buried years ago.

Brian sensed something was off with JD. So he began talking. "Ms. Washington."

"Tracy," she corrected.

"Okay, Tracy," Brian replied and smiled. "I'm a federal investigator working on a case with JD and your name came up."

"My name?" Her expression was marked with confusion.

"Yes, in connection with the case," Brian clarified.

"I can't imagine why my name would come up in connection to any case, federal or otherwise. Are you sure it's not another Tracy Washington?"

"Tracy," JD spoke up, "does the name Albert Day mean anything to you?"

"Yes, he's my brother," she frankly replied.

"The brother who taught you how to dance, cook and play ball? That brother?"

"Yeah," she replied, surprised he remembered that. "He's the only brother I'm aware of. Why?"

"Then we do have the right person," Brian stated.

"When was the last time you saw or spoke with your brother?" JD asked.

"At graduation, about two years ago. Why do you ask? Is he in some kind of trouble?" Tracy sat forward, put her arms on the desk and nervously began to rub her hands together. She began a small prayer that Jeffrey would not tell her Turk was dead.

"Is he okay?" she reluctantly asked.

"You haven't heard from your brother in two years?" Brian asked in a tone that did not sit well with Tracy.

"No," she replied edgily.

JD could see Tracy was uncomfortable with the conversation. He knew from experience she would revert into a shell and no one would get any answers. Her brother meant a lot to her and JD had an uneasy feeling that the case was not going to go as smoothly as he had hoped. He reached over and took Tracy's hand in his. "Tracy, the case I'm working on involves your brother. He is not hurt, but he is in trouble."

"What kind of trouble?"

"I'm not at liberty to say. But I need to ask you some questions."

She trusted Jeffrey, so answering questions for him was not an issue for her. "Okay."

"Does your brother have any connections to your business?"

"This business?"

"This one or any other you may have," Brian interjected.

Tracy really did not like his tone. She pulled away from JD, sat back in her chair and turned to Brian. "No, he doesn't and I don't have any other businesses, Mr. Thompson. Ashley and I started this business when we were at Harmon. You know that, Jeffrey."

JD, sensing the tide changing, stood. "I know, Tracy, but I had to ask." He smiled. "I'm sorry we had to bother you with this. But this case puts me in a very awkward situation."

"I seem to do that to you a lot," she commented. "But I understand you have a job to do."

"Thanks for seeing us on such short notice, and I'm sorry it had to be under these circumstances."

"I'm sorry, too, Jeffrey." She stood and turned to him. "I don't know what Turk has gotten himself into, but would you please give him this card. Ask him to please call me if I can help him in any way."

JD did not like what was about to go down or how it would affect her. He was feeling a little guilty right about now. He knew he was about to take her brother down and that bothered him. Her brother was the only family she dealt with and she loved him. But he had to be honest with her. "I am not sure I can help him with this. But I will give him the message."

Wondering why JD had stopped the questioning, Brian stood and walked towards the door. "Needless to say, you will contact us if you hear from your brother," Brian stated.

"Needless to say I will not, Mr. Thompson," Tracy replied.

"You do realize that would be obstruction of justice."

"Brian, I'll be out in a minute," JD cut in.

Brian looked at JD then stepped outside.

JD exhaled. "I'll make sure he gets the message."

"Thank you, Jeffrey."

He reached out and squeezed her hand. "It will be alright, Tracy. I'll make sure of it." He started to walk out, but turned back to her. "Oh, and by the way, it's not bad," he stated as he shook his head.

"What's that?" she asked.

"The changes in you," he replied. She blushed.

"You look good." He smiled. "The best part hasn't changed at all."

"What part is that?" Tracy asked bashfully.

"Your smile. You still have that smile that could brighten any room."

"Thank you," she said with a shy smile.

He returned the smile and walked out the door.

Once they were outside, Brian turned to JD. "Are you going to be able to handle this case objectively?"

JD looked at him confused. "Yeah, why in the hell did you ask me that?"

"Because you seem to have gotten a little distracted in there."

"No, I'm straight, man, I just got a...." He searched for the words. "I've got a feeling about this one."

JD opened the door and got into the car. Brian slid in on the driver's side.

"Do you believe her?" JD asked.

"Yeah, I do. However, to be on the safe side I'll do a financial check on the business and see where it leads," Brian replied.

"Yeah, follow the money." JD thought for a minute. "The problem is, not only do I believe her, I know we are going to hurt her when everything comes out, and I don't like that," he angrily commented. Then he continued, "We have to use her to pull Day out and I don't like that."

"Is there anything you like about this case?" Brian asked with a grin.

"Not a damn thing," JD replied. "Brian, I know this girl. She is not knowingly involved with her brother's dealings."

"Were you ever involved with this woman?"

"Yes and no," JD replied. "She was nineteen, Ashley's roommate and best friend, when I met her." He smiled.

"The yes part?" Brian looked over at him and grinned. JD looked over at him, then turned away.

"I pulled away, hmm. I thought she was too young at the time." JD thought back.

"And now?" Brian asked curiously.

JD looked out the window, shook his head. "There's more to this than what we know, and I don't think it's going to turn out good. I just don't like the idea of taking her through any unnecessary changes."

When JD returned to the office it was late. He wanted to catch Calvin before he left for the weekend. On his way to Calvin's office Mrs. Langston buzzed him. "Mr. Harrison, you have a call on line two."

"Would you take a message, please?" JD asked.

"The gentleman indicated it was important and would not give his name," Mrs. Langston replied.

"Okay, put it through, Mrs. Langston."

This type of call was normal for JD. Most of his informants would call anonymously, but this was the last thing he needed right now. Informants could take up a lot of time. He needed to get with Calvin to help him figure out how to get Day without using Tracy.

"JD Harrison."

"Al Day," the voice stated. "We need to meet."

JD sat down in his chair, took out a pen. "When and where?"

"Field overlooking canal walks, your private investigator and my lieutenant, one hour."

The line went dead. JD dialed Calvin's number. "My office now," he said and hung up.

JD sat back in his chair. *What in the hell is going on here?* He liked to control his cases, but this case was controlling him and he did not like that. First the reconnection with Tracy, causing him to change the way he normally handles a case; and now this. He had to take a moment to think.

When Calvin came through the door, JD pointed to the chair. Calvin knew JD was about to start talking, but did not want a response. He needed a sounding board to get his thoughts out into the open. Calvin sat and JD started running through the day's events, including the phone call. He stopped and looked at this watch. He had forty-five minutes before the meeting, which was about fifteen minutes away. He called Brian and told him to meet him in the garage in thirty minutes. Then he turned to Calvin. "Synopsis?"

"Day knows you met with his little sister, that's why he's calling. He could only know one or two ways: Brian told him or she told him, and I don't think it was Brian. If we work on the premise that Tracy told him that means she was not truthful with you earlier today and you read her wrong. Which don't usually happen to you with women. You and I spent time with Tracy; she is a pretty honest person."

JD sat up. "When did you spend time with her?"

Calvin looked at him. "Want to focus here? Other possibilities, could he know about the case and if so, how, and why would he be calling you? Is there a possible deal in the works? If so, that would solve your problem with using Tracy. You just got this case this morning and it is giving you a run for your money. Take control before it starts controlling you. Do the meeting on his terms, let him talk; see where it leads. We still on for Maxi's tonight?" Calvin asked as he stood.

"Yeah, unless something comes up with this meet," JD replied.

They walked out of the office to the elevator. While in the elevator, JD asked, "When did you spend time with Tracy?"

Calvin smirked and put his hands in his pockets. "After graduation, remember? She didn't have any plans. I didn't like the idea of her being alone, so I took her to dinner to celebrate."

"I do remember that. She was a little shy around the family. I don't think she ever got over Uncle Joe."

"Shy?" Calvin laughed. "That herd of people you call a family would scare Joan of Arc. Hell, they scare me and I'm used to them."

A moment of silence went by and Calvin began to laugh. "So what did you two do?"

"I knew that was coming."

"What?"

The elevator door opened and they saw Brian at the SUV.

"We ate dinner, what do you think?" Calvin answered. "Watch his back, B," Calvin said shaking his head as he walked to his car.

"I got him," Brian replied. "See you at Maxi's."

Brian got in the car. He reached under the seat and pulled out his Magnum to make sure it was loaded. He slipped it in the back of his pants, then checked to make sure his department issued revolver was loaded.

"The meeting is at the field overlooking the canal walk. Tucker will be with him," JD said, referring to Day's top lieutenant, whom he had read about in the reports.

"Why Tucker, why not Tate?" Brian asked.

"He selected people we each trust the most. If we see Tate, I know he will be handing me some bullshit."

"What do you think this is about? He couldn't know about the case unless Ms. Washington told him," Brian remarked.

"I don't think that's what happened."

"JD," Brian warned, "it's too early in this case to close your mind to anything, I don't care how phat she is. You don't trust anyone until you know the facts. If she did not tell him, why is he calling? It's not as if we've done a lot of legwork on the case yet, so nothing could have slipped. So what is it about?" Brian expressed in a rather insistent manner.

"I guess we will find out when we get there," JD replied.

JD understood exactly what Brian was saying to him, and he was right. He had to put Tracy out of his mind, for now. This case was too important for so many reasons to mess up over, what, feelings. Hell, since Vanessa, JD had stopped dealing with feelings mainly because he hadn't had any. On top of that, how could he instantly want to protect someone he really did not know? Yes, Tracy has been around the outskirts of his life for the past six years, but only as Ashley's friend. When he had decided she was off limits, he had put her completely out of his mind. Well, maybe not completely. It was a little difficult at times. The week Tracy stayed at his house really set his career in motion. For a while, every time he was in his office Tracy would cross his mind. He had felt so alive and carefree when she was around. It wasn't easy for him to forget. Now this. In the past, JD managed to keep a distance between them. Now this case was bringing them together again.

Tracy was a little restless after the conversation with Jeffrey so she went home early. Ashley had left and was not coming back to the office. She told Tracy she had a dinner meeting with one of the new clients and would be home late. Tracy took advantage of the tranquility of the condo and crunched some numbers. Her thoughts went to Turk, the brother who always appears out of nowhere whenever she needed him. She had not seen or heard from him since graduation. As she looked back, things had really gone pretty well for her since that day. There was really no need for him to show up. Now it seemed like he might need her help and she had no way of finding him unless she broke her silence and contacted her mother. Then she remembered what Turk had said: "I got you out; it's up to you to stay out." Calling her mother was out of the question. Her mom would just remind her how she had ruined her life. Or how ugly she was and how she was going to end up being somebody's whore. *How did I ever make it through that shit? Turk,* she thought with a smile. Turk kept her going all those years when her mom mentally beat her down. All Tracy ever wanted from her mom was her love. But for some reason, she couldn't have that. Turk used to tell her, "Don't worry about Mom; I love you enough for both of us."

Tracy went back to crunching her numbers on her laptop. She remembered her first laptop...

She was 17 and it was Christmas Eve. She didn't expect much. Her mom always had something else to do with her money than spend it on "childish things." Turk came by earlier that day. However, he had a terrible argument with Lena so he left. Something about a Christmas tree. Lena dressed and went over to Tracy's sister Valerie's house. She was having people over and asked her mom to bring Tracy, but she said no. Valerie knew how her mom was when it came to Tracy, so as soon as she thought Lena had left she called Tracy. "Merry Christmas, Tracy."

"Merry Christmas, Valerie," Tracy replied merrily.

"I have a gift for you."

"You do? What is it?" Tracy asked with excitement.

"It's a surprise. But I'm gonna keep it here so nothing can happen to it."

Tracy knew what that meant, so Mom would not know about it. "Okay, thank you. I didn't have any money, but I made you something. Are you coming over tomorrow?"

"No," Valerie replied, "we are doing dinner over here. Didn't Mom tell you?"

"No, she didn't say anything. Well, I'll bring your gift over tomorrow," Tracy offered, thinking her mom planned on taking her.

"Okay, I got to go now. Make sure the doors are locked."

"Okay," Tracy said as she hung up the telephone.

Tracy turned on the television then stretched out on the floor and fell asleep. When she woke up, Turk was on the couch asleep. He had put up a little artificial tree that came with lights on it. There were gifts under the tree, all with Tracy's name on them.

"Oh, snap," Tracy exclaimed, waking Turk up. "Can I open them, Turk, please?"

Looking at the clock and smiling at his sister's eagerness he agreed. "Okay, it's after midnight."

Turk sat on the sofa laughing at her. "You sure you don't want to wait until tomorrow?"

"No, well, maybe I'll hold one out for tomorrow."

Tracy started opening gifts. Most of them were clothes and shoes, and there was a leather jacket. Her favorite gifts were a gold necklace and a laptop. Tracy felt like she had died and gone to heaven. She put the necklace back under the tree and started working on the laptop.

She stopped and said, "Thank you, Turk. Thank you so much. I got something for you. Well," she said sadly, "it's nothing like what you have given me. But I saved my lunch money to get it for you." She handed him a small box.

Turk opened the box. Inside was an engraved ID bracelet that read, "To My Big Brother, Love T." He looked at it and smiled. "Thank you, Sugie."

"I didn't have enough money to put my whole name on it."

"That's okay, I know who T is. Where's your mother?"

"She went to Valerie's house."

"Why didn't you go?"

"I don't know," Tracy shrugged her shoulder.

"Okay. Look Sugie, I got to meet some people. Give me a hug, and I'll see you next time."

"Okay, Turk. Thank you so much," she said, hugging him.

Tracy was sitting on the sofa working on the laptop when her mom came in. "Hey, Mom, look what Turk gave me for Christmas."

Her mom looked around the room. It seemed like she was getting angrier with every item she took in. "What is this shit?"

Recognizing the tone, Tracy closed the laptop down and put it behind her. "They're my Christmas presents from Turk," Tracy replied innocently.

"Well, it's going the hell out my house."

Tracy's mom began picking up the things under the tree and boxing them back up. When she came to the leather jacket, she put it on. "Hmm, I could use this."

Then she opened the box with the gold chain and smiled. "I always wanted one of these," she said, and put the box under her arm. Tracy knew not to ask any questions. That would only lead to her mom yelling and cursing at her. When her mom went into her bedroom with the boxes, Tracy grabbed the laptop and took it into her bedroom. She put it under her mattress then went to bed.

Whenever her mom would leave the house during the Christmas break, Tracy would pull out the laptop and work on it. When Tracy came home after the first day back to school from winter break, she went into her bedroom to pull out the laptop and it was gone. Tracy came out of the room upset. Her mom was at the kitchen table. "Where is it?" Tracy asked.

"I sold it," her mom said coolly.

"That's stealing—it wasn't yours to sell," Tracy yelled.

"Who in the hell do you think you're yelling at? Anything that's in my house is mine. I can do what in the hell I want to do with it. That includes you. If you don't like it you can take your little ass and live somewhere else. Or your ass can go live on a street corner for all I care. You ain't gonna turn out to be nothing but a whore anyway."

"Why do you hate me so much? I ain't never done nothing to you, Mom," Tracy cried.

"You never done anything to me," her mom yelled. *"Look around, you little bitch, do you see my husband anywhere? NO! I'll answer it for you. He ain't here because of you. Yeah, I sold your damn computer and got good money for it. If your ass was halfway decent looking I would put you on a corner and make you earn your keep."*

Tears were flowing down Tracy's face. How could the woman who gave birth to her hate her so? *"I will leave here one day and won't ever look back,"* Tracy said calmly.

"Don't wait for someday, get your ass out here now," was her mother's reply.

Tracy went into her room and closed the door. She knew her mom would eventually stop and leave. Tracy called Turk and told him what happened, but begged him not to say anything to her mom.

Tracy wasn't sure what happened after that. The next day Tracy had her laptop back and her mom never said another word to her.

Tracy closed her laptop and wiped the tears from her eyes when she heard Ashley come in about an hour later. "Tracy, contract signed, dated, Is dotted and Ts crossed," Ashley yelled while coming up the steps. "Girl, I was on point tonight. The charm was rolling out 'cross the table, like you spread butter on one of Mama's hot rolls. I was goooooood. And this is for you," she said, handing her the envelope with the contract and a twenty-five thousand dollar commitment check enclosed. "Our first major client! I am so psyched, let's go have a drink."

"You mean you are not already drunk?" Tracy replied, displaying a tearful smile.

"No, I didn't drink during dinner. I needed to stay focused and close the deal, which I did. Now we celebrate."

When Tracy did not respond, Ashley turned to her. "Hey, what's up? You seem a little down."

"Jeffrey and a friend of his, Brian Thompson, came by to see me today."

"My brother JD and Brian? Why?" Ashley asked with concern.

"They wanted to know about Turk."

"Your brother?"

"Yes."

"Why?"

"I'm not sure, but Jeffrey said he was in trouble."

"Was Brian with him in a professional capacity or were they just hanging out?" Ashley asked.

"Professional, I'm sure. He was the main one asking questions. Why?"

"Well, Brian works for the federal government and I think JD is working on a case with him."

"That's what the Brian guy said."

"That means, whatever your brother is involved in is big."

Brian pulled up to the entrance of the field and stopped the car. He stepped out and walked up the hill to look around. It was an open area and unless there was a reason to, no one would venture in. He could see a vehicle had just been through, so he knew Day was already there. Brian wanted to make sure there were no surprises. He did not have time to send someone out to scout, prior to the meet, which, he was sure, was what Day had intended. There was no way in hell Brian was going to let JD walk into anything he was not comfortable with. In addition to being his personal friend, JD was a "good guy" committed to the justice system. That was rare and Brian was not going to let anything happen to him. "Okay, we can roll," Brian announced when he got back in the car.

JD did not think twice about his safety. He knew Brian had his back no matter what. Approaching the site they saw two people, Day and Tucker. That immediately relaxed Brian. He knew Tucker from earlier years and he had a certain level of professional respect for him. They were both about the protection of their man. JD knew, by seeing Tucker, whatever Day was about to tell him, he could trust. For whatever reason, Day did not want his people to know about this meet. Brian got out of the car and JD followed. Tucker stepped forward to frisk Brian. "I'm carrying," Brian said as he took a step back.

Tucker grinned. "So am I. Since that's understood, let's move on."

JD put his hands on the hood of the car and Tucker frisked him. Day did the same on their car and Brian frisked him.

"Good," Tucker said.

"Good here," Brian countered.

"The one and only JD Harrison in the flesh." Day chuckled as he and JD stepped to the side. "I got much respect for you, man, and I like your style. No bullshit; just straight to the ass whipping. Motherfuckers don't stand a chance with you on them."

"Is that why you called me, to give props?"

"Naw, man, I'm ready to let this go. So this time I'm going to save you some steps."

"How's that?"

"I'm going to give you me. But I won't come cheap."

"I'm listening." JD put his hands in his pocket and put his head down, the way he does when he's trying to reason something out.

Day watched JD's every move. He trusted this man, followed his career and knew what he was about. But this was not a simple thing he was about to ask him to do. "You are going to arrange a deal for me through the attorney general only, none of your people."

JD looked up.

"I'll explain. Hear me all the way out first."

JD put his head back down. "Okay, continue."

"I will give you me and a few of your people who belong to me."

JD did not show any expression, but his mind was racing. *We got dirty people in the DA's office.* Now all he wanted to know was who. "In exchange for what?"

"You have to give me your word you will protect Sugie."

"And who the hell is Sugie?"

"You know her as Tracy Washington, my little sister."

JD smiled at the nickname. Day caught the smile; he knew JD was the right person for the job.

"What does Tracy have to do with this?" JD held his breath, not sure what the answer would be.

"Nothing," Day replied. "She doesn't even know what I do or where I am and I want you to keep it that way."

"That will be difficult," JD responded, relieved. "The arrest is going to have media coverage and if not, the case will."

"There will be no trial. I'm going to plead to whatever you bring me."

JD stood up and faced Day. "Why?"

He glared at JD and stated, "My little sister is the only thing in this world that is good and pure to me. I have spent my life protecting her. Now someone in your office has put her in danger and the only way to continue to protect her is to give myself up."

"You do realize the best I would be able to give you with what I have is forty years, federal time," JD stated. "You're willing to do that without question to protect your sister?"

"You met her, Harrison—wouldn't you?" Day laughed. "I got into this to keep her off the street. Tracy is doing good. I can let go now. But I can't protect her from certain people. You can."

"Who are you trying to protect her from, your people or mine?"

"Now see, man, that's what I like about you, a brother who listens. That's why you got my respect. But, before we go any further, I need your word as a man, that you will protect Sugie, with your life if need be."

JD didn't have to think about that one. Without hesitation he replied, "You have my word. I will not let anything happen to her."

Day turned to Tucker, who was standing near the car, and nodded. Tucker pulled an envelope from the car and handed it to Brian. Brian opened the envelope and started to read. Day turned back to JD.

"The package your man has will be all you need to begin an investigation of the people you need to clear out. You have three people in your office that will have your back no matter what might come out: Johnson, Thompson and Langston. Everyone else is politically motivated."

JD looked at Day.

Day glared at him, "No one else," he said without flinching.

"Why me?" JD asked.

"I've watched you. You're what they call a good guy. Then there's Sugie. I know you're gonna look out for her. But I didn't choose you. The people who involved my sister picked you. You are good, take no motherfucking prisoners, and I like that. But this case was given to you to pull me out. He knew you would make the connection of Sugie and me while working on this case. I believe his game plan was to find her, leak her name and whereabouts to one of the organizations we have beef with. I don't have to tell you how they would use her to get to me. Her name was put in there purposely. There's only one person who could have given you that name and that's the person who is trying to bring me down," Day explained.

"Okay, I'll bite—who's trying to bring you down and why?"

Day looked at JD. "You've already figured that out." He laughed. "The why is because I killed Sugie's father years ago and he helped me clean it up. Ever since then I would steer him in the right direction on some things to help him win cases, and he began rising in the legal system. He in turn let me run my business. Now I'm a threat to his aspirations, which I really don't give a shit about; he leaves me the fuck alone, I leave him alone is my motto. He used you to make the connection and lead others to Sugie to weaken my power base. He knows I run a clean business; I only kill those who try to kill me. But if a fucker puts a hand on Sugie, I will retaliate and there would be a war. I don't want her caught in the middle. If I go in, it will be on my terms and Sugie is no longer in harm's way. No reason for a war, which I am sure I will conveniently die in. Whatever time I need to do to keep her safe, I can handle. When you bring him down, you will be in line for his position." Day stopped and watched for JD's reaction.

JD shook his head. "I don't deal in politics; it's a dirty game."

"So, what you doing with the senator's daughter?"

"Entertaining myself," JD replied with a smile.

Day laughed. "I heard that, my brother."

JD smiled. He liked this man, but he had a job to do.

"I will give you 24 hours to make the deal," Day stated. "After that I go to Plan 2."

"What is Plan 2?"

Day looked at him, then, turned to walk away.

JD understood. "Day, why did you kill Tracy's father?"

Day looked down at an old bracelet on his arm, walked back to JD. "The bastard tried to put his hands on my baby sister. You will hear from me in 24 hours," he announced. He got into the car with Tucker and left.

Brian walked over to JD. "Do you know who is in here?"

"Yeah, Gavin."

Chapter 4

JD was tense with all that had taken place in the last two days. The deal was made for Day and the investigations into the other individuals had begun. He was at home attempting to relax away the thought of Tracy, but it was not working. He needed a distraction, he thought as the telephone rang.

"Hello," JD answered.

"Well, Mr. Harrison, if I was an insecure person I would think you didn't like me."

"I had a few hectic days," JD replied with a smile.

"Okay, I'll take that. Want some company?"

"Sure."

"Good. Open your front door."

JD opened the door and Carolyn Roth stepped in. He hung up the phone and closed the door behind her. She kissed him, dropped her trench coat to the floor and started up the stairs.

"Always ready for anything," JD said, smiling as he watched her naked body go up the steps.

"The question is, are you?" Carolyn asked as she reached the top of the stairs.

"Sounds like a dare to me."

"Up to the challenge?"

Boy, was he ever. A few hours later, Carolyn screamed, "Damn, JD, you can wear a sister out."

"You challenged." JD smiled. "I countered."

"Alright, you got me," she answered back as she laughed.

He reached across her to discard the condoms they had used throughout the evening.

"By the feeling of things, it doesn't seem that I have conquered you yet," she said as she attempted to mount him. He stopped her.

"Okay, I know, not without protection." She grinned. "But I do have other ways of handling that."

As she went down on him, he wondered why she wasn't able to satisfy him tonight. Carolyn wiped that thought from his mind in a matter of minutes. Carolyn never doubted her ability to satisfy a man. Convinced she had succeeded, she got up to leave.

"I'm sure that will keep me on your mind for a day or so."

What she did not know was his mind was already on someone else.

JD got up the next morning feeling a little more relaxed. He called Carolyn and thanked her for the evening. He always made sure he did a follow-up call, no matter the outcome with the ladies the night before. He felt it was the gentlemanly thing to do, and women loved the sensitivity. After the call he took a shower. He was trying to find the words to tell Tracy about Al, but the words did not come. He decided to go to the one person who always had an answer to his problems.

"Hey, Mom," he said as he walked through her back door.

"Good morning, son. Want some breakfast?" his mom asked.

"Yeah," JD replied as he kissed her cheek.

"Eggs with cheese good for you?"

"That'll do, thanks, Mom."

"You got court today?"

"No, just in the office."

She put a cup of coffee in front of him. As he put in cream and sugar he smiled, remembering Al, referring to Tracy as Sugie.

"What you grinning at?" his mom asked.

"Nothing, Mom."

They began talking about nothing in particular, but Martha knew her son. If he came by this early in the morning, he needed to talk. So she listened without questions, knowing he would eventually get around to what he had to say. He was just like his father in that way. He couldn't show a weakness like needing somebody to talk with; that was just not manly. When she finished cooking, the eggs with cheese had turned into a plate of eggs, bacon, hash browns and toast. She sat at the table across from him. "You talked to Ashley yesterday?"

"No, I was busy all day. What's up with her?"

"Oh, not her; it's Tracy."

JD looked up from his plate. "What's wrong with Tracy?"

"Ashley said she's been a little down about something for the past couple of days and she's not talking about it. She wanted some advice on how to help her. You know Tracy. She walks around with that beautiful smile of hers all the time dealing with things on the inside. She needs to learn how to talk things through. I told Ashley to be patient; she'll eventually talk to her about what's bothering her. She always does," his mom laughed lovingly.

JD began moving food around his plate. Martha knew he was ready to talk, now, so she sat back.

"Mom, I have a case involving Tracy's brother. He will be arrested sometime this week. I feel like I should be the one to tell her, but I don't know how," JD explained.

"Just tell her straight; don't mince words on that," his mom suggested.

"I don't want her to hate me for incarcerating her brother. He's the only family she has."

My, my, his mom thought, *JD caring about Tracy's feelings, hmm.*

"Son, Tracy is a smart girl. She knows if her brother is doing something illegal, he is going to jail. You are doing your job; she is not going to hold that against you. Just be honest with her, whatever you do. That girl does not deal well with lies."

"Mom, I just don't want her to feel alone when this happens," he said with a sigh.

"She's not alone. She has Ashley, me and you."

The conversation went on as JD finished his meal. He kissed his mom on the cheek and left.

"Well, well, James, honey," Martha said talking to the ceiling, "I think your son has found the one. Let's see, it's April. Yep, by the end of the year we can expect a wedding."

Across the city, Ashley was preparing for work. She was surprised to hear Tracy in her room.

"Tracy, are you going to work?" she asked.

"Ashley, do you think you could handle the office for me today? I'm not feeling that great."

"Okay, I can do that. Are you spending the whole week in the house?" Ashley asked, concerned.

"No, I just need a little time."

"I know what's going on with your brother is getting to you, but you can't hide in this house forever. Eventually, you will have to deal with what's happened and move on. Just ask JD where things stand and stop worrying. JD is a man of his word. He said he would work things out and he will."

"You know, Ashley; it's easy for you to move forward when things happen, because you always know one of your many family members will have your back. I don't have that luxury. So if I choose to sit in this house and not put on the smile everyone thinks I should have, forgive me. I'm sure I'll get back in touch with myself soon and everyone will be happy again."

Ashley raised her eyebrow at Tracy. "Feel better now that you have that off your chest?"

Tracy looked at Ashley regretfully. "I am so   ry. I didn't mean to put that on you. Just let me have a few days to ge   self back on track."

"Okay, Tracy needs a few moments to herself. I'm leaving now so Tracy can have some alone time," Ashley said in a very perky voice.

They both started laughing.

"Give me a hug." Ashley sighed. "You will be just fine. Call JD; see what he can tell you. I'll talk to you later. I have to go play boss."

"See you later." Tracy smiled.

Instead of calling, Tracy decided to go to JD's office. As she got off the elevator she looked around for some directions. A very attractive older woman at the receptionist desk called out. "May I help you with something?"

"Yes," Tracy replied with a smile, "I'm trying to locate Jeffrey Harrison's office."

"You're in the right place," Mrs. Langston replied. "Do you have an appointment?"

"No, I'm sorry; I should have known I needed an appointment. I'll just try to reach him later."

Tracy had turned to walk away when Mrs. Langston said, "Let me buzz his office; he may be free."

Tracy, having second thoughts, replied, "Thank you, but that's okay, I don't want to be a bother."

"No bother, honey, hold on. Mr. Harrison, there's a—what's your name, dear?"

"Tracy Washington."

"There's a Tracy Washington here to see you. I'll let her know. He'll be right with you."

Now Tracy really wished she had not made this trip. Her stomach was doing the flip and flop thing it does when she was nervous. Seeing her discomfort, Mrs. Langston asked with a reassuring smile, "May I get you anything while you're waiting, Ms. Washington?"

"You wouldn't happen to have some Pepto-Bismol back there, would you?" Tracy replied smiling.

"No," Mrs. Langston replied and laughed. "I have something better." She motioned her hand for Tracy to come closer. "Homemade sugar cookies. They're wonderful, if I may say so myself. Would you like one?" she whispered.

"Okay, thank you. Why are we whispering?"

"Because they're our secret," a voice from behind declared.

Before Tracy turned she knew it was Jeffrey. She turned and thought, *my Lord, that's a good looking man, especially in a suit.*

"Quick, Mrs. Langston," he said over Tracy's head, "hit me with another."

They both looked around to make sure no one was looking. "Okay, Mr. Harrison, but that's your quota for the day."

JD took the cookies and put them in his suit pocket. Tracy smiled at the two of them. He was taken by that smile again, and Mrs. Langston noticed his reaction.

"You should do that more often," he said.

"What?" Tracy asked.

"Smile," he replied. "Come on let's go to my office."

He put his hand on the small of her back. It felt as if it naturally belonged there. He guided her down the hallway to his office.

Mrs. Langston watched the couple. "Hmm," she observed.

"As you can see, I'm spoiled. My mom cooked breakfast for me and Mrs. Langston bakes cookies for me," he commented with a smile.

Tracy smiled up at him. "You're fortunate to have so many people who love you."

"Have a seat," JD offered. "You have people who love you, too, Tracy."

"There's only one I know of and that's why I'm here." She exhaled. "I don't want you to compromise your position here, but is there anything you can tell me about Turk?"

JD gazed at her with a frown. "Who is Turk?"

"Oh, I'm sorry. My brother—Turk is short for Turkey," she replied, shaking her head to disregard that part of the conversation. "It's a long story."

He smiled. "I love these names you two have; you call him Turk; he calls you Sugie."

She smiled. "Yes, he does."

"Al is doing okay. I met with him the other day."

She smiled. "He's not hurt or anything like that?"

"No, he's not," JD assured her.

"Okay." She breathed a sigh of relief.

JD was glad he could ease her fears a little.

"You actually saw him?"

"Yes, I did."

"Is he somewhere I can see him?" she asked with a gleam in her eye.

JD sat forward. He knew what he was about to say would take that gleam away. "It would not be safe for you to see him right now, Tracy. He is very concerned, with good reason, for your safety."

Seeing the disappointment in her eyes, he walked around to the front of the desk where she was sitting and hunched down beside her. "Tracy, Al made a deal and he will be going away for a long time. The only thing he asked of me in return was to make sure you stayed safe and I gave him my word that I would make that happen. Right now, it is very important to keep your connection with him confidential. You being anywhere near him could cause a problem."

He saw the tears begin to form in her eyes, but they never fell.

"I understand," she smiled sadly. "Thanks for this. At least I know he's okay."

She picked up her purse and stood to leave. "Turk is the only person who cared anything about me one way or another. He's protected me all my life. It's going to be hard to let that go."

JD stood to walk her to the elevator. Now it was his job to protect her. She stopped and asked, "He doesn't want to see me, does he?"

JD would not lie to her. "He can't, not now."

Tracy looked down, so JD would not see the hurt within her. "Okay, well, I'll let you get back to work."

Sensing her disappointment, JD smiled. "Tracy, trust me, this will be okay. I'll walk you to the elevator."

"Jeffrey," she said while walking down the hallway, "where's my cookie?" She stopped directly in front of him and stuck her hand out. "Give them up."

They stood there watching each other as if it was a standoff. He pulled the cookies from his inner pocket, and gave her one.

"Thank you," she said and bit into the cookie.

"You're a cookie thief," JD declared. "We don't play with the cookies."

She began to laugh. "Mrs. Langston," Tracy said, "thank you for the cookies. They made life a little easier to swallow."

"You are welcome, Ms. Washington. Please come back to see us. It's not often we get to see such a beautiful smile."

"Thank you," Tracy responded blushing. "I'll try. Jeffrey, thank you for making the time for me today."

"Anytime you need me just come by or call, I'll be here," JD replied with a little more enthusiasm than he planned.

Tracy smiled and the elevator doors closed. JD stood there staring at the door.

"She's a beautiful woman with a beautiful spirit; it's not often you see the two together," Mrs. Langston commented.

JD turned. "Yes, she is, and you are right, it's not often you see it." He smiled and began walking down the hallway. *Not often at all*, he thought. He entered his office and picked up the phone then dialed a number.

"We need to meet. I need you to do something for me; it's a deal breaker. You asked me to trust you, now I need you to trust me. Previous arrangement; one hour earlier."

Tracy went home feeling a little relieved, but trying to deal with the thought of never seeing Turk again. It's official, she was really alone in this world. No family to turn to if something went wrong or just if she needed something. She wiped that depressing thought from her head. She put her hair up in a ponytail, changed into a pair of jeans and a midriff blouse and began concentrating on her project. At least she could get a couple of hours of work in before Ashley came home. The telephone rang and she answered.

"Tracy, hi, it's Jeffrey."

He called himself Jeffrey, not JD. About time he noticed that, Tracy thought as she smiled.

"I really did not like the way things went today. I know you were disappointed. Let me make it up to you. Come go for a ride with me."

"Jeffrey, I'm not in the best of moods and I'm not dressed to go out."

"I'll have you back in about an hour," JD appealed.

"Okay. Do I have time to change?"

"No, I'm out front and we are on a time schedule."

"Okay, I'll be down." *What the hell,* Tracy thought, *she needed the company.* Tracy grabbed her keys and purse and went downstairs. Jeffrey was standing at his black 750 BMW as he opened the passenger door for her.

"Jeffrey, where are we going? As you can see I have on jeans and you're in a suit, driving the Beamer. It's going to be embarrassing if anyone sees you with me like this."

She looked sexy as hell to him. "Embarrassed? What are you talking about?"

"Cynthia said you never ride in a Beamer unless you are dressed, people will be looking."

He looked at her and shook his head. "Cynthia? Get in the car."

Tracy shrugged her shoulders "okay" and got into the car.

The things women tend to care about are beyond me, JD thought as he pulled off.

"You are a highly intelligent woman. Explain to me, why do you listen to Cynthia of all people?"

"I usually don't, but she seems to know about things like that. I don't."

"Things like what?"

"Things like cars, men and what people do and do not care about."

"Does Cynthia have a man?"

"I don't think so, but she has had plenty."

JD smiled. "I bet she has, but has she been able to keep one?"

"Not so far."

"Okay, wouldn't it be better if you listen to one of your friends who has a man?"

"In theory, that would be a sound decision, but a difficult one."

"Why?"

"I don't have any friends who have a good history with a man."

JD laughed. He had forgotten just how honest Tracy was. "Here, you have to put this on."

Tracy looked at it. "Why am I putting on a headband?"

"It's not a headband; it's a blindfold."

"No, it's not, it's a headband," she answered with a laugh.

"Okay, it's a headband that I'm making into a blindfold; now put this over your eyes," JD declared, a little frustrated.

"Why?"

"Because, where I'm taking you is a surprise."

"Why?"

"Because it is; now put this on."

She just looked at him as if he had lost his mind. Recognizing the "I'm about to go off on your ass" look, JD explained. "Look, before you go off on me, I really need you to put this on before I go any further."

"Why?"

"Because, I don't want you to see where we are going."

"Okay." *That's simple enough*, she thought as she put the blindfold on. "It's still a headband."

JD smiled and drove on. He had forgotten, honesty works for her.

"Where are we going?" Tracy asked after a few minutes.

"It's a surprise," JD replied. Seeing she was a little uneasy, he held her hand. "Do you trust me, Tracy?"

She hesitated. "Yes." Then she closed her hand around his. Tracy was a little nervous. She had not really been around Jeffrey for this long in a while.

"What have you been up to since graduation?" he asked.

"Just work," she responded. "I see you've been doing very well with your career."

"Things have been okay."

She nodded.

"Those folks with the propensity for violence keep me pretty busy," he said, smiling.

She laughed. "Yeah, well, there's quite a few of them out there, you know. I'm surprised you remember that conversation."

"I remember every conversation we've had."

Tracy did not want to go back there. She had buried those hurt feelings and did not want to bring them back up. The sad part was, she still hadn't dealt with the rejection from him. She had just crawled back into her shell and stayed there. JD was sorry he took the conversation that way. She became silent. He was sure he hurt her back then, but that was not his intention. Hopefully this little trip would make up for that. He stopped the car.

"Are we here?"

"Yes," JD replied. "Tracy, don't get out of the car until I tell you it's okay."

She shrugged her shoulders. "Okay."

JD got out of the car. Tracy thought she heard voices, but she was not sure. Getting a little nervous, she called out, "Jeffrey?"

"Yes, I'm right here."

"May I take off the headband?"

"It's not a headband; it's a blindfold. And no, not yet."

"Okay." Tracy sat there.

The door opened. "Okay, you can get out now," JD said as he extended his hand to help her.

"Okay, may I take off the headband now?" Tracy asked.

"It's not a headband, it's a blindfold."

She put her hands on her hips. "We're not going through this again?"

"Yes," he said, a little exasperated, "you can take it off now."

As she took it off she saw Brian. "That's not much of a surprise."

Brian's eyebrow went up. "I'm insulted."

"You'll get over it," she said.

Jeffrey laughed and turned her around.

"Turk!" Tracy screamed, then ran full speed ahead and jumped dead into his arms. Turk grabbed her and hugged her tight.

"Hey, Sugie. Man, you look good. It's so good to see you."

She put her head down into his shoulder and begged him. "Please don't leave me here alone. Let me go with you wherever you're going."

Turk looked over his shoulder at Jeffrey.

"This is why he did not want to see her," Jeffrey said to Tuck and Brian.

"He hates telling her no," Tuck said, "or seeing tears in her eyes."

Turk set her down. He stood her straight up, held her at arms' length. "Sugie, I'm going to prison. You cannot go with me."

"I know that, but I can move to the town where you will be. That way I can come and visit."

Turk just looked at her. She had grown into a beautiful woman, but all he could see was his little sister, and he smiled.

"I don't want to be alone anymore, Turk," Tracy said with tears streaming down her face.

JD turned his back to them. He could not deal with seeing her upset. Brian took his hand and ran it down the length of his face to hide his emotions. Tucker put his head down and turned away. Turk took her hands in his. "You are not going to be alone. You have people who care about you and a life to live."

Tears flowed down her face as he talked. She listened and tried to control the tears.

"You will never be alone, Sugie. I will always be here, just like before, nothing is changing. If you ever need to reach me for any reason, just tell Harrison. No one else, unless he says it's okay, do you understand?"

"Yes."

Trying to make her smile, he stepped back. "Damn, Sugie, you are all that and some more. Why don't you have a man looking out for you?"

"Because I got tired of you scaring them off and gave up."

"Oh, yeah; I did do that, didn't I?" Turk laughed. "Sugie, look at yourself, you can have any man you want. Just make sure he's worth it."

"Oh, now you will let me have a man? All my life growing up it was stay away from those knuckleheads; they ain't no good." She smiled.

"Well they ain't, but I might be willing to let up a little bit, if he's worth it."

"Thanks a lot. But it's a little late; nobody wants me now."

Everybody looked up at each other, Jeffrey, Brian and Tucker, and then looked at her.

"Shit, I don't believe that," Tuck sneered.

Turk glowered over her shoulder at Tucker and he turned away. Brian and Jeffrey both laughed. "Where the hell did you get that idea?"

"Cynthia tells me that all the time. Apparently she's right. Never had one and don't see any in the near future."

"Who in the hell is Cynthia and why you letting her control you?"

"Don't ask," JD stated.

Turk looked at him.

"We have to go," Brian announced, looking at his watch.

The tears were starting to form again, but Tracy held them back this time. She did not want Turk seeing her for the last time with tears in her eyes.

"As soon as I can I will let you know how I'm doing so you won't worry. I've been taking care of myself for a long time, Sugie, and I'm still here."

"I know. I love you, Turk."

"I love you, too, Sugie."

He hugged her tight. "What about Harrison? He's a man," Turk whispered in her ear.

"He's way out of my league," Tracy replied.

"You sure about that, little sis?"

"Yeah, I'm sure, and so is Cynthia."

"Cynthia, huh. Okay, I got to go." He kissed her cheek, and then got into the Suburban with Brian.

Tracy waved goodbye to Turk and Brian pulled off. She stood there and watched as the Suburban drove out of sight. JD went to her and put his arms around her. She put her head on his chest and quietly let the tears flow. He held her and tried to console her, as every tear seemed to go straight to his heart. He looked at Tucker as he gave the motion that they had to go. "Tracy, we have to go now."

She nodded, lifted her head, and wiped her tears. "Okay."

JD put her in the car and closed the door. He went over and shook Tucker's hand. "Good luck, man."

"You too," Tucker replied. "I'll follow you out."

JD nodded and got into his car. As they were pulling off, she asked, "Jeffrey, do I have to put the dumb headband back on?"

He grinned and said, "Blindfold, blindfold!"

"Headband," she replied.

He took the headband and threw it out of the window. She smiled with tears in her eyes. He took her hand in his and held it. She laid her head back and fell asleep.

Every woman JD had ever dealt with played some kind of game. This woman sitting beside him was different. She was simple, honest, beautiful inside and out. She affected him in a way that made him feel like a man. Not in the sexual way, but in the love, honor and protect way. Well, since it was his thoughts, he admitted: she was sexy as hell to him. But, now a few things from the past were a little clearer to him. The incident with Uncle Joe was a reminder in some way of what Al took her from. JD remembered the conversation they had years ago. Now, he thought, she might be right. He would not ever knowingly break the law, but the right circumstances, like the thought of someone hurting her, would make him have the "propensity for violence," as she put it. He smiled to himself. Yet again, she's off limits, but this time because of the case.

Jeffrey pulled into his mother's driveway and turned the car off. His first instinct was to kiss Tracy's hand to wake her, but he couldn't do that. So he squeezed her hand.

"Hey, time for some real TLC," he said.

Tracy opened her eyes and turned towards him. She smiled at him and looked around.

"We're at your mom's house?"

"Yeah. Come on, let's go inside."

"Okay," she said sleepily.

"Does your mom know we're coming?"

"No."

"Jeffrey, we can't just stop in without calling, that's rude."

He raised an eyebrow. "Not with family."

"Yes, with family, too."

"Where did you get that from?"

"Cynthia."

"I should have known. I have to keep you away from her," he said and put the key in the door. "Hey, Mom."

"JD?" his mom called out.

"Yeah, I have someone who needs your dinner."

"Tracy." Martha said as she came into the living room. "Hi, honey, how you doing?" She gave Tracy a hug.

"I'm fine, Mrs. Harrison. How are you?" Tracy replied with a smile.

"Oh, honey, I'm just fine. Y'all come on in the kitchen; I got dinner on the stove. Tracy, it's funny you came by, I was gonna call you later."

"You were? Did you need something?"

"Oh, no, honey, I was just gonna check on you. Ashley said you were feeling a little down and I just wanted to tell you I was thinking about you."

"That is so special, thank you."

"Well, you're here now. I can feed you. That always makes you feel better."

Tracy smiled. "Thank you, Mrs. Harrison. May I help you with anything?"

"No, honey. Just sit down at the table and tell me about your day."

"I had an okay day. How was yours?"

JD smiled. He knew Tracy had a hell of a day and did not need to be alone. This is what she needed today, family. He stood in the doorway, loosened his tie and watched his mother work her magic on Tracy.

Ashley came over after work. JD had called her earlier and gave her a summary of the day. They were all sitting out on the patio eating dinner and talking when JD received the call from Brian that all was settled and well. JD took Tracy by the hand and walked her over to the swing set at the end of the yard. He sat her in the swing and told her about Al. She nodded. "Okay. I know you will do what's right by Turk and he trusts that you will, too. You just need to wrap it up and seal the deal, right?"

"Right," he replied with a smile.

Desperate now to talk about anything except Turk or her future, she sighed. "Why does your mother's flower bed stop there?" Tracy turned and saw where the other side stopped. "And there, like it's a gap."

JD stood to see what she was referring to. "Oh, that." He smirked. He walked over to the area and she followed him. "My dad was putting a border of flowers around the fence for my mom. He never had a chance to finish it before he died." He hunched his shoulders and sighed. "I keep telling her I will finish it, but I haven't yet."

"Why not, you've been too busy?"

"Not really, I could do it on a weekend."

"JD, are you making promises and not keeping them?" she joked.

He turned and smiled back. He liked the way her eyes lit up when she smiled. "No."

Tracy could see he was having a difficult time expressing his feelings with this.

"When I look at this it reminds me of my dad. I'm afraid if I finish it, I might forget him. Hmm," he frowned. "I have never said that out loud. Thought it, but never said it."

"How long has he been gone?"

"Eight years this summer," he replied as he put his hands in his pockets.

Jeffrey is such a proud man, Tracy thought. *It has to be difficult for him to say he's afraid of something.* He and Ashley were so much alike. She looked at him. "You know, Jeffrey, when someone touches your heart, and I mean truly touches your heart, you can never forget them. Your dad will always be a part of your heart; he will not be forgotten." She looked up at the sky, then back to him. "Seems like you have a few things to wrap up."

She turned and began walking back to the house. He stood there for a moment and then followed her. As they walked in silence, JD thought, *It's so easy to be around her; no drama; no pretenses. Damn, she scares the hell out of me.*

Ashley and Martha sat on the patio and watched the two of them.

"Mom," Ashley said, "do you see what I see?"

"Yep," Martha replied.

"Is that okay with you?"

"She's your friend, are you okay with it?"

"Do you think JD's ready for her?"

"You know, honey, if you had asked me yesterday, I would have said no, but after what I've seen and heard today, he's definitely ready. The question is: does he know he's ready? Your brother's been out there playing around for a long time. He may have a hard time letting the lifestyle go. Tracy may not understand that."

"I see it a little different," Ashley said. "I think the question is, does Tracy even know what's happening? The girl is naïve when it comes to men; no experience, clueless. JD's background with the women may scare her off."

"Well, honey, she knows something, because she's got your brother's interest."

Ashley and Martha laughed, and went into the house.

Chapter 5

Ashley beamed with pride as she and Tracy rode the elevator to the 12ᵗʰ floor of the state building. She had finally contributed to the company she and Tracy started during their junior year at Harmon. Well to be honest it was really Tracy. As a way of making money Tracy began working for a small business in the Norfolk area as a filing clerk. In the course of her job, she began making suggestions on how organize and work more efficiently. The owner was so impressed with the outcome of Tracy's suggestions that she introduce her to a few other mom and pop business owners in the area. Tracy seemed to have the same magical touch for them. Her boss suggested Tracy start an efficiency business that specialized in small business organizations. One of the top reasons small businesses failed was because the owners knew their tasks very well, but did not know the business end. Tracy began with 3 small businesses that she acted as a consultant to help organize and then ventured into suggestions on investing their capitol. The only problem was Tracy was not a people person, so explaining to people what she did was difficult. That's where Ashley came in. She had no problem talking to people and loved to boast about Tracy's IQ. So, she began talking to other business owners about what Tracy was capable of and Next Level Consulting was formed. Ashley would set up meetings to get the clients interested. Then Tracy would go into the business and assess the need. She would put a proposal together then explain it to Ashley, who would in turn present the project to the clients for a very reasonable fee. By the end of their junior year they had 6 clients with five-year contracts. At the end of their senior year they had twenty. By the time they graduated, Next Level Consulting was grossing enough income to give both six-figure salaries.

At Next Level Consulting, things were progressing. Proud of the fact that she had initiated and closed their first major deal, Ashley set up a meeting for Tracy and the Commissioner of Special Services, James Brooks to meet. He signed the contract, but wanted to meet with the person At Next Level who would be handling employee development. The meeting was held at the state office, which was located on Broad Street in the downtown Richmond. When Ashley and Tracy stepped into the office, there were several people present. Ashley stepped forward. "Hello, Mr. Brooks, it's good to see you again. This is Tracy Washington, owner and developer for Next Level Consulting."

Tracy extended her hand. "Good morning, Mr. Brooks."

"Ms. Washington, it is indeed a pleasure to finally meet you." He smiled. "Let me introduce my staff: Angel Brown, human resources, Herman Kraft, accounting, and Karen Holt, assistant commissioner."

Ashley began the program. "Good morning, everyone. If you will take a seat, we can get started."

She waited a moment while everyone took a seat and settled down.

"Thank you. My name is Ashley Harrison. This lovely person is Tracy Washington. We are the owners of Next Level Consulting. Before we get started, we would like to take a moment to thank you for entrusting your organization with us. Now, we will show you how we plan to reward that trust. I will be handling the presentation and Ms. Washington, our efficiency expert, will be available for technical questions."

Ashley gave a clear, concise presentation, not leaving anything to chance. Tracy answered all questions regarding how the tasks would be accomplished. The two of them together could convince a drowning man to buy a case of bottled water.

After the meeting James approached Tracy. "Ms. Washington," he said in a rich, deep voice, "Ashley tells me you are the person who actually put together the package for our organization."

"Yes, I am."

"I must say I'm more than impressed and a little astonished."

"Astonished?" Tracy questioned. "Why?"

"The layout of the plan is nothing less than brilliant. I have no doubt if the plan is followed this agency will experience the efficiency level we need to serve the public."

"I believe that also. That's what you were looking for. Did you doubt our ability to deliver?"

"Usually that level of comprehension and detail comes from experience. You don't appear to be much over the age of 18. Yet you have a firm grasp on the pulse of the business world."

Tracy thought for a moment. This was the very reason she preferred not to deal with clients, because of her tendency to say exactly what came to mind, which, on most occasions, was not very tactful.

"Mr. Brooks, I genuinely believe there was a compliment in that statement. I am certain that it was not a question of the integrity of our company."

He smiled. "You are very protective of your company. That's admirable. But please know I was simply admiring your work."

"If that's the case, please accept my apology. And, yes, I am very protective of our reputation. We are a young organization, as you mentioned." She smiled. "I'm afraid our reputation is all we have at this point."

James was more than a little taken with this beautiful young woman standing in front of him.

"Well, Ms. Washington, I will be open to accept that apology over lunch. Will you join me?"

Tracy frowned a little, then smiled. "In case you haven't picked up on this little tidbit, I'm not the people person in our organization. Believe me, there is a reason for that. I'm certain I would bore you to death. So before I cause more damage than I already have, I'll pass on lunch."

"You know, a simple no would have sufficed," he said with a laugh. She laughed with him. James's heart leapt at her smile.

"Do you know your face lights up when you smile?"

Tracy stepped back. She was a little uncomfortable with the way the conversation was going. Sensing her uneasiness, James commented, "Please know I don't mean to be offensive and normally I am not so forward. But I am more than a little impressed with you."

Tracy blushed. "Thank you."

"Are we ready to wrap up?" Ashley asked as she approached.

"Yes, I believe we are," Tracy replied. "Mr. Brooks, it was a pleasure." Tracy extended her hand.

"The pleasure was entirely mine." He took Tracy's hand and held it. She pulled away after a moment.

"Good day, Mr. Brooks," Ashley said as they walked away.

Tracy turned back and smiled.

JD could not sleep. He would usually call Carolyn or some other lady to help him relax, but not tonight. His mind kept thinking about Tracy. So he called Calvin instead.

"Hey, man, you asleep?" JD asked.

"Well, let me think about that for a minute, JD." Calvin yawned. "Not anymore. What's up?"

"I'm trying to work on this plea agreement and I need your help."

"I thought the agreement was 40 years on the kingpin charge and 10 on the racketeering, to be served concurrently."

"That was it, but I need to do something a little different," JD said and then went silent.

When JD did not continue, Calvin asked, "What are you not telling me?"

"I need something that would satisfy Gavin, the AG's office, and not be devastating to Tracy."

For some reason, that was very important to him. It should not play a role in his decision, but it did. He did not want to destroy the trust he saw in Tracy's eyes the night before. Calvin sat up in bed, turned to look at Jackie, lying next to him. He did not want to leave that woman tonight.

"Alright, man, you better be glad I love you like a brother. I'll be there in 15."

JD had a drink waiting for him when he arrived. Calvin took the drink and looked at JD. "Tracy, huh?" Calvin smirked.

JD turned and started talking about the case. Calvin sipped his drink and wondered to himself how JD was going to pull this one off. He had no doubt that JD would find a way, but it was always amazing to see his mind at work.

The arraignment was held at 8:00 A.M. in Judge Margaret W. Mathew's courtroom. Judge Maggie, as JD referred to her, was tough but fair, and he knew he could trust her to do the right thing by Al. The deal took place with the Attorney General, JD, Calvin, Day's attorney and of course Al. One officer and a clerk reporter were in the courtroom. Al accepted the deal and the conviction was sealed with sentencing guidelines and location. No one outside of that courtroom knew where Al Day was going, and JD wanted to make sure it stayed that way.

Day's information was damaging enough to make a few people in the homicide division very uncomfortable. The information on Gavin could be harmful to someone running for political office. JD was convinced the whole story had not surfaced yet. His instincts told him something was missing. He decided to hold off on the information Al gave him until he was sure what took place. JD believed Gavin made this information surface because he wanted Al out of the way before he made a bid for the governor's office. However, he wasn't convinced Gavin would have Al killed. However, this left enough doubt for JD not to trust Gavin on this case. Therefore the only people privy to any information were JD and his select few.

As JD left the courtroom he knew he had a few things to wrap up in his life. There was no better time than the present. He placed a call to Carolyn and arranged to see her that evening. Upon his return to the office, he checked in with Mrs. Langston. "Hello, Mrs. Langston, everything okay around here?" JD asked as she handed him his messages.

"Mr. Roberts is looking for you, has been all morning. Every 15 minutes or so. It's about time for him right about now. Hmm, what do you know, there he is. Mr. Roberts, guess who I found for you?"
She looked at JD and started laughing under her breath.

"Thanks a lot, friend," JD joked. "Gavin, they tell me you've been looking for me, what's up?" JD asked while reading his messages.

"JD, let me talk to you for a minute."

"Sure, your office or mine?"

"Yours will do."

"That's good; at least I know I'm not being fired." JD winked at Mrs. Langston.

They walked to JD's office. He closed the door, put down his briefcase, then sat at his desk.

"What can I do for you, Gavin?"

"Well, I received a call from the Attorney General himself congratulating me on a job well done with the Day case. Now, I'm sure you can imagine my surprise to find out the case is a done deal."

"Oh, yeah, that was wrapped up this morning. Made an offer, Day accepted, the court had an opening. The AG got it in on the docket; closed the deal. Indictment, conviction and sentencing all in one day. I tell you, Gavin, I like the way they operate over there. No bullshit back and forth trying to get deals approved." JD sat forward, put his hands across the desk, and glared at Gavin. Gavin knew JD very well. The tone in his voice and the look on his face told him JD had something but wasn't talking.

"Anything I should be aware of?" Gavin questioned.

"Not at this time," JD said, sitting back, "but I will let you know if anything comes up."

"So you found Day's sister?" Gavin smirked.

"Wasn't hard, but you knew that. Here's something else you should know. She has my protection now. As long as she is happy, I'm happy."

"JD," Gavin said as he stood, "if I didn't know better, I would think that sounded like a threat."

"No," JD replied as he stood. "It would only sound like that if there was something to be threatened by. You have no reason to be threatened by me, unless something happens to her. As far as I'm concerned, it's business as usual."

Gavin acknowledged JD's statement by nodding his head and walked out of the room.

JD exhaled. "One issue wrapped up, on to the next."

Gavin went to his office and made a call. "Harrison knows something, but he's not going to talk if you stay away from the girl," Gavin stated.

"Harrison is just like his father, straight as they come. How do you know he won't come after us?"

"I don't think he has us, I think he has me. We can't take any chances on this. I'm the one who stands to lose everything I've worked 20 years for. All we want is Day silent. She is our assurance that he won't talk. As long as JD has a hand in this nothing will come out."

"Are you sure of that, Gavin?"

"He gave his word. But to be safe, I have something that will keep him occupied."

Tracy was already in the office working when Ashley got in around 8. "What the hell did you do, come in at dawn?" Ashley asked while pouring a cup of coffee.

Tracy looked up. "No," she replied laughing. "I got in around 7 and started working on Brook's project."

"Oh, yes, my first closer, you must make that one good. My reputation is on the line," Ashley boasted.

"Well, I've got to give it to you, you made a good deal. I taught you well." Tracy smiled and stepped around to the front of her desk and gave Ashley a high five.

"I feel like I'm contributing now, not just hanging on your skirt tail."

Tracy looked at her with a frown. "You always contributed."

Ashley sat down on the sofa next to the door. "Yeah, but not like you. All I did was talk to people. You put the packages together and keep the ball rolling. I just bring them in. It's your work that keeps them sending in their friends for consultations."

"It takes both pieces to make the company successful," Tracy said and sat on the edge of her desk. "I can't persuade people like you can and your mind can't work like mine."

"Girl, you are so right. That piece you put in about matching employee contributions in the investment plan was really a deal sealer. James loved it," Ashley exclaimed.

"That's good to know; tells me he's into his employee's well-being and personal growth."

"Okay, whatever." Ashley took a sip of her coffee. "So, what's up with you and JD?"

Tracy tilted her head to the side and got up. "What are you talking about?"

"I saw you two in the yard talking the other night."

"Oh, that was about Turk and what he is doing with the case."

"Looked like a lot of hand holding to me."

"It was a rough day."

"That's all?"

"Yep, that's all."

"Tracy, you know I love you like a sister, and I have never steered you wrong."

"Bullshit," Tracy replied with laughing.

"Okay, okay, okay, once or twice," Ashley said, and put her hand up, "but I was still trying to look out for you."

"Okay, I give you that. But?" Tracy said, waiting for Ashley to continue.

"JD's my brother and I love him, but you know he's a player. He has not had one serious relationship since Vanessa, way back when."

"Okay." Tracy raised her eyebrow. "And?"

"You are a very serious type person and I don't want you to get hurt."

"Hurt by who?"

"It's whom, not who," Ashley stated.

"Oh, now you are giving me English lessons?"

"No, I'm just saying, I did not want you to misread JD's attention to you yesterday. I know how you used to feel about him," Ashley said, as she eyed Tracy over her coffee cup.

"Ashley, I might be a little naïve, but I'm not crazy. I know there is no way Jeffrey would even be remotely interested in me. Please, I don't have what it takes to be on the front of anybody's magazine cover and that's what he goes for. So don't worry about that, I have not lost my senses, yet. I know my place; Cynthia taught me well."

Ashley got up. *Yep, she still has feelings for him.* She smiled to herself. "Well, that's not how I meant it, but okay." Ashley shrugged her shoulders. "I just want to make sure you are not setting yourself up for disappointment like you have a tendency to do."

Tracy smiled. "Thanks for looking out, but I'm straight on this one." When Ashley left, Tracy closed her eyes and thought, *okay, remember your place, get that man out of your head, NOW....*

Ashley went to her office called her mom. "Mom, I tried to feel Tracy out. She has such a complex about JD. Getting them together is not going to happen without our intervention."

"Okay, I'm in honey, just tell me what to do," Martha replied.

"Well, I'll lay the groundwork, you just follow my lead."

"Good job today," Calvin commented as JD joined him at Maxi's bar. "You managed to get Gavin his 'kudos' from the governor, satisfy the AG and Day. That's a hell of a job for one day."

"Jack straight," JD said to the bartender.

"Coming up, JD."

"Thanks, man. I appreciate you listening last night. I needed a sounding board," JD stated as he took his drink. "You got a minute or do you have plans with Jackie?" JD motioned to Calvin to take a booth.

"Yeah, what's up?" Calvin asked as they took a seat.

He hesitated. "Do you love Jackie?"

Laughing, Calvin responded, "Man, why are you asking me some shit like that," ready to give the typical male response.

"Well, do you?"

Seeing JD was serious, Calvin replied, "Yeah, but I will take the Fifth if you tell her. Why you ask?"

"How do you know?"

"I am not sure what you mean."

"How do you know it's love and not lust?" JD clarified. "I mean, there are millions of women out there. What is it about this one that makes you want to be with just her?"

Calvin smiled. JD needed guidance. He had not allowed any women to get close to him. Calvin thought at one time Vanessa had penetrated that thick skin of his, but that ended. Now, apparently someone was making him think of a one-on-one again. The last thing Calvin wanted to do was to hand him that bullshit most men tell other men.

"Well, you're right; there are a lot of women out there. But I haven't found one, other than Jackie, that makes me want to go home every night," Calvin confessed.

If this was the way he could help JD experience what he has with Jackie, he would break the male code, tell him the real deal.

"It doesn't matter what we do or where we go. I just want to be wherever she is. There were times when we had plans to go out to dinner or to one of Carolyn's functions, but instead we stayed home, alone, and loved it. I enjoy taking the time to get to know her; hearing about her day and all the crazy shit Carolyn is up to. It's the craziest thing." Calvin laughed. "All hell can break loose at work. But when I go home, Jackie knows just what to say or do to calm me down."

As if a second thought just hit him, Calvin added, "Oh man, when it comes to sex, you haven't felt anything until you make love to a woman you actually love and she loves you back. There's nothing like it. It doesn't matter if it's a 'I got to have it now on top of the kitchen table' or a session you planned with the candles and shit."

He hesitated for a moment. "I would give my right arm for Jackie if she asked. But she would never ask. Because she loves me with the same intensity that I love her and that's what makes it good." Calvin stopped.

JD thought for a moment and smiled at his friend's happiness. "What happens when she leaves? How do you cope with that?"

"What makes you think she's going to leave?"

"They always do," JD responded, "one way or another. Look at Vanessa. I loved Vanessa; she left. Look at Mama. She loved Daddy with all her heart and he left."

In all the years Calvin had known JD it had never dawned on him JD was afraid of being abandoned.

"Your dad did not abandon you, JD, or your mother."
JD flinched.

"As for Vanessa, well let's examine that, JD," Calvin said. "Did you really love Vanessa, I mean really? If Tracy had been available to you back then, Vanessa would have been history long before she actually was."

JD looked at Calvin.

"Yeah, I knew you had a little thing for Tracy back then," Calvin stated. "Apparently it was deep enough that you still feel it now, six years later. So I ask you again, did you really love Vanessa or was she just a convenience?" Calvin sipped his drink.

"As for your mom," Calvin said with a chuckle, "she has a smile on her face every time I see her. It's the same smile she had when we were little and your dad came home from work. You should ask her why she's still smiling. Oh, just so you know, I don't worry about if or when Jackie may leave. I enjoy having her in my life one day at a time. If she leaves, at least I can say, I know what it felt like to be truly in love."

Calvin watched JD for a moment. He knew his reconnection with Tracy was what prompted this conversation. He remembered JD struggling with getting Tracy off his mind and using Vanessa to do it. Calvin also knew Carolyn would go after Tracy if JD started seeing her. Carolyn could be a devious bitch.

"JD," Calvin started, "hear me out on this. I'm going to say this with all the respect and love a man can have for a brother, and you know I'm down with you for whatever, have been since kindergarten." Calvin wanted to be sure he said this right. "I know you. Been through many women with you. Hell, shared one or two with you. Tracy isn't the type to understand the hit-and-run game that men play. She's the type you love and cherish, always. When she loves, she loves totally. When she trusts, if she trusts, she trusts totally. The two are one in the same for her. Don't play with her emotions. Remember what this girl has been through. She's been on her own all her life, except for her brother, and now he's gone. Tracy does not need you to come in, hit it and leave; she doesn't deserve that. Don't play with her; be sure of your intentions."

JD was glad Calvin was his friend. Whether he wanted to hear it or not, Calvin would always give him a straight answer. "I'm not going to hurt Tracy. To be honest, she scares the hell out of me." JD chuckled, and then finished his drink. "I'm glad you and Jackie have each other.

Don't let Carolyn or anyone else mess you up. Speaking of Carolyn, I'm running late. I'll check you later."

Calvin watched as JD left. He pulled out his cell and dialed. "Hey baby, what are you doing?"

Tracy was still in her office integrating the notes from the morning meeting into the Brooks file. As she keyed the notes into the computer, she remembered the conversation with James Brooks. *Why would a man like that be interested in her?* Tracy wondered.

James Brooks was an accomplished man. At the age of 30, he was named the Metropolitan Area Business Man of the Year. He had written several articles on management in the future. Every agency he headed was rated number one or two in the state for employee satisfaction. This was the fourth agency a sitting governor had commissioned him to head. Unfortunately, it was one of the largest in the state and had poor morale issues. He was placed there to clean up the agency, but had been met with a lot of resistance.

Tracy pulled out his bio: James Avery Brooks; age, 35; Harvard Business, Master's in Public Administration; he married at the age of 26 to his college sweetheart, divorced five years later. They had one child, a son, James Jr., 6 years old.

Tracy smiled looking at the picture of James that accompanied the bio. *The picture does not do him justice*, she thought. Maybe this could be the person to get her mind off Jeffrey. She was 24 years old now. She had put up a shield when she was 19 and had never let anyone in. It didn't appear anything would ever happen with Jeffrey. Cynthia had always said he was out of her league.

Tracy remembered when she and Ashley returned to campus from that spring break. Cynthia came by the room to see Tracy, which should have been her warning.

"What in the hell made you think you could go after JD Harrison?" Cynthia yelled at her.

A little startled, Tracy asked, "What are you talking about, Cynthia?"

"I saw you two in the sunroom at the club the other night."

"There wasn't anything to it, don't sweat it, Cynthia." Tracy turned her back and continued working.

"You do realize you are not his type. I mean, you don't have anything to offer a man like him. You don't even look the part and you're from the wrong side of the tracks, if you know what I mean. Just because they let you in their house don't mean you get to play with the big boys."

"I get it, Cynthia. You don't have to keep going on about it. I get it, okay," Tracy yelled.

"Oh, don't tell me your feelings are hurt—what did you expect? JD Harrison is the cream of the crop, girl. You can't even clean the bottom of his shoes. I'm just trying to keep your dumb ass from getting hurt. Make sure you remember that," Cynthia said as she left the room.

Tracy closed the bio on James Brooks. *Cynthia would probably say the same thing about Brooks,* She thought, smiling to herself. When she looked up, James Brooks, all 6 feet 2, 220 pounds of him, was standing in her office doorway.

"Good evening, you're working late. Now why doesn't that surprise me?" James smiled. "Do you always leave your door unlocked after hours?"

"I guess the receptionist did not lock it when she left this evening," Tracy replied, surprised. "Is there something you need, Mr. Brooks?"

He smiled. "That's a loaded question, Ms. Washington. And please call me James."

The picture really did not do him justice. She smiled. "Mr. Brooks, it is a little late and I was just about to leave. Was there something in particular that brought you here?"

"Yes, your smile."

Tracy sat back in her seat, not sure what to say.

"Before you say anything, hear me out," James said as he took a seat. "It's not in my nature to pursue a woman. I don't have the time for it. Before you walked in my office today I was curious, to say the least. Your proposal impressed me and that's not easy to do. That's why I asked to meet with you. When you walked into my office today, I was totally knocked off my game. You were a very pleasant surprise." He sat forward. "All I'm asking for is a chance to get to know you a little better, nothing more."

Tracy blushed. "Thank you. Mr. Brooks, I'm not a very sociable person. This company keeps me busy. Even if I did take time to get to know a person, it would not be one of my clients. It's a matter of principle"

"Your reputation?"

"Yes. You know the business world. Two young females, trying to run a business. The appearance of impropriety alone could kill us. That's why I keep my personal and professional lives separate. I'm sure a man of your intelligence understands that."

James smiled and stood up. "Hmm, another rejection. I do understand, but I will not concede defeat just yet."

Before Tracy could respond, Ashley, Cynthia and Rosaline came through the outer door. "Hey, Tracy." Ashley burst through the door then stopped when she saw James. "James, hello."

"Hey ho, what's going on?" Cynthia called from behind Ashley. "Oh, excuse me, I didn't know someone was here," Cynthia remarked somewhat surprised.

"Good evening," Rosaline said.

"Um, Mr. Brooks, I really don't know these people," Ashley joked.

Cynthia hit Ashley in the back and then extended her hand. "Cynthia Thornton. And you are?"

"James Brooks." He shook her hand while smiling. "It's a pleasure to meet you."

"Rosaline Taylor, and the pleasure is ours," Rosaline added, extending her hand.

"Ladies, I was just leaving." He turned to Tracy. "Ms. Washington, hopefully we will have an opportunity to continue our conversation at a later time." James smiled.

"I'll walk you to the door," Tracy replied as she stood.

"Good night, Mr. Brooks," Ashley said as Tracy and James walked out of the office.

"I apologize for that." Tracy smiled.

"No apology needed. Have a good evening, Tracy."

"You too, James."

James hoisted an eyebrow. "You see, we are making progress."

She smiled and locked the front door.

"What was James doing here?" Ashley asked from the door.

"He had one or two questions for me," Tracy replied. "What are you guys doing here?"

"Cynthia has a favor to ask." Ashley hit Cynthia on the shoulder.

Tracy could see Cynthia was contemplating her question. "Why don't we all sit down. What do you need, Cynthia?"

Cynthia inhaled. "Well, Rosaline and I have been talking about starting a business together. You seem to have a knack for putting together good business packages. So we were wondering, if you had the time, would you put one together for us."

Tracy rolled her chair back to her file cabinet, opened one of the drawers and pulled out a file. "Here you go. If you need capital, let me know." Tracy handed the file to Cynthia. The folder read "TNT Event Planning."

"How long have you had that?" Ashley asked, smiling at Tracy.

"Since the day we were in the kitchen talking about putting Rosaline in a restaurant."

"Damn, this is good," Cynthia commented. "I can even follow this."

"There's a building over on Mechanicsville Turnpike that would be perfect for a starter place. It's large enough to house functions and your offices. Cynthia, you are so good at planning and decorating. You could hook that place up in no time." Tracy smiled.

"We could have a grand opening and invite potential clients to a private event," Cynthia remarked enthusiastically.

"Girl, with the right people in the place, we may get a few hits," Rosaline added.

Ashley sat on the corner of Tracy's desk. "That was really special, Tracy. Now why was James really here?"

Tracy smiled. "He asked me out earlier today and I turned him down."

Ashley's mouth fell open. "You are not serious. Why did you turn him down?"

"'Cause she's stupid—that's a fine ass man that just left here," Cynthia responded.

Tracy looked up at Cynthia. "Well your gratitude lasted all of five minutes."

"Thank you for the plan. I'm sure with your help this will work. But you're still stupid if you turned that man down."

Tracy got up and grabbed her purse. "I'm going home now, ladies. Let me know if you want to look at that building, Cynthia. Ashley, I will see you at home."

"Wait, don't go," Cynthia pleaded, "I do have some questions about this. Please."

"Even from you, that 'please' will work. What do you have questions on?"

Chapter 6

JD went home, showered and changed before he went to pick up Carolyn. He intended to break things off with Carolyn tonight. After his talk with Calvin, he wasn't sure what to do. He knew something was happening to him whenever he was around Tracy. He didn't think it was love, but what would he know. He just knew he had to be honest with Carolyn about his feelings for Tracy. JD knew she would not take this sitting down. Carolyn had plans for him, but he told her from the beginning, he had no interest in politics or a long-lasting relationship with her. He was about to hurt her and he knew it.

He rang the doorbell. Carolyn opened the door and seductively answered, "Mr. Harrison, it's so nice of you to come by this evening, kiss kiss."

JD stepped inside. "Carolyn, you look wonderful as always," he replied as he kissed her on her cheek.

She raised her eyebrow. "That wasn't quite what I had in mind when I said a kiss."

Carolyn clutched his arm and he gently pulled away. "What's up, JD?"

"Carolyn, I was planning on us going out, but would you mind very much if we talked here?"

"Talk?" Carolyn remarked as she walked by him. "No, I don't mind."

He sat and she sat next to him on the couch. "Carolyn," he began, "I need to tell you about someone I know. I've known her for a while but hadn't seen her until recently."

Carolyn sat up. He saw her claws coming out. "An old girlfriend?" Carolyn testily asked.

"No," he replied, "I've never been involved with her."

Carolyn breathed a sigh of relief. "Okay, but you feel the need to tell me about her. Why?"

"Yes," he paused. "Because I think I might have," he hesitated, "feelings for her." He stood up and walked over to the fireplace. "Things are a little crazy right now. I seem to be going through an epiphany or something. I need to tell you about it."

Carolyn was experienced in masking her feelings. Hell, she was the daughter of a politician. If someone said Mt. Rushmore had fallen on her Mercedes, you would never know from looking at her that she was upset.

"JD." Carolyn smiled and walked over to where he stood. She put her hand on his back. "We said in the beginning if either one of us met that special someone during our journey, the other would step aside. Are you asking me to step aside?" Carolyn was playing the "I'm not into drama" card with him at the moment. She would have to explode later.

"I don't want to mislead you, Carolyn," he stated. "The feelings I have for this person are different from anything I have experienced before. I don't know where it's going to lead. But I need to find out."

"So you are not currently involved with this person?"

"No, but I want to be."

"But does she?"

"I don't know," he replied, unsure of himself.

A little relieved, Carolyn thought, *I still have time to work on him.* With that, she did what every woman does when they are trying to hold on to a man: stroke that ego.

"You are one hell of a man, JD Harrison. Whoever ends up with you will be a very lucky woman."

He looked at her, a little stunned at her response.

Carolyn smiled at his expression. "Did you expect the drama queen to come out?"

"To be honest, yes."

"You and that damn honesty." She laughed while caressing his biceps. "Believe it or not, I can control the drama." She stepped away. "With you, I care about the aftermath. Regardless of what our outcome may be, I want to continue to be a friend to you. Someone you can turn to for whatever, whenever."

JD turned to look at her, not really believing what he was hearing.

"Don't worry," she said, "I'm okay. It's just that I care about you and value your friendship. I would never do anything I thought would jeopardize that."

Carolyn knew she had caught him off guard, so she continued. She sat on the bar stool and crossed her legs. "So, tell me about her."

JD developed a newfound respect for Carolyn. Either she was playing him and doing a really good job at it, or she really meant what she just said. Or maybe he was in a funk right now. Whatever, he was just glad there was no drama tonight. He had been through enough for one day.

Nevertheless, he definitely was not going to tell Carolyn anything about Tracy.

"No, I don't think I will do that," JD replied with a smile as he sat beside her at the bar.

"You look so tense, JD. Relax. We are both adults and we knew from the beginning what we were getting into. It is sweet that you cared enough to tell me about this person. Thank you." She ran her hand over the bulge in his pants. "Did I do that?" She seductively smiled up at him.

He looked down at her and sighed. "Hmm, you were always able to get my attention."

"You seem to be in need of some attention." She squeezed him gently as she kissed his cheek. "Friends don't leave friends in need," Carolyn offered. "Whatever you need, JD, whenever."

No man in his right mind could ignore a beautiful woman saying something like that to him. *What the hell? It's not like I'm committed to Tracy yet.* He kissed Carolyn and began to rub his hands over her thighs.

Bingo opening; he can't love her but so much, Carolyn thought as she ran her hands down his body and unbuckled his pants. She shed his pants and briefs from his body and went straight for the kill, taking him into her mouth in one swoop. JD grabbed both sides of the bar in an attempt to brace himself from the feel of her tongue moving against him. The edges of her teeth were gently touching him. As she moved him in and out of her mouth with precision, he felt himself expanding at her touch. He reached for her head to let her know she was approaching the danger zone and pulled her head away just as he felt himself release.

They both slid to the floor side by side. Carolyn moved to mount him, but he stopped her. He pulled her to the side and held her. "We can't do that."

"I know, I know," she stated, "no protection." She hit him in his chest and they laughed. *Damn,* she thought, *will this man ever let his guard down?*

"Are you in love with this person, JD?"

Rising up on his elbow, he looked down at her. "I don't know, Carolyn. I don't know what it is."

"Well, take your time and find out. In the meantime, I'll be here."

JD was stunned. This was not the Carolyn he knew. "Let me make sure I have this right. You are going to be here available for me while I try to sort this thing out. Why?"

"Because I care," Carolyn replied.

"And what do you get out of it?"

"My friend," she smiled sweetly.

They talked a little longer, then JD took a shower and left. Carolyn picked up the telephone. "I'm free after all. Do you want to get together?" She paused. "No, I'll come to you."

She hung up the telephone. *Okay, JD,* she thought, *let's find out who your little love is.* Carolyn jumped in the shower, changed her clothes and left.

Chapter 7

The next morning Ashley was in the front of the office talking to Monica when JD pulled up. Monica was looking out the front window.

"There's that fine brother of yours. I saw him on TV last night talking about the gang activity in North Side."

"Yeah, that was taped a couple weeks ago. What's up, big bro?" Ashley asked as JD entered the office. "What are you doing out and about early this morning?"

He kissed her on the cheek. "Hey Squirt. Good morning, Monica, you're looking good this morning."

"Not as good as you." Monica smiled flirtatiously.

"If I was just a little bit younger, you wouldn't stand a chance," JD flirted back.

"Oh, please, please, don't let a little thing like age stop you," Monica said and stepped forward.

Ashley stepped in between both of them. "Your mom would kill you and JD both, so back off."

JD laughed and asked, "Where's Tracy?"

"She's in a meeting with James Brooks," Ashley replied.

"From Special Services?" JD questioned.

"Yeah."

"He's the commissioner over there, isn't he?"

"Yep."

"What's he doing here?"

"We just signed a contract to revamp his agency."

Impressed, JD responded, "We're not moving on up to state contracts now, are we?"

"Yep, and I closed the deal the other day."

"Get out, lil sis, I'm proud of you. I didn't know you had it in you."

James and Tracy stepped out of her office. "You are sure I can't change your mind on my invitation?" James said with a smile.

"Thank you, Mr. Brooks, but it's a matter of principle for me," Tracy replied.

"I'll accept that for now, but I will ask again."

Tracy looked up and saw JD. *Damn, that man looks good early in the morning.* Tracy and James walked over.

"Good morning," Tracy said to everyone. "Mr. Brooks, this is Monica Scott, our administrative assistant"

"Hello, Mr. Brooks, we have spoken on the telephone," Monica responded.

"It's nice to meet you in person," James replied.

"This is Ashley's brother, Jeffrey Harrison."

"Yes, we have been in each other's presence, but never officially met." James extended his hand.

"It's an honor to meet you, Mr. Brooks," JD said and extended his hand.

"I have followed your cases," James remarked. "I am very impressed with what you have been able to accomplish in some of our neighborhoods."

JD shook his hand and replied, "Thank you for that, but we still have a long way to go."

"Yes, we do, but you're young and you have time," James replied as he patted JD on the shoulder then turned to Tracy. "Ms. Washington, I look forward to speaking with you again."

"Thank you for coming by, Mr. Brooks."

"James," he said while smiling at her.

"You have a good day, sir." Tracy smiled.

"Principles, huh? We have to work on that," he replied and left.

She closed the door and all eyes were on her as she turned. "What?" Tracy asked.

"That man was flirting with you, Ms. Tracy," Monica responded.

Tracy ignored the comment. "Good morning, Jeffrey." She smiled and walked towards her office.

Now, JD wasn't sure of too many things, but one thing he did know: he did not like James Brooks. "Hello, Tracy," he managed to say as she walked by. He wasn't sure what hit him. Could it be jealousy? No, not JD Harrison, jealous? But the sight of Tracy with Brooks did piss him off.

Ashley watched the scene and laughed to herself. *JD is jealous. I would have never thought the day would come that I would see my big brother jealous over a woman. I love this,* she thought.

"Well, JD, are you here to see me or Tracy?" Ashley asked.

"Both, actually."

Tracy stopped and turned. "You need to see me?" she asked, surprised.

"Yes, just for a moment."

"Okay, come on in," she said and motioned towards the office.
JD went towards Tracy's office and said, "Ashley, I'll be in to talk to you in a minute."

"Alright, I'll be in my office."

As the door closed, Monica said, "Damn, my girl has gone from no man in years to two good looking men in one day."

Ashley laughed. "Moni, this could get interesting."

Tracy sat behind her desk as JD sat in the chair directly in front of her. "What's going on, Jeffrey?" she asked.

"You look nice this morning," he said with a smile, trying his best not to question her about Brooks, which was what he really wanted to do.

She blushed and bashfully replied, "Thank you." *He's just being polite*, she told herself, *don't read anything into this, remember your place.* "You look pretty good yourself, but you always do."

He smiled. "Tracy, I was in court yesterday with Al. He pleaded guilty on all counts and was sentenced yesterday."

She closed her eyes and sighed. "How long?"

"It's a sealed case and I can't say, but he will be away for a long time."

Tracy held her head up and forced a smile. "Okay, that's a wrap, right?"

JD smiled at her. "Yes, it is. He will be in a federal facility that is actually one of the best we have. He will be comfortable."

"Comfortable behind bars—isn't that a contradiction in itself?"

"I guess you could look at it that way," JD replied. "I rather look at it that he's alive, with a better chance of survival in there than on the streets."

Tracy looked up and laid her head back against her chair. "Maybe you're right, Jeffrey; either way there is nothing I can do about it now." She exhaled and smiled. "Thank you for all you did to help him and me through this situation."

"You are welcome." JD sat forward, took her hand in his. "Tracy, if you need to get in touch with him for any reason, just let me know and I will arrange it. But remember, for a while we don't want anyone to know where he is."

"Is he in some type of danger?"

"No, but Al knows things that some people may not want to get out."

"I understand," she said, nodding her head with a sad smile.

"It'll be alright," JD said as he stood and pulled her around the desk. He put her head on his shoulder and held her. *Holding her felt like the most natural thing in the world to him*. He smiled. "If you need anything, anything at all, even if it's to talk, call me, okay?"

Every particle in Tracy's body was calling for help at that moment. Having him this close to her again, comforting her, felt like everything inside of her was coming alive; she did not want to let go.

God, JD prayed, *please help me to release this woman*. He held her a moment longer than he should have, but he couldn't just let go. Her touch made his heart pound so loud, she had to feel it. He brushed her hair back from her face as he lifted her head from his shoulder, and looked into her eyes. What he was feeling at that moment was more than just comfort. He wanted to kiss her and knew it would be returned with no hesitation from her, but he couldn't; he made that mistake before.

JD knew Calvin was right. Tracy had been through too much in her life for him to play games with her. He had to be sure of his feelings before getting her involved. *But damn, it feels so good holding her right now*. He ran his hands down her arms and stepped back, still holding her hands.

"Tracy." JD didn't know what to say. He didn't know how to tell her what he was feeling. "There is something about you that scares the hell out of me."

Puzzled, Tracy swallowed. "I'm not sure how or why, but I don't mean to." She stepped back.

JD smiled. "I have to go now. I'll talk to you soon."

Tracy stood there. She really wanted to kiss that man. Then Cynthia and Ashley's words went through her mind. *Remember your place.*

"Okay," Tracy managed to say, and, "Thank you for everything."

JD opened the door and walked out. Tracy fell back into her chair and realized she had been holding her breath. She released air out again and again and again until she felt she had some kind of control of herself. *How can one man's touch affect her so deeply?* Everything in her was screaming. She laid her head on her desk. *God, please help me; please help me with this man.*

It took all the willpower JD had not to kiss Tracy. He exhaled and knocked on Ashley's door.

"Hey," he said as he walked in, sat on her couch and put his feet up. He needed a moment to compose himself. "Have you ever felt like you're in a nightmare and if you could just find the right door to open, you'd wake up and everything would be alright? No, not just alright, but as it should be."

"No," Ashley answered, and then cut to the chase. "But I know Tracy is at a crossroad in her life and she is going to need to reach out to someone. The question is who: you, Brooks or someone else?"

JD sat straight up. "Brooks! He is too old for her. He's got to be hitting 40."

Ashley laughed and shook her head. "Actually 35, not much older than you, and don't let James fool you. He's a charming man and very intelligent. Just Tracy's type. Hell, Brooks could charm my drawers off."

JD's eyebrows went up. "Ash, you got a thing for Brooks?"

Ignoring his question, she asked, "Did you think you were the only one that was attracted to Tracy? Hmm, my conceited big brother." She shook her head.

JD stood up and walked towards Ashley. "You didn't answer my question."

"And I'm not going to. JD, Tracy is a very lonely person. Hell, sometimes I think she likes it that way; no chance of getting hurt. But she has so much love in her. I can tell you this: whoever is lucky enough to get her will have love for the rest of his life. Once Tracy commits to something or someone, that's it, door closed."

"I have to clean up some things before starting anything with Tracy, Ashley," JD said with his hands in his pockets, looking down at the floor as if the answer to his dilemma was down there. "I know what you are saying is true. But honestly I don't know where I am with Tracy. I can tell you there is something in here," he said, pointing to his heart, "for her. It has been for a while, but I don't know what it is. I'm not going to take a chance on hurting her while I'm trying to sort out my feelings. But I know I have to do something, so I started with Carolyn."

"What did you do with her?"

"I talked to her last night. I told her I had feelings for someone else." Smiling, JD continued, "It actually went better than I thought. As a matter of fact, her reaction surprised me."

"JD, be careful. Carolyn is very vindictive. Did you tell her who Tracy was?"

"No."

"Thank goodness. You know you men do stupid things when you're getting some."

"I'm not that stupid. I know Carolyn very well. That's why I can't be with Tracy yet. I don't want Carolyn to go after her and I know she will try."

"So how are you going to stop her?"

"By getting her mind on exactly what she wants."

"And what's that?"

"The governor's mansion." JD sighed. "I've never worked for a woman. They were always there."

"Well, this is not just any woman for you, JD."

"I know." He shook his head. "I don't have the slightest idea when it happened."

Ashley laughed. "Spring break a few years ago."

"You're right." He heaved a sigh. "I don't want to make a mistake with Tracy. I don't want anything that I've done in the past to interfere with our future. When did life get to be so damn complicated?"

"Life and love have always been complicated. Shit, you know that."

He looked at his sister and wondered when she grew up. "When did you get so smart about life and when did your mouth get so nasty?" JD leaned across Ashley's desk.

"Well, life I learned from mom and the mouth I got from you."

"I love you, lil sis."

"I love you too, JD."

He kissed her forehead.

"By the way, what did you need to talk to me about, other than Tracy?"

"Oh, yeah, Mom wants me to give you a birthday celebration so I will be having lunch with Cynthia today to work out the details."

"Okay. Nothing fancy, and make sure you invite James Brooks."

JD raised an eyebrow. "Okay."

"JD, Tracy is going to be an uphill battle. First you will have to convince her she is worthy. Then you have to protect her from Carolyn's wrath. But I got your back," Ashley said as she hugged him.

JD entered his office around 11:00 A.M. He retrieved his messages and cookies from Mrs. Langston and was sitting at his desk when Gavin knocked on the door. "JD, it's nice of you to join us today, or are you still out?"

"Sorry, Gavin, I had to take care of something this morning. Did you need me?"

"Yes, I got a call from the AG's office. They want you to handle the Gonzalez case."

"The 13-year old who was killed?" JD asked.

"That's the one."

"Why federal?"

Gavin put the file on JD's desk. "RICO—gang related death. They want the gang brought down, and since you brought down Day so easily, they believe you could lead this one also."

JD heard the mockery in Gavin's voice. "If you have an issue with this, Gavin, you can assign it to someone else. I won't challenge that decision."

Gavin looked at JD. He respected JD's work and knew he was good. "No, the fact of the matter is, if anyone can bring them down, it's you. I know that."

"Is the Day issue behind us, Gavin, or will I hear about it again?" JD asked, giving Gavin one of those "let that shit go" looks.

Gavin put his hands in his pockets. "It's done. Who will you need on this case?"

"Give me a minute to review the file. My mind is not there right now." JD sighed

"I can see that—personal or professional?"

JD looked at him.

"Look, regardless of what info you got from the Day case, I'm still the same person I was last week. If you need to talk, I'm here."

JD didn't say anything, so Gavin began to walk out.

"Gavin, are you going to take a run at the AG's office?"

Gavin hesitated. "I'm considering the governor's office. Why?"

"You plan on taking Carolyn with you?"

Gavin put his head down and smiled. "You know about that?"

"I know Carolyn. She only steps out when it benefits her."

"You pissed?" Gavin asked.

"No, I'm done with that. It wasn't serious, at least not for me. What about you, Gavin?"

"She could be very useful in a political campaign, " he said, smiling.

"Yes, she could, but more importantly, she could win one by her sheer talents alone." JD smiled, remembering the last time they were together.

"My Lord could she," Gavin replied remembering last night. Satisfied he had laid the foundation with Gavin, JD picked up the Gonzalez file. "I'll get on this case and let you know what I need."

"Whatever you need, you'll get," Gavin said and walked out.

JD put the file on the desk, walked over to the window as his mind went back to Tracy. He knew what he felt for her was real. Holding her today was as natural to him as breathing. Nothing in his life had ever felt so right. He looked up to the sky. "God, help me with this woman."

Chapter 8

James called Tracy and asked for a lunch meeting. He promised it was business that he did not want to discuss at the office. They agreed to meet at The Croaker Spot, a restaurant on historical Second Street in downtown Richmond.

"Hello, James," Tracy said as he stood at the table to greet her.

"You look wonderful." He smiled.

"Thank you," Tracy replied. "So what's going on in the office?"

"Unfortunately, my management team is not pushing the reform to the employees as we had asked. We have to find a way to get the employees on board without using the management team."

The waitress came to the table. They placed their order and she left.

"Is it everyone on your management team?"

"No, just one or two of them," James replied.

"Well, the best way to go around them is for you to go directly to the employees."

"That would take a while. We have eight hundred employees across the state."

"Alright, then bring the employees to you. Have an event announcing the incentives. Once you get them there, the incentives will sell themselves."

"I agree with that, but how do we get the employees there? Their trust level of management is unbelievably low."

The waitress returned with the food.

"Thank you," Tracy said to the waitress, then turned back to Brooks. "Give them free lunch. Have a luncheon for all employees, with you serving them. While they are there, have Ashley do a presentation. Since all employees can't be there all at once, have the lunches in shifts."

Tracy said grace, bit into her sandwich and continued. "During each lunch shift, have a drawing for a hundred dollars to go towards the winner's incentive package. If you foot the bill for the luncheon, Next Level Consulting will put up the door prize money." Tracy started eating her fries. "You know what? I have the perfect company to handle the event. It's a new company that we just took on as a client. As a matter of fact, you met the owners the other night."

"At your office?"

"Yes, that's why they came by, for a business plan."

James raised an eyebrow.

Tracy smiled. "I know, they may seem a little wild, but they are really good. Cynthia planned every event there was at college. If Ashley, Cynthia and Rosaline were not involved in an event, it was not worth going to."

"So I heard," James said. "One of the members on the management team remembers Ashley from college."

"Really? Which one?"

"Karen Holt, my assistant commissioner."

"I don't remember a Karen Holt at Harmon."

"I don't think she went there," James said. "I think her husband did."

Tracy stopped eating. "David Holt?"

"Yes, is that an issue?" James asked, noticing Tracy's expression.

"No, it shouldn't be," Tracy said with a little hesitation.

James smiled. "Well, we have been here all of 20 minutes and you have found a solution to a problem that I have been thinking about for days. How in the hell do you do that?"

Tracy sighed. "It just comes to me, and I have no idea where it comes from. Ashley says I freak her out with that."

"Speaking of Ashley, there's her brother." James stood then extended his hand. "Hello, Mr. Harrison, how are you?"

"I'm fine, thank you," JD replied. "Hello, Tracy."

"Hello, Jeffrey." Tracy tried to smile but it didn't work. Tracy's heart sank when she saw the woman Jeffrey was with. She grabbed Jeffrey's arm possessively while he was still looking at Tracy. James noticed how uncomfortable Tracy had become.

"Hello, Carolyn," James spoke.

"Hello, James," Carolyn said as she kissed his cheek. "It's good to see you again. It's been a while."

"You two know each other?" JD asked.

"Yes, Mr. Brooks and I have met before."

JD continued. "This is Tracy Washington. Tracy, this is Carolyn Roth."

"It's nice to meet you," Tracy responded while extending her hand.

Carolyn noticed the change in JD's demeanor the moment they approached the table. "Tracy, it's nice to meet you also," Carolyn replied. "Now how do you two know each other?"

JD hesitated.

"I'm Ashley's business partner," Tracy replied.

"Your sister, Ashley?" Carolyn looked to JD for clarification.

"Yes." JD smiled.

Carolyn loved it when other women checked her out. She could tell Tracy was doing just that, checking her out from head to toe. Carolyn was doing exactly the same thing. This cannot be the woman JD is interested in. This person is not even close to his type. She seems plain, ordinary, compared to her.

Tracy felt like a rag doll, looking at the woman with Jeffrey. She was simply beautiful, graceful and confident. All the things Tracy was not. That's the kind of woman Jeffrey is supposed to have on his arm. Even Cynthia would have to agree to that. Tracy turned away from the couple.

"How are you, Tracy?" JD asked.

"I'm doing well, thank you."

"It was good seeing you. Enjoy your lunch," JD stated and walked away.

James sat back down. He watched Tracy for a moment. That freethinking spirit that was there minutes ago was gone. "So" he started, "that's why you are not available?"

"What's that?" Tracy asked.

"Harrison," James said as he took a drink.

Tracy laughed. "No, I'm not in that league."

"You're right. Believe me, you are far above Carolyn."

Tracy smiled and looked at Carolyn again. "I don't think so."

James wiped his mouth with his napkin. "Oh, she is a beautiful woman, but it's not always about what's on the outside."

"Of course it is." Tracy smirked. "Any man who says it's not, is not being honest with himself."

"Is that so?" James exhaled.

"Sure."

"I disagree," James replied. "What's on the inside is very important. I don't care what a woman looks like. If she can't carry on an intelligent conversation, all you have is a shell with no substance. And the shell diminishes with time."

"It's rare for a man to think that way. Usually the body is the first thing a man looks at."

"Oh, and women don't look at a man's body or bank account?"

"It's not important." Tracy shook her head. "Like you said, the body and looks will go. And I have my own bank account."

"Like you said, it's rare, especially for a woman, to think that way," James responded.

Tracy looked at her watch. "You know, I need to get back to the office. I will contact Cynthia about the event and give you a call on their availability."

James could tell seeing Harrison with Carolyn Roth was unsettling for Tracy. At least he knew who he was up against. "Alright, I'll give you a call a little later," he replied. "Thank you for the solution. I think it will work."

She smiled and extended her hand. "It will work; I'll make sure it does. I'll talk to you later."

James watched her as she left.

JD watched until Tracy was gone, wondering what in the hell she was doing with Brooks.

"So," Carolyn said while pretending to look at the menu, "that's the person who took your attention from me."

JD never acknowledged Carolyn's statement one way or another. "How's things with Gavin?" he asked and changed the conversation.

JD went back to the office and waited on Calvin to review the Gonzalez file. His mind went to Tracy and James Brooks. He wasn't used to competing for a woman's attention; he always had it. He could not imagine Tracy with any man but him. But James Brooks concerned him. From all accounts, Brooks was a decent, respectable man. Then JD remembered her reaction to Brooks the morning he was there; the interest was there on Tracy's part. He exhaled. Now he questioned Tracy's feelings for him. There was no way he could be wrong about her reaction to him. But then again, this woman confused him like no other. He thought back to the morning in her office. He had to step back from her; she never stepped back from him. He remembered the puzzled look she had when he did. She'd had the same look at the club a few years ago.

"No," JD said aloud to himself, "there's no way she would choose him over me." He had to believe that.

"No, what?" A voice came from behind him.

JD turned and it was Calvin. "Hey, Calvin. You ready to go over this case?"

"Sure, as soon as you tell me why you are talking to yourself."

JD walked over and closed the door. "I don't know why I'm concerned about this," he said, "but one of your revelations regarding Tracy turned out to be real."

"What revelation?"

"The one about someone else being interested in her."

"Please tell me you are not surprised by that?" Calvin said, laughing at him.

"No, I just never thought it would be an issue," JD replied with a sigh.

Calvin shook his head. "Tracy is the type of women most men dream of. She's very easy to look at, attentive, easy to talk to about anything and makes you feel like you are the only man on the planet when she looks at you. In what world did you think no one else would notice her?"

JD smiled. "I don't know, Calvin. Why is it that I'm just seeing all of that?"

"Because you're just realizing what's important in life. You weren't ready to see it then; now you are."

"I'm not sure how to proceed now. I had a plan, but now that I've seen her with James Brooks I'm afraid to take a chance on losing her."

"James Brooks from Special Services? Whew, heavyweight. Is she really that important to you, JD, or is this a situation of JD just not wanting to lose out?"

JD smoothed his tie down and really thought about Calvin's question. "Calvin," he said with the seriousness he used in court to sway a jury, "I can't tell you why, but I know down in my gut that Tracy is not just another woman for me." He hesitated for a moment then smiled nervously. "I'm not used to being insecure about a woman. I'm lost here. I need help with this one."

"Okay," Calvin stated, "if you are serious, throw your plans out of the window. They don't work anyway. Don't play games with her. She's not Carolyn or Vanessa and you know that. Step out on faith. Let her know what you feel."

JD left the office late. He was reviewing the Gonzalez files and decided he would get more accomplished by using his computer at home. The system Tracy taught him years ago was still very effective for the type of research he needed on this case. This particular gang appeared on the surface to be dangerous and extensive. JD knew he was going to need additional help. He needed to make some calls to get his team together. Since this was a Latino gang, he was going to need someone on board that spoke the language. Then he would need a representative from the AG's office on board full time until the case was done.

JD's house phone was ringing as he walked through the door. He looked at the number and answered the call. "Hey, Mom."

"JD, a package came here for you today. It's heavy."

"Where's it from?"

"Lowe's."

Lowe's? JD thought. He didn't remember ordering anything from there. "Okay, Mom, I'll come by Saturday to get it. How are you doing today?"

"Just fine, son, just fine."

"Mom, I need to make some calls, so I'll have to talk to you later."

"Okay, son, talk to you later."

JD worried about his mom being at the house by herself. The neighborhood had changed so much. But she loved that house and was not leaving it. He refocused, and then called Brian.

Chapter 9

JD looked at his watch. It was well after six in the evening. He had spent the last two weeks focusing on the Gonzalez case. The event from the case was heart wrenching and he needed a break. Whenever his mind was free, thoughts of Tracy would creep in. JD walked over to the window of his office. He shared the scene with Tracy one night. He smiled as he thought about the gift she sent to his mother's house. When he opened the package from Lowes, the note thanked him for his help with Turk and reminded him to wrap things up. JD checked his watch again. *It's not that late*, he thought, and decided to call her.

"Next Level Consulting," Tracy said into the phone.

"Hi, Tracy, it's Jeffrey."

Her heart skipped a beat at the sound of his voice. "Hello, Jeffrey."

"Are you busy?" he asked.

"No," she replied. "Everyone's left for the day."

"Am I holding you up?"

"No, I still have some work to do. What's wrong?"

"Why do you think something is wrong?"

"I can hear it in your voice. You sound a little stressed," she replied.

Damn, how did she pick up on that? he wondered. "Sorry about that." He smiled. "I was just going over a case that's not sitting well with me."

"What's it about?"

"A 13-year-old girl died during a gang initiation."

Sounding very concerned, she said, "I'm sorry to hear that. What happened?"

"It wasn't good." He sighed.

"Hmm, that much I know; she died, it can't be but so good. What happened?"

JD smiled, then sighed. "She was um, gang raped. That was her initiation, a gang rape. Thirteen years old, probably still a virgin, but the people who did this did not care. They just had their way with her, without a moment's thought of her well-being. The medical examiner said she was probably unconscious after the 10th one."

"Hmm." Tracy sighed. She could hear the frustration in Jeffrey's voice. "How many were there?"

"At least 20."

"With so many assailants and DNA, it's going to be difficult to get a conviction."

"Yeah," he replied, his voice rising, "it will, but I told the medical examiner I wanted everyone we could identify. I want each one of those bastards to pay for what they did to that child. Cases like this piss me off." He caught himself. "Whoa." He stopped and remembered whom he was talking to—no, yelling at. "Hmm." He exhaled. "I am sorry. I lost it there for a moment."

"You don't have to apologize." Tracy smiled. "You're very passionate about your work. There's nothing wrong with that."

"I don't know about that. It's cases like this that keep me up at night."

"That's not good," she replied. "Have you talked to the girl's parents yet?"

"No, we usually don't deal with the parents from this office."

"Why not? I'm sure her parents would like to know someone other than them cares about what happened to their daughter. It would ease their minds to know someone is seriously looking into what happened and not allow their daughter's death to be in vain. Besides, it may help you to talk to someone who would be just as passionate about the child as you. Who better than the parents? Let them know who you are and what you are going to do to get justice for their daughter. Tell them what steps you are going to take to make sure this does not happen to another child. It will certainly help them to sleep better at night, and it will help you, too."

JD hesitated. He had not spoken with her in weeks and here she was helping him cope yet again. It wasn't so much what she said—as a prosecutor he knew this—but having her reiterate the sentiment was good to hear. "How do you do that?"

"Do what?"

"Know just the right thing to say to make me feel better."

Tracy smiled. "Did I succeed?"

"Yes, you did," he replied, hesitating to say anything more. "Thank you, for being there for me."

"I'll always be here, Jeffrey," she said. Silence. *Too much*, she thought, *clean it up, girl, quick, clean it up.* "What did you call me for?" She asked as she cleared her throat.

Trying to remember why he called, he said, "Oh yeah. I wanted to thank you for my gift."

"Oh, it arrived," she said with excitement. "Did you wrap things up?"

"As a matter of fact, I did." He smiled.

"Have you forgotten anything about your dad?"

"Just the opposite," he said, a little excited. "Memories started to flood my mind." He laughed.

"That's a good thing."

"Yes, it was. Thank you."

"You are very welcome." Tracy smiled.

Silence again, but JD wasn't ready to hang up the telephone. "Are you going to be in the office long?"

"I don't know; it depends on how much I can get done on this project," she replied.

"Don't stay there too late."

"I won't."

"Well, I guess I'll talk to you later."

"Okay." She started to say "bye," but then she said, "Umm, Jeffrey?"

"Yes," he answered, sounding a little anxious. Silence again.

"Nothing." She shook her head. "That's okay. I'll talk to you later."

"You sure?"

"Yeah, I'm sure."

"Alright," he said, disappointed.

Neither one wanted to end the call; it seemed like another moment lost.

"Tracy, have you had dinner yet?"

"No, I haven't."

"Would you like to go grab something?"

Silent, Tracy was trying to gather her thoughts. *Have dinner with him or go home to a lonely dinner; hmm, let me think.* "Sure."

Releasing his breath, he said, "Alright." He smiled. "I'll be over to pick you up in about 15 minutes."

"Okay. See you soon."

Tracy went into her restroom to freshen up. She looked in the mirror. Her hair looked a mess. She plugged in the hot curlers, then washed her face, brushed her teeth and used mouthwash. A girl should always be prepared for whatever; one never knows. *Oh stop that*, she thought, remembering the last time she saw him with that gorgeous woman. She could not compete with that. Just like Cynthia said, "Jeffrey is a player and a high stakes player at that. You don't get to play in his league. Remember your place." Tracy curled her hair, and then changed her shoes. She had worn her white linen trousers with a white sleeveless tee, a red linen blazer and white sneakers to work. She had not intended to go out tonight. However, just in case a client stopped in, she had her red heels under the desk. Jeffrey was 6 foot 4; she was 5 foot 6. She changed into her heels, which gave her another three inches. Maybe that would help her look like she belonged with him. Tracy was looking in the mirror putting on some lip gloss, and then she stopped primping. "You will never look like you belong with him," she said aloud to herself.

"Who are you talking to?" JD asked from her office.

Tracy stepped back to see him standing by her desk. *Damn, I'm going to have to put a bell on that front door.* She smiled. "Hello, Jeffrey."

"Hello, Tracy." He smiled. "Who are you talking to?"

"Myself," she said as she unplugged the hot curlers.

He walked over to the bathroom doorway. "Are you going to continue this one-on-one conversation or can we go get something to eat?" Looking around the restroom, he said, "Man, this is nicer than some bathrooms in people's homes. You two have some of everything in here." He stopped and looked around. "Please explain why you have a shower stall in here?"

"Now, that's a dumb question. You are talking about two women who like looking fresh. One never knows when the man of her dreams may walk through the door. Besides, an office would not be complete without a shower."

"My office doesn't have a shower. And there are no dumb questions, only curious people seeking to be educated." JD leaned against the doorjam. "And you know, more times than not, the person of your dreams could be standing right in front of you and you may not recognize it."

Raising an eyebrow, she thought, *No truer words have ever been spoken.* "Touché, Mr. Harrison, I stand corrected." She walked past him into her office. "And you are right."

"On which point?"

"Both." She smiled. "Are we ready to go?"

He walked towards her. "Yeah, let's go."

JD drove his car to a building on Fifth Street near the old John Marshall Hotel in the downtown Richmond not 10 minutes from her office and about five minutes from his. They walked down about five steps from the sidewalk to a double entry door. Jeffrey took a card out of his wallet and slid it down an electronic sensor. The door opened. An older, very distinguished looking gentleman dressed in a black suit greeted them in what one would call a vestibule. "Good evening, Mr. Harrison. Your table is ready and your meal will be served shortly."

"Good evening, Mr. Brown," JD replied. "Please, JD would be fine."

The gentleman opened the door to one of the most elegant rooms Tracy had ever seen. There were a number of people inside, but it was not crowded. JD put his hand on her back and pushed her forward. "What is this, Jeffrey?"

"This is the Renaissance."

"The nightclub?" she asked, very surprised.

"No, the nightclub is upstairs with the public entrance. This is the private club."

"My goodness, this is really nice."

The Renaissance was just that: a place where you could revitalize yourself. There was a bar area but no stools surrounding the bar; there were tables and chairs in the open area for those who wanted to take a seat. The décor was a rich burgundy, black and gold. The area made you feel like royalty just standing there. As they continued walking, they came to a section that was about midway through the building. The area to the far left had huge flat panel TVs mounted on three walls. Burgundy and black sofas were arranged in a semicircle around each TV for direct viewing. The room was sound proof with double glass doors leading into it. Closer to the left were six pool tables with enough room between them not to interfere in anyone's game or conversation. Pool sticks of all sizes and quality lined the walls. To the right were several plush card tables that were sectioned off, with four tables in each section. Each section had a tournament bracket board mounted on the wall. As they walked on, they came to another set of double doors. A man dressed in a black suit was standing behind a podium. Jeffrey handed his card to the man. He swiped it, gave it back to Jeffrey.

"Mr. Harrison, they are ready for you."

Two other men opened the double doors. The area was exclusive, with enclosed booths. You could only see people as you walked past to get to your station. Each station had French glass doors with gold trim that slid open, individual music systems, soft leather sofas that allowed you to adjust the distance between you and your guest, and a personal waitress or waiter.. Tracy was so in awe , she did not know they had reached their station. Trying hard not to act like she was out of her element, which she was and she knew it, Tracy stepped inside the station and noticed the gold plaque on the door was engraved "Jeffrey Daniel Harrison." Tracy slid into a seat and waited for the waiter to leave before speaking. "Jeffrey, can they hear us in here?"

"No," he replied, wondering why she asked the question, "why?"

"Well," she began, "when they said your table was ready, they literally meant your table." She pointed to the name on the door.

JD smiled, took off his tie and put it on what appeared to be a nightstand. Then he placed his cell phone and keys there.

"Are you getting comfortable?" Tracy asked.

He smiled. "That's what this place is to me; somewhere I can be comfortable, just like home."

"Jeffrey, if your home is like this place, you've got to be doing something illegal. Is there something you need to tell me?" she said jokingly.

"Are you impressed?"

"Yes." She hesitated. "Are you trying to impress me?"

He didn't answer, but he was.

Tracy looked around. "I have never seen anything like this."

"You've been too sheltered."

"Well, yeah, but sheltered or not, this is awesome. How do you know about this place and how did you rate your own private room?"

"My friend Douglas owns this place."

"I believe your drinks are here." The waiter stepped aside to allow the waitress in with an iced tea for Tracy and a Heineken for Jeffrey. Both waiters left the room and closed the door.

"You ordered ahead?" Tracy asked.

"Yeah, I do it as a courtesy. That way it won't take so long to get your food."

"What did you order?"

"A couple of steaks, baked potatoes and salad."

She smiled, nodding her head in agreement. "Why do you get a beer and I get an iced tea?"

Damn, she was beautiful, he thought. "Because I had a hard day and need a beer and you don't drink."

"Are you driving?" she asked.

"Yes."

"Then you should not be drinking either."

"A beer has a point-two alcohol level. Point eight is the legal limit. I think I can have one or two."

"Actually, for your size and weight, you can have four before you are remotely affected."

JD laughed. "You kill me with that kind of stuff."

Tracy smiled. "I turn most people off with that kind of stuff, but I can't help it."

"It doesn't seem to turn James Brooks off," he said. *Damn, he didn't mean for that to come out.*

Tracy looked at Jeffrey. "Where did that come from?"

JD sighed and shook his head. "I didn't mean to say that."

"James Brooks is a very intelligent man. He can hold a conversation about anything. But he's a client, nothing more," Tracy offered.

JD took a drink and looked around uncomfortably, clearing his throat. "I had no right to go there."

Changing the subject, Tracy asked, "How often do you come here?"

"When I need to relax or think."

"Which is it tonight?"

He looked up at her, took a swallow of his beer and said, "Relaxation."

Tracy didn't realize it, but she had been sitting up the whole time. She squirmed a little.

"Sit back, relax. I swear nothing will happen to you in here." JD smiled.

Tracy sat back, placed her purse on the seat beside her and crossed her legs. She looked at him. "Why are you so tense, Jeffrey, is it the case?"

He sighed heavily. "This type of case tends to bring out the worst in me."

"Are you going to talk with the girl's family?"

It felt good having someone to talk to about his cases. Normally, he would have to work his way through the madness. "I will," he stated. "You know, my dad used to tell me all the time, the worst thing parents go through when a child dies before they do is not knowing what happened or the guilt of not being there when their child needed them. He used to make it a point to be able to answer those questions for the victim's family."

Tracy listened to him. His eyes were full of wide-eyed innocence when he talked about his dad.

"Jeffrey, what happened to your dad, was he sick?"

The expression on his face turned to anger instantly. A flash of hatred came into his eyes as he looked away from her. The waiter knocked on the door. Tracy motioned him to wait.

JD looked at her. "You're waiting for an answer?"

"Yes." She nodded.

When Tracy looked at him, it made him feel like he was the only person in the world. The night at his mom's house he had felt the same way. *How does she do that?* It's as if she was reaching into his soul and making him reveal his all to her. But this subject was and always had been off limits for anyone. JD looked over and motioned the waiter to come in. He came in, set the plates on the table with all the condiments and asked if there would be anything else. JD answered, "No, thank you." The waiter stepped out. They both said grace and JD began eating. Tracy sat there and waited. "It smells good and I'm starving," she said, "but I'm waiting for an answer."

JD hesitated. "He was killed in the line of duty," he replied angrily.

Tracy began eating her salad. *Time to change the subject,* she thought. "I noticed a number of pool tables outside the door. Are they reserved for special people or can the public use them?"

Thankful she let the subject go, JD asked, "Do you play?"

"No." She stopped. "I win," she said and continued eating.

"Oh, you do?" he said with a questioning tone.

"Yes, really," she said with a tone of challenge.

"Is that a challenge?"

"Of course not, Jeffrey," Tracy said while shaking her head, "I wouldn't challenge you at anything."

"Oh, now you are attempting to pull me in."

"I'm sitting here eating my salad." She laughed. Tracy continued to eat and then said, "But I am good."

"Alright, that's it," he replied, wiping his mouth with his napkin and placing it on the table, "let's go."

JD opened the door. Tracy stood and turned to face him. "I don't want you to get upset when I beat you at this game," Tracy said very seriously.

Confident with his skills, he replied, "Are you backing down from this challenge?" He slid the door open.

He looked so serious and kissable. "Let's go," she said.

As they entered the area with the pool tables, Tracy noticed the place had gotten more crowded. The crowd made her a little uncomfortable, not quite as sure of herself.

JD noticed the change in her instantly. He walked up behind her. "Are you backing out?"

She smiled and sucked her teeth. "Pick a table, and I promise to make it quick."

He went over to a table, patted it and smiled. "I'll take you right here."

The people seated at another table turned to look as Tracy walked close to him and smiled. "You sure you want to do this?"

He took off his jacket laid it across a chair. He took down two sticks and handed one to her. "I'll be a gentleman and let you break."

She smirked. "Jeffrey, are you sure?" She laughed again. "You really want to do this?"

He looked at her as if she had lost her mind. "You really think you can beat me at this?"

"Yes," she replied as she laughed.

"Okay," he said, "you break."

She sighed heavily. She walked over to the end of the table with the balls and began talking the game. She broke, and several balls fell into the pockets. "You see, Jeffrey, what a lot of people don't understand, pool is a game of precision. It's all about calculation. I'll take the stripes, just to make it interesting." JD noticed more solid balls fell than stripes, so he was a little surprised she selected the stripes. He began to roll up his sleeves thinking, *Okay, she's got a little game,* but he wasn't worried.

"It's about knowing the positions of the balls and the distance the ball has to travel." She hit two stripes, one going into the pocket in the middle on the left and the other going into the right pocket at the end of the table. "Knowing just the right amount of power needed to get the balls to travel the distance to each pocket." Calling the next pocket, she continued. "Being able to calculate just the right angle to connect with the balls to get them to go in the direction you want." She stood up and watched the ball go into the pocket. She walked around the table and stood before him. "Kind of like what you have to do with men, or so I've been told." She smiled. "Excuse me," she said. He smiled and stepped back. Three stripe balls were left. She bent over the table. "Ten in the right center pocket."

"You can't make that shot," he whispered in her ear. "You should go for nine in the left pocket."

She stood up and turned to him. He was standing so close. Tracy could feel his warm breath on her face. She looked up, and then seductively asked, "Are you trying to take me out of my game?"

He bent his head down to her ear. "Yes," he whispered.

My goodness, he has wonderful eyes. Taking in a breath, she said, "Excuse me."

He stepped back. A few people had gathered near the table watching the game. One of the guys spoke, "Hey, JD," he said laughing. "What you been into?"

"Getting my ass kicked right now," he replied.

Being that close to Jeffrey had distracted Tracy. She had to take a moment to exhale before she took the shot. Tracy knew she could make the shot; she had made it several times before with Turk. She set the stick against the table, took off her blazer and untucked her blouse.

That unnerved JD. Now he was watching the movement of her body, more so than the shot she was about to take. *Damn, that woman has a body on her,* he thought.

Tracy picked up her stick, looked at him and repeated, "Ten in the center right pocket." As she leaned across the table, JD's friend looked up at him, "Whenever you get tired, I'll happily take an ass whipping from her."

Tracy hit the 10 ball. It banked against the left side of the table and went into the center right pocket.

"Yes! Nothing but net," she said as she walked past JD smiling. "Now, just for you, nine in the left pocket."

JD made a mental note, *Don't ever let her break.* But it was all good. He liked seeing her confident and comfortable with him, just enjoying life.

Tracy put the end of the stick on the floor, put her hands on her hips and looked up at him. "Which pocket would you like the 12 ball to go in?"

JD blinked when she asked the question. She was sexy as hell standing there, with that stare from her light brown eyes going right through him. "Anywhere you want it to go."

"You do realize I'm going to win this game?"

"There will be others," he responded with a smile.

"You promise?" She smiled.

He looked at her and knew he meant what he was about to say. "I promise, there will be many more."

She smiled, and then banked the ball against the end of the table where he was standing. It landed in the pocket at the end of the table. A small crowd that gathered cheered, "Man, that was a shot."

She looked at JD. "I'll make it painless: eight ball, corner pocket." The ball dropped in the corner pocket. She walked to the end of the table where he stood, gave him her stick and announced, "I'm starving, let's eat."

JD smiled, put the sticks up, grabbed their jackets and walked out of the area.

"You do know that only a very secure man could take an ass whipping like that and walk away with his head up."

JD turned to the voice that made the statement. "Doug, hey, man," he said as they shook hands.

"It's been a while, JD; it's good to see you."

"Same here, man. How's everyone?" JD asked.

"Doing good, man, doing well," Douglas replied. "Who's your guest?"

"This is Tracy Washington. Tracy, this is the friend I told you about, Douglas Hylton. He's another one of my boys from high school."

"This is a very nice establishment you have here, thank you for having me."

"Hello, Tracy, I'm glad you're enjoying your visit," he replied.

"Business looks good," JD commented, looking around.

"Can't complain, man. Let's go back to the Chambers," he said, referring to the dining area.

They all walked back to JD's room. Someone had placed their plates on heaters to keep the food warm.

"You two finding everything satisfactory?"

"Yes, but I reserve the right to complain about your pool tables later," JD said laughing. "I think they are rigged."

"I think you just got your ass whipped." Doug laughed. "Look, I'm going to let you two get back to your evening." Shaking JD's hand, he added, "Don't make it so long next time, man." Douglas smiled at Tracy. "It was nice meeting you."

"You, too," Tracy replied.

"Have a good evening." Doug turned and left.

"You set me up," JD said. "Who taught you to shoot pool like that?"

"My brother."

JD laughed. "I should have known. Is there anything you are not good at?" He was not expecting to get the answer he got.

"People," she said. "I'm not good with a lot of people."

"I don't buy that," JD said as he started eating. Tracy actually did what JD thought was impossible. He was able to let go. He didn't feel as if he had to impress or prove anything to her. He could relax and talk freely. "You are a beautiful, intelligent woman and sexy as hell. So far, I know you got game with the b-ball court and on the pool table. You are by far the easiest person to talk to, at least for me."

Tracy never looked up from her plate. Beautiful, sexy. It was confusing hearing this from him.

JD continued, "Ashley talks about you like you are her own personal guardian angel and so does Monica. Rosaline thinks you are one of the most generous people she has ever met. Cynthia is jealous as hell of you and Mama, well she thinks you are an angel sent down by God himself just for me."

Tracy sat back listening to the things he was saying and she couldn't believe he was talking about her. Noticing her reaction JD stopped talking. Her hand was lying on the table. He put his hands over hers. "Tracy, what's wrong?"

She swallowed hard. "What do you think, Jeffrey? We have been tiptoeing around each other for a while now. Do you feel the same things I do when we are close to each other or is it just me?"

He sat there for a moment. Tracy called his card and she was right, they had. He had to get this out. Tracy did not retract the question, even though her mind was telling her to. *Take it back,* her mind was saying, *you don't want to hear this answer.*

Jeffrey put his fork down and moved to sit beside her. He put his hands behind her head and gently rubbed her neck. He exhaled. "Tracy." He kissed her forehead and then rested his head against hers. "I'm not good at this, so bear with me."

Jeffrey was too close to her. Tracy was having problems breathing again. *Hold your head up,* she told herself. *You asked the question, now be woman enough to accept the answer.* She held her head up and looked at him as he talked.

"I'm not sure how to answer that question." JD hesitated. "I've asked myself that question over and over since Al's case." He smiled and continued talking and playing with her hair. "At first I thought I was just fulfilling my promise to Al to protect you and make sure you were okay. But then things got to the point that I wanted to see you, to talk to you." He hesitated and exhaled. "Not one day has gone by in the last two weeks that you haven't crossed my mind. And lately, when I have days like today, I find myself wanting to be with you. You have a way of knowing what to say or do to make even my bad days okay." He smiled. "The other day when I saw you with Brooks, I didn't like it. I thought I was going to lose it." He laughed nervously, and then looked into her eyes. "I would love nothing more than to be with you, but there are issues concerning you and," he breathed heavily, "and my past that I need to address before I can do that."

Tracy could not believe Jeffrey was saying these things to her. He was feeling the same as she was feeling. Too many moments had been wasted, but not this one. Tracy wanted to feel the way she did at the club a few years ago. She placed her hand on the side of his face and as he leaned into it, she gently kissed his lips.

The kiss was innocent and her lips were soft, and JD wanted more. Just a little more, he thought as he returned the kiss. But the sensation of her touch was too much to resist. He needed to taste her, so he allowed his tongue to lightly cross her bottom lip.

Something stirred within her at his touch. Whatever it was, Tracy wanted more, and she parted her lips a little. JD pulled back a little, pushed her hair from her face and looked at her. There was no mistaking what he saw there and he wanted all she was offering. JD wanted Tracy. Whatever it would take, he was going to have her. He pulled her closer as he leaned in and kissed her, again parting her lips in search of her tongue. Their tongues found each other and a small groan escaped her throat as Tracy began to relax in his arms. As hard as he tried, JD couldn't stop himself; the kiss went deeper and for a moment he actually lost control. His mind had told him to pull away before, but not this time. Tracy placed her hand on his chest and what felt like a wave of hot liquid surged through him. As he held her, JD decided he was going to have her.

Tracy did not want this moment to stop. Since she was 19, she had waited for this moment and now, he was ending the kiss. JD placed his hand over hers and held it against his chest. He did not want to pull away completely. As he pulled his lips from hers and looked into her eyes he knew she was feeling the same thing he was.

He smiled at her. "Did I answer your question?"

"That wasn't the answer I expected," she said and lowered her head.

"What did you expect?"

"Oh, something like, Squirt Two, you know I love you like a little sister."

"Hmm," he laughed, "I've never looked at you like a little sister. I called you 'Squirt' to remind myself that you were off limits back then." JD rested his head against hers. "Tracy, I don't have a lot of experience at relationships. I have been with a lot of women in the past and some issues may arise. I'm going to make mistakes here, so please be patient with me."

"I'm not experienced at this either, Jeffrey." She smiled. "So, we will make mistakes, learn from them, then move forward."

"I just don't want to do anything to hurt you," JD confessed. "I would walk away before I do that. I want to do this right."

"You want to cultivate the relationship."

He laughed. "Yeah, I do."

Relieved to have come to this point, they sat there talking and laughing with each other for hours. Neither wanted to leave that room. Tracy knew in her heart that once they left that room something would destroy the moment they had just shared. That's just the way her life went. JD did not want to leave because he knew what issues he had to address to do right by Tracy. Some of those issues were not going to be easy. But he was determined to make it happen.

Chapter 10

It was 8:30 A.M. when Brian walked into the DA's office. Calvin was at the receptionist's desk talking with Mrs. Langston.

"Good morning, good people, how is everyone?" Brian asked.

"Brian," Calvin said, shaking hands and bumping shoulders. "Man, what are you doing here so early in the morning?"

"Good morning, Mr. Thompson, how are you this morning?" Mrs. Langston asked.

"I'm pretty good this morning, Mrs. Langston, and yourself?"

"Fine, thank you."

Brian turned to Calvin. "JD asked me to meet him here at nine. I decided to come in early, knowing how he is when he first gets a case like this."

"Same here," Calvin replied. "Whenever JD gets a case involving a child, he is hell to deal with until he gets the person responsible."

"Maybe we should put a call in to Carolyn now, to try to ease his mood," Brian suggested.

"Gentlemen!" Mrs. Langston reprimanded the two friends.

"Well, it works," Brian, replied laughing.

"Maybe, but I believe Ms. Roth is seeing Mr. Roberts now," Mrs. Langston replied, trying to clean up the subject. "Is it a bad case, Calvin?"

"Yeah, I'm afraid so," Calvin responded. "A 13-year-old girl was killed during a gang initiation."

"Any case concerning children and gangs usually puts him in a bad mood for days." Mrs. Langston shook her head.

"You better get your oven ready, Mrs. L.," Brian suggested. "We are going to need it."

"I've already put Jackie on notice. It will be long hours until this case is closed," Calvin added.

The elevator doors opened and JD stepped out. "Good morning, everyone. "Mrs. Langston, you look too good to be behind that desk today. Why don't you take the day off and bake us some of those oatmeal raisin cookies," he said smiling broadly.

"Well, Mr. Harrison, I would if you signed my paycheck instead of Mr. Roberts."

JD laughed. "Well, just tell him I gave you the day off. Hey Calvin, Brian, glad you could make it in early. Let's take this to my office," he said, walking off.

Calvin, Brian and Mrs. Langston stood there for a moment, stunned at JD's disposition. The men followed him down the hallway.

"Have a seat; I have to make a quick call," JD said as they entered the office.

Standing at the window in his office, overlooking the city, he pulled out his cell phone and pushed a button. He played nervously with his tie. "Good morning, sunshine," he beamed. He dropped his head as Tracy began to speak.

"Good morning to you. Did you sleep well?" she asked.

"No, I couldn't sleep once I got home. I worked on the case."

"I couldn't either," she said, blushing. "It is the next day, right?"

"Yeah, it is." He replied with a smile.

"This is real, right? You're not calling to say it was some kind of dream, are you?"

"Yes, it is real, and no, it was not a dream," he said firmly.

Tracy sighed in that sweet voice JD loved to hear. "Okay."

He smiled. Brian and Calvin sat there a little puzzled.

"Are you going in to the office today?" JD asked.

"I'm already in. We have the Brooks presentation this morning."

"Oh, yeah, the one you were supposed to work on last night," he joked. "Will you be free for dinner tonight?"

"Yeah, especially since I did not get a chance to eat last night."

"I know. I forgot about the food, too." He laughed. "I owe you one."

Turning while he was laughing, JD noticed Calvin and Brian were watching him curiously. He honestly forgot they were there. "I've got to go. I'll call you when I wrap up here," he said and pushed the end button on the phone. "Gentlemen," JD said while pulling a folder from his briefcase, "we have three main targets to bring the Latin Eagles down."

Brian grinned. "No, my brother, it's not going that way. Who in the hell were you talking to on the phone that has you swinging from the chandelier like that?"

Calvin didn't have to ask—he already knew. "Decided not to follow your plan?" Calvin asked, smiling.

"The plan went out the window." JD sat down laughing. He leaned back in the chair and crossed his legs, still laughing. "Calvin, if there's such a thing as heaven right here on Earth then I was there last night and if I do this right, I will spend the rest of my life there."

"Tell me you did not hit that last night?" Calvin said.

"Hit what?" Brian asked.

"No, I'm not even pressed for that." JD laughed. "The shit is funny." He exhaled "It was like you said, I just want to take my time and really get to know her; you know?"

"Get to know who, damn it?" Brian demanded.

JD and Calvin replied "Tracy" at the same time.

"Come on, B, keep up, man," Calvin said.

Brian looked at JD. "You sure that's a wise move?" he asked. "I mean, you did just convict her brother on federal charges."

JD exhaled. "B, I don't know if it's the right move for me professionally or not. But I gave her up before because of my career; I can't let her go again, not now."

He stood, pulled the bulletin board out and pinned three faces on the board. "As I was saying, gentlemen, these are the targets to bring down the Eagles. We have two additions to our group for this one. They should be arriving at nine."

Mrs. Langston's voice came on the intercom. "Mr. Harrison, Ms. Rivera and Mr. Graham are here to see you."

"I'll be right out," JD replied and exited the room.

"What in the hell did I miss?" Brian asked.

"Did you think he just let Carolyn go for nothing?" Calvin asked, not really expecting an answer.

"Carolyn don't have shit on the head job Tracy put on that man," Brian replied. "Damn near makes me want to have some of that."

Calvin laughed. "Yeah, man, he's done."

JD walked back in the office. "Gentlemen, meet Magna Rivera, specialist on Hispanic gangs from D.C. and Dan Graham from the AG's office. They will be with us throughout the entirety of this case. Ms. Rivera; Mr. Graham; my right arm and partner Calvin Johnson; and head of security, Brian Thompson—both of whom I trust with my life.

"Let's take a seat and get started. The wheels are   motion on this case, so let's get caught up." JD handed each person a file with a detailed plan of action on each target identified. "This is the plan; it's your job to make it work."

They began reviewing the files and worked through lunch. JD suggested they wrap up around four. That would give him a chance to catch Gavin up on the events of the day, give Ms. Rivera a chance to get settled in and give him a chance to make a trip he promised Tracy he would make.

"Brian," JD called out as everyone was leaving the office, "let me talk to you for a minute."

"I'll catch up with you guys later," Calvin said and left with the others.

"B, I need you to make arrangements for me to see Day as soon as possible. I don't want him to get word about me and Tracy off the street. I need to tell him in person."

"Alright, man, I can do that."

"I need another favor. I need you to take a ride with me."

"Where are we going?"

"Blackwell."

Brian gazed at JD. "Give me 10 minutes, I'll set it up."

JD and Brian crossed the James River using the 14th street Bridge. As they pulled into the Blackwell area of Southside, it was easy to see the illegal activity going on. The Latin Eagles had control of a 25-block radius. All of the high-rise apartments were under gang control; no one entered or left without permission from Juan Cortez, their leader.

Brian pulled the Suburban in front of the 25th Street high-rise and turned to JD. "The white Expedition to the right and the Chevy Caprice to the left are us." Brian was not a man to be caught off guard. He had his revolver in his hand as they got out of the car. JD entered the high-rise first, Brian directly behind him. There were several Latinos sitting on the steps and another group down the hall to the right of them.

"What's up?" A man's voice came from stairs above. "Y'all in the wrong place." Men in suits did not frequent the high-rises. They were either Social Services or cops; either way, they were not welcome.

"We are looking for Lisa Gonzalez's parents," JD politely stated.

"They live on the third floor. What you want with them?" A young man asked.

JD ignored the question and walked towards the steps. No one moved. He looked at the group to determine who the leader was, then glared at the man doing the talking. "I'm District Attorney Harrison. I don't want any problems. But, like I said," Brian put his revolver in clear view, "I am going to talk to Mrs. Gonzalez. How that comes about is up to you." JD stepped closer to the man and asked, "What's it going to be?"

The other group moved closer to the steps. Brian cocked his gun then pointed towards the group. "Who's first?" he asked.

Two men with sawed-off shotguns walked in the door behind Brian to support him and flanked the doorway.

"Man, it ain't got to be all that." A voice came from the top of the steps. "It's all good, let them up."

Brian lowered his gun. The boys at the bottom of the steps got up. JD and Brian went upstairs; the armed men stayed at the doors.

"Mr. Harrison," the man at the top of the stairs asked, "what brings you to our part of town—slumming?"

"Taking care of some business with the Gonzalez family," JD replied.

"They don't have nothing to say to you, man."

"That's cool, but I have a few things to say to them."

"You a bold motherfucker to come down here. You know Juan is going to have your ass for this."

JD and Brian laughed. "Juan controls you, not us," Brian replied.

JD knocked on the door and a little girl opened it. He stooped down and smiled. "Hello, what's your name?" A woman came up behind her. JD stood. "Mrs. Gonzalez?"

"Yes."

"My name is JD Harrison. I'm the district attorney handling your daughter's case. May I have a moment of your time?"

"Si, come in." JD stepped inside. Brian guarded the door.

"Why a DA got secret service guards?" the man asked Brian.

"The man is connected like that," Brian smirked..

"Y'all know you suppose to clear shit like this through Juan. He ain't going to like this."

"In case you missed the point before, we don't give a damn what Juan likes or don't like."

"You can't disrespect the man's turf like this and don't expect retaliation."

Brian looked at the man. "Do I look worried to you?"

An hour later, the door to the apartment opened. JD stepped out. "Thank you for taking the time to listen, Mrs. Gonzalez. I will be in touch."

"Thank you, Mr. Harrison. It's good to know somebody cares."

"You have a good evening, ma'am."

"You, too, Mr. Harrison, and thank you."

JD turned and left the building with Brian. Once they were in the car, the two men with the guns left the building and got into the Chevy Caprice. The Chevy pulled off, Brian next, and then the Ford.

"That's a lot of coverage for just a DA," one man said.

"Yeah, and they weren't all secret service."

"How you know that?"

"Sawed-off shotguns are illegal. Let Juan know we had visitors tonight. See how he wants it handled."

Once all three vehicles were back in the downtown area of Richmond, Brian signaled an all clear. The other two vehicles pulled away and Brian hit Interstate 95 heading toward the federal prison in Petersburg.

"How did it go?" Brian asked.

"Pretty well. I'm glad I did this, it felt good," JD replied.

"Well, let's hope your next conversation goes as well." Brian laughed. "I made arrangements for you to see Day within the hour. You up for it?"

JD smiled. "Hell no, but I have to do it."

"No you don't. The man is in prison and it's not a damn thing he can do about you being with his sister."

"It's a matter of respect, B. If this was my sister I would expect no less."

It was getting late, but JD had to do this before word got to Al about him and Tracy. He prayed all the way to the facility that Al would understand. He respected Al for taking the steps he did to protect Tracy. JD felt as though he owed Al at least that. Well, as far as that went, he also owed Gavin. It was because of them he was able to reconnect with Tracy. Damn, that's twisted. All JD knew for sure was he couldn't turn back. Even if Al did not accept his relationship with Tracy, he could not give her up, not now, not ever.

The warden met JD and Brian at the front entrance. "Mr. Harrison, you indicated this was a sensitive matter you needed to discuss with Al, so we set you up in my conference room. No one will disturb you there. A guard will be outside the door, if you need him."

"Thank you, we will not be long," JD replied.

"You want me in there with you?" Brian asked out of concern for his friend.

"No, thanks B, I got to do this on my own," JD said as he entered the room.

"Harrison," Al said as they shook hands.

"Al," JD replied and shook hands.

"I didn't expect to see you, much less hear from you this soon. It's only been a couple months. What's up, man?" Al asked.

"How are you doing in here, Al?"

"Life's okay; it ain't great, but I'm surviving."

"Good. I wanted to fill you in on Gavin, but I also need to talk to you about Tracy."

"Tracy?" Al questioned.

"Yeah," JD said, clearing his throat, "but first Gavin." He filled Al in on the agreement he made with Gavin to keep him off Tracy.

"I can hang with that as long as he keeps his word," Al replied.

"He will or I'll have to kill him myself."

"Harrison breaking the law." Al said laughing. "I think you better leave that one up to me."

JD smiled. *That damn propensity for violence. Alright,* he said to himself, *stop putting this off, talk to the man.*

"Thanks for the update, but that's not why you're here," Al said, sitting back in the chair.

JD looked down and held his head back up as Al was talking.

"You're not good at bullshit, Harrison. You're a straight shooter. What gives, man? What's got you so nervous?" Al laughed.

"You're right." JD smiled. "I need to talk to you about Tracy."

Al sat up and asked, "What about Tracy? Is she alright?"

"Yes, Tracy's fine," JD replied with a broad smile.

"She's alright?" Al said watching JD closely, wanting some reassurance.

"Believe me, she's fine."

Al noticed JD's tone and change in facial expression when he talked about Tracy.

"I, um, wanted to tell you in person I've been seeing Tracy," JD said, looking closely at Al.

"Alright, so what's the problem?" Al asked, not quite sure where JD was going.

JD stood up. He was pretty sure Al did not get his meaning. "Al, Tracy and I have been seeing a lot of each other and to be honest, I'm in love with her, I think."

The casual atmosphere changed immediately and tension filled the air. Al abruptly stood up. "You've been fucking my sister, Harrison?" Al yelled.

Okay, now he understands, JD said to himself as he watched Al approach him aggressively. JD stood his ground. "No, but make no mistake; it's going there," JD yelled back with just as forcefully.

"I trusted you with my sister and you take advantage of her. Then you got the nerve to come in here and tell me about it. Man, have you lost your damn mind?" Al yelled.

Trying to keep things calm, JD stepped back and took a deep breath. He put his hands in his pockets. "Yes, Al, I have, and it was your damn sister who took it."

Al stood there and stared; JD's response took him off guard. Al paced a little, and then stopped. He started walking on the opposite side of the room from JD. Al needed to think for a minute. *Well, he did tell JD not to let any knuckleheads mess with her.* He stopped and stared at JD. *He was a good guy, clean cut, good family and an honest man. If he really loved her, he would protect her with his life.* He stopped again and looked at JD. "What happened with the senator's daughter?"

"I had to let that go before I started anything with Tracy," JD replied as he watched Al's thinking process.

Al looked at him. *That was decent,* he thought.

JD continued. "I did not set out for this to happen. But to be honest, man, it happened years before I even met you. I didn't want this to go any further until I had a chance to talk to you about it. But know this, Al,

I don't care if you agree or not, I am going to be with her. I'm only here because Tracy loves you. That makes your reaction important to me."

This is a bold motherfucker standing here, Al thought. He liked that. "You do know I can have your ass killed, even from in here."

"I realize that. But it won't change anything. I would still love her and she would still love me," JD replied. "Either way, I'm here; do what you got to do, but I can't let her go again, not now."

Al sat down at the other end of the table. "Do you realize what position this will put you in? You're a fucking DA, involved with the sister of a convicted criminal. Man, if that shit gets out, your professional career is gone."

"That's possible." Both men were talking calmly now. "Al, I'm damn good at what I do."

"Shit, you ain't got to tell me," Al said, "I'm in here."

JD leaned against the back of the chair. "If they want to let me go because of my relationship with Tracy, then so be it. I will offer to walk if this becomes an issue. But there's another angle that concerns me."

"What's that?"

"If this gets to your people, they may think you are working with me. That could cause problems for you."

"You mean when, and that's if they don't already know," Al said. He shook his head. "It might cause an infraction or two, but nothing I can't handle. Does Tracy know you are here?"

"No," JD replied.

"How do you think she will feel about you jeopardizing your career for her?"

"She would not be very happy with it," JD responded.

"Tracy is not stupid. She has thought this through, Harrison. She usually see things a little clearer than the average person. Don't try to keep her out of the loop. Talk this over with her. If she tells me she wants to be with you, then I'm alright with it. But JD, let me warn you, if you hurt my little sister, DA or not, I will kill you."

Chapter 11

The Special Services agency luncheon, which was catered by TNT Event Planning, was managed with a relaxing flair. Tracy was very proud of the professional manner in which Cynthia and Rosaline handled the event. James was very pleased with the outcome. Ashley and Tracy were able to pull the employees into the scheme of things, and James added his own personal touch. He sat down and spent time talking to as many employees as he could, discussing his plans for the agency. Some employees felt comfortable enough to discuss some of their individual issues.

The employees were pleased James took the time to talk with them. Unfortunately, some things came out about upper management he would have to address immediately. James and Tracy arranged to meet later to discuss a strategy on how to deal with the major issues. To make the event as appealing as possible, invitations had been extended to family members.

"Ashley Harrison, you look better than you did in college."
Ashley froze. She did not need to turn around to know who was there. She continued to put her papers away. "Hello, David," she responded.

"What, I don't get any love here?" he said with his arms spread open. Ashley turned around to face him. "Isn't that your wife over there?" she asked curiously.

He put his arms down. "Ashley, we are just two old friends saying hello. There's nothing wrong with that."

Ashley knew this man meant her no good. If he could, he would take her right there in the room with his wife watching. "We're not old friends, David. And yes, I think there is something wrong with that. I'm sure your wife would agree."

Ashley cleared her throat to catch Tracy's attention. Tracy looked over James's shoulder and saw the expression on Ashley's face and the object of her discomfort. Tracy sighed.

"What is it?" James asked as he followed Tracy's attention path.

"I'm sorry, James, excuse me."

A little concerned with the expression on Tracy's face, James said, "No, I'll go with you."

As they approached it was apparent Ashley was uncomfortable talking with David. James did not like talking to the man or being in his presence for any amount of time. He went to Ashley, put his hand possessively on her shoulder and extended the other. "Hello, David. How have you been?"

"Brooks," David said, "I'm doing well."

"David," Tracy sourly spoke.

"Tracy Washington, how in the hell are you?" He looked her up and down. "You are looking good these days."

"Thank you," she said, but her words were tinged with disdain.

"I should have known if one was here the other was not far away."

"It's a good thing we are like that." Tracy smirked.

"That was a great presentation you two gave," Karen Holt said as she stepped beside her husband.

"Yes, it was," James agreed looking down at Ashley. "You two gave us that jolt we needed. Ashley, may I speak with you a moment?"

"Sure," she said with a smile. "Excuse us."

James put his hand on the small of her back as they walked away. David noticed the action and turned to his wife. "Honey, are you about finished here?"

"I just need to go to my office for a moment. I'll be right back," she said and walked away.

David looked at Tracy. "Damn, girl, if I had known you were going to turn out looking this fine, I would have hit that back in the day."

Tracy smirked. "You may have tried, like you did with everyone else. But you would not have made it; not man enough for me." She turned and walked away.

"Ashley, are you okay?" James asked.

"Yeah, I'm fine," she replied with a wry smile. "James, I am truly sorry this happened here. I had no idea David was Karen's husband."

James shook his head. "It's not an issue, Ashley. Please let it go."

"Well, thank you for the rescue."

David watched the exchange between Ashley and James. *Hmm, we will talk again, Ashley.*

"You ready, babe?" Karen asked as she walked up behind David.

"Yeah, I'm ready. What was all the hoopla about today?"

"James had the efficiency experts do a presentation for the employees," Karen answered.

"How did they do?"

"Great, those two are really good."

"Yes, they are," he said as he looked back at Ashley. "It's good to see some HU girls did learn something."

Ashley walked away once David and Karen left the room. She was embarrassed with the scene.

"Is she going to be okay?" James asked Tracy.

"Yes," Tracy replied. "That was a really bad situation, James. Thank you for stepping in."

"It was no trouble." He looked at Ashley. "She's not as tough as she puts on, hmm?"

Tracy smiled. "No, she's not. But she does put on a good front."

Not knowing what the issue really was, James did not say anything more. But he had become very fond of both of the ladies from Next Level Consulting and, hence, very protective. "If he becomes an issue, be sure to let me know."

Tracy looked at her watch. "It's still a little early. Would you like to meet at my office around three to go over some of those issues you mentioned?"

"If you have the time that would be great. I'll bring Angela along. I want her to hear some of these accusations."

"Alright," Tracy replied. "I'll see you at the office."

Tracy went to help Ashley pack up. She pushed Ashley with her shoulder. "The asshole still looks good," she joked.

Ashley started laughing. "He did look good."

"Look, Ashley." Tracy pointed to Cynthia approaching James.

"Oh, no." Ashley laughed. "We need to help James."

"You know, I think Cynthia may have met her match with James."

Ashley shook her head. "You're right. Cynthia couldn't get or hold a man like James."

Tracy looked at Ashley. "Is there something you're not telling me about James?"

"No. Is there something you are not telling me about James?"

Tracy smiled brightly. "Not about James."

Ashley looked sideways at Tracy. "What you talking about, Tracy?"

Tracy laughed. "We'll talk later."

Tracy, Ashley, James and his human resource manager, Angela, were going over several issues raised by employees at the event when JD walked through the door. "Hello, Monica, is Tracy busy?"

Hearing Jeffrey's voice, Tracy smiled. "Excuse me for a moment."

Seeing the smile on Tracy's face, Ashley raised an eyebrow as she walked by. Ashley stood in the doorway of the office and watched as JD and Tracy approached each other. When they met, JD grabbed her hands and looked down into her eyes. "Hello."

"Hi." Tracy smiled back. He then kissed her as if they had not seen each other for days.

Ashley smiled and said, "Excuse us" to James and closed the office door behind her. She stood there watching them, as did Monica. They both were enjoying the moment, as were JD and Tracy.

JD hesitantly broke away and just smiled into her eyes. "It's been an interesting day. I just finished wrapping up a few things. So I thought I would stop to say hello before I went home."

Tracy smiled back. "Would you like to say hello again?"

He smiled and kissed her again. This time he put her hands around his waist and his around her shoulders and gave her a long, hard sensuous kiss that made Monica exclaimed, "Damn."

Ashley cleared her throat. "Excuse me, umm, Tracy, we have a meeting going on in here."

JD pulled away, because Tracy wasn't.

Sighing, Tracy said, "I've got to go back in."

He kissed her softly on her lips, rubbed her upper arms, not really ready to let her go. "Alright, call me when you are finished."

"Okay."

"Ash, Monica, I'll talk to you guys later." JD turned and walked out the door. Tracy watched every step until he was gone.

Monica looked at Tracy, then at Ashley, then back to Tracy. "You okay, Ms. Washington?" she smiled.

"No, Monica, I'm not, I can't breathe right now."

"Shit, me either." Monica laughed.

"Tracy," Ashley said, laughing, "we have people in your office. We need to get back to them. Okay. Breathe, Tracy, breathe."

She did, several times.

"Better?" Ashley asked.

Tracy sighed heavily. "Yes."

"Okay, no harm done. Let's go back in now, and before you go anywhere tonight you're going to tell me what you were doing until four o'clock in the morning." Ashley opened the door and pushed her in before Tracy could object.

They wrapped up the meeting about 30 minutes later. Ashley was walking everyone to the door as James asked to speak to Tracy for a few minutes.

"Sure," Tracy replied.

James closed the door after everyone left. He exhaled "Harrison? Do you know what you are doing, Tracy?"

Tracy looked at him and then down at her desk. "That's a little personal," she said.

"In case you haven't noticed," he replied, smiling, "I take things with you personally, Tracy. I am sure I shouldn't, but that's me."

"James," Tracy started.

He put his hand up to stop her. "Tracy, you are a special young woman. I respect and like you, probably more than I should. But with that said, please know this: I don't want to see you hurt," he said sincerely. "If you ever need me for any reason, all you need to do is call, any time."

Tracy smiled and lowered her head. She liked James. Not the way she liked Jeffrey, but as a friend. Tracy had to talk to someone about what was happening and she felt she could trust him. "This is all new to me, James." She smiled while putting her hands on her hips. "I don't know where this is going. I'll admit I'm scared to death." She let out a nervous laugh. "This man is totally out of my league and I don't have the slightest idea," she hesitated, "why he wants me. All I can say is: I'm on board for the ride and just have to see where it takes me."

James looked at her with that smile on her face, laughed, walked over to her and gently kissed her lips. "I know exactly why you." He turned to walk out the door.

"James." Not knowing what to say to him, she said, "Friends?"

"Always. I'll be in touch and please don't forget what I said: any time, any reason." He smiled.

Once James and Angela were gone, Ashley was standing in Tracy's doorway with Monica. Tracy was sitting at her desk.

"Okay, what gives?" Ashley asked with her hands on her hips.

Tracy sat there, not knowing what to say or how to say it. She started shaking her head with disbelief and laughing. She put her hands over her face and laid her head on the desk. "Oh God, oh God, oh God, oh God." She looked up at Ashley and Monica, tears started coming down her face, and she still couldn't say anything.

Tears were coming down Ashley's face now. "It took you two long enough," she cried.

Tracy really started laughing and crying all at the same time. Ashley and Monica joined in.

"I want to know every detail," Ashley stated.

"Me too," Monica joined in.

Chapter 12

Life was good, JD thought. Having Tracy in his life this way was what
he needed; he just hadn't known it. After talking to Al, he was ready
to take the relationship with Tracy to the next level. He did not want to
rush her, but it was getting hard for him to be with her without making
love to her. JD accepted the realization that Tracy was now a part of him.
He loved being with her and watching her become more confident about
him. Tracy was at a point where she could be herself around him, like
she was that day in his office years ago. JD could kick himself for letting
her go back then, but he was going to make sure it did not happen again.

Every now and then it seemed Tracy became a little uneasy around
his friends or when they went to certain places. The average person
would not notice, but he could tell, and so could Ashley. To anyone else
Tracy appeared to be the most confident person in the room. But now,
she was becoming more comfortable with him. Every so often one of his
old girlfriends would stop by the table and say hello while they were out.
JD would introduce Tracy, and most were very polite. However, one or
two of them let their jealousy show. Tracy would say hello and excuse
herself to allow him time to get the situation under control. He loved her
tactfulness, but didn't like her being in that position. There was even a
time when the two ran into Carolyn, who was now very angry with him
for not returning her calls. She made it very clear to everyone in the club
that night JD and Tracy were now on her proverbial "shit list."

JD admired the way Tracy handled herself in that situation. He
apologized and vowed not to let it happen again. But for a week or so
afterwards Tracy would not go out in public with him. He tried to
understand and be patient, but he could not help himself. He had gotten
to the point where he wanted her with him, wherever he went. To be
clear, JD did not mind staying in with her. Hell, he would be content to

come home from work, take her in his arms and just be with her for the rest of his life. But he knew with his career, they would eventually cross paths with Carolyn again. This was one of his issues and JD was going to have to find a way to control it. He did all he could to reassure Tracy he had no interest in anyone but her. Nevertheless, Tracy had developed a serious complex when it came to Carolyn.

About a week later, after a lot of begging and pleading, JD persuaded Tracy to go jogging with him in the park. She was hesitant, but decided to go anyway. As luck would have it, they had just come out of the park when they ran into Carolyn and Jackie. JD was carrying Tracy on his back and her arms were around his neck. The two were laughing and not paying attention to their surroundings when they heard her voice. "Taking your little friend for a piggyback ride, are we, JD?" Carolyn asked.

JD put Tracy down. "Oh, shit," he whispered under his breath. "Hello, Carolyn," he replied.

Tracy immediately started brushing her hair down. She felt so insignificant around Carolyn.

"Hello." Carolyn sneered.

"Hi, JD, Tracy," Jackie spoke.

"Tracy, you remember Carolyn," JD said as he held her close.

"Yes, hello, Carolyn."

"Oh, yes, I remember meeting you now. You were with James Brooks if I remember correctly."

"Yes, he's a client of mine."

"Really, is that all? I was under the impression there was more going on there."

JD pulled Tracy a little behind him. "Where's Calvin, Jackie?" he asked.

"I thought he was at the basketball court with you."

"No, I didn't make it today."

"Well, what are you two up to?" Carolyn mischievously asked.

Tracy held on to Jeffrey's hand. "Just hanging out," he replied, in a warning tone. "How is Gavin?"

"Gavin's fine," Carolyn replied testily.

"Well, we are going to go now," Jackie interceded. "It was nice seeing you, Tracy. Bye, JD," she said as she turned to Carolyn. "Come on, Carolyn, it's time to go."

Carolyn put her hands on JD's chest. "I'm sure we will talk later." She smiled seductively. "Bye, Tracy." She snickered.

JD looked at Tracy and could see the immediate effect Carolyn had on her. "Tracy, she is nothing for you to be concerned about."

Tracy laughed and tried to pull her hand away. JD was not going to let go. They had come too far to slide back because of Carolyn. He pulled her to him. "Hey, we won't let outsiders come between us; not now, not ever." He kissed her long, hard and deep, then picked her up over his shoulder, smacked her butt and walked to the car. Tracy couldn't help but laugh at him.

When they got back to the condo, JD asked, "Where's Ashley?"

Tracy put the key in the lock and replied, "It's Saturday. She is probably out shopping with Cynthia."

They entered the foyer at the bottom of the staircase that led to the living room. "Hmm, that means we are alone." He smiled mischievously as he picked Tracy up over his shoulders and carried her up the stairs.

Tracy laughed. "Look, Tarzan, you better not drop me."

As they reached the living room, he stopped at the hallway leading to Ashley's master bedroom and looked in. "Just making sure," he said laughing. He proceeded through the living room, just past the fireplace, to the door that led to Tracy's master bedroom. He walked in and threw her on the bed. "Me Tarzan, you Jane." He jumped on the bed beside her.

She smiled. "I'm not sure I'm speaking to you yet."

"Alright." He stretched. "Then you'll listen."

"Wait," Tracy said, "is Carolyn Roth in one of the closets waiting to jump out at me?"

JD laughed. "I certainly hope not."

He pulled her on top of him. She straddled her legs on both sides of him. She sat there with her hands on his chest and he covered them with his. Now JD's mind was having a private battle, trying hard to stay focused on what he needed to say to her—but Tracy sitting on top of him was playing havoc with his concentration. Even in her sweats and ponytail she was a vision of pure sexiness. The white cotton tee shirt she was wearing showed the form of her breasts, her flat stomach and tiny waistline. Yes, he was having a very difficult time thinking clearly.

She squirmed to settle herself, but he reached out to stop her. "Don't do that," he said as he wrapped his hands around her waist and adjusted himself. He smiled at the sight of her and realized she had no idea what she was doing to him. "I'm sorry about Carolyn. She is one of those issues I told you about," JD began.

Tracy looked down at him. She hesitated to have this talk, but knew it was needed. "Jeffrey, we really need to talk about her. I remember thinking the first day I saw the two of you together that Carolyn was the type of woman you should have beside you. She is beautiful and full of self-confidence." She shook her head. "I don't have any of that. Cynthia has told me for a while now that I did not fit into your world; maybe she is right," Tracy said sincerely.

"Tracy." JD stopped her. "Listen to me, babe, I need you beside me." He smiled at her. "With all your little quirks and insecurities. As for Cynthia, I ask you again: Why do you listen to her? I am not so sure she is a friend to you, Tracy." She wiggled a little, and he held her still. "Don't do that," he said, and then continued. "A friend would not do the things Cynthia does to you. I see, she is a friend to Ashley, not you."

"She may not be a friend to me, but she is real with me. Cynthia never once concealed her feelings towards me. She has always been honest about that. I have to respect her for that, and she has my friendship, whether she wants it or not."

"Alright, you can think that way if you want to; I have different thoughts on her," JD replied irritably.

"Cynthia is not important, but Carolyn and Turk are. Jeffrey," she said, looking down shyly. "I don't know a lot about relationships, sex or things that happens between a man and a woman. But," she hesitated for a moment, "I know I love you and I would not do anything intentionally that I thought would hurt you. It would be too much like hurting me. My connection to Turk would hurt you professionally if it was ever exposed. So," she breathed heavily, "before this goes any further, I will step aside with no drama, no issues and no bad feelings."

JD let her waist go and folded his hands across his chest. "Oh, you would?" he exclaimed.

"Yes," Tracy replied sadly.

"You mean as in leave me, not see me anymore?" He asked almost in a whisper.

"Yes," Tracy said, missing the vein that was threatening to explode in his neck. "I'll just step aside."

"And on what planet do you think I would let you?" JD bellowed.

Tracy raised her eyebrow. "Don't raise your voice at me," she said as she tried to move.

He held her in place. "Then talk like the intelligent woman I know you are and not like a stupid little schoolgirl."

Tracy did not like the tone or volume of JD's voice and began to move off him. He grabbed her, pushed her backwards, and then rolled on top of her. JD was mad; not pissed, not a little upset, but mad. *How in the hell could she even think about leaving me now?* He thought.

Tracy could not believe how quick and strong JD was. As she looked up, recovering from the sudden moment, she actually thought she would see fire coming out of his nose any moment. His breathing so heavy with anger, she knew instantly she had said something wrong. She looked up at him with innocent eyes, "I take it this was not a good time to say that."

JD looked down at her and he wasn't sure if he saw fear or confusion in her eyes. Either way, he did not like what he was seeing. Taking a moment to compose himself, he adjusted her beneath him placing his legs on the outside of hers and relaxed his body. "There will never be a good time for you to say that to me, Tracy. I love you. I don't think it, I don't wonder about it. I know I am in love with you. The thought of you leaving me for any reason is unacceptable."

JD gently pushed her hair back off her face with his finger, looked at her and smiled. What he saw reflected in her eyes was all he could ever want or need in a woman: Love. It surprised him when he said he loved her, but he did. He gave her a feather-touch kiss. "Right now I am not interested in Carolyn, Cynthia or Turk. All I'm interested in is right here," he said, looking up and down her body.

Tracy didn't know if it was the way Jeffery was looking at her or the fact that she could feel his manhood against her thigh. Whatever it was caused her body to respond with a need to feel more of him. She placed her arms around his neck and pulled his lips to meet hers in a passionate kiss. His hands ran down her body and she followed his lead with her own exploration. Her hands traveled up his muscular arms, across his wide shoulders and down his back.

Jeffery wasn't sure if it was the kiss or her hands exploring his body, but the heat between the two of them was unbearable. He reluctantly left her lips to pull her shirt over her head, exposing her breasts. He kissed each mound, but then returned to her lips when she gently moaned. He kissed her gently at first, but the intensity grew as he parted her lips with his tongue and dwelled deeper.

He instinctively pulled her closer, but it wasn't close enough for Tracy. She wanted to feel his naked skin against her, so she tugged at his shirt. Jeffery stopped and pulled the shirt over his head and threw it to the floor. As he began kissing the base of her throat, Tracy reared her head backward. He heard her moan softly and felt her body begin to move beneath him. He ran his tongue down to her breast, circling one while he caressed the other with his hand. He sucked, licked and massaged both, getting his fill, until her nipples were erect.

Tracy held him tight, not wanting the warm feeling that was surging through her body to stop. She pushed her body closer to his and ran her hand down his back. Just the touch of her hand on his naked skin almost rendered Jeffery senseless. He released her breasts and went back to her lips, kissing her with an urgency that she matched.

He moved to her side, not breaking the kiss, then ran his hand down her flat stomach to her thighs. Reaching inside her sweatpants he moved her panties to the side, and then pressed against her warmth. He heard a moan escape in her throat as she pressed her hips up to his hand. His mind registered how soft and moist she was, and he needed to feel more. He slipped a finger inside and reveled in her reaction. Jeffery moaned. *She was wet and ready. Stop, damn it, stop; something isn't right.* But his fingers were not listening, as another one entered her.

There was an invasion in her body that Tracy had never experienced, but she wanted more of it. She pressed her body upward into Jeffery's hand and held him so tight he couldn't think. Jeffery was losing control, and that was unusual for him. He broke the kiss, pulled his hand away, and whispered, "Please stop," as Tracy continued to move under his hand. He was trying hard to get control of the situation, but Tracy did not want to stop. She didn't want him to stop and now she was truly confused as to what she had done wrong.

Jeffery lay there beside her, breathing hard, not moving a muscle. "I am sorry," she said breathlessly almost in tears. "I don't know what to do, now."

Jeffery shook his head. "Shh," he said as he turned his head and kissed her cheek. "It's not you. I shouldn't have," and he stopped mid-sentence as it began to dawn on him. He moved his hand out of her panties, and then rested his hand on her stomach. Disappointed, Tracy dropped her hand to the bed. He sat up on his elbow, holding his head up with his hand, and looked down at her. She was lying there with her eyes closed. Tracy knew something was about to happen, she was so close. She had no idea what, but she longed to find out. Jeffery smiled. "Look at me, Tracy."

She hesitantly opened her eyes and he saw the uncertainty in them. He could not believe what he was experiencing. She immediately looked down, feeling a little ashamed of her actions, when he put a finger under her chin and forced her to look at him. "You've never made love before, have you?"

She looked back down, bit her lip and exhaled. "No," she said as a tear escaped her eye.

He kissed the tear away and smiled. She gave a fake laugh to hide her nervousness. "That's funny, right. I've lived a quarter of a century and never had sex. Just what you needed." She looked down and continued to bite her lip.

Still trying to rein himself in, he asked, "Why would that upset you?"

"Here I am trying to get you to stop looking at me like I am still the 19 year old you met years ago and I really am still a little girl."

He looked down at her body and laughed. She looked up at him as if he was losing his mind. She tried to get up, but he pressed down on her stomach with his hand, stopping her. "I'm not laughing at you. Well, yes, I am, but not for what you think. Squirt, you may be a lot of things," he said, looking down her body again, "but you are definitely not a little girl."

More in control now, he kissed her again. In that moment he knew he could never let her go. He stopped the kiss, but allowed his lips to remain on hers and whispered, "Don't ever talk about leaving me, Tracy. Not having you in my life would hurt me more than I could ever explain right now. My career is what it is: just what I do. You," he said, smiling at her, "are my life, my future. None of it matters without you."

Tracy still couldn't look at him. "You don't have this problem with Carolyn Roth, do you?"

Jeffery laughed deep and hard. "Hell, no," he said, still laughing. Seeing her reaction, he said, "I'm sorry." He cleared his throat and changed to a serious tone. "You're being serious, aren't you?"

"Yes," she said and hit him in the chest, but left her hand there to travel down to his abs.

He closed his eyes at her touch as she explored and prayed for control. "Jeffery," she said shyly, "could you make me feel like that again?"

He opened his eyes to see her innocently looking up at him. When he asked God for this woman, he had no idea how precise he would be. He said a private *Thank you and please forgive me, Lord*, for he certainly was not going to deny Tracy the pleasure she was seeking.
"Yes, I can." He smiled and began passionately kissing her.

He placed a trail of kisses from her neck down to her stomach, then pulled her sweats and panties off in one smooth move. As he examined her body with his eyes, he knew he had to pace himself, but he had no idea how he would be able to do that looking at her. "Jeffrey," she called out nervously to him.

He heard her voice shake, so he kissed her forehead. "Do you trust me, Tracy?"

She thought about that for a minute. "I'm lying here with no underwear on; I better trust you."

He laughed at her as she smiled back at him. *There was no denying it, he loved her*, he thought. He stood and closed the bedroom door, took off his sweats and went back to the bed beside her.

Tracy gasped and thought, *He is a good-looking man, especially with his clothes off.*

Kissing the base of her throat he ran his hands down her body as if he was trying to memorize every inch. She placed the palm of her hand on the side of his face. He turned and kissed the inside of her hand then began to kiss her lips as he moved her hand down to his manhood. Her eyes opened with a surprised look. He smiled, and then guided her hand around him as he continued to kiss her. Jeffery knew instantly that was a bad move. He moaned and then slowed his actions as he realized he was losing control at her touch. He ran his hand down the same path as before until he reached the warmth between her legs. His fingers slipped easily into her moistness. Just the feel of her was stripping his control. He never had a problem with control, why now? He moved down her body strategically placing kisses. She was moving to the rhythm of his fingers inside of her as he kissed her inner thighs. The kiss sent an instant sensation through her body. She was responding to every touch from his hands and his tongue.

Tracy didn't know exactly what was happening to her, but whatever it was she didn't want it to stop. Jeffery gently parted her legs and began to softly kiss the very center of her. Knowing he had to brace her for his next endeavor, he placed his hand on her stomach. Her sweetness was undeniable and he indulged in the untouched treasure that was now his. Her body immediately jerked, as he knew it would. She reached out and took his hand, as he, concentrated on pleasing her; nothing else mattered. She moved her hips downward to take everything he had to offer and he increased the movement until he could feel she was losing control. Tracy cried out in pleasure. It felt like a tidal wave had just hit inside her body. Jeffery held still until the very moment he felt her climax.

He reached up, and entwined his fingers with hers. She grabbed his other hand and held on for dear life. He felt her body jerking and immediately laid back on top of her and held her. Her breathing was so labored he began to gently kiss her. He rolled over and pulled her to him; he held her until her trembling began to subside.

"That's just the beginning, isn't it?" Tracy asked breathlessly.

Jeffery pulled his head back so he could see her face. She looked up at him. "Oh yeah, there's a lot more to come," he grinned.

She smiled. "Okay," she said in a very sweet, sexy voice.

Jeffery rolled back on top of her as he raised her arms above her head. He looked into her eyes. "Tracy, there is no turning back now. It's you and me; no one else from this moment on." He kissed her lightly on the lips. "Just you." He spread her legs with his thigh. "Just me," he said again while kissing her.

Tracy could hear Jeffery talking to her, but she was getting lost in the kiss, and at this point she would agree to anything he said as long as he continued to make her body feel alive. He positioned himself to enter her, temporarily breaking the kiss. Breathing just as heavily as she was, he looked down at her. "Tracy, this is going to be uncomfortable for a minute, I'm sorry. But I promise it will only hurt for a minute, okay?" he whispered.

"Okay," she whispered as she blinked.

Jeffery smiled. He loved to hear that from her. He slowly entered her and tried to go slow, but she was moving with his every motion and he was about to lose control. Tracy felt him enter her and she knew instantly this was the answer to her curiosity. She began to embrace what was giving her so much pleasure.

Jeffery increased his rhythm to keep up with Tracy's body movements. When he reached her blockage, he began to kiss her deeply. He entwined his tongue with hers. He couldn't hold back any longer, he held her tight and pushed through, then paused. He heard the cry rise in her throat and proceeded to kiss her passionately to take away the discomfort. Tracy squeezed his fingers as her body tensed under him. His body was protesting but he held back. He wanted Tracy to enjoy this moment and remember it with a smile. He continued to kiss her through the hurt, and when she returned the kiss he began moving slowly within her until he felt her responding to him.

Once he felt her body relaxing and moving in rhythm with his, he went deeper and deeper into her. She pushed her hips upward and he followed her rhythm. They were simultaneously losing control. He released her hand, reached under her body and pulled her closer to him. She wrapped her arms around his back and held on tight. They were both moving feverishly to reach their climax. As he pushed deeper and deeper, Tracy held him close. She wanted more of him, all of him, and he conceded, giving all he had. The explosion that followed left them both clinging to each other, sweating and breathing heavily, neither of them wanting to let go. The two bodies seemed to have merged with each other, creating one.

When he was able to move, Jeffery held Tracy's face in his hands and kissed every inch. She began to giggle, and then started laughing, and so did he. His chest was vibrating from the laughter. They lay there laughing and holding each other for a few minutes. He looked down at her and could see the laughter in her eyes. "You're laughing now," he chuckled, "but you're going to be pissed at me tomorrow."

"No, I won't," she smiled.

"Yes, you will," he replied. "You'll see." Rubbing her forehead gently with his thumb, he added, "But it'll go away in a day or so."

"What will go away?"

"The soreness." Jeffery sighed heavily as Tracy looked up at him with those eyes that seemed to look straight to his soul. He kissed her and said, "I love you, Tracy Washington, don't you ever doubt that." He kissed her and they started all over again. They went on through the night until the wee hours of the morning, when they fell asleep in each other's arms.

Jeffery woke the next morning with Tracy asleep in his arms. *Lord, thank you for all you have bestowed on me. But if her body responds to me like this with no knowledge, what is she going to be like when I've finished teaching her?* Jeffery thanked God for answering his prayer and asked for guidance to make her happy for the rest of her life.

He watched Tracy sleep and thought of the barriers he let fall last night. He did not use protection. That was irresponsible on his part. Jeffery had never had sex without protection; he just didn't do it. With Tracy, it never entered his mind, but it should have. A few issues could arise from that. AIDS—it was important for both of them to be tested. Jeffery did not want to jeopardize her life or his. He knew he was clean and she hadn't been with anyone; he smiled at that thought. Still, they both should be tested. Pregnancy. Wow, that's a thought. For some reason it did not scare him the way it used to. He could see having babies with this woman.

Jeffery got up, went into the bathroom and started to run a warm bath for her. His thoughts went to what Calvin told him about making love to Jackie. He smiled. *Damned if he wasn't right.* He had never made love the way he did last night with Tracy. He came out of the bathroom and looked at her. They were now one and he liked it that way. He began thinking about her statement to him about the propensity for violence. He smiled. *Damned if she wasn't right.* He knew he would kill anyone who tried to take her from him. He had never experienced jealousy over a woman in his life. But now, he would take someone's life to protect her. He knew it was selfish, but from this moment on he wanted to be her everything. He saw her stir in the other room.

"Good morning," he said from the doorway.

Tracy looked over, saw him and smiled brightly. "Good morning."

Jeffery walked over to the bed to kiss her.

She put the sheet over her mouth. "Yuck mouth."

He pulled the sheet down, kissed her, tongue and all. "Now we both have yuck mouth."

She laughed, moved her leg and moaned. "Ohh." She rubbed her thigh.

"That's just the beginning," he laughed.

She blushed, and then laughed with him.

"Okay," he said laughing with her, "you're laughing now, but you won't be laughing when you have to go to the bathroom. But I can't help with that. However, I can help with the muscle soreness. Come on."

He pulled the sheet away from her.

"Jeffery," she screamed and pulled the sheet back, "I don't have on any clothes."

He looked at her and laughed in disbelief. "You don't need any clothes on."

A frown came on her face. "Jeffery!"

He just looked at her. "I saw every inch of you last night. No need in trying to hide it now."

He pulled the sheet off, picked her up and carried her into the bathroom. He sat on the side of the tub. "Test the water. Make sure it's not too hot."

Tracy put her toe in. "No, it's fine."

He set her down in the tub, and went back into the bedroom.

Tracy sat there for a moment thinking, *what in the hell did I do to make my legs so sore?*

When JD came back into the bathroom, he saw the puzzled look on her face. "What's wrong?"

She looked down, a little embarrassed by the thought of last night. "My legs hurt."

He sighed; relieved that was all it was. "Oh that," he said while pulling off his sweatpants.

She inhaled and covered her eyes. "Jeffrey, what are you doing?"

He climbed in the bathtub behind her. Tracy held her breath when she realized what he was doing. His private part rubbed against her as he was sitting in the tub. "Umm, you want to get that thing off my back?"

"Oh, it's a thing this morning? Last night you couldn't get enough."

Stomping her foot in the water, she exclaimed, "Jeffrey!"

He pressed against her and kissed the back of her head. She blushed, as he settled her back against him. He took the sponge from her and started washing her and Tracy began to relax. He smiled. JD was glad she was becoming comfortable. "Now, about your legs. You have now experienced a real man between your legs."

"Oh, really, is that what you are, a real man?"

"Damn right." JD laughed. "Seriously, you never used those muscles in that way before and it's the same as when you first start to exercise. Every muscle in your body hurts until you become used to it." She let that answer sit for a moment and began to enjoy him washing her with the sponge.

"Jeffrey?"

"Yes."

"Will it always be like that?"

"What, making love?" He kissed the back of her neck. "Actually, from now on it will be better."

Tracy laughed. "I don't think that's possible."

"Well, next time you will not have the discomfort you did last night."

Closing her legs, she remembered the pain. But she also remembered it went away and another feeling replaced it. "Jeffrey?"

"Yes."

"Did I...um...did I, you know...um, satisfy you?"

He kissed her cheek. "Yes, you did, very much so."

She released her breath, and relaxed against him again.

"Now I have a question for you."

"What?" She asked with a smile in her voice.

He put her head under his chin. "Why didn't you tell me you'd never been with anyone before?"

She sighed. "Cynthia said—"

"Not 'Cynthia said' again."

"Do you want to hear this?"

"Shit, no, not if Cynthia said it."

She sighed. "Well you asked."

"Okay, okay, what did Cynthia say?" JD asked, not really interested.

"Cynthia said a man like you would not want someone with no experience. A man like you didn't have time to teach someone how to satisfy him. You needed someone who knows what to do."

"Tracy," he said, cutting her off, "I will ask you this question again: does Cynthia have a man?"

"No."

"Then stop listening to her." They both laughed.

He moved her forward to wash her back. She pulled her knees up, put her arms around them, and laid her head on top of them. They sat quietly for a moment, both content with the sensuousness of the moment. He leaned forward over her back, kissed her, and felt himself becoming aroused again. He had to clear his mind from that. She was too sore for him right now. He pulled her back against his chest. "Tell me what happened yesterday."

"Umm, let me think, oh, yeah, you took my virginity," she said, laughing.

He smiled, put his head against hers. "Yes, I did, and enjoyed every moment of it." He kissed her head. "But that's not what I'm talking about."

"Oh." She laughed. "What are you talking about?"

"Why does Carolyn make you so uncomfortable?"

She sat quietly for a moment, thinking, and then asked, "Why do you want to be with me, Jeffrey? I have nothing to offer you. I'm not Carolyn, Cynthia, Karen, Denise or whoever else I haven't met yet."

He put his arms around her. "I'm with you, Tracy Alexandria Washington, because I love you. You have all that I will ever need or want, and that's your heart."

She smiled. "You've had that for a number of years now."

He smiled and relaxed against her. Listening to her talk made him realize her insecurities came from people like Cynthia and Carolyn constantly telling her she didn't belong. And they were right, she was above them. "Please don't allow other people to destroy what we have," he said, "and they will try. We are stronger as two than we are as one. Just remember, we can withstand anything together."

As she reclined in his arms, she wondered if it could really be like he said. Could they really be together? "Jeffrey?"

"Yes," he answered, not sure if he had convinced her.

"I'm hungry; let's get something to eat."

Relieved, he hugged her tight, and thought, *I'm hungry, too, but not for food.*

Chapter 13

A few weeks later Jeffrey was in the office reviewing the Gonzalez case when Gavin knocked on the door. "Hey, you got a minute?"

"Sure," JD said, looking up from the file.

"JD, I received a call from the *Times-Dispatch* requesting an interview with you concerning the Blackwell neighborhood. Apparently a reporter got wind of the visit you made on the Gonzalez case. They spoke with Mrs. Gonzalez, who is singing your praises to everyone from the editor of the newspaper to the governor."

"She's a nice lady." JD smiled.

"Yeah, well, the AG thinks this will be good publicity for the office and so do I. Now, I know you turn down interviews and I understand your reasons why. But I'm asking you to reconsider this request."

"Gavin, I don't want the publicity. I just want to work the case as effectively as I can."

"I understand your position, but consider this. Next year is an election year. You will be in a position to get any assistance you request, with any case. You will have access to AG's office or the governor's office if you do this interview."

"Why this one?" JD asked. "I have refused many interviews in the past."

"The Hispanic vote is up for grabs. You've made an impression on the Hispanic community. In addition to that, you have the African-American community wrapped up. Whatever direction you go, they go. Both parties are aware of your popularity among both sectors. They are going to be grabbing at you to help capture that group. Now, I know none of that is important to you, but being able to get whatever you need from the AG on cases without red tape or hesitation is something you will need now and in the future. JD," Gavin pleaded, "do this one interview. I told these people I would talk to you personally. Help me save face here."

"You shouldn't have promised them anything, Gavin."

"I did not make any promises. I know better, but work with me on this one."

"No personal questions?" JD said with a questioning tone.

"None, and if any come out, you can throw her out," Gavin replied.

"Her—her who?"

"Victoria Murillo."

"Alright, Gavin, I'll make arrangements to meet with her."

"Well, she's here," Gavin said.

"I thought you didn't make any promises."

"I didn't. I just said I would ask." Gavin smiled. "I didn't want to give you a chance to change your mind in case you agreed. Ms. Murillo, please come in," Gavin said while opening the door. Victoria Murillo walked into JD's office.

Victoria was a beautiful young woman. She was about five feet eight inches, slim at 110 pounds with an almond skin tone. Her hair was jet black, flowing down to her waistline, with big brown eyes full of aspirations. "Mr. Harrison, thank you for meeting with me." Victoria smiled.

JD extended his hand. "Ms. Murillo."

"Well, I'm going to leave you two. Ms. Murillo, it was a pleasure meeting you."

"Thank you for your assistance, Mr. Roberts."

"If you need any further assistance, let me know," Gavin said as he closed the door.

"Have a seat, Ms. Murillo," JD said, pointing to the chair.

"You are a difficult man to pin down, Mr. Harrison."

"I rarely do interviews unless it is helpful in a case."

"So I've been told by everyone I have contacted regarding you."

JD could read women very well. He noticed she was checking him out the minute she walked in. "Why is this interview so important?"

"Are you questioning my motives for this visit, JD?" Victoria said with a flirty smile.

"Yes," JD replied, leaning back in his chair.

"Why?"

"Because, frankly, I don't see how a tragic story about a young girl's death and a subsequent visit to the child's mother would qualify for good pleasure reading."

Victoria was taken aback a little by his sharp-toned response. "You take your cases a little personally, don't you, JD?"

"Is that question on or off the record?"

Victoria frowned, wondering why he asked that. She replied, "Nothing we have discussed so far has been on the record. I usually let someone know when they are on the record."

"So you are feeling me out," JD stated. "Why?"

"What makes you think that?" She laughed.

"You are a reporter; everything is on the record. Yet I noticed you did not pull out a recorder nor are you taking notes. What is it you want from me, Ms. Murillo?"

"Boy, you don't pull any punches do you? No small talk, just straight to the point." She chuckled.

JD just looked at her. "The question is still on the table, Ms. Murillo. What do you want?"

Victoria was impressed. Most attractive men in power positions tend to be just the front man. There was usually someone in the background with the brains. But this man was the real deal. He was serious about his work. Sitting forward she said, "You are right, JD, I'm not here to do a story. But I will write one as if we did an interview. I'm here on behalf of Mrs. Gonzalez."

While Victoria was talking, JD looked at his watch and wrote a note, but was listening very intently.

"She did what you asked of her and was able to get a small group of people from the community to meet with you."

Not knowing if she could be trusted, JD did not acknowledge the conversation with Mrs. Gonzalez. He did not want to take a chance on anyone else in the family being harmed by Cortez or any of his people. He did not know Victoria Murillo and wanted an opportunity to have her checked out prior to discussing anything with her. "Excuse me for a moment." JD hit the intercom. "Mrs. Langston, would you step in my office for a moment?"

"Yes, sir," Mrs. Langston replied

"How do you know Mrs. Gonzalez?" he asked.

"I grew up in Blackwell. My mom still lives there with my little sister. She and Mrs. Gonzalez are friends and have been for the past 20 years."

A knock came at the door. JD stood and handed the note to Mrs. Langston. "Would you handle this for me please?"

"Yes, sir," she replied.

"Is Ms. Rivera still here?" JD asked.

"Yes, sir."

"Would you ask her to step in here, please?"

"Yes, sir."

"Mrs. Langston, would you please stop that?" JD asked.

"No, sir. Mr. Harrison, will there be anything else?" Mrs. Langston asked with a smile in her eyes.

"No, thank you, ma'am," JD replied with a smile.

Mrs. Langston stopped, looked at JD then at Ms. Murillo. "Mr. Harrison," she said with a smirk.

JD smiled and sat back down. "How many brothers and sisters do you have, Ms. Murillo?" JD asked, returning to the conversation.

Victoria made note of the playful exchange between the two. It was nice to see he had a playful side. "Are you interviewing me, JD?" she asked.

"Yes," he said, being very serious.

"I have two brothers and a sister. One of my brothers is a member of the Latin Eagles and the other is a victim. I'm trying to keep my sister from going down the same trail as Lisa Gonzalez," she replied with a little irritation in her voice.

Magna knocked, then stepped into the office and took a seat.

"Why should I believe you are here on behalf of Mrs. Gonzalez and not your brother?"

"Hector," Magna interjected.

"Hector," JD repeated.

Victoria smiled. "You guys work quick. Look, I went through a lot to get to you. So all my trouble will not be in vain, let me give you this message. The group would like to meet with you. However, meeting anywhere in the neighborhood would be dangerous for them. Therefore, you would need to make arrangements outside Juan's turf and at a time that would not be suspicious." She got up to leave. "Thank you for the interview, Mr. Harrison. Oh and if you or your people want to follow me, I'll save you some trouble. I'm going home, which is 126 North Elm. You can check that out later if you like." She smiled at JD. "You have a good evening."

"You do the same, Ms. Murillo," JD said as Victoria closed the door.

"What did you get on her?" JD asked Magna.

"From what we could get on short notice she is on the up and up," Magna replied. "She started with the paper right out of college and has an anchor position in the works with WWBT12. Here's the kicker. Back in high school she was Juan's girl."

On his way home from the office, JD placed a call to Maxi's and made arrangements to reserve her conference room. He asked her to keep the meeting confidential. He knew Maxine would know what to do. JD hung up the telephone then called Tracy to see where she was.

JD loved going home these days. He and Tracy had spent every day and night together since the first time they made love. He thought the sex was so good because of the excitement of him being her first lover. However, as the weeks passed, nothing changed. Just the opposite happened: he couldn't seem to get enough of her. It was so unreal, he thought. It actually pissed him off when he had to leave her to go to work. The guys noticed he hadn't been to Maxi's in a couple of weeks.

JD laughed to himself, remembering that Brian had asked him one day, "Man, what in the hell are you doing, hitting it 24/7?" When JD just smiled, Brian threw his hands up in the air. "I'm so jealous."

JD pulled into his garage and went inside. Tracy must have heard the door because she was coming out of the kitchen with a dishtowel wiping her hands off as he entered the room. She threw her arms around JD's neck. "Hello, handsome," she said, then kissed him, long and deep.

JD grabbed Tracy around her waist, pulling her feet off the floor. He walked her backwards to the sofa where they both collapsed. "Hello to you," he replied once he broke the kiss. "Hmm, how was your day?"

"Long," she replied. "What about you?" She smiled up at him.

JD was caressing the back of her neck as they talked. He told her about the day, including the meeting with Ms. Murillo.

"And how gorgeous was she?"

"Oh, she was hot. She had dark, mysterious eyes and long legs," JD said grinning, "but not my type."

"Oh, really, why is that?"

"Because she wasn't you."

Tracy closed her eyes and exhaled. "Good answer, Mr. Harrison." She pulled him down and kissed him. Dinner was late that night, but no one complained.

The next morning Calvin met JD coming down the hallway. "Everything is set for this afternoon," Calvin said as they entered JD's office.

"Good, I spoke to Mrs. Gonzalez, she did send Ms. Murillo. She will be facilitating things between us from now on. Mrs. Gonzalez indicated at least 10 people will be in attendance tonight, but she said it will be a tough crowd," JD explained to Calvin.

"Man, if anyone can convince them, it's you."

Magna walked through the door. "Things on my end checked out. Murillo has no connection with Juan Cortez or her brother Hector. There was an apparent blow-up about the brother joining the gang and Murillo walked out. She is an untouchable, per Juan's orders. Right now her main goal is to keep the little sister out, especially since Lisa Gonzalez's death."

"Where's Brian?" JD asked.

"He is making transportation arrangements for you and Mrs. Gonzalez. Dan's on his way," Magna answered.

"Dan's here," he said as he walked through the door. Everyone sat.

"It's important that we are able to convince this group that we can do something to clean up their neighborhood," JD started. "Synopsis."

That was Calvin's cue. "We are going to have to provide a force of police power in that neighborhood for an undetermined amount of time. We can't waiver on this. We need the police force visible at all times. As soon as they suspect we are easing up, Cortez's group will stomp on that neighborhood—starting with whoever they think opened the door to let us in."

"We also have to make sure the sentences Juan's people get will keep them behind bars long enough to give the good people time to reclaim," Magna added, as Brian entered the room and took a seat.

"Brian." JD acknowledged his entrance. "Dan, will the AG's office guarantee the force Calvin is speaking of?"

"Maybe," Dan replied.

"I can't go in there tonight with a maybe. I need a guarantee before we ask these people to put their lives in danger. Contact the AG, get me a guarantee," JD replied.

"You got it." Dan left the room. "Brian, what do you have for me?" JD asked.

"We know you and Mrs. Gonzalez are being watched. We arranged for her to come here. We will take you and her to the meeting in another vehicle. If they are watching either of you, they will think you two are here. That will keep the others in the clear."

"That will work," JD replied. "Calvin, should we put Gavin in this loop?"

"Not yet," Calvin replied. "Let's keep a lid on this until we need to bring him in. These people are taking a chance on us. No one out of this circle should know about this meeting."

"I agree," Magna said.

"I agree," Brian seconded.

"Alright, it's just us," JD responded.

The meeting took place without interruption. The group was actually larger than expected. A few business owners shared their concern about the illegal activity that caused people to go outside for services they provided right in the neighborhood. Others who expressed their concerns at the meeting were people who wanted to go home at night without fear. "People live in the projects not because they want to, but because they have to. Does that mean they have to live in an environment that is not safe for them or their children?"

"When our children try to go to school, they have to endure thugs trying to get them to sell drugs or do other things for them. We should not have to live like this. What can you do to help us?"

JD did not have an answer to all of the questions that they threw at him. It hurt him to his heart to hear the desperation in their voices. They wanted a normal life for themselves, but mostly for their children.

"I don't have all the answers to solve all the things you have mentioned tonight. But I can eliminate the cause of your problems, which is the gang activity. As you all know, we received indictments on some of the key people in the organization that is holding your building hostage, Mrs. Gonzalez."

"Yeah, but will they just get off like before?" one person yelled.

"I don't take cases to court I can't win," JD replied. "The suspects we have will be sent away for a very long time. I am going to be honest. As long as Juan Cortez is out there, he will just replace and rebuild. Therefore, until we get him, things will continue the way they are. We have to hit him from both directions. We will do our part with the law. You must do your part by standing up and fighting back for your neighborhoods."

"Man, are you crazy? They have guns and thugs that will kill us just for looking at them wrong," another person responded.

"I believe you," JD said, "but at some point, you've got to say enough is damnit enough. When Lisa Gonzalez was killed, that was enough for me. What is it going to take for you? Maybe your daughter, or your son?"

"So, Mr. Harrison, what can we do? Where do we start?"

Magna interjected, "Start simple, nothing fancy or anything that would cause suspicions. Like a simple community day or block party. Anything that would bring people out as a community, showing a united front."

"But they will show up, too."

"Yes, that's the whole point. Let them see you doing nothing but living, having a good time with each other. Rather than everyone running into their homes at night out of fear, do some cooking, have music; invite your neighbors out of their homes just for one night. Then after that, just start small conversations regularly with other people in the neighborhood, start building alliances. Take one small step at a time."

JD kicked in. "They did not take over this neighborhood in one night. You are not going to get it back in one night. It will take time, but you've got to start somewhere."

"Well, we could just throw an old-fashioned block party," Victoria offered. "Pot luck, everyone bring a dish. Get a DJ, for some sounds. Have some activities for the children."

"Yeah, but how do we keep the thugs out?" someone asked.

"You don't want to keep them out," JD said. "You plan the block party; we will provide security for that night." A few murmurs went through the room. "Not to make any arrests, just a show of force to keep things under control. If they don't bring no mess, won't be none."

The group laughed.

"It costs money to do even a small block party—where is that supposed to come from?" someone asked.

"We'll find a sponsor. Hell, I'll pitch in myself, but you all have to remember, I work for the state, I am not a rich man." JD smiled.

The group laughed and began talking amongst themselves.

"The group is laying plans for the block party," Magna said to JD. "I think you may have them."

"Maybe. Your input was on time. Thank you."

"Let's hope it works."

"Oh, I think it's a good start," Victoria said, walking over. "This is the first time in a long time I have seen them with even a little ray of hope. JD, I just might forgive you for that interrogation you put me through." She laughed.

"Yeah, well," JD replied, "sorry about that. But I was not going to put Mrs. Gonzalez at risk. I did not know you; I wasn't taking any chances."

"Well, I'll do my story on you with just hearsay." She smiled. "You didn't check out my place the other night. I was wondering why."

JD just looked at her.

"Word has it you're off the block. Can I get a confirmation on that?" Victoria asked flirtatiously.

Magna started to walk away, guessing that the woman was making a pass at JD, and knowing she did not want to be a part of it. JD's answer stopped her in motion.

"Yes, that is true, and I could not be happier," JD replied with a smile. Magna smiled. A man actually admitted to this very attractive woman that he was not available.

"Can I quote you on that?" Victoria asked, blinking back, not believing he turned her away.

"Yes, you can."

Victoria smiled and walked away. Magna looked at JD and smiled. "It must be love, JD."

"What's that?"

"You just told that gorgeous woman you were not available to her or anyone else and then you told her she could publish that info. It must be love."

After the meeting was over, JD was pleased with the outcome. He called Tracy to see where she was—his place or hers. Tracy met JD at the top of the stairs.

"Hey, you," she said as they exchanged a loving kiss. "How did your meeting go?"

"Better than I expected. The community is planning a block party to show a little unity and hopefully start opening some lines of communication among other neighbors. All I have to do is come up with a sponsor and security."

"What do you need a sponsor for?"

"Well, most of the people in that neighborhood are living paycheck to paycheck. They can barely feed their individual families, much less provide food or money for a block party."

"Next Level could sponsor it," Tracy offered.

He smiled, kissed her, and then said, "You don't have to do that, but thank you."

"Well, why not? What would you need, a couple thousand?"

"I don't think so," he said, then looked at her. "You have a couple thousand you can give away?"

"Well, it wouldn't hurt us. Actually, we could use it as a write-off for tax purposes. Tell them whatever they need the funds will be provided, but don't tell them by whom," she stated.

"Why?"

"There's no reason for them to know."

JD hesitated. "Let me think about that. I'm not sure I want to get you involved with this," he said, shaking his head.

"Oh, I can be a part of your life with limits," she said testily.

"No, don't take it like that," JD said, "it's just I'm not too crazy about my girlfriend giving money for one of my causes. It's a man thing, baby."

"It's a man thing," she repeated, now irritated. "Okay" she said, "let it be a man thing." She got up from the sofa. "It'll be a man thing and your ass will be broke with no money. Yeah that's a man thing. You got this community to at least try to come together on something, but they are going to go broke trying to do it because it's a man thing. Okay, that makes sense, Jeffrey."

"Are you upset?" Jeffrey teased as he lay back on the sofa watching her pace.

"Yes, because that's stupid," she replied with a little attitude.

He got up, picked her up over his shoulder and headed to the bedroom.

"Jeffrey Daniel, you put me down right now!" Tracy demanded.

"Okay," JD said. He threw her on the bed, and down on top of her he went. "You're kind of sexy when you're mad." He smiled at her.

"Well, you kind of stupid with that man thingy," Tracy said smiling, "but you are so damn good looking with those dimples."

That was that. They were in for the night. During the middle of the night, JD woke Tracy up and asked, "Your company makes enough money to pay Ashley, Monica and you a salary and still have money left over to give away thousands of dollars?"

Still half-asleep, Tracy answered, "Yeah, the company grossed close to one this year." She closed her eyes.

JD shook her again. "One what?"

"What?" she asked, still half asleep.

"One what?" JD pressed.

"About one million," Tracy replied, then went back to sleep. He started to wake her again, but decided to ask her in the morning.

Tracy told Ashley about the conversation with Jeffrey the next morning at the office. That day during lunch, Ashley paid JD a visit at his office. JD was in a meeting with Magna, Dan, Calvin and Brian when Ashley walked in. "Excuse me, I don't mean to interrupt, but Mrs. Langston was not at her desk."

"That's okay, Ash, come on in." JD smiled. "I think you know everyone except Magna. Magna Rivera, my sister, Ashley."

"Hello," Ashley said. Dan was sitting there clearing his throat.

"Oh, this is Dan Graham from the AG's office."

"Hello," he said with a crooked grin and lust in his eyes.

"Hello." Ashley smiled, noting the look.

Ashley kissed Calvin. "Hey, Squirt." Calvin smiled.

"Hi, Brian," Ashley said.

"Whatsup girl, you looking good," he replied.

"I can't help it," she replied then turned to JD. "I have this check for you for the block party. Now, before you hit me with the, *It's a man thing*," Ashley started, "let me say this to you. You're my big brother and I love you. But if you ever turn down an offer to help people because of your dumb pride I will kick your ass myself."

"Ashley, you do realize you are in my office talking to me like this in front of people I work with?" JD replied, a little embarrassed.

"Calvin, Brian, is this upsetting to you?" she asked.

"No, I've seen him do it to you plenty of times." Calvin smirked.

"Yeah, me too," Brian agreed.

"Magna, Dan, have I offended you?" Ashley asked.

"No, I'm good." Magna smiled.

"You can stay as long as you want and say whatever you want," Dan replied.

"Thank you, Dan," Ashley smiled.

"Oh, you're welcome," he replied. Calvin and Brian started laughing.

"JD, call the people. Tell them you have the funding to have that block party and if they need more just let us know. And do not argue with Tracy about this. Don't ever argue with her about money. The company is doing very well and so is she. Don't be one of those men who have a problem with their woman making more money than him; you're so above that."

"Are you finished?" JD asked.

"Yes." Ashley smiled.

"Good, now get the hell out of my office. I will talk to both you and Tracy later."

"Okay, I love you." She grinned and gave JD a hug. "Goodbye, everyone; and Dan, it was so nice meeting you," Ashley said flirtatiously.

"Get out, Ashley," JD yelled.

"I'm gone," she said and left.

"You know," Magna said, "I'm going to quit my job in D.C. and move here just to see what happens around here next." She laughed. "I loved that."

"Oh, you think that's funny?" JD asked.

"I do, I do," she replied with a smile.

"Dan, you like your coffee a little dark, don't you?" Brian asked jokingly.

"That was a good-looking woman," Dan said. "Baby got back is all I can say"

"Excuse you!" JD roared. "That's my sister you're talking about."

"Oh, yeah, sorry about that, JD. She's a very attractive woman," Dan smiled.

"How much is the check?" Calvin asked while laughing.

JD glanced at the check. "Twenty-five hundred."

"What?" Magna exclaimed. "That will really fund a nice block party. You're not going to give that check back, are you?"

JD hesitated. "No, we'll call Victoria and tell her we have the funds for the block party."

"Good." Magna exhaled.

"Hey, JD, man, just out of curiosity. How much money does Tracy's company make?" Brian asked.

Calvin hit Brian. "Man, don't ask a question like that, what's wrong with you?" He turned to JD. "But if you want to answer, I won't stop you."

All eyes were on JD, waiting for an answer. "I don't know what she makes," JD replied, agitated. "I never asked." No one said anything. All sat there waiting for a reply. "The company is worth close to $1 million," JD replied with a small frown on his forehead.

"Damn," the group replied in unison.

Chapter 14

The block party was held a week later, since an anonymous sponsor signed on and provided the funds needed immediately. The AG's office provided security, mostly volunteers. JD held a meeting with some officers he knew and they brought in a few friends. The city gave permits to block off a section of Hull Street for the party. JD talked with Gavin about the party, who in turn talked to Carolyn about it. Carolyn in turn mentioned it to her father. Ashley mentioned the party to Cynthia and Rosaline. They each pitched in to help with setting up the food. Victoria got a popular radio station to donate some airtime and a deejay for the event.

When JD and Tracy got there, the party was in full bloom. The senator, the AG and the DA's office was fully represented. It warmed JD's heart to see the outpour of support from people on his behalf. The first person he searched for was Mrs. Gonzalez.

"Hello, Mr. Harrison, do you see this? Can you believe this turnout?" Mrs. Gonzalez exclaimed with excitement.

"It's a little overwhelming, isn't it?" JD replied looking around at the crowd. "Mrs. Gonzalez, this is Tracy. Tracy, this is Mrs. Gonzalez."

"It is so nice to meet you, ma'am." Tracy smiled.

"You, too. Are you Mr. Harrison's girlfriend?" Mrs. Gonzalez beamed.

"I think so," Tracy replied.

JD laughed.

"You got a good man. Look at all he's done for us. He is a man of his word, and you don't find that nowadays," she said. "You hold on to him."

"I'll try. What can I help you with?" Tracy asked.

"Oh, honey, you don't have to do a thing but eat and enjoy the people. Victoria, come here, honey," Mrs. Gonzalez called. "Meet Mr. JD's girlfriend."

"Victoria Murillo." She extended her hand to Tracy.

"Hello. Tracy Washington."

"This is a good thing JD has accomplished. Looks like a good turnout," Victoria commented.

Mrs. Gonzalez came back with a plate. "Tracy here, sit; sit."

"I'll tell you what, Mrs. Gonzalez, I will sit if you sit and talk to me," Tracy replied.

"Oh, honey, I have too many people I have to recruit for the real work, but Victoria will keep you company."

Mrs. Gonzalez left. Victoria and Tracy sat at a table. "So you are the woman that has taken JD off of the market?" Victoria asked.

"I don't know about that," Tracy replied, not sure where this woman was going with her comment.

"That's what he told me, and I hope it's true because I put it in print," Victoria responded.

Senator Roth walked up to JD and pulled him away. "Hell of a turnout, son," he stated.

"Yes, sir, it is," JD said, looking back to where Tracy was. "Let's hope it's effective."

"If you get 10 people in addition to what you already have to turn out in a community like this, count it as a success," the senator replied with a smile.

"Well, thank you for taking the time to support it."

"JD, whatever you need, whenever you need it."

"I appreciate that, sir."

Carolyn spotted JD and her father talking and decided to interrupt. "Well, hello stranger, it's been a while. Are you alone?" Carolyn asked, looking around.

"Carolyn," her father said, "not here, not now."

"I'm just saying hello," she replied.

"Hello, Carolyn, and no, I'm not alone," JD replied with an icy voice.

"Oh, Tracy's here?" Carolyn asked, attempting to locate Tracy. Carolyn was still very livid over the last conversation she had with JD. He did not like what she said to Tracy at the park and he had let her know it. He made the mistake of telling her what effect it had on Tracy. "There she is, let me go say hello," Carolyn exclaimed, and then walked away.

"I'll take care of that for you," the senator said as he went after Carolyn. JD walked behind him and Magna, who was nearby watching the scene that followed.

"Tracy," Carolyn called out with a sweetness that was filled with loathing, "I see you are still hanging in there." The senator walked up as JD and Magna stood behind Tracy. Victoria sat there taking in the action.

JD jumped in. "Senator, this is my friend Tracy. Tracy, this is Senator Roth; and you know Carolyn."

"Hello, Senator, it's a pleasure to meet you," Tracy said, extending her hand. She turned to Carolyn. "To answer your question, Carolyn, yes I am still around and I plan on being around for a while. Now you can get used to it or not. The choice is yours. But you will not do this at an event like this. It is not the place or time. Here's my card. Whenever you need to talk, call me. But do try to contain your anger towards me here, today."

Gavin walked up. "Everything okay here?" he asked, crossly looking at Carolyn.

"Yes," Carolyn replied with serious attitude, "everything is fine."

"Good, let's go," Gavin responded. "You all enjoy yourselves," he said as he guided Carolyn away.

"It was really nice to meet you, Tracy," the senator said. "The next time I need to put Carolyn in her place, I'm calling you." He smiled and walked away.

Tracy sat back down. JD rubbed her shoulder and sat beside her. "You okay?" he asked.

"Yes, I'm okay. Go mingle. The people here need your attention right now," Tracy replied.

He kissed her and said, "Alright."

"I got her," Magna said to JD as he walked past her. "Hey, ladies, may I join you?" Magna asked. Tracy wondered if this was another one of JD's issues she would have to deal with.

"I'm Magna Rivera. I'm working on the Gonzalez case with JD."

"Hello," Tracy replied.

"Hello, Magna," Victoria said. Speaking in Spanish, Victoria asked, "Did she just tell the bitch off or what?"

Magna, speaking back in Spanish replied, "I couldn't have done a better job myself."

Tracy looked at both of them, and stated, "I could have, but I didn't think smacking her would make for good publicity."

Realizing she had understood everything they said, Victoria laughed and gave Tracy a high five. "Alright now, Carolyn Roth has finally met her match."

When Gavin got Carolyn to himself, he calmly said, "Listen to me very carefully, Carolyn, and look at me when I say this so there will be no misunderstanding here." Carolyn looked away as he was talking. "Look at me," Gavin ordered in a no-nonsense tone.

Carolyn turned towards him. "I am announcing my candidacy for governor. I am going to the mansion. You need to decide here and now whether or not you are going with me."

Carolyn started to say something and Gavin stopped her. "If you decide you are going with me, your pursuit of JD Harrison will cease at this moment. If you do not believe you can control yourself when it comes to him, walk away now." Carolyn did not like Gavin talking to her in this manner, but she could not afford to aggravate him more than she already had. He may indeed be her only avenue to the mansion. "You are still here," Gavin affirmed. "Say it, are you with me or not? Before you speak, know that contrary to what you think, I have no problem walking away from you. Now, what will it be?"

"I'm with you," Carolyn replied.

"Good." He kissed her forehead. "This subject will not be discussed again," Gavin acknowledged and kissed her. "Let's mingle."

JD, Gavin and Dan spent a good part of the day talking to people— not asking any questions, just meeting people and talking about the neighborhood. Brian began to see one or two of Juan's people filter in. Just as it began to get dark, the streetlights came on and Juan himself arrived with his entourage. You could feel the change in the mood almost instantly. A few people began to leave, some stayed. Brian appeared out of nowhere and just stood behind JD. "B, nothing happens here," JD instructed. "This has gone well. Make sure it stays that way." Brian followed JD's request. He made sure his men kept their tempers in check even during one or two incidents where Juan's people stepped out of line.

But nothing disrupted the day. It was a huge success all around. The residents of the community actually got to enjoy their neighborhood. Mrs. Gonzalez was able to get more people involved with her group. JD got a little more information that might help with the case. Victoria got a story for her paper. Yes, it was a good day. Unfortunately, there were underlying currents flowing through Carolyn and Juan that would cause damage in the future.

James was in the office working that Saturday. He usually got more done on Saturday than during the week. While going through the files on his desk, he came across the report from his investigators. After the incident with Ashley, James wanted to know David Holt's story. He leaned back in his chair, pulled out the report and began to read.

Holt was a football star at Harmon the year Ashley was a freshman. He had a reputation with the ladies and did not like the word no. David and Karen got together during their freshman year and have been together ever since. While Karen attended another nearby school, David felt he could play. Apparently, Ashley was going out with David his senior year. Ashley got wind of Karen and broke things off with David. David did not take the break-up well and had a few public arguments with Ashley. The story was that Ashley was studying in the 24-hour study room which was adjacent to the library on campus. David followed her there and tried to have his way with her. Tracy went to meet Ashley and walked in during the act. Tracy got the campus police, but the report was squashed at the request of the head football coach. However, a copy of the report was kept just for the record. From that point on, David had issues with Ashley and Tracy. Apparently, neither Ashley's brother nor any members of her family were made aware of the incident. Only Tracy knew. James smiled to himself. Those two really stick by each other.

His mind drifted to Tracy; they could have been good together. She had a mind and a determination to succeed that matched his. That was rare. He stood up, went over to the window and could see the festivities taking place across the river in Blackwell. Tracy had a certain innocence about her, a kind of vulnerability that was attractive. James did not have a problem getting women. His problem usually was losing interest in them. He had not met many women who stimulated him mentally. Tracy Washington did. She challenged him at every turn. But now she was with JD Harrison, a young man he truly respected and admired. For someone so young, he had a drive and determination about him. He wanted to do the right thing by people and did, from what James could tell. Yes, as soon as he realized Tracy was attracted to Harrison, James had him investigated. If he had to concede to anyone, he would concede to Harrison. Tracy and Harrison were going to be good together, if Harrison could keep the women from his past out of the picture.

James had resigned himself to being only a friend to Tracy. James sat back down, put the report back in the folder and filed it away. Now, how was he going to handle this situation with David Holt and Ashley Harrison? For the moment, James thought to let things be. But if Holt steps out of line with Ashley, he would have to intervene. *Ashley Harrison,* James thought, *she appears so confident and self-assured.* But he could see how vulnerable she was with Holt. Ashley, maybe. He smiled and moved on to other things.

Chapter 15

Jeffrey and Tracy were becoming a public couple, attending functions that ranged from the block party to formal dinners with the governor. As much as Tracy loved being with JD, being around some of his friends intimidated her. Tonight's function was mandatory for JD to attend but the more Tracy thought about it, she really did not want to attend. She was sure Carolyn would be there and Tracy did not believe she could take another night of being belittled by the green-eyed vixen. Tracy did all she could to let JD know her feelings, but he was relentless; he wanted her there with him. Tracy tried to solicit Ashley's assistance with JD on this matter, but her friend only reprimanded her for allowing people to affect her in such a way. Instead of helping Tracy avoid the event, Ashley took steps to make sure Tracy made a hell of an appearance. Ashley told JD not to pick Tracy up; she would meet him at the function.

The music was playing, and for a change it was decent—a nice blend of music that everyone could enjoy, a little old school, a little new—not the elevator music that normally played at a formal function. The Governor's Ballroom was as elegant as always and as impressive as the guests in attendance. The customary guests were there. All of the top offices of the state were represented, including James Brooks. Since Brian, Magna and Dan were currently a part of the DA's office, they attended as well.

All signs indicated Cynthia and Rosaline had another successful affair underway. The crowd appeared to be enjoying the friendly banter and refreshments, particularly the open bar. Standing at one of the many flowing bar stations were JD, Calvin, Brian, Magna and Dan. When Carolyn approached, Calvin tried to give JD a heads-up, but was too late. "Good evening, everyone, are you all enjoying yourselves?" Carolyn asked in a very suspect tone. Everyone politely acknowledged her. "Good evening," they replied in unison, as all eyes went to JD.

"JD, you look ravishingly handsome tonight," she commented.

"Thank you, Carolyn, and you are beautiful as always," JD responded politely.

"Well, I do try, you know." Carolyn beamed at the compliment.

"You do well at it." Brian smiled, admiring the low-cut gown Carolyn was displaying.

"Thank you," she smiled brightly, loving every moment of the attention. Stepping closer to JD, she asked, "JD, you're not flying solo tonight, are you?"

JD took a respectable step back then replied, "No." He looked at his watch. "I don't think so." He searched around the room for Tracy.

"Well, I wouldn't want you to get lonely. Let me know the outcome," Carolyn offered seductively. "We are still friends, aren't we?"

JD looked at Carolyn as if she had lost her mind.

"I don't think that will happen." JD smiled.

"My Lord in heaven," Daniel said, looking over JD's shoulder, "grant me the words I need to take her home with me tonight."

"What?" Brian asked, laughing and looking in the direction of Dan's admiration.

Calvin knew exactly what Dan was referring to and smiled as he saw the look on Carolyn's face.

Brian touched JD on the shoulder and pointed towards the door. "I'm so jealous." He smiled.

JD turned and had to catch his breath.

Tracy entered the room and she was breathtaking. She stood at the table talking to Cynthia; her back was to them, literally. The black dress that graced her body was cut down to the lower back. It had a strand of diamonds, sparkling against her skin, hanging from her neck to the middle of her back. The rest of the dress was form fitting, falling just above her knees. She wore a pair of three-inch black sandals with diamond straps around her ankle. She turned towards them. Her hair was up in a French roll with bangs swayed to the side, revealing a pair of one-strand diamond earrings which accented her face perfectly. JD stood there for a moment. He always thought she was beautiful; he didn't need convincing. But tonight Tracy totally dominated the room, especially for him.

Tracy was surveying the room, feeling as if a hundred pairs of eyes were on her, and they were. When she spotted JD, she smiled nervously and began walking towards him. JD melted at the stunning woman who looked at him with so much love. He put his glass down and walked toward her, but before he could reach her James Brooks showed up at her side, which infuriated JD. "Hello, Tracy." James smiled.

Tracy turned towards James, taking her eyes away from JD for a moment and smiled. "Hello, James, how are you this evening?" She shook his hand.

"Wonderful and you are beautiful," James replied in his rich baritone voice.

"Thank you," she said as JD approached. She turned back to JD. "Hello," she said with a smile that made his heart sing. JD put his hand on the small of her back possessively, pulled her to him, and then kissed her. "You're late." He smiled back.

"I know, I'm sorry," she apologized. "Jeffrey, you remember James Brooks."

"Yes," he said, shaking his hand. "How are you this evening, Mr. Brooks?" JD asked resenting the way Brooks was admiring Tracy.

"I'm fine, JD. I was just telling Tracy how beautiful she is this evening," James replied, gazing at Tracy from head to toe.

"Tracy is always beautiful, Mr. Brooks," JD replied with a touch of possessiveness.

"I agree," he said, noticing the look of irritation in JD eyes. "You two have a good evening. Try to save me a dance, Tracy," James said as he excused himself.

"I'll do the best I can, but this man is priority tonight." Tracy smiled.

"I'm patient," James replied and walked away.

Tracy turned to Jeffrey again. JD was looking down at her smiling, but Tracy could tell the smile did not go all the way to his eyes. Thinking something was wrong she looked down, put her hand on her stomach and sighed. "What's wrong? Is it too much?" she asked nervously.

"No, you are stunning," JD replied as he gave her the once-over.

"Thank you," she said smiling. "Then why are you frowning?"

"I'm contemplating if I'm going to have to kick Brooks' ass tonight," JD stated with a half-hearted smile.

"Jeffrey!" Tracy exclaimed as she leaned into his chest laughing. "I don't believe you said that." She kissed him on the cheek.

He smiled. "I have some people I want you to meet."

JD took Tracy's hand as he looked back at James Brooks.

JD could tell Tracy was nervous. She was clutching his hand tightly as they walked across the room. A number of eyes were watching the couple, most of them wondering what had come over JD. He was never one to fawn over a woman in public. Others were watching the couple and then watching Carolyn, wondering how she was going to handle JD's attention going elsewhere. Either way, Tracy was very aware of the crowd's eyes. JD rubbed his thumb across her hand as a calming motion. She looked up at him and smiled just as they reached his group of friends. "Everyone, this is Tracy." JD smiled. "Tracy, you know Calvin and Brian."

"Hey, Tracy." Calvin smiled.

"Hi, Calvin." She kissed him on the cheek.

"Mr. Thompson," Tracy said with a smile on her face, but not in her eyes.

Brian smiled and replied, "Ms. Washington, I see I'm not forgiven yet."

"I'm still contemplating that." Tracy smirked.

Laughing, JD continued, "You've met Magna Rivera and this is Daniel Graham. They're working on the Eagles case with us."

"Hello, Magna, Mr. Graham."

"Oh, please, please, call me Daniel," he said, smiling.

"Okay, Daniel."

"You've met Calvin's friend Jackie and, of course, Carolyn."

"Good evening," Tracy politely responded.

Carolyn stepped up to Tracy. Everyone held their breath, not knowing what to expect. "Well, hello again, Tracy," Carolyn said as Tracy stepped a little closer to Jeffrey. "I think we should make some time to talk privately, as you suggested before. Although we have nothing in common, we could compare notes on JD. I may be able to teach you a thing or two about him."

"Really?" Tracy asked, raising an eyebrow.

"I know I could and I promise it will be worth your time," Carolyn said while looking at JD.

"Let's dance," Jeffrey suggested, pulling her away from Carolyn and walking towards the dance floor.

Tracy looked back at Carolyn as they were walking away.

Carolyn was infuriated and everyone knew it. *How dare this little bitch walk into the room? This is my territory and she just crossed the line,* Carolyn thought.

"Jackie, we need to talk," Carolyn said. Calvin knew Carolyn was about to involve Jackie in one of her "get that bitch" schemes.

"Come, Jackie, let's dance," Calvin said as he took her hand, not giving her time to decline. They joined Jeffrey and Tracy on the dance floor.

Jeffrey was holding Tracy close while they were dancing. He could tell she was a little tense. "Are you okay?" he asked, smiling down at her and hoping to change the mood.

"No," she replied angrily, then looked into his eyes. "I hate it when you do that," she said.

"Do what?" JD smiled.

"Look at me like that and make me forget what I'm mad about."

He smiled at her and pulled her closer, allowing their heads to touch slightly as they continued to dance. "Are you mad at me?" he asked while his hands played on her back.

"Yes," she said, pouting.

He pulled his head back a little to look into her eyes. "Talk to me; what's on your mind?"

Tracy felt a little silly now looking at Jeffrey. He was there with her, not Carolyn; what did she have to be upset about? She looked into those dark brown eyes she loved, smiled and jokingly replied, "I'm wondering if I'm going to have to kick Carolyn's ass tonight."

Jeffrey laughed, kissed her on the forehead, pulled her closer and enjoyed the rest of the dance.

After presentations were made and pictures were taken, JD was talking with Gavin, Senator Roth and a few men she did not recognize. Tracy did not want to intrude, so she took a seat at the bar then searched around the room. The crowd in the room seemed to have doubled since the presentations. It appeared to Tracy that everyone wanted a minute to talk to Jeffrey. She watched him and smiled. Just like so many others, Tracy loved that man. For a moment she wondered why he loved her. Looking around the room, she saw so many beautiful women. The bartender interrupted her thoughts. "Would you like something?" he asked with a smile.

"Chardonnay, please," she replied. Tracy sat and sipped her wine. A voice came from behind and shocked her. "So, you're with the man of the hour tonight," David Holt said as he walked up behind her. Tracy immediately looked around the room for Ashley. She spotted Ashley and James on the dance floor. *Hmm, that's interesting*, Tracy thought, then turned to David. She stood, then stepped back away from him. He was standing too close. David was a political analyst. She assumed he must be working for one of the many politicians in the room. "What do you want, David?" She asked in a frosty tone.

David looked her up and down, then grinned. The look made Tracy uncomfortable, so she took another step away from him and looked around the room for Jeffrey. He smirked. "I'm working, but could always find a moment for pleasure. Where's Ashley? If you are here I'm sure she is." He spotted Ashley on the dance floor. "I see Ashley is with Brooks again. What's up with that?"

"Go to hell, David," she stated, then started to walk away.

David grabbed her arm with a subtle jerk. "Don't ever walk away from me," he scoffed.

"Take your hands off that woman before I break your fucking neck," Brian demanded coldly without a blink. David looked at Brian, then released Tracy's arm. "You okay, Tracy?" Brian asked as he stepped between the two of them without taking his eyes off David.

"Yes, thank you," Tracy replied. The last thing she wanted was to be the cause of a scene.

Brian looked at David. "This is not a good situation for you, my friend. We can do this quietly or not, doesn't matter to me," he stated, standing toe to toe with David. David looked at Tracy then at Ashley and sneered. "Tell Ashley I will be in touch." Then he walked away.

Brian waited until David was out of hearing range, and then stared at Tracy with a raised eyebrow. "Who in the hell was that?"

Tracy sighed. "David Holt, an old friend of Ashley's."

"What is he doing here, or better yet, what were his hands doing on you?"

"I don't know why he's here. But we've run into him a little too much lately."

"If he's a problem you should tell JD about him."

"It's not my business to tell, it's Ashley's."

"Then why was he grabbing on you?"

Tracy gazed at Brian. "He doesn't like me very much."

Brian smiled. "Well, I'm not sure about you yet myself, but I will not put my hands on you."

"Thank you, Brian," Tracy said sarcastically.

"Where is Ashley?" he asked. Tracy pointed to the dance floor. Brian located Ashley. "Who's with her?" he asked.

"That's James Brooks, one of our clients."

Brian surveyed the room and saw David watching Ashley and James on the dance floor. Brian did not like the look on David's face; he had seen it before. David was sizing up the enemy. Brian went over to the couple on the dance floor then tapped James on the shoulder. "Excuse me; may I have a moment with Ashley?" Brian asked.

James looked at Ashley. "He's a friend of JD's who I'm going to smack in a minute." Ashley smiled. James smiled then stepped aside. Tracy walked over and began dancing with James. James looked at Tracy searching the room. "What's going on?" he asked.

"David Holt is here."

"Where is he?" James asked. Tracy pointed to the opposite side of the room. "Is there a problem?" James asked.

"A small one, but Brian is handling it."

James looked over at Ashley on the dance floor with Brian. "Who's the guy?"

"Brian, he's a federal agent and a friend of Jeffrey's."

"And Ashley's?" James asked.

"Yeah, I suppose so," Tracy replied.

As Brian and Ashley danced, she gave him a brief explanation of David's behavior, without details. Brian had known Ashley since she was a little girl and he could tell this guy frightened her. What bothered Brian was the fact that he knew Ashley was not an easy person to scare.

There had to be more to the story than she was saying, but Brian did not push any further. "Ashley, you need to tell JD about this guy."

"Brian, David is harmless," Ashley stated.

"Well, your harmless friend just grabbed Tracy in a way that JD would have killed him on the spot if he had seen it."

Ashley stopped dancing and ran to Tracy. "You okay?" Ashley asked as she reached James and Tracy.

"Yeah, I'm fine," Tracy reassured Ashley.

Not wanting to draw attention, all four of them left the dance floor and returned to the table. Ashley and Tracy sat at the table while Brian surveyed the room. "James Brooks, Brian Thompson," Ashley said to introduce them.

Brian shook James's hand. "How are you doing, man?" Brian asked, then turned back to Ashley. "What are you going to do, Ashley?" Brian asked, a little agitated.

JD walked up. "What's going on?" he asked, sensing the tension.

Each of them looked to Ashley. Ashley looked from James to Brian. There was no way she was getting into this tonight. She shook her head at JD. "We have a dilemma, trying to decide which one I'm going home with." Ashley sighed. Tracy and James started laughing.

Brian smirked. "You wish."

JD looked at the group as if all of them were losing their minds.

James extended his hand to Brian. "Thank you. I'll take her from here, Mr. Thompson. Let's go." James laughed as he took Ashley by the hand and walked away from the table.

Not sure what to think, JD looked at Tracy. "Did I miss something?"

"Just a little bit." She smiled. "Come dance with me." The couple went back to the dance floor while Brian made a mental note to keep an eye out for David Holt.

As the evening progressed, JD introduced Tracy to so many people, there was no way she would be able to remember all their names. It seemed the people he introduced her to accept her being there with him. Tracy even found a moment to talk to Brian and forgive him for his actions when they first met. She actually enjoyed being with JD and his friends.

They were in the middle of a conversation when Jackie suddenly excused herself and asked Tracy to join her in the ladies room. This time, JD squeezed Tracy's hand. He knew Jackie and Carolyn were as thick as thieves and wondered why Jackie would invite Tracy anywhere. Jackie had not said much to Tracy all night, but Tracy agreed to join her. JD held on to Tracy's hand, and looked at Jackie, who quickly looked away. JD scowled. Noticing his reaction to the events, Magna offered, "I'll join you," then smiled at JD. "I'll keep an eye on things."

JD looked at Calvin. "What's she up to?" They both looked around for Carolyn. She was nowhere to be found. "Damn," JD exclaimed. "Do you see her?"

"No, man," Calvin replied. "Don't worry. Tracy can handle herself."

"Not against Carolyn, Calvin. Carolyn will try to tap into every insecurity she can find in Tracy and believe me, she will find some."

"You can handle that, JD. You have nothing to worry about."

"I don't know, Calvin. I don't want to mess up here," JD sighed with a worried look on his face. "I don't feel good about this situation. Right now it's scaring the hell out of me."

Calvin was sensing some insecurity in JD. He really did not understand why. Everyone in that building saw the two of them on that stage tonight. There was no doubt in anyone's mind that those two were in it for the long haul.

Earlier in the evening JD had been honored with an award from the attorney general. He escorted Tracy to the stage with him to accept the award. Calvin knew that was JD's way of letting everyone know, Tracy was now a permanent fixture in his life. But, for some reason, JD was unsure of himself. Calvin smiled at the thought as he saw Mrs. Langston about to leave. "Mrs. Langston, are you on your way out?"

"Yes, I am," she replied.

"Before you go, would you go into the ladies room and tell Jackie I need to see her right away. Tell her it's important."

"Be happy to," Mrs. Langston replied, and then she turned to JD. "You made me very proud tonight. Not just with your promotion, but with your choice for life. Make sure you invite me to the wedding." She leaned down and kissed him on the cheek.

"Thank you, Mrs. Langston." JD smiled.

As Jackie, Tracy and Magna entered the ladies room, Jackie went directly into one of the stalls. Tracy went over to the sink, looked in the mirror and started washing her hands, wondering why Jackie asked her there. "You know, I was never one of the girls who went to the ladies room in a group," Magna laughed.

Tracy laughed back. "Me either."

Magna walked over to the sink next to Tracy and hunched her. Magna whispered, "Sooo, what's up?"

The door to the ladies room opened and Carolyn walked in.

"Never mind, we are about to find out," Magna said and stepped aside. Tracy looked towards the door and sighed, "Here we go."

"Tracy," Carolyn said with a fake smile, "how wonderful. Now we a have chance to talk one on one, without interference."

"You mean without Jeffrey." Tracy smiled. "Why?"

"Well, I thought it was important for you and me to talk. You seem like a nice person and from what I see you really care about JD. Well, I care about him, too. I would hate to see him make a mistake that could affect his future." Carolyn hesitated.

"Okay," Tracy said with a touch of annoyance. "I'll bite: what mistake is that?"

"Tracy," Carolyn sighed, "it is important that you take what I have to say in the right context and know I have JD's well-being at heart. JD and I were involved with each other, and I do care what happens to him. You do realize JD is completely out of your league. He is not the average Joe you are probably used to. I'm sure even you can see that about him. JD has a political future, where he will be able to help people in this state and maybe eventually around the world. I'm not sure JD even realizes what he is destined to do. Your involvement with him may very well hurt him. Your background is not suited for JD or his future. Let's say 'family connections' could cause him problems. Now, I know you have no intentions of hurting JD in any way, I can see that. I really can. But just think about it for a moment, Tracy. If your connections ever get into the wrong hands, think how it will affect JD, his future."

Tracy took a paper towel to dry her hands. She was hurt by the things Carolyn was saying and thought she was probably right. But there was no way in hell she was going to show that to Carolyn. "I take it you have the type of connections that would easily help Jeffrey's career." Tracy smiled.

"Impressively so." Carolyn smirked. "But that's a moot point. JD and I are not seeing each other. Although we remain very close friends." Carolyn let that hang in the air for a moment. "As a matter of fact, I'm seeing Gavin Roberts now—you know, JD's boss. I just don't want to see JD's career damaged because he wanted to get between the legs of a home girl." She laughed. "As soon as he gets over the novelty of being with someone from the street, he will turn right back to women of culture—you know, the kind he is used to. I give it a month or so. That's how long it usually takes before JD gets bored."

Tracy took a step back. *This so-called woman of culture is nothing but a bitch in designer clothing,* Tracy thought. But she was not going to let this person get to her.

"Oh, I'm sorry. I did not mean to hurt your feelings. We are just talking woman to woman here, keeping it real, you know what I mean," Carolyn said, stepping closer to Tracy. "Please tell me you are not under the misconception that JD is in love with you." Carolyn snickered. "Honey, that's so sweet. But you're in the big league now. You're just the flavor of the month. JD will be moving on."

"I take it you were last month's flavor," Magna said, growing tried of Carolyn's attempt to intimidate Tracy.

Rolling her eyes, Carolyn turned to Magna. "Do I know you?"

"I'm here to use the bathroom, but you are interrupting me with all this bullshit you're giving her."

Mrs. Langston walked into the room and immediately sensed the uneasiness. She looked around the room. "Am I interrupting something?" she asked.

"No, Mrs. Langston, please come in," Tracy said, regrouping from the puncture wounds Carolyn had left with her remarks. Tracy prepared to leave the room, but stopped. "Carolyn, thank you for your concern. It's good to know Jeffrey has someone like you to protect him. You may be right. I may not be the person Jeffrey needs in his future to have the career you believe he is destined for. But I think that's his decision to make; not mine or yours. JD knows who I am and where I'm from. Whenever our—" she hesitated searching for the word, "novelty begins to interfere with his career plans, he'll end the relationship; as he did with you. However, I believe your concerns about his future are truly sincere. I plan to have a candid discussion with JD on the topic. Now, if that's all, I would like to return to what's left of my evening." Tracy turned to walk out the door then noticed Jackie standing to the side. She smiled. "Thank you for the invite, Jackie. It was very enlightening." She left and Magna followed.

"Jackie, Calvin said he needs to see you right away. He said it's important," Mrs. Langston said, looking at Jackie, wondering what part she played in the scene.

"Thank you, Mrs. Langston, I'll be right there," Jackie replied.
Tracy returned to the table and sat beside Jeffrey. She sipped her wine, then looked at Magna.

"Nice comeback. Are you okay?" Magna asked.

"Yes." Tracy smiled. "I'm fine."

Jeffrey put his hands on her back and asked, "Do we need to talk?"

"At some point, but not tonight," she said, looking into his eyes.

He smiled at her as he rubbed her back. "Are you ready to go home?"

She smiled back, put her head to the side and said, "Now that depends—your place or mine?"

JD hesitated for a moment, then kissed her gently on the lips and looked into her eyes as if she was the only person in the room. "Mine; you have a tendency to get loud."

She hit him on the arm and laughed. "Then yes, I'm ready to go," she replied.

JD and Tracy got up to leave just as Jackie returned to the table. Carolyn walked up behind her. The tension in the air was thick. Jackie took her seat next to Calvin. Calvin could see Jackie was a little disturbed about something, but did not say anything. "You two leaving so early?" Carolyn smiled.

"Yes, we have other plans tonight," JD politely replied while giving Carolyn the look of death.

"Well, have a good evening." Carolyn smiled confidently, knowing her words had cut Tracy deeply.

Tracy took JD's hand. "Good night, Magna. Calvin, I hope you enjoy the remainder of your evening."

"Good night," Calvin and Magna said simultaneously as JD and Tracy walked away.

"You little bitch," Magna sneered at Jackie. "I'm sorry, Calvin." Magna pointed to Carolyn. "Her, I understand. She wants the man back. But what's your excuse for setting someone up to be hurt like that?"

Calvin looked up at Jackie and asked, "What did you do?"

Chapter 16

JD and Tracy rode home in silence. He knew something went down with Tracy and Carolyn, but wasn't sure what. JD did not like drama, or drama queens, and he was not sure how Tracy was going to react to whatever Carolyn said. But if he had to go through drama to keep Tracy in his life, he would. Tracy understood him so well. She knew and understood what was important to him and why. Most of all, she listened to him and motivated him. She made him want to be better.

His mother had recently told him, "If that woman could move you to finish this flowerbed after all these years, you need to marry her." JD smiled at the memory. His mom had called him to the house and said a package was there. When he went by to pick it up, he found a stone, just about the same color of the stones in the flowerbed in her backyard. The stone was engraved, "In loving memory of James T. Harrison. Once you've touched the heart, you are never forgotten." At that moment, JD had no doubts about Tracy being a part of his life. He took off his jacket, pulled the tools from the shed and finished the flowerbed. Afterwards he and his mom sat in the yard and talked about his dad for hours, things he had forgotten and things he loved about his dad. He needed that closure to move on to the next level of his life and Tracy gave it to him.

JD wondered why Tracy didn't see just how important she was in his life or the impact she had on him. After taking her suggestion to visit the Gonzalez family, he was able to think clearly about the case. To add to it, the publicity from that visit created a buzz for him professionally. He received letters and calls from the community, thanking him for caring enough to visit one of them after the death of a child. The governor's office called Gavin and gave him kudos for having such a caring DA on staff. The news coverage about the neighborhood brought in several leads about illegal activity in the neighborhood. People came forward wanting to help clean up the neighborhood. Tracy did that for him. *Damn*, he thought, *I should have paid closer attention.* He knew she was uncomfortable about going to this event. He didn't understand why, but he knew she was.

Tracy's mind was racing and she did not say much during the ride home. The last thing in the world Tracy wanted was to hurt Jeffrey's career. She knew all that bull Carolyn said tonight was to get her away from Jeffrey. Tracy did not want to give Carolyn the satisfaction of knowing just how close to home she hit this evening. Cynthia had told Tracy for years she was not good enough to be around a person like Jeffrey. Well, the point was driven home tonight. As much as she loved Jeffrey, Tracy did not believe he could truly love her. The women in that room tonight were the ones who could get him to the next level. She knew Jeffrey needed to marry a socialite like Carolyn or Cynthia. They had the looks, the money, family connections; they had it all. There was nothing she could do for this man but get in the way of his future. His popularity was growing with communities he was trying to clean up. People recognized him on the street from being in the paper so much. Jeffrey was receiving invitations from senators and the governor all the time. Different politicians wanted his endorsements. He would not give them to anyone because he did not want to be typecast as anybody's man. He did not want to lead people astray, and people would follow his lead, because they trusted him. He liked being free to support whomever and whatever cause he wanted to. Jeffrey had won the respect of his colleagues by bringing in indictments that led to convictions. He was a man of his word and everyone loved him because of it, and so did she.

Tracy knew the day would come when she would have to let him go. Despite Carolyn's reasons, Tracy knew she was right. Her own family ties could hurt Jeffrey's career. A DA involved with the sister of a convicted criminal. That would not look good in any light. It would have to come out at some point. Tracy closed her eyes. She had to let him go. She could not stand the thought of Ashley or Mama Harrison hating her for hurting Jeffrey's career. Hell, she couldn't stand the thought of Jeffrey hating her. *Yes, it was best to let go now,* she thought. Besides, Jeffrey had plenty of women friends. She had to settle for that and nothing more.

Jeffrey reached over, took Tracy's hand into his. "Talk to me, Tracy. Tell me what happened."

She inhaled, and told him about the conversation. When she finished, Tracy said, "That's why I have to give up on being with you. Eventually someone would try to use me against you."

JD's body tensed, and his heart skipped a beat. Neither of them spoke again until they reached his home. As they entered the house, JD pulled off his tie, and Tracy walked past him into the living room. JD prayed, "God give me the words to make her understand," then followed behind her.

He wrapped his arms around her tightly and whispered in her ear, "It's you and me, remember." He squeezed her tight.

"You and I both know being together can hurt you professionally," Tracy said as she pulled away from JD. "I know you are not accepting that, but it is true, and I don't want to hurt you in any way. Like it or not, Carolyn Roth is right on that point. If information about Turk gets out, how will the people in the community react?"

JD grabbed her again and tightened his arms around her. Tracy felt his chest swell and it frightened her a little. Impatiently he said, "Did you not understand what I said—there is no turning back. I'm willing to fight for that; why aren't you? Is it something else, Tracy?"

She pulled away from him again. "No, Jeffrey. I can't take the idea of someone like Carolyn Roth trying to use me against you. That's all it is."

"Tracy." JD took a moment. He did not want to lose his temper, especially with Tracy. But if she kept this up, JD knew he was going to explode. "When you accompanied me on that stage tonight it was because from now on every oath I take I want you next to me, for the rest of my life. I need you beside me, guiding me. That's why God put us together. All this other bullshit...."

"How you going to speak of God in one sentence and use profanity in the next?" Tracy asked.

JD gazed at Tracy, relaxed a little, then smiled. "He knows I'm a little pissed right now, he'll forgive me. Now, back to the bullshit. You do realize Carolyn has her own agenda here? It had nothing to do with my well-being or yours."

"I know that." Tracy sighed.

He walked over to her, still a little frustrated. "I don't know how to help you deal with people like Carolyn. People can only hurt us if we let them. I don't plan on letting them. Just so you know, I will leave the DA's office before I give you up." JD walked to the bar between the family room and kitchen and poured a drink, while Tracy sat at the bar. JD watched her intently and thought. He was an attorney and made a living at convincing people to see things his way. Why was it so hard to get Tracy to understand she belonged with him? He took another drink as he watched her with her head lying on the bar. He smiled. She looked so precious, like a little girl in her own fantasy world. JD wanted to be a part of her fantasy. "Where did you get that dress from?" he asked.

She looked up at him. "From Penne." Tracy put her elbows up on the bar, and then put her hands under her chin. "Don't you like it?" She smiled up at him. The smile was in her eyes as well as on her lips. JD knew she loved him. Anytime a person could deal with the shit that Carolyn dished out, and still be able to smile at him like that, he knew it was love. He leaned back against the counter. This was the second time she had mentioned leaving him. JD could not explain the way that made him feel. But he did not like it. "Marry me, Tracy," he said without thinking.

Tracy's heart skipped. The look on her face was of pure shock. "What?" she asked, not sure she had heard him right.

JD put the glass down and walked around the bar. He got down on one knee, looked up at her and proclaimed, "Tracy Alexandria Washington, I promise to love all your doubts away; to keep you safe and happy all the days of my life. Please, Tracy, marry me."

Tracy got down on her knees with him. Everything in her wanted to yell "*Hell, yes.*" She couldn't get the words out. "Did you understand anything I just said to you about hurting you or your career?"

"Yeah, I heard that. And I ask you again. Will you be my wife?"

Tracy stared at JD with an intensity that made him feel unsure of himself. Jeffrey had never felt so vulnerable in his life. He thought for a moment she was going to say no and he wasn't sure if he could handle the rejection; not from her.

"Yes," she said.

JD smiled. "Yes? Wow, yes," he said again, not believing what he heard. He kissed her.

"Yes," she said again.

He took her face in his hands then proceeded to kiss every inch. Then he stopped suddenly. Both of them were on their knees laughing. "We should call Carolyn and thank her," JD said.

"Oh no, please don't call her." Tracy laughed. "Let me have this moment before she tries to take it away."

He held her and held her tight. "No one is going to take this away from us." JD exhaled. "No one."

While it was impromtu moment, JD had no second thoughts about asking Tracy to marry him. He held her tight and prayed she had no second thoughts about saying yes. They lay on the floor of Jeffrey's family room talking through the night. They decided to tell Mama Harrison, Ashley and Pastor Smith only, until they were ready to make a formal announcement.

The article in the Flair section of the *Times-Dispatch* covering the governor's reception had the picture of the governor, Tracy, JD, Senator Roth, Carolyn and Gavin. The caption read, "Political couples of the future?" The article went on to mention the awards given to Jeffrey Harrison and the possible announcement of Gavin Roberts's bid for the governor's office. In the same article there was a smaller picture of Jeffrey and Tracy while he was taking the oath. Victoria, the author of the article made this statement:

Now ladies, on a sad note for any of you with thoughts on conquering the heart of JD Harrison for yourself: you are out of luck. This reporter has it on good authority (JD Harrison himself) that he is off the market. I know, ladies, the news hurt my feelings, too. But meeting the lucky lady in person helped. She is a beautiful, intelligent young woman with a heart of gold. No, they are not engaged, but I suspect that will not be far away. I'll keep you informed. In the meantime, ladies, I will be on the lookout for the next someone for our lonely hearts to daydream about. You can count on me.

Carolyn's rage hit the fan when she read that article. *You may have won this battle, you little bitch, but the war has not been fought yet.* Carolyn vowed to find a way to cause problems, but in a way not to piss off Gavin. Gavin had not proposed yet and Carolyn did not want to take a chance on angering him. She could not do anything to jeopardize the mansion, but she knew someone who could certainly put a wrinkle into Tracy's day. Carolyn picked up the telephone and called an old rival. She smiled as she dialed the number. "Time for some fireworks."

Chapter 17

After the governor's function, James and Ashley sat in the lobby of the hotel and talked for hours. James was certain Tracy would not be home and did not like the idea of Ashley going home alone, with David Holt slithering about. He invited Ashley to stay the night at his place, in his guest room, of course, and she accepted.

Ashley did not get a good look at James's house when they entered that night. The next morning it startled her to see the size of his home. As she came down the stairs she noticed there were at least three bedrooms, each with an adjoining bathroom. The staircase led to the center of a huge foyer, which Ashley estimated was big enough for at least fifty people to stand in without touching each other. To her right as she descended the stairs was what appeared to be a family room or den. To the left was the dining room and kitchen area. That's where James was sitting reading the paper. Ashley brushed her hair down hoping it was not tangled or standing up on top of her head.

"Good morning." She smiled as she entered the room. "You just happen to have women's clothes in your house?" She asked, tugging at the robe she had on. *Please say they belong to your sister,* Ashley thought, laughing to herself.

James smiled. "One never knows when a beautiful woman may need to stay over. One must be prepared at all times," he said as he set the paper aside and pulled a chair out for her.

Ashley smiled. "All of this was not necessary, you know." Ashley sat in the seat and crossed her legs. She put her elbows on the table and rested her head in her hand. She inhaled and looked at James. He was a handsome man with very strong features. To Ashley, James was the epitome of what a man sitting at the head of a table should look like. He reminded her so much of her dad; not the way he looked or his size, but his very presence. James was a proud, private, reserved man on the surface. *I know there is some fire under all the public persona,* Ashley smiled to herself.

"Would you like some breakfast, ma'am?" A voice startled Ashley back to the present. A somewhat older, attractive woman of either Mexican or Spanish decent was smiling at her with a maid outfit on.

"Just coffee would be fine," Ashley replied as she pulled her robe tighter around her waist. She had no idea someone else was in the house with them. As the maid left the room, Ashley reached over and took the toast and a slice of bacon off James's plate.

James smiled. Ashley did not seem intimidated by him at all. "Are you hungry?"

"Starving," she replied.

He laughed. "Clair would have fixed you breakfast, you know."

"I would feel guilty making someone cook for me. But that's okay, I'll eat yours," she said as she pulled his plate in front of her. Clair came back in the room and saw Ashley eating James's food. She put the coffee in front of Ashley.

"I'll fix you another plate." She smiled at James then left the room.

"Thank you," Ashley said to the woman's back.

"Her name is Clair," James said as he pushed the sugar and cream towards her.

"Thank you," Ashley said. "Is she your maid or just your cook or more?"

James gazed at Ashley then smiled. "Clair is housekeeper and a little of everything you just said; with the exception the 'or more.'"

"Why do you have a housekeeper?" Ashley asked as she continued to eat. "For that matter, why do you have such a big house?"

James laughed. "I have a housekeeper because I do have a big house which I do not like to clean. And I like to eat, but can't cook, therefore, I have someone to cook for me."

Ashley smiled, but never stopped eating. "Doesn't it bother you to have someone waiting on you hand and foot?"

"No. I pay her very well to do just that," James replied.

"Oh," Ashley said as Clair returned with a plate of food for James. "Thank you again," Ashley said as Clair left the room. "And the house: why such a big house for one person?"

"You are full of questions this morning," James replied.

"If you want to know something you have to ask, or else you will go on wondering," Ashley replied in a very nonchalant manner.

Changing the subject, James put the paper in front of Ashley and said, "Your brother made the paper again today."

Ashley smiled as she picked up the paper. "Oh, what a nice picture of him and Tracy. It really was a nice function last night. Thank you for letting me join you at your table." Ashley smiled.

"I don't recall allowing anything. If I remember correctly, you told me you would be there."

"You could have said no." Ashley smiled.

"And miss the pleasure of your company or the drama of David Holt? I don't think so"

James saw Ashley's disposition change instantly at the mention of David Holt. Ashley appeared to be so lighthearted and charismatic. But the mere mention of Holt revealed a vulnerability that did not sit well with James. He noticed it the day of the luncheon and again last night. Ashley was shaken by Holt's action, although she would never admit it.

"You ready to tell me about David Holt?" he asked as he began drinking his coffee.

"You know, my mom is going to kill me," Ashley said in an attempt to get James off the subject. "I'm supposed to meet her at church this morning."

James picked up the cordless phone. "Call her; let her know you will not make it today."

Ashley hesitated. "I don't want to talk about this right now."

James set the phone on the table. "It's not an option at this point. Call your mother. Let her know you will not meet her at church today. When you finish, we will talk about David Holt."

James watched her mind working. She was trying to come up with some clever statement to cover up her fear. But he was not going to let her deal with this situation alone. Ashley noticed James was staring at her. She really wanted to get to know this man. But how would he feel about her once she told him about David? Ashley never discussed the incident involving David with anyone, not even Tracy.

"Nothing you say to me will be revealed to anyone, if you don't want it to be," James said as if reading her mind.

Ashley hesitantly called her mother. "Hey mom, I'm being held hostage by a very attractive man and I will not be able to meet you at church today." She put the phone back on the table beside James. "Mom will be saying a prayer for you," Ashley advised James.

James smiled. "Thank you. I'm sure I need it." He waited.

Ashley sighed. "What do you want to know?"

"Everything."

Ashley related the story to him just about the same way the report read. The difference was the fear he heard in her voice. "I was stupid," she began. "I thought I was in love, you know. One night Tracy and I decided to meet and study in the study hall next to the library." Ashley looked down at the plate as if she was ashamed of what she was about to tell James. That part upset James the most. She swallowed then continued to play with the food on her plate. "David got there a few minutes after I went in the room. He said a lot of dumb shit I didn't want to hear. When I told him that and tried to walk away, he went off." She was quiet for a moment, then tears rolled down her face. "He threw me against the wall, then jumped on me with all his weight." She hesitated as the memories came back. "He pulled my clothes off. I fought him. I really did, with everything I had, but he was so strong. He held me down with one hand; I couldn't move. It didn't matter what I did, I could not get him off of me."

James went around the table to where she was, pulled her into his arms and just held her. He rubbed her back as she continued telling him what happened.

Clair walked in the room. James shook his head for her not to say anything; she went back into the kitchen. He lifted Ashley in his arms then carried her into the family room. He sat on the couch with her in his lap and held her until she had calmed down. Here she was, this very confident, independent woman with everything going for her. No one would ever know she had been carrying this around with her all these years. "Did he actually...?"

Before James completed the question, Ashley shook her head. "No."

"Okay, did you ever tell your brother about this?" James asked.

She shook her head. "No."

"You and Tracy are the only ones who know?"

"David knows," she said as she sniffled.

"That all happened, what, five years ago. Why is he bothering you now?" James asked.

"He had a problem with the way Tracy and I handled things," she sighed. "Since the coach cleared everything up for him, I felt he could do whatever he wanted with me. Tracy didn't like the idea of him having that kind of control over me. So she wrote an article and had it published in the school paper with his description." Ashley laughed through her tears. "He was so mad, but there was nothing he could do about it because she never named him. See, David has a very distinguished birthmark on his butt and when Tracy entered the room she saw it. When his girlfriend heard about the article she broke up with him." Ashley began to laugh more. "Life got interesting after that. Tracy never got involved in anything. I mean nothing until then. She was my rock until I was able to get my backbone back."

Ashley stopped talking. She did not like feeling this vulnerable with James or any man. She had to get out of this situation. She attempted to stand, but he held her still.

James could sense she was uncomfortable now that she had revealed the event. "I know at this moment you feel vulnerable; as if you just exposed yourself to me." He kissed her forehead. "I'm honored you trust me with this. I would never reveal what you shared with me today with anyone. What you do have to worry about is what I'm going to do to Holt if I ever see him near you again."

Ashley looked up at James; he truly was a fine man. Ashley surveyed James's face as she sat there. He had thick eyebrows over deep brown eyes, with a very commanding baritone voice that was comforting to her. She smiled. "I must be losing my touch. I stayed in your house overnight. Here I am sitting in your lap with nothing on but a robe and you have not made a pass at me. Why is that?"

James smiled and pulled her closer. She was back to Ashley now, full of life and a mischievous spirit. He could see it in her eyes and he liked it; he liked the idea of her. "You can try all you want to keep from talking about this, but it is not going to work. There is nothing you can do to avoid this conversation."

Ashley reached up and kissed him. Startled, James pulled his head back a little and looked at her.

Why in the hell did she do that? He thought. His body's response answered the question for him as he leaned forward to return the kiss.

Ashley was surprised by the feeling she was getting inside. She had been with other men since David, but none who touched her emotionally the way James did. James got lost in the kiss for a moment, but when his body began to react to Ashley in a way that James did not expect, he knew he had to pull away. James was a careful man, a man who liked to stay in control. He did not get involved with anyone on any level without thinking it through. James slowly pulled away from the kiss. "I guess I was wrong."

Ashley smiled at him then tilted her head to the side. "You are an extraordinary man, James Brooks."

He smiled back. "You are a woman of many talents, Ashley Harrison. One of which is using that wonderful wit of yours to keep people away."

She began kissing his neck. "Are you really as composed as you appear?" She kissed the other side of his neck. "Or am I really out of my league here?" She stopped and waited for his response.

Ashley was getting to him and James knew it. He stood up and set her on the sofa. "I always stay composed." He smiled. He turned to walk away; he needed some space from her.

Ashley stood and grabbed his arm. "It's Tracy, isn't it? Are you in love with her, James?"

James thought for a moment. "No, I'm not in love with Tracy."

Ashley did not believe him. She thought that since Tracy was with JD, she might have a chance with James. Now Ashley knew she was wrong. She dropped her hand from his arm. "I'm going to go upstairs to get dressed." Ashley was a very proud young woman and strong minded.

There was no way she was going to stay where she did not feel she was wanted.

When Ashley left the room, James exhaled. He rubbed his chest. "Damn, that was hard." He closed his eyes trying to compose himself. Ashley really got to him. He laughed.

Ashley came back downstairs a few minutes later. "I'm ready to go," she announced angrily.

"Are you okay?" James asked, sensing uneasiness in the room.

"I'm fine; would you take me to my car now?"

James smiled. "Sure," he replied.

He drove her to her car. Ashley did not speak during the ride. Her mind was on what just took place at James's house. Did she make a complete fool of herself in front of the man she had deemed her soul mate? He may have pulled away from her on the first kiss, but the second was different. Ashley was sure he was into it as much as she was— if not more.

"Ashley, you are not usually this quiet; talk to me," James said, wondering what she was thinking.

"Will our conversation stay between us?"

"I will not tell a soul; you have my word."

She exhaled and smiled. "Good."

When they reached her car, there was a note. The note simply read, "All is not forgotten, you owe me one."

"Who is it from?" James asked.

"No name. I'm sure it's from David."

She crumpled the paper up then put it in her purse. "Thank you for everything, James," she said without looking at him. If nothing else, Ashley was raised to handle rejection with dignity. She unlocked her car and got in.

"Ashley, are you going to be okay?" James asked, leaning against the driver's door.

"I'll be fine, thank you." She smiled, and then pulled off.

Chapter 18

During the next week Magna, Graham, Calvin and JD made cases on two members of Latin Eagles. However, their leader, Juan Cortez, remained elusive. The arrest of his men left a bitter taste. Revenge was on his mind. "He fuck with my family, I fuck with his." That was the word from Juan. Juan knew killing a DA would bring too much heat on his organization. Nevertheless, he had to let it be known, in no uncertain terms, a price will be paid if you fuck with the Eagles. This Harrison man had disrespected him by coming on his turf and interfering with his neighborhood. Now he had three of his good men locked up and families scared they would be next. He had to send a message aimed directly at Harrison

Morning briefings were mundane, but necessary, for Brian. It was a time to review the week's activity with a clear mind, no interruptions. Something in one of the reports caught Brian's eye. One of the surveillance tapes had a member of the Latin Eagles on it in an unlikely place. He began to watch the tapes intently. *There he was again, but why, why there*, Brian wondered. He continued through the tapes and spotted the same man again. "What the hell?" He placed a call. "Jones, the tapes you brought in this morning, when and where were they taken? Are there any more? Bring them up. Yes, now," Brian said. He continued through the tapes; there were at least four occasions where an Eagle appeared near or around the Next Level office. It did not bother Brian at first. He figured the Eagles had a man on JD and JD must have gone to see Tracy. Jones brought in the other tapes.

"Jones, take these down," Brian said as he handed reviewed tapes to the man. "Have stills made every time you see this guy. I want stills of him and everything around him. I want to see what he sees."

"Yes, sir," Jones replied.

Brian began talking to himself. "What the hell are you up to, Juan? Why is your man uptown? That's not your turf," he said, almost singing. Brian turned on the CD player; Everett Harp came through the speakers. "Ahh, jazz. Thinking music." He looked closer at the tapes. "It's there; I just need to find it. The answer is there." Humming to himself, he said, "Just keep watching and it will show its ugly face, it always does.... Who you looking for, Juan?"

In the frame Brian was observing, Juan's man was standing across the street from Next Level Consulting. On the other side of the street were Tracy, Ashley and James Brooks. JD was nowhere around.

Not sure what to make of it, Brian contacted his superiors and requested permission to put a man on Tracy. When that was denied, he tried Ashley; the agency denied that also. Their only concern was the protection of JD Harrison.

Later that same night, JD was in his home office preparing for the third trial. His office was directly across the hallway from his bedroom. Before Tracy came back into his life, he only had a desk and a bookcase in the room. Tracy, being the organizational person, redesigned the room. She added a mahogany wall unit with bookshelves and file drawers on both ends at the bottom. Of course, all files were neatly arranged. A BOSE stereo system with surround sound was on the middle shelf. All of his law books were displayed along with awards JD had received. Against the wall to the right of his desk were a leather sofa and a matching chair in front of his desk. The wall next to the door had a twenty-seven-inch television. It was actually more professional than his office downtown, and more comfortable.

Tracy knew that when Jeffrey was dealing with a case, he would spend more time in that office than in the bedroom. That much had not changed. JD got just as caught up in cases as he always had. Now he had someone to help him through the rough moments. This case was going to be a little more intense because it dealt with Juan's little cousin. Juan's little cousin was the closest person in the organization to Juan. If JD could get him to turn, they may have a shot at Juan. But so far JD had not been able to penetrate that bond.

Tracy reached over for Jeffrey but he wasn't in bed. She knew exactly where to go. She put on his shirt that was on the floor and walked across the hall to his office. "Did I wake you?" JD asked.

She walked around the desk, put her arms around his neck and kissed his cheek. "No, you didn't wake me," she said. "Why are you looking at those inaccurate bank statements?" she asked yawning.

He laughed. "They only look bad because you are half asleep."

"No, they are inaccurate, look." She pointed to the sheet. "That's a fudged number."

"What do you mean, 'fudged number'?" he asked.

"They don't add up," she said, lying on the sofa. "Put them in your calculator; that bottom line should be an additional 10 percent."

JD added the column of numbers and saw that Tracy was right: the bottom line was wrong. "How did you know it was wrong?"

"I could see it," she said.

"You were just standing here for a minute, how could you see that?"

"I don't know." She grabbed a pillow and put it under her head. "My mind remembers numbers at a glance." She closed her eyes, thinking the conversation was over.

JD looked over at her. She was lying there with her thighs exposed under his shirt. Now how was he supposed to concentrate? He sat at the end of the sofa then put her legs across his lap.

"Explain," he said.

Tracy opened her eyes and looked at him. "Okay," she started, "I can look at a number or you can give me a series of numbers and I can add, subtract, multiply or do whatever with that number in my mind."

"Without a calculator?" he asked.

"Yes," she said, then looked at him. "Are you challenging me again?"

"Yes," he said. He reached over for the calculator on the desk. "The figure at the bottom of the page is...."

"Stop," she said. "Let me tell you: 128,562.58."

"That's not right; the total at the bottom is 115,706.33."

She sat up. "And it's wrong. Take 128,562.58 and multiply it by 10 percent, 12,856.25, now add your figure to that figure: 115,706.33 plus 12,856.25 equals 128,562.58. Someone is skimming 10 percent off the bottom line figure."

He did the calculations on the calculator that she did in her head. He looked at her. "You remembered all those numbers?" Looking at her amazed he asked, "How do you do that?"

"I don't know. Turk can do it, too."

"Get the hell out of here," he said, surprised.

"No, I don't think I will." She positioned herself on top of him and kissed him.

He responded to her kiss. Suddenly he stopped. "Wait a minute, hold that thought." He set her back at the other end of the sofa and called Calvin.

"I guess the honeymoon is over," Tracy said and went back to bed.

"Calvin, get over here, I think we got Juan."

JD turned the information over to the DA's tax accounting division. The next day JD had subpoenas issued against several bank accounts. Two days later, Juan was arrested for five counts of tax evasion, which carry federal time of 10 to 15 years, each. All bank accounts and assets with Juan's name or social security number on it were frozen. The total take on all accounts plus current market value of the assets was well over $2.3 million. The DA's office telephone lines blew up with requests for interviews and details of the arrest.

This hit Juan's organization hard financially. Needless to say, Juan was going to retaliate.

JD met with Mrs. Gonzalez. He explained they may not be able to convict Juan on Lisa's murder, but they could get him off the streets with these other charges. She was pleased with anything that would protect the neighborhood. JD felt pretty good about the outcome of the case. He knew it would not satisfy the need for justice on Lisa's death. But it was something.

JD could not wait to tell Tracy about the subpoenas. He called her office, but she was in a meeting. So he decided just to tell her at home. JD was wrapping up his work that afternoon when he received a call from Carolyn. "Are you leaving for the day?" she asked.

"Trouble, what are you up to now?" He laughed.

"That's not funny. I just wanted to know if you were free for drinks tonight."

"With you? In what world?"

"There is no reason we can't be civil to each other, JD."

"You're right. Let me change my answer. No, I'm not free. I have plans."

"With Tracy?"

"Yes."

"JD." Carolyn hesitated. "Are you serous about this girl?"

"Carolyn, I don't want to play these games with you." JD waited.

"Are you and I really at a point where we cannot have a decent conversation?"

"You made it that way, Carolyn. Now I have to go." JD hung up the telephone. Alarms started going off in his head. He knew something was up. His first instinct was to call Tracy, just to make sure things were okay. He called from his cell on his way out of the office. She was still in a meeting, so he headed home.

JD got out of the shower, dried off and wrapped a towel around his waist. He wanted to call Tracy to tell her what happened with the case. *She was in a meeting earlier, maybe she is free now,* he thought. He walked out of the bathroom into the bedroom and picked up his cell. Tracy had called. "It rang about 10 minutes ago," a voice said. JD turned to see Vanessa was lying on his bed naked. "I didn't think it would go over very well if I answered it." She smiled.

JD staggered back against the dresser. He had not seen or talked with Vanessa since last year.

They had a little arrangement. Whenever she came into town they would get together. Vanessa knew where he kept the spare key; that way she was able to let herself in when he was not home. He did not think to call Vanessa when Tracy came into his life. Tracy walking in on this scene began playing over and over in his mind. JD knew he had to do something quickly. Unfortunately, a certain part of his anatomy was not cooperating with him. The sight of a fine, naked woman lying on his bed was hard to ignore. Especially Vanessa, the one he let get close enough to know his likes and dislikes. She knew his weakness and he wasn't sure he would be able to resist her.

JD wasn't sure how this came about, but he knew it was a trap and he did not like being trapped. "Where's the key?" JD asked.

"You have the key, JD." Vanessa smiled.

"The door key, Vanessa, where is it?" he asked again.

"Everything we need is right in this room," she said as she walked over to him with nothing on but a pair of stilettos. *Down boy; down,* JD said to himself. Vanessa kissed him right at that spot just beneath his throat and ran her hands down his chest to the towel. *Damn,* he said to himself; he was responding to her touch. As he pushed her away, Vanessa pulled the towel. "Well, hello, Mr. Harrison, it's been a while," she said, seeing him spring to life. "It's good to see I still have an effect on you," she said as she started to bend down.

JD pulled her up, looked away from her body into her eyes. "Vanessa you got to get the hell up out of here. Where is the key?"

Looking disappointed, Vanessa replied, "Downstairs on the table."

JD grabbed his robe. "Get dressed, Vanessa," he ordered as he walked by her.

"But I really don't want to," she said seductively.

While running downstairs to get the key, JD dialed Tracy's cell. "Come on, baby, pick up," he said to himself. "Shit, no answer."

Vanessa put on JD's shirt that was lying on the floor and followed him downstairs. She was not going to let this opportunity get away from her.

He could only resist her for so long. "Payback time, Tracy." Vanessa smiled.

When JD got downstairs he began looking for the key. He had to get the key back in its place outside and relock the deadbolt before Tracy got there. She would knock and wait before using the key. That in turn would at least give him time to get Vanessa dressed and out of his bedroom. Getting her out of the house was out of the question.

"JD," Vanessa said, "you know Carolyn told me you had lost you mind. I'm beginning to believe she is right."

JD frantically looked around the room for the key. "When in the hell did you and Carolyn become friends?"

"We're not; she just called out of concern for you." She paused watching him. He really was concerned about this shit; she was amused seeing him this flustered. "You want me to believe this one little girl is able to take care of all your needs? JD, I know you, know your appetite. There is no way in hell that girl could do for you what I did for you."

JD stopped. "She's grown up, Vanessa. But you are right, what she does for me is different."

"Really, well, I am not here to cause problems for you and Tracy."

"Ha, that's funny, Vanessa. You are here to do exactly that. Now where is the key?"

Vanessa stepped directly in front of him and he stopped. "JD, calm down," she said. "I don't think I have ever seen you this rattled. Let me help you to relax. Do you remember how good we were together?" She reached under his robe and began to stroke him. JD's body was not cooperating with his mind and for a split second he contemplated taking this one moment. Vanessa was good, but he also knew this was a set-up. He had to get Vanessa dressed before Tracy came by.

Vanessa had other plans in mind. She knew his weak spot and went straight for it. Now on her knees she began to kiss him on the very part of his body that was betraying him. "I'll leave if you want me to," she said while taking him in her mouth.

"Damn!" JD grabbed her head, but hesitated a moment too long. Tracy walked through the door.

JD pushed Vanessa away and closed his robe, but he knew it was too late. "Tracy!" he started, "I can explain this."

Tracy took a step back to survey the situation. Vanessa was on her knees in front of Jeffrey with her mouth on him. Yeah, that about covered it, she thought. "You can explain this? How?" Tracy coolly asked. Tracy looked at Vanessa getting up with Jeffrey's shirt on. One of the very shirts Tracy would pick up off the bedroom floor to put on. "I'm sorry, it seems I have interrupted something," Tracy said with a tremble in her voice.

Jeffrey walked over to Tracy, took her hand then closed the door. "Tracy, baby, this is not what it seems," he said nervously. As the words came out of his mouth he knew it was lame.

Vanessa walked over to them smiling and leaned against the banister. "Tracy, it's so nice to see you again. It's been a while," she said, her voice dripping with mockery.

Tracy looked puzzled. "Do I know you?"

"Oh," Vanessa replied smiling, "you don't remember me. That's sad. You interrupted my life and you don't even remember. Baby girl, that's irony."

"Vanessa!" JD bellowed.

Vanessa rolled her eyes at JD, then continued, "We met about five years ago. Yeah, you came home with Ashley for spring break. I was JD's girlfriend at the time. I can remember like it was yesterday how he swore to me there was nothing happening between the two of you. Now, look at us all here together again."

Tracy looked at Vanessa. "I'm sorry if I caused you any pain, it was not my intent. Can you say the same?" She turned and looked at Jeffrey. "It's not a good feeling."

JD saw the hurt in her eyes. "Vanessa, tell her nothing happened here," JD growled. Tracy turned to leave, but JD had his hand on the door.

Tracy put her hand on the knob. "Jeffrey, I want to go."

"Vanessa, tell her!" JD yelled.

Tracy pulled on the doorknob. "Jeffrey, let me out," she said.

"No, Tracy, listen to me, baby, nothing happened here," he said almost pleading for her to believe him.

Vanessa sat on the bottom step and watched the action. She saw the look that Tracy gave Jeffrey to make him release the door. Tracy pulled it open but then Jeffrey grabbed Tracy just as she was about to walk out the door.

"Tracy, listen, this is not what it seems. This is Vanessa and Carolyn playing games. Don't, baby, don't fall for this."

Tracy looked at JD with such hurt. "You fell for it, Jeffrey, not me." Tracy slowly removed her arm from Jeffrey's grip, walked out and closed the door behind her.

JD ran up the stairs past Vanessa. He put on a tee shirt, sweatpants and sneakers. He turned to Vanessa as they passed each other on the stairs: "Lock the door and don't ever think about coming back."

Chapter 19

Tracy truly believed her heart was coming out of her chest and she couldn't stop it. She was trying to drive but could not get the picture out of her mind. She can't compete with someone like Vanessa. Hell, she wasn't sure how Vanessa got all of Jeffrey in her mouth, but she did. How could she compete with that? Tracy's mind was racing from being pissed at Jeffrey for falling for this, to being pissed at herself for not knowing how to do what Vanessa was doing.

When she reached for the key and it wasn't there, she knew something was not right. She should've walked away. But the door was cracked open and Jeffrey never left his door open. She laughed and cried at the same time. *Vanessa got him good.* Tracy laughed to herself; Vanessa wanted her to walk in on them. Tracy parked her car and went inside her condo.

Entering her home, Tracy was still numb from what she had witnessed. *Jeffrey said he could explain. That should be interesting to hear.* She stopped and sat on the step, trying to rationalize what she saw.

"Tracy," Ashley called, "is that you?"

Tracy exhaled, then got up. "Yes."

Ashley appeared at the top of the steps. "What's wrong?" Ashley asked as Tracy walked by.

Tracy noticed Cynthia sitting at the breakfast bar. "Hi, Cynthia," Tracy said without stopping. As she walked to her bedroom she remembered Cynthia telling her this would happen; she would end up hurt dealing with Jeffrey.

"Hey ho," Cynthia said to Tracy's back. When Tracy did not reply, Cynthia looked at Ashley. "What's up with her?"

"I don't know." Ashley started walking toward Tracy's room as the doorbell rang. "Cynthia, get that, please," Ashley said.

Cynthia pushed the button. "Who is it?"

"JD."

Cynthia pushed the button to unlock the door, then sat back and crossed her legs. "Hmm; this ought to be good."

JD came up the steps as Ashley was coming out of Tracy's room. "What happened?" she asked.

JD hung his head. "Is she in there?"

"Yeah," Ashley replied.

"I'll talk to you later," JD replied, then walked into the room and closed the door.

Ashley walked into the kitchen, pulled out the cherry vanilla ice cream, grabbed two spoons and sat on the opposite side of the bar. As she gave the spoon to Cynthia she said, "Dig in; it's going to be a long night."

Tracy came out of her bathroom to find JD sitting in the chair by the door. "Tracy," JD said exhaling, "you know this was a set up. I know what you saw, but Tracy, nothing happened. You walked in at the very time Vanessa wanted you to. I know what it looked like, but nothing happened," he emphasized as he walked over to her.

Tracy stepped back. He hung his head and closed his eyes as Tracy spoke. "She called earlier today and told me you two had a sexual relationship that's been going on for a while. She wanted to make sure I was ready to play in the 'big league.'" She made the quotation gesture with her hands. "Hmm," she said, shaking her head, "I thought as long as I had some of you I could play along." Tears began to form in her eyes. "But, umm...," she continued, shaking her head as she tried to hold back the scream in her throat, "I, I think not. The thought of it and the reality of it are two totally different things," she said. "I can't do it."

"Tracy, I'm not asking you to," Jeffrey said. "That's not something I would ever ask of you." He touched her on the shoulder, but she shrugged him off. "Tracy," Jeffrey said, trying to reign in his temper. This whole situation was now beginning to piss him off. Driving over, he thought he would explain what happened and Tracy would be okay. But things were not going that way and he was on the verge of losing his temper. Tracy walked around him to the other side of her bed. "Tracy, don't let them do this to us," he said. "This was nothing but a set up, Tracy, don't you see that?"

"Did you want to have sex with her tonight, Jeffrey?" Tracy asked.

If there was ever a time in his life that JD needed to lie, it was now. "Tracy." Jeffrey put his hand on his chest. "I'm a man," he said, "and a naked woman was lying on my bed; yes, I wanted to, but I didn't."

Tracy lowered her head to hide how much that answer hurt her. She needed to get away from him for a minute, just to clear her head. She walked out of the room into the living room and grabbed her keys to leave. Jeffrey came up behind her and put his arms around her; he put his head on her neck and kissed it. "Please don't do this, Tracy; don't leave, please don't leave."

She tried to pull away but he would not let go. "Jeffrey, let me go," she said just a little too calmly for him.

"Tracy, I can't, I can't let you go." Jeffrey was afraid if he let her go she may not come back. "I know what you saw hurt, but baby, please, please believe me—nothing happened." He was squeezing her, trying to get through.

"Let me go, Jeffrey, I just got to go." Tracy was losing control as she felt the tears beginning to drop. When she looked up and saw Ashley and Cynthia watching them she closed her eyes. She did not want to cry, not in front of Cynthia.

JD took the keys out of her hand. "Tracy, I'm asking, no, begging you to believe me. I didn't do what you are thinking. I love you, Tracy. Just let me explain what happened." He kissed the side of her face. "I love you."

Tracy needed to get away, so she turned to face him. "You want to explain, okay, explain."

He hesitated, searching for the words. "It wasn't what you think you saw," he said.

"No," Tracy said, "I think I saw your dick in her mouth; what did you see?"

Her words shocked him. Tracy wasn't just hurt, she was angry and he caused it. It never dawned on him that Tracy was capable of being angry; he never saw this side of her. He did not like being the object of her anger. "It was a set up, Tracy."

"Jeffrey, you are a prosecuting attorney. How many times have you heard that? Now, how many times did you believe it?" When he did not respond, she turned quickly as the tears started to fall and she lost her balance. JD caught her and they both fell at the top of the steps.

"Let her go, JD," Ashley said, now crying along with Tracy.

JD wrapped his arms around Tracy and would not let her go; he couldn't. His heart was breaking. He couldn't believe this was happening. "Tracy," he pleaded, "this is what they want: to come between us. Don't let them win."

"Jeffrey, from the day I met you I never thought about being with anyone else, in any way, only you," she cried. "Can you say the same?"

He could not answer that question honestly; it would cause too much damage. Jeffrey rocked Tracy back and forth like a baby; he could feel the tears dropping on his arm. Each drop burned his skin, representing the hurt he caused her.

When he did not respond, Tracy whispered, "Please Jeffrey, please let me go."

He hesitated; not wanting to cause her more pain, he kissed the back of her head and released her.

Tracy got up, went down the steps and out the door without looking back. Ashley ran past Jeffrey and followed Tracy. Jeffrey sat there at the top of the steps with his face in his hands, wondering what in the hell had just happened.

"Hmm..., you were always concerned about me hurting her feelings," Cynthia said in a matter of fact tone. "Who do you think hurt her more, you or me?"

JD ran his hands down his face wiping away the tears, got up and walked away not answering the question. He knew what Cynthia said was true; he cut Tracy deeply.

Ashley was watching Tracy pull away as JD approached. She saw the devastation in his eyes and decided now was not the time for the words she had for him. "Let her go. When she comes back, you will appreciate the love she has for you more. Give her some time, she'll get past it," Ashley said. "Love is new to her and you, too. You both have things to learn; give it time."

JD hugged Ashley, got in his car and pulled off.

When Ashley went upstairs, Cynthia saw the worried look on her face. "They will be okay, he loves her. Which is freaking amazing to me, but whatever, they will work it out."

JD felt empty and alone for the first time in his life. He was blessed with family and friends who loved him, and a full life, but at this moment none of it mattered. The only thing that would take the emptiness away was Tracy's love. He allowed the past to take it away, but he only had himself to blame. JD called Brian from his cell phone and asked him to put a search out for Tracy. He needed to know where she was and that she was okay.

Tracy was hurt and had no one to turn to. Ashley was her best friend, but also JD's sister, and she could not put her in the middle. Tracy called James, but hung up before he could answer. She really did not want to be around anyone. She was hurting, and like any wounded animal she needed a place to hide to lick her wounds. She needed to clear her mind and think. She pulled into the Omni Hotel downtown and got a room. When she entered the room she threw her purse on the table and fell across the bed. She was exhausted, hurt and empty. She just needed to close her eyes and think.

As JD entered his home, he put his keys on the counter and saw the key and a note: "What goes around, comes around, V." He had tried not to let his past hurt Tracy, but here it was. JD sighed. It really wasn't the past, he hesitated; he had let Vanessa get to him. How was he going to fix this? JD knew what Tracy saw; he knew it hurt her. And he knew better than anyone why this cut her so deep. How could he let this happen? He picked up the key and threw it with all his force against the front door. The doorbell rang; JD jerked it open, hoping it was Tracy.

"Sounded like a bullet was coming through the door," Brian said stepping inside. JD bent down and picked up the key. "What's up, JD, what's going on?" Brian asked.

JD threw the key on the countertop, walked over to the cabinet in the kitchen, and pulled out a bottle of Jack Daniel and two glasses. Brian sat at the breakfast bar and took one of the glasses; JD poured. JD swallowed one shot straight down and poured another. Brian took the bottle out of his hand. "You have court tomorrow, man."

JD pulled up a bar stool, sat and told Brian what went down. "JD, you knew Carolyn and Vanessa were out to do this; you should have warned Tracy."

Brian's cell rang. "Talk to me," Brian answered. "Where? Thanks, man. I'll take it from here." He hung up the phone. "We got her, she's at the Omni downtown."

JD didn't move.

"You're not going to talk to her?" Brian asked.

JD shook his head. "No, she's not hearing me right now." JD swallowed hard, holding in his emotions.

Brian could see the hurt in JD's face. He finished his drink. "I'll go," he offered.

"Make sure she's okay. I don't want her to be alone," JD said dejectedly.

"Alright, man, I'll be in touch," Brian said and left.

JD called Tracy's cell; her voicemail picked up. "Trac, I know you don't want to talk to me right now, but baby, please know I love you. I would never do anything to betray your love or your trust in me. Please just call me. Let me know you are, okay? Please, Tracy." He hung up the phone

Tears flowed as Tracy played the message from Jeffrey. The idea of her causing him pain was difficult for her to handle, but at the moment her pain was deeper and she had to deal with that before she could deal with Jeffrey. A knock at the door interrupted Tracy's thoughts, but she

ignored it, thinking someone had the wrong room. When the knock occurred again, Tracy opened the door. When she saw it was Brian, she closed her eyes and walked back into the room.

"What are you doing here?" Tracy asked.

"Hello to you, too," Brian replied as he closed the door. "I'm here checking on you, of course."

Tracy put her hands on her hips. "Jeffrey called you?" she asked angrily.

"What do you think?"

She looked away and exhaled. "Did he tell you what happened?"

He walked towards her. "Yeah, he told me."

Tears streamed down her face.

Shit, Brian thought, *not the crying.*

Tracy put her thumbs in the back pocket of her jeans then bit her bottom lip. The tears began to flow.

"Oh shit, don't do that," Brian said almost begging. But she couldn't stop. He walked over and put his arms around her. "Okay, okay, it's going to be okay," he said thinking, *Shit, shit, shit.*

Tracy wrapped her arms around his waist and broke loose against his chest.

Oh, shit, Brian said to himself. "Alright now, now, it's going to be okay. Shh, shh." He guided her to the sofa, consoling her until she began to settle down. He grabbed the box of tissues that was on the table and handed one to her.

"You can stop patting my head. I'm not a dog, you know," she said through the tears.

He smiled. "Look," he said, "I'm not good at this sensitive kind of stuff. You have to get Calvin for that." Still holding her, he added, "I'm just here as a substitute. JD didn't want you to be alone," Brian said as he looked down at her. He didn't understand her being this upset; this kind of thing happens all the time, women get over it. Brian began talking, hoping she was ready to listen to reason. "You realize this was a set up, right?"

Tracy nodded. "Vanessa advised me of her intentions. I honestly did not think Jeffrey would get caught up in it."

"He didn't," Brian said, sitting back. "He's a better man than me. I would have been all up in that," he said, shaking his head in disbelief. Tracy pulled her legs up to her chest and put her arms around them. She sucked in her teeth at Brian and he laughed.

"I'm glad you are getting some amusement out of this," she said. He pulled her legs out from under her arms and pulled her onto his lap. He tucked her head under his chin and put his arms around her attempting to comfort her.

"Tracy, JD loves you. His relationship with you is not about sex, you know that. There is something more there. I know it seems to you something happened. But JD said nothing happened and I believe him."

"I think I believe him; I want to," Tracy said looking up at him. Brian was caught off guard for a minute; those innocent eyes of hers were getting to him. He tucked her head back under his chin so he could not see them. "If you believe that, why are you so upset?"

"He wanted to, Brian. If I had not walked in at that time, would he still be able to say nothing happened?"

"I don't know, Tracy," he said. "But you are dealing with a what-if, and no one can answer those."

"Brian, I can't compete with women like Vanessa and Carolyn. They know how to do things I don't when it comes to sex. What happens when Jeffrey wants those things and I can't give them to him? Will he turn to Carolyn or Vanessa?"

"What things are you talking about?" Brian asked, not sure what she was referring to. "You are a woman, he's a man. What else is there to know?"

"I'm not very experienced," Tracy said in a whisper.

Wondering why she was whispering, Brian whispered back, "Experienced in what?"

She exhaled. "Sex, Brian," she said, exasperated.

He laughed and laughed and laughed until she hit him in the chest.

"Okay, okay, I'm sorry," he said. He looked down at her. "How old are you?"

"I'll be 25 next month."

"And you never did the do before JD?" he asked in a surprised tone.

"No," she replied, "and I don't know how to go about learning. I mean...." She sat up. "I can take a book and learn anything and everything. But I don't know the mechanics to put what I read about into action. You know what I mean."

"Well, that's because sex is about emotions; you can't control them all the time and you definitely cannot learn about it from a book. It comes with experience." He smiled. As he looked at her, he realized she was serious. "Have you discussed this with JD?"

"No, I can't talk about this with him."

"Hell yes, you can. That's who you are supposed to talk to about shit like this."

Tracy put her head back on his chest and he wrapped his arms around her. "Brian, I think Cynthia was right. Jeffrey is not going to wait around for me to learn how to please him. You're Jeffrey's friend, Brian, can you teach me? Can you teach me how to do the things to keep him away from Vanessa and Carolyn?"

Brian prided himself on being a man that was up for just about anything, but he never expected this. He stared at Tracy and the longer he stared the more he realized she was serious. She was genuinely asking for his help. His mind began to filter between the angel on one shoulder and the devil on the other. *This is your boy's girl—you have to ignore your libido and do the right thing,* came from one side of his brain. *Man, she asking you to teach her. Look at it as helping JD,* came from the other side of his brain.

Brian decided to help her in the best way he could. He set her at the other end of the sofa then stepped away. "Don't you ever ask a man to teach you anything like that again unless it's JD, do you understand me," Brian yelled while standing over her. He put his hands on his hips and was shaking his finger at her as if he was reprimanding a child. "Never," he yelled, "ask a man to do that, especially a man like me." Not trusting what he would say next, he simply said, "Shit," and turned and walked out of the room. He stopped in the hallway, turned to go back to the door. Then he said, "Hell no, hell no," stopped, looked down at his groin. "Stop it; damn it, stop it," he said, talking to himself. He walked the hallway for a few more minutes trying to compose himself. After a few minutes he pulled out his cell phone. "Hey, I got her," Brian said agitated.

"Is she okay?" JD asked, concerned.

"Yeah, but I'm not staying in that room with her," Brian yelled.

JD sat up in the bed. "What's happened, B, did you upset her?"

"Did I upset her?" Brian could not believe JD had the nerve to ask him that. "Hell no, she upset the hell out of me," Brian yelled and hung up the phone.

Brian walked the hallway a little longer, and then went back into the room. Tracy was still sitting on the sofa with her legs folded up under her chin. She looked up at him with tear-filled eyes. "I'm sorry, Brian. I didn't mean to put you in the middle. I don't know what to do."

Brian wanted to help her and JD with this one, but not in the way she asked him to. He walked over to the sofa, took her in his arms and held her. "I'm sorry, too. I didn't mean to yell. But right now what you need is to hear some facts of life. First, never ask anyone but your man to teach you anything about sex. Second, you need to understand, there is a distinct difference in sex and making love. What went on between JD and Vanessa was an attempt from her to have sex with him, nothing more. The reason women like Vanessa and Carolyn have to resort to the things they do is because they have not been fortunate enough to meet that one person God put on this Earth for them to love. You and JD have been blessed with that. I know JD knows that and I believe you do, too." He kissed the top of her head. "You two are going to go through situations like this, and believe me, it will make your relationship stronger."

"Does it have to hurt so much?" she asked.

"Anything that has to do with the heart will hurt from time to time," Brian replied, "but the feelings you get when things are right outweigh the hurt." He smiled at the thought. "Now, what you saw tonight was one of the hardest things for a man to resist and Vanessa knew that. Any man, with the exception of the man above, would waver at the thought of a beautiful woman giving him head."

"What is that?" she asked.

He looked down at her with a frown on his face. "A blow job," he said. She still looked at him as if she did not understand. He thought for another moment. "Okay, oral sex," he said.

"Oh!" Tracy said, and settled back down on his chest.

Brian was pleased he was able to clarify that for her. He continued, "Vanessa took advantage of that and used it against JD tonight."

"But he fell for it, Brian," Tracy said. "How do I stop that from happening again? I don't know how to give him—" she hesitated, "what you said."

"A blow job?" Brian said, smiling and thinking, *It's going to be a long time before JD gets that, hell she can't even bring her self to say it.*

"Yeah, that," she said.

"You give JD so many other things, Tracy. If he wants that from you he will teach it to you. But don't ever ask a man like me to teach you."

"Why, you're not that bad?"

"Because I will turn your ass out, girl," he said shaking his head back and forth. "You wouldn't know what in the hell hit you." They both laughed.

He put her head back down on his chest and rested his chin on top of her head. *If she only knew what he was thinking at that moment she would not be laughing, she would be running out that damn door,* he thought. "It's late, let's get some sleep."

He adjusted himself and held her until she dozed off. Brian had not understood why JD had given up all women for this one until now. This is the type of woman you are supposed to leave the single life for. Brian smiled, envying his friend. JD had the best thing a man could ask for: the love of a good woman. Brian fell asleep with his friend's woman in his arms.

Chapter 20

The arraignment of Juan Cortez was scheduled for 9 a.m. and JD had not gotten any sleep. He was up all night worried about the situation with Tracy. Ashley called around 6 a.m., concerned when Tracy did not come home. She hoped JD had been able to calm Tracy down and she was with him, but that wasn't the case. JD gave Ashley the rundown on what had actually happened. Ashley knew Carolyn was involved in some way, but did not know about Vanessa.

When JD finished his call with Ashley, he called Tracy's cell; she didn't pick up. JD never felt so guilty about anything in his life and he vowed he would never hurt her again, it hurt too damn much.

JD went to the office early, thinking it would take his mind off Tracy. She did not believe him and that cut him deep. Why would she doubt his word? He had never lied to her about anything. How could she doubt him now? JD didn't notice the elevator door open, and it began to close on him, but he caught it. Damn, he needed to concentrate today. The Cortez case was at a critical point; he needed to clear his mind. But he didn't know how. The only thing that would calm him was talking to Tracy, but that wasn't happening.

He went into his office and put his briefcase on the desk. Calvin walked in behind him. "You're in early this morning," he said.

JD turned. "Hey, Calvin." He put his hands in his pockets and walked over to the window.

"What's going on, JD?"

"I think I lost Tracy last night."

Calvin laughed. "I don't believe that; Tracy is crazy about you."

JD hung his head. "She walked in on Vanessa at my place last night."

"Man, what is wrong with you? Why in the hell did you have Vanessa at your place?"

"I didn't, man. She used the key I keep outside the door and let herself in. She undressed and was lying across the bed when I got out of the shower. She left the front door open; Tracy walked in, as if on cue."

"Where is Tracy now?"

"At the Omni with Brian."

Calvin raised an eyebrow. "What is she doing at the Omni with Brian?"

JD put his hand up. "Long story." Exhaling and frustrated, JD asked, "How do I fix this, Calvin? She didn't believe me when I said nothing happened."

"Did anything happen?"

"No!" JD replied. "Well, it might have looked that way." He hesitated. "Vanessa had just gone down on me when Tracy walked in. It took me a minute to push her away."

"But not soon enough for Tracy not to see." Calvin smirked.

"Right," JD replied.

"Have you talked to Tracy?"

"I tried; she's not listening, yet." JD sighed.

"Then give her time. Tracy loves you; she will work through it."

JD unbuttoned his suit jacket and sat in his chair. "I can't lose her, Calvin. Not now."

"Have you called her this morning?"

"Yeah, she's not picking up."

"Have you heard from Brian this morning?"

"Not yet."

Calvin cleared his throat. "Don't you think you should call Brian, just to make sure Tracy's okay?" JD looked at Calvin then picked up the phone to dial Brian.

"She's okay," Brian said walking through the door. JD hung up the telephone as Brian closed the door. "Don't be trying to put no shit in that man's head," he said to Calvin. He looked at JD. "Don't you ever put me on detail with that woman again."

"Is she okay, Brian?" JD asked anxiously.

"Yeah, she's hurt as hell, but she is okay. Give her a little time, both of you will be okay," Brian said, taking a seat.

"Why did you close the door?" JD asked, puzzled.

"Because I didn't want anyone to overhear what I am going to say to you." Brian shook his head and sat forward. "Man, you have my sympathy. I understand why you have lost your mind over that woman. She's beautiful, intelligent and green as hell." He pointed at JD. "You have been keeping secrets, my brother. Tracy was a virgin before you...."

JD did not respond. "You don't have to answer; she told me," Brian said, sitting back in his chair. "That's why she is taking this petty shit so hard, man. She doesn't think she knows how to satisfy you sexually. She believes you will eventually turn to Vanessa or Carolyn for that satisfaction."

"Damn, Brian, she told you all of that?" Calvin asked.

"Oh, we had a sister-to-sister kind of talk. But wait, it gets better." JD sat there not saying anything. "Then she asks me to teach her how to satisfy you," Brian said, looking at JD with a firm look on his face. JD stood up as if he was going after Brian. "Sit your ass down; I ain't for no shit out of you after what your woman put me through last night!" Brian demanded firmly.

"What did you do, B?" JD yelled at Brian.

"Not a damn thing; I got the hell out of that room. It took me damn near an hour to talk myself down."

Calvin started laughing and couldn't stop. JD and Brian just looked at him. Calvin almost fell out of the chair, he was laughing so hard. Brian turned to Calvin. "That shit wasn't funny."

JD sat down, put his head in his hand and began laughing. "I can't believe Tracy actually asked you that," he said laughing. At that moment, JD was grateful Calvin was finding the humor in this situation. If he had been alone with Brian, JD wasn't sure they would all be laughing. JD looked at Brian. "You all right, B?" he asked, understanding Brian's experience with Tracy.

"Man," Brian said, "I gave her a good talking to and told her not to ever ask a man some shit like that. You better start teaching that girl and I mean like right damnit now."

Calvin was out of the chair on the floor.

JD was still laughing. "She can be a little frustrating. But man, if I teach her anything else right now, I wouldn't be able to stand it. She wears me out."

"Then why does she think different?" Brian asked.

"I don't know, man," JD said laughing.

Calvin was up now. "Alright, man, I'm sorry. But I would have paid money to see you with her last night."

"I'm sorry, too, B. Man, I should have warned you," JD apologized.

"You mean she was telling the truth about the virgin shit and all?" Brian asked.

Sitting back in his chair, JD replied, "Tracy is a very honest person; she wouldn't lie to you."

"Then you need to fix this shit as soon as possible and keep me away from her. You lucky you're my boy, I know that. I'm going home to take a shower. Shit, two or three of them," Brian said as he walked out the door.

Calvin, still laughing, said, "It's time for court, JD, you ready?"

"Yeah, let's do this," JD replied.

In court, Juan pleaded not guilty on all counts and a trial date was set for a month later. On his way out of the courtroom, a bailiff gave JD a note. The note said "An eye for an eye." JD asked the bailiff who left the note, but the bailiff did not know. Brian read the note and set the security team in motion immediately. JD's home and office were set up with surveillance. Brian and two alternates were assigned to JD personally. Gavin was advised of the heightened security level then Magna, Dan and Calvin each had an agent assigned to them until the trial ended.

Two days had passed and Tracy still was not responding to JD's calls. Her absence from his life was taking a toll on JD and everyone around him. It was simple: a part of him was missing and it was the very heart of him. JD begun lashing out at everyone for the smallest things, but when that fury was directed towards his mother, Brian knew things had to change.

JD's mom went to his house to cook dinner for him. Ashley told her about Tracy and Martha was worried about her son. While cooking dinner, she decided to clean up a little, and started with the bedroom. When JD got home that evening he ate dinner with his mom and went upstairs to shower and change clothes. Martha was clearing the table when JD ran downstairs yelling about the bed linens. The smell was different; Tracy's scent was gone, now he had nothing. Martha smiled at her son and softly said, "Anger will not change what happened; only love will. Tracy touched your heart, and you touched hers. Neither of you have forgotten the other. Fix this, Jeffrey Daniel, and fix it now."

Brian went by the hotel to see Tracy, as he had for the past two nights. He told her what happened and that she had to go home before Mama Harrison killed JD.

JD was in his office going over security details when Tracy called. Seeing her number on his cell phone prompted him to answer immediately. "Babe, where are you?" he asked.

"At the park across from your office."

JD walked over to the window and looked out, then smiled when he spotted her. "I'll be right there, just stay there; babe, please, just stay there."

"Brian, I got to go. You all stay here and finish this," JD said and headed out.

"Stay on this," Brian said, rushing to catch up with JD.

"What's that all about?" Magna asked Calvin.

"A personal matter," he replied. Calvin walked over to the window. He saw JD as he entered the park and spotted Tracy. Calvin smiled. "Magna, watch this." Magna walked over to the window and watched.

Tracy saw Jeffrey walking towards her and her heart began to beat faster as he closed the distance between them. She put her arms up around his neck; he grabbed her around her waist and just held on.

"I love you, Tracy. I'm sooo sorry," he said as he kissed every inch of her face. "I should have warned you about Vanessa. But I swear I did not touch her, Tracy. I did hesitate for a moment, but it would not have happened, please believe me," he pleaded.

"I believe you."

He held her face cupped in his hands and smiled. "You do?" he asked, emotionally drained. JD Harrison, who had the respect of the governor, senators, powerful people, knew that to have this woman believe him meant more than everything in the world to him.

"Yes, I do," she said. "Brian explained some things to me." She lowered her head. "I'm not going to pretend I understand all of it, but I'm not willing to give up on us just yet."

JD kissed her with all the passion he had within. "Don't ever leave me, Tracy." JD sighed heavily. "Don't ever do that again."

"Okay," she said in that voice that drove him crazy.

He took her by the hand. "We have some things to talk about," he said, "starting with Brian."

They walked through the park and talked for a while. Brian stayed right behind them every step. He saw his men as they joined in flanked on both sides of the couple at a distance. JD explained what had happened with Vanessa. He tried to explain what she did to Brian and the position she put him in with her request. Tracy told JD about the conversation she had with Brian. JD was a little surprised; he never would have thought Brian could be that patient. But it did let him know just how much of a friend he had in Brian. JD told Tracy undoubtedly that he was more than satisfied with their lovemaking and he had no thoughts of being with anyone else. Tracy asked him if he would teach her to do "that blow job thingy." JD shook his head and smiled at her. "I have to keep you away from Brian." When JD and Tracy left the park that night, there was no separating them. Their bond was tight, impenetrable, and both of them knew it.

Tracy returned to work the next day and was revealing the details of her nights away with Ashley. Ashley was looking at Tracy in disbelief; she couldn't believe Tracy would ask Brian, of all people, to teach her anything. They were laughing so hard, neither of them noticed James was standing in the doorway. "Hello, ladies." James smiled.

They both turn towards him. Tracy continued to laugh and said, "Hello, James."

Ashley stopped laughing and seemed to tense up. "James," Ashley said and turned away.

Tracy noticed the change in Ashley's disposition but did not comment. "Did we have an appointment?" Tracy asked James.

"No, I decided to stop in to check on you two," he replied while looking at Ashley.

Tracy got a strange vibe from Ashley and James. She remembered getting the same feeling at the dinner the week before. "That was very thoughtful of you," Tracy said, attempting to make small talk. "Wasn't it, Ashley?"

"Yes, well, James has shown signs of being a thoughtful person, at times," Ashley responded without looking up.

Okay, now Tracy knew something was up. Ashley was not her normal throw-everything-to-the-wind, flirty self. Tracy looked from James to Ashley and then back to James. James had a frown on his face telling Tracy to leave, while Ashley's signs were telling her to stay. "You know what, I left, umm...something out front. Would you excuse me for a minute, James?"

"Sure," James replied as Tracy left the room. "She's not a good liar."

"No, she never has been," Ashley said. "What can I do for you, James?"

"You have not returned my calls and I would like an explanation."

"I have returned all calls related to the project. There is nothing you and I need to discuss."

"I disagree," James responded. "I think we need to discuss what happened between us, maybe over dinner?"

"Why, because Tracy is unavailable?"

"Tracy's not unavailable," James stated. "She's not married; she's not dead."

"No," Ashley said, "she's just in love with another man."

"This has always been the case, for what I can ascertain. But that does not make her unavailable," James replied.

"Why were you calling, James?"

"I have missed talking with you. Your calls had become a nice routine in the morning."

"I'm sorry, James, I don't play second," Ashley stated as she went to walk by him.

James gently grabbed her arm. "I never asked you to play second to anyone and I'm not asking you that now. Yes, I was interested in Tracy. I will never deny that. She will always have my friendship. But that is all it is, a friendship. I want more than that from you." He kissed her gently. "The ball is in your court. You know the numbers." James walked out of the office.

Tracy came back into the conference room. She closed the door then sat down at the table Ashley was standing over and waited. Tracy knew the routine so well. There were many nights Ashley would come into the dorm room and need to talk. She would never give Tracy any background on whatever was on her mind. Ashley would start with what she was thinking at that moment. Tracy knew to sit and wait; Ashley would eventually start talking.

"I really like him, you know," Ashley started, "from the very beginning. He reminds me so much of my father and JD. Isn't that funny," she smiled. "I would have never believed another man was out there like them; I was wrong." Tracy moved to the other side of the table to see her friend's face. Ashley had never talked about her father before. Tracy did not want to miss any of what Ashley was about to say. "I excelled on this project because I was trying so hard to impress James Brooks. But he did not pay me one bit of attention. It was always you." Ashley's words stung Tracy a little, so she lowered her head as if feeling ashamed. Ashley saw Tracy's reaction. "I knew you were in love with JD and James did not stand a chance," she said with a faint smile. "I thought, why not, I'll take a chance. No matter what I did he didn't see me. When David showed up at the function, James got into this protective mode. It made me feel special. Safe. After the function he insisted I stay at his place. Nothing happened; I slept in his guest room. The next day I told him about David. Can you believe that, Tracy? I have never told anyone about that night, but I told James. For the first time since it all happened, a man made me feel safe, secure; you know what I mean." She hesitated for a moment, and then continued. "I kissed him and it felt so right. For a moment I thought he responded, but I guess I was wrong." She smiled faintly.

"What did he say when you told him how you felt?" Tracy asked.

"Hmm, see that's the thing. I didn't really tell him." She laughed nervously. "I asked him if he was in love with you."

Tracy hung her head. "What did he say?"

"He said he wasn't. I didn't give him a chance to say anything else."

"You two haven't talked since then?"

"No, he's called several times, but I think, no, leave it be."

"Ashley, you should at least talk to him; hear what he has to say."

"I know how he feels about you, Tracy; how do I deal with that?"

"I don't know what he might have felt for me. But he told you it was a friendship and that's all he offered to me, nothing more." Tracy smiled.

"If you had opened that door, Tracy, he would have run in."

"Life is too short for what-ifs. Maybe you should talk to the man. He seems to be genuinely interested in you."

Ashley smiled at Tracy. "Do you have feelings for James?"

"No. I mean, I like James very much. But I am in love with Jeffrey."

Ashley smiled. "If you are so in love with my brother, what possessed you to ask Brian to teach you how to give head? Girl, don't you know that's a conversation for your girls, not your man's best friend," Ashley said laughing. "I would love to have been there to see Brian's face."

Tracy began blushing. "I did not ask him to teach me that, not exactly."

"No need in you blushing now. You should have been blushing the other night."

Going back to the original subject, Tracy asked, "Are you going to talk to James?"

Ashley shrugged her shoulders. "I'll think about it."

"You know, I think you are scared to really explore the possibility of James. He is very sophisticated and a little conservative. He may be out of your league." Tracy smirked.

"I know you are not challenging me," Ashley claimed

"Prove me wrong. Show me you can get and keep James Brooks. Talk to the man."

Chapter 21

Ashley was parked outside when James pulled into his garage. The night she was there she had not paid a lot of attention to his home. But while she was waiting for him to meet her, she got a good look at his house; it was enormous, yet elegant. For a moment Ashley thought Tracy may have a point; maybe she was out of her league.

"Oh hell, no, I'm not Tracy. No one is out of my league."

As James approached, Ashley got out of the car. "I realize this was short notice. Will I be interrupting any plans?" she asked.

James walked over to her car. "No. I would not have agreed to see you if there were a problem."

Ashley stood there, not certain where to go from here.

"Are we going to talk out here or would you like to come inside?"

Why did she feel unsure of herself around him, Ashley wondered. "Inside," she replied.

As they entered the house, Clair came from the back. "Hello, Clair," James greeted.

"Good evening, sir. Good evening, ma'am. Dinner is on the stove. Will you need anything else this evening?"

"No, thanks, Clair. You have a good night," James replied.

"You, too, sir; ma'am."

"Good night," Ashley said.

James walked into the family room; Ashley followed. He had made up his mind to allow Ashley in his life days ago. But she had to accept him on his word about Tracy. He could not do that for her. James did not allow people to get close. He had been through hell with his first wife and was determined not to go through that again. For him to consider allowing Ashley in just a little was a feat, but at this point Ashley did not see it that way. James went over to his bar. "Would you like something to drink?" he asked.

"No, thank you. I just need to talk."

He smiled, walked over, took her hand and set her on the sofa next to him. "Talk."

Ashley hesitated then began slowly. "James, I am more than a little attracted to you. I think you know that. But the situation with you and Tracy concerns me. Tracy is not just my partner; I consider her part of my family. I would never do anything to hurt her or betray her trust. If you have feelings for Tracy, then I can't be involved with you in any way."

James put his glass on the table. "Did you come over here to talk about Tracy?"

"Yes, I really need to get this cleared up."

"You could have discussed that on the telephone. You didn't have to come here for that conversation."

"James, you are avoiding the question." Agitated, she stood up and walked towards the door.

"I didn't hear a question," he replied.

"Well, give me a response to my series of statements," she said with a little attitude.

"I understood everything you said," James replied.

"You know what, I'm not doing this again," Ashley said, looking around for her keys. She thought she was ready to open up, try to feel something again. But she just didn't have the patience. She liked James, she really did, but his alpha male personality was pissing her off.

James watched her. It was like she was trapped and needed to be rescued. He went over to the foyer and picked up her keys. "Are looking for these?" Ashley reached to take them; he closed his hand then put them in his pocket. "I don't think you should leave just yet."

She put her hands on her hips. "James, give me my keys. I want to go."

He walked away. "No, you don't. You are running away again. I'm not going to let you do that." Ashley stood there. *No, this man is not playing this game with me,* she thought.

"We are going to talk, but we are not going to talk about Tracy. We are going to talk about you and me," James firmly stated.

Ashley put her hand up to her forehead. "You are being an ass. We can't get to you and me until we clear up Tracy."

Now James was getting a little frustrated. "Ashley," he said calmly, "I am not a man to answer the same question more than once. At this moment you are trying my patience. I'm not going to answer any more questions about Tracy."

"Then we don't have anything to talk about. May I have my keys?" Ashley held her hand out with the other on her hip. James handed her the keys. "Thank you," she responded.

James really did not understand what more he could say to ease her concerns about Tracy. She asked the question, he told her no. He even went to her a second time and explained further. In his mind that should be it. Ashley turned to go out the door. James had mixed emotions, but he was certain he did not want her to leave. As she opened the door she reached around her and pushed it closed. He pinned her against the door, then kissed her passionately. Ashley responded with just as much passion. James's reaction surprised him, but he couldn't let her walk out of that door.

James placed kisses from her neck down to the top of her breast. Her blouse was constricting his movements. "You don't need that," James said as he pulled her blouse over her head and returned to the spot where he began. Her skin was as smooth as silk and tasted as sweet as honey as he ran his tongue from her breast then down to her navel.

Ashley touched the side of his face and guided him back to her mouth. As James devoured her mouth, he took the keys from her hand and dropped them on the table. James put her arms around his neck, picked her up by the waist, and started climbing the stairs. The heat generating from their bodies caused James to stop midway up the stairs. They fell, unable to walk any further, momentarily ending the kiss. James looked down into those big brown eyes of hers. "For the third and last time, Tracy is a friend. I was interested in her. I am now consumed with you."

Ashley was lost in the kiss, but she heard what she needed to hear. She looked up at him, pulled his tie off, and began unbuttoning his shirt. "I thought you never lost your composure, Mr. Brooks."

She pulled his shirt over his head and threw it up the staircase. Ashley inhaled. James had smooth broad shoulders and abs that revealed regular workouts. Ashley ran her hands down his chest. It never occurred to her that James would look so good under his tailored suits. She stared up at him, groaned, and kissed his chest.

"You keep doing that and I am going to lose more than my composure," James growled as he turned over and pulled her on top of him. He was kissing her neck as he unzipped her skirt then pushed it down her long legs. Ashley slid down his body, leaving a trail of kisses down his chest, removing his belt and sliding his pants down the stairs.

What on Earth am I doing? James thought. He was always so conservative when it came to sex and women. He was always in control. He pulled her back up to his lips, kissing her as he carried her up a few more steps. They fell again, and laughed, but did not lose contact.

Ashley could feel James growing against her leg. *Can I handle this man,* she wondered as she wrapped her legs around him. That was the leverage James needed. He placed his hands under her rear and carried her into his bedroom, dropping her shoes along the way.

They fell across the bed. James never had any concerns about pleasing a woman, but he wanted to please Ashley beyond reason. For him it was important for her to experience the wave of emotions she had stirred in him. As he held her close to his heart, Ashley began to kiss the base of his throat and took control, rising above him with the grace of a gazelle. She groaned. It was a perfect. Like a finger sliding into a glove. She slowly began moving against him with smooth, powerful strides. James encircled her waist, guiding her body over him. The pace increased, becoming more powerful with each stroke. Her head fell back as they moved closer to that moment of ecstasy. Wanting to feel her in his arms, James sprang up, holding her tightly as he kissed her exposed neck until they both cried out the other's name in unison. They sat there entangled with each other, trying to ease their racing pulses. Ashley dropped her head to his shoulder and he stroked her back as they sat there. Her breath against his ear caused him to react, and he could feel himself growing inside of her again. With her legs still around his waist he leaned backwards, ran his tongue from her throat down to her breast. He pulled out, picked her up and placed her standing on the bed against the headboard while remaining on his knees. He ran his tongue around her navel down to the very core of her. When Ashley was to the point of her knees buckling beneath her, James placed his hands on her hips and guided her body down, then entered her at full force, again. Ashley called out his name with such passion that James nearly lost his control. Ashley took in every inch of him, and there were a few. She held on tight as he continued to fill her like no other before him. With each compelling stroke he took control of her body. Their release was so overwhelming, he fell backwards and her body followed like a chain reaction. James held her until the waves from their bodies subsided.

By the time they fell asleep, it was time for them to get up, but neither could move. James heard Clair and remembered the clothes they left on the stairs. He looked down at Ashley. She was on his chest and his arm was wrapped around her back, holding her close to him. He realized he never let her go once they fell asleep.

That surprised James. He did not consider himself an affectionate man. In the past he would have sex with women then leave at what he considered an appropriate time. With his wife, she would turn to her side of the bed and sleep. Ashley stretched in his arms and he liked the feel of that. He surveyed her body as she slept, and smiled; Ashley had long, firm legs. James thought she had the legs of a runner. For the first time in years James actually wanted just to stay in bed with her beside him. The thought shocked him back to reality; he had to go to work. He didn't want to wake her, so he put a pillow under her head and slipped out of bed.

Halfway through his shower, the door opened and Ashley stepped inside, kissing his back.

"You are not shy at all, are you?" he asked as he turned to her. James wrapped his arms around her as he kissed her feverishly.

"No," she said as she began kissing his chest, then down to his stomach. He grabbed her before she went any further, pulled her up against the shower wall, held her with one hand and braced with the other hand as he entered her. Water from the multiple showerheads was pulsing from every direction, which enhanced the sensation of their simultaneous release.

By the time they finished their shower, Clair had folded the clothes and placed them on the bench at the end of the bed. When Ashley saw the clothes, she gasped with humiliation. "She didn't see us, did she?" James laughed as he walked into one of his closets. "It's a little late to be bashful now."

"We left our clothes on the stairs. Oh my goodness, I am not going to be able to look that woman in the face," Ashley exclaimed.

James came back into the room still in his towel, but with a suit in his hand. He placed the suit on the stand and then grabbed her around the waist. He could not believe Ashley was that self-conscious. He tossed her across the bed and landed on top of her. James knew he was running late but she was so damn sexy in that towel and her damp hair up in a ponytail. He looked down at her. "You know, I measured your legs while you were asleep." He smiled as he wrapped her legs around him.

She laughed. "Did we ever go to sleep?"

"Just for a minute." He laughed. "We really did not talk last night."

"Would you like to come to my place for dinner tonight? If you are free, I mean. We could talk then." Ashley did not want to take anything for granted here.

"Can you cook?"

"Quite well," Ashley replied.

"Then I will be there." He smiled.

They dressed then went downstairs. James went into the kitchen. "Clair, I'll have to pass on breakfast this morning. And I have plans for dinner tonight, but you may want to fix a sandwich or something. I don't know if she can cook."

"I heard that," Ashley commented.

James smiled. Clair returned the smile. "It's good to see you smiling, Mr. Brooks."

James did not realize he was smiling. He bashfully turned away. "Have a good day, Clair."

"You too, sir," Clair replied as she watched the two leave.

When they reached Ashley's car, James noticed a note on the windshield. Ashley read the note and was a little unnerved. Ashley handed the note to James.

After reading it James asked, "Ashley, are you involved with Holt in any way?"

Ashley could not believe he asked her that. "No!" Ashley replied with a touch of irritation.

James took the note and put Ashley in the car, then closed the door. "I'll follow you home

Chapter 22

No formal announcement was made but it was a foregone conclusion, Gavin was going to run for governor. The Roth family hosted a fundraiser to assist with financing his campaign. JD reserved a table and invited a few friends to join him and Tracy. To JD's surprise, Ashley's date was James Brooks. Tracy was aware of the relationship between Ashley and James, but JD still had no idea they were involved. Tracy smiled when the two arrived. It was good to see Ashley excited about a man, especially since that man was James.

JD was a bit unnerved, but was cordial towards James. Actually, JD was a little too busy keeping Tracy away from Jackie and Carolyn to be concerned with James. After the incident at the last function that they all attended, Calvin had a long conversation with Jackie. He did not ask but told her she would not be a part of any future schemes against JD and Tracy. Jackie had to choose for the last time to whom she was loyal — him or Carolyn. Jackie promised Calvin she would stay clear of anything involving his friend.

When Jackie saw Carolyn approaching the table, she excused herself and walked to her. While Jackie and Carolyn talked, Ashley and Tracy took a walk, leaving JD, James and Calvin at the table. "So, JD, how is the case going? Are you going to convict?" James asked.

"On all five counts," JD replied with confidence.

"Yeah, thanks to Tracy. I swear, man, we need to hire her," Calvin responded.

"I don't think the DA's office can afford her." James smiled.

"You're right about that," JD said. "Besides, I like having her to myself, I don't want to share."

"I must say, JD, I'm pleasantly surprised. You two have been hanging in there for a couple months now. Tracy is happy and you appear to be on top of the world. I'm happy to see it," James acknowledged.

Gavin approached the table. "Happy to see what?" he asked.

"JD and Tracy," Calvin replied.

"That is surprising." Gavin smiled. "I didn't think it would last this long, but I'm glad it has." He laughed. "The time has given me half a chance with Carolyn." JD smiled. "You know I would not stand a chance if you were still available," Gavin said laughing. "There was a time not long ago we all lived vicariously through JD. Every week it was a new woman."

"Some weeks it was two or three," Calvin added. Calvin and Gavin at the same time said, "So many women, so little time." They laughed. JD laughed with them.

"That was the motto," Gavin said.

"But then he ran across Tracy again." Calvin smiled pleasantly.

"You knew Tracy before?" James asked.

"Yeah," JD said, sitting back. "We met when she was a sophomore in college." He smiled. "She was only 19 at the time. I was working with the DA's office."

Calvin and JD at the same time said, "Jailbait." They laughed.
"Referring to Tracy that way kept JD's mind off of her." Calvin laughed.

"But you two ended up together anyway." James smiled. "That's called fate."

"Yes, it is; you can't mess with that." Gavin smiled.

"No, you can't," JD said, "and I wouldn't change anything about it or Tracy. God knows I love that woman."

"Here, here. To fate, the past and the future," James toasted.

"And the love of a good woman," JD added.

Each man had picked up his drink to toast when a voice came from behind them. "What woman would that be, JD?" JD turned to see Vanessa standing behind him.

"Speaking of the past." Calvin squirmed.

JD instinctively looked around for Tracy. He was not going to let her be ambushed by Vanessa or Carolyn again. "She's out on the balcony," Vanessa informed him.

JD, Gavin and James stood. "Vanessa," JD said.

She took the seat between Calvin and JD and crossed her legs, exposing her thighs. JD made the introductions around the table.

James wasn't sure why, but the friendly mood at the table had changed. He excused himself and went to search for Ashley. Gavin joined James's retreat and Calvin followed.

"It seems I cleared the table," Vanessa confirmed.

"You usually have that affect on people," JD said as he took a drink.

"So you didn't answer my question: what woman?" Vanessa asked.

JD smiled. "Did I not make myself clear the other night?"

Vanessa looked away. "JD, you've been with Tracy all of what, six months?" She looked at him. "We were together for damn near two years; this is all I get?"

JD just raised an eyebrow. "What do you want, Vanessa?"

"I want you to admit that I was right five years ago." JD looked around, avoiding the question. "Well, you don't have to answer. It seems you two made it through the events of last week. That's good," she said sincerely. "You two may have the real thing."

"And that means something to you?" JD asked sarcastically.

"Yes, JD, it does; I care about you."

That pissed JD off. "You care about me? You come in town with the sole purpose of interrupting my life with Tracy because you care about me? Do me a favor: don't give a shit about me from now on."

JD got up from the table and joined Tracy.

"Dance with me," he said, leading her to the dance floor. Ironically, Luther's "Going out of My Head" was playing. JD laughed as he put his hands around her waist.

"What's so funny?" Tracy asked.

"People have told me I have lost my mind over you, and they are right." Tracy smiled and JD pulled her closer and whispered, "Have I told you that I am totally in love with you?" He kissed the side of her temple.

"No, you haven't told me that, not totally. Did you tell Vanessa that when you were talking?"

He looked into her eyes. "In no uncertain terms."

They continued to dance quietly.

Later in the evening, Carolyn was introducing people to Gavin's campaign staff, which included David Holt. As they approached JD's table, David excused himself and went in the opposite direction. David did not want to have a confrontation with James in front of Carolyn, his candidate's future wife. As he walked away, David noticed Ashley and Tracy were on the balcony. He looked back to make sure James was still at the table, and then stepped out onto the balcony. "Hello, Ashley," David said.

Ashley froze. David walked up. "Do you think we could talk privately?" he asked while sneering at Tracy.

Ashley stepped back. "No, and why have you been leaving notes on my car?"

"Why have you been avoiding me? I just wanted a chance to talk to you. We have some unfinished business, Ashley," David replied, fuming.

"Any unfinished business you may have with Ashley goes through me," James insisted from the doorway.

Ashley walked over to James. "Let's go, James, this isn't important," she pleaded.

James looked at her. "It is important that David and I talk. You can leave now."

"James," Ashley implored, "it's not necessary."

"Ashley, go with Tracy," James ordered in a tone that let Ashley know not to question. Tracy took Ashley's arm and pulled her through the door. James looked at David. He didn't like this man the first time he met him with Karen. James walked past David over to the balcony. He wanted to find a way to stop the stupidity David had started with Ashley.

"David, I noticed Karen hasn't been to work in a week. How is she?" James inquired.

David stepped forward. He looked James up and down. Then he smirked to himself. *This man don't have shit on me; he can't handle Ashley,* he thought as he took a drink. "Karen's good," David replied.

"I'm glad to hear that. What unfinished business do you think you have with Ashley?" James asked with his back to David.

David smiled. "That would be between Ashley and me. It's not your concern."

James turned to face the man and laughed to himself. *I could choke him, throw him over the balcony and just walk away.* "I'm making it my concern, and as such I don't like it when anyone makes Ashley's life difficult. You are making her life a little trying and I'm uncomfortable with that. When I'm uncomfortable I have this nasty habit of trying to change things. This means I have to change you or, at the very least, what you're doing to her. I am a very determined man and usually succeed in things I set out to do. You are now on my list of things to handle."

David saw the irritated look on James's face. "Brooks, I don't know what Ashley told you, but you seem a little intense. Lighten up, man." He laughed nervously.

James smiled and walked up to stand next to David then looked at him. Since James was facing the ballroom, he saw Ashley watching what was taking place on the balcony. James wondered if she was nervous for him or David. "I don't like you, Holt; never did. Make no mistake about who you are dealing with here. From this moment on, you don't go near Ashley."

"Brooks, I think you got it a little backwards. Ashley still wants me." David smiled.

James smiled, but never acknowledged what he said. "If you go anywhere near her again, you're going to have to deal with me. Now son," James said as he reached up to knock something off David's lapel, "if you don't know, you better ask somebody. This is the only warning I will give." James stepped away, turned back and smiled. "Tell Karen to take her time. Make sure she's okay before she returns to work." James walked back into the ballroom. He sat at the table next to Ashley as if nothing at all had happened.

Carolyn caught David as he reentered the ballroom. "David, I saw that exchange with James. Is there anything you need to tell me?"

David smiled. "Everything is fine."

"For your sake, I hope you are right. James Brooks is not someone we can afford to have against us. He is heavily involved with the Democratic National Committee and a major contributor."

David looked Carolyn over from head to toe. He smiled, then asked, "How in the hell do these old men end up with these fine women? First Ashley with Brooks; now you with Gavin. I wonder; can Gavin handle all your needs?"

Chapter 23

The first day of a trial was usually a day of anguish for JD. However, today he was calm and ready. Compared to the last three days, the trial would be tranquil. This Labor Day weekend had been a special one for them. Martha had her annual cookout that Saturday with everyone in attendance, including Uncle Joe. JD invited everyone connected to the Gonzalez case, including Dan and Magna. Cynthia and Rosaline were there just to hang out, not working. Ashley invited James, but he was unable to attend.

The music was jamming, the food was good and the different conversations were hilarious. Inside the house a few card games were under way. Every now and then you could hear someone yell, "B-town, next." Outside, grills were at full blast, Uncle Joe at one, Calvin at another. Picnic tables were spread out across the yard. At the corner of the yard, where JD had finished off the flowerbed, was a portable dance floor with lights hanging above.

The house and yard were full of people when "Candy," by Cameo, hit the speakers, and everyone headed to the dance floor. With such a crowd on the floor, the deejay continued with one or two additional upbeat songs, until it seemed people would fall out if the tempo did not change soon. When the deejay played, "I Was Made to Love You," by Gerald Levert, JD got down on one knee and made it official. He asked Tracy to marry him before his friends and family. As he placed the diamond ring on her finger, there wasn't a dry eye in the house, including Brian's.

The next day at church, Pastor Smith made the announcement of their engagement during the morning service. He asked JD and Tracy to come to the front of the church. The congregation stood behind them and said a prayer of togetherness. Everyone at that service left with a touch of the spirit in their heart. The Sunday paper had an article about the engagement with a picture of the couple from a previous event.

Monday was spent answering phone calls about the engagement, or receiving congratulations. Tracy was overwhelmed by the number of calls and stopped answering the telephone. JD could see her nervousness and decided to take her to the Renaissance for dinner, just to get away. They were greeted by a few people who had heard about the engagement. But once they entered JD's room, the two had alone time. That was Tracy's first taste of JD's popularity. He knew a lot of people and a lot of people knew and loved him.

By Tuesday, JD was actually looking forward to the trial. He asked Tracy to come to court, to see for herself how things would turn out. When they arrived, the steps of the courthouse were crowded with reporters and cameras. Only three cameras from the local stations were allowed in the courtroom. When court was called to order, Tracy, Dan and Magna took a seat right behind JD. Brian sat at the end of the bench next to Tracy. Tracy was excited; she was about to witness Jeffrey's talents for the first time.

JD's presence in a courtroom was impressive. He introduced himself to the jury, then methodically explained the prosecution's case. He systematically explained how the evidence pointed to Juan. Then he explained the defense's case and demonstrated each loophole that existed in their theory of corruption. The jury was very attentive and JD made sure not to lose any of them with large words or complicated conclusions. Then, the defense attorney stood and rendered her version of events and how the so-called evidence may have been tainted during the change of possession. After the defense attorney finished, the judge called a 15-minute recess before calling witnesses.

The courtroom was packed with a mixture of people. Some Tracy recognized from the block party, including Mrs. Gonzalez and Victoria. They all stood as the judge left. JD stepped behind the swing gate and stood next to Tracy, Mrs. Gonzalez and Victoria. He explained his strategy for Juan once they got the convictions on this case. Then he would begin the manslaughter case against Juan as the leader of the gang involved in Lisa's death.

Magna, Dan and Calvin were still at the prosecutor's table as Brian observed the actions of some men in the back of the court. "Mr. Harrison," one of them called out. JD and Tracy turned toward the voice. Brian immediately stepped in front of JD and pulled out his revolver. Three Hispanic men pulled revolvers out, all pointing towards JD. Brian fired first, hitting one in the shoulder. JD grabbed Tracy, tucked her under him, and fell to the floor as another shot rang out. Magna pulled out her weapon and returned fire at the remaining targets as she pushed Dan and Calvin to the floor. Brian hit another assailant just as a bullet grazed his arm. Magna took the last shooter out.

At the sound of gunfire officers came from all directions with weapons drawn. Brian went to the floor where JD and Tracy landed. Seeing blood, Calvin yelled out, "Get an ambulance! Now," he exclaimed.

JD moved. "Tracy," he called out. She did not answer. He turned her over and saw blood on her face. He was feeling over her body feverishly to determine if there was any other wound. "Tracy," he yelled.

Tracy moaned and reached for her head, which felt like it had been hit with a brick. She looked up at Jeffrey, and then noticed all the confusion in the room. "Jeffrey?" she called.

"You okay?" He smiled while hugging her.

As they pulled apart, Tracy saw blood on her hands. "Jeffrey?" she questioned. He did not reply. Tracy looked in Jeffrey's eyes and saw them beginning to close. She clung to him, holding him upright. "Brian!" she screamed out.

Brian looked at Tracy and then at her hand and saw the blood. He began removing JD's jacket exposing the wound in JD's back. Tracy immediately began to place pressure on the wound to stop the bleeding. Brian yelled, "Clear the area now. JD! Shit, JD, open your eyes! JD, talk to me, man, give me something," Brian called to him. JD did not respond. The courtroom was cleared of everyone except officers and those that were injured.

"Jeffrey, please open your eyes," Tracy cried, still holding him up, applying pressure to the wound. "Please baby, please open your eyes." JD closed his hand around her waist but never opened his eyes. She smiled, a little relieved by his movement. "Okay, okay. I'll take that. It's going to be okay. I am right here." She kissed the side of his face. "Right here."

Tracy was terrified. Never in her mind did she ever imagine a scene like this. Her heart was pumping so fast she could not catch her breath. The paramedics came in and tried to assess JD's injury. They tried to move Tracy, but she was not letting go.

Brian turned to her. "Let go, Tracy." She looked up at him with tears of fear in her eyes. Brian took her hands from around JD as the paramedics pulled him back. They turned JD over and started working on him.

After assessing the injuries, the paramedics put him on the gurney, attached an oxygen mask and began moving him out. Brian helped Tracy up, and they all followed the gurney to the ambulance. TV cameras were everywhere; police taped off the area and secured the scene. Brian cleared a path for Tracy and the paramedics, while Calvin and Dan helped with other injured people from the shooting.

As they put JD in the ambulance, Brian assured Tracy, "We'll be right behind you."

"Okay," Tracy replied, and she got in.

Brian started walking towards his vehicle, while calling ahead to the hospital to set up security. When he and Magna reached the Suburban, he got in the driver's seat. Magna got in on the passenger's side. They both took a minute to breathe. She reached for his hand and held it. He squeezed her hand and said, "It'll be alright," and pulled off at full speed.

Tracy prayed and talked to Jeffrey all the way to the hospital. It was only a 10-minute drive, but it seemed like it took forever. When they finally arrived at the hospital emergency room, police officers lined the entrance. JD was not just a DA to them—he was the son of one of their own; he was family.

Gavin was already there when the ambulance pulled in. "Tracy, all the emergency information has been given to the nurse." Tracy wasn't listening. She stayed with Jeffrey as they entered the trauma room. They began to cut Jeffrey's clothes away.

Tracy stood there, stunned at the amount of blood she saw. Brian walked up beside her and she grabbed his hand, not taking her eyes off Jeffrey.

"Why would someone do this to him?" she asked. "Why?"

Brian could not speak. He always thought of JD as invincible; nothing ever took him down, and this wouldn't, it couldn't.

Calvin came in and stood next to Brian. JD was not going to leave them. They had been together since grade school. *JD would never leave them.* That was the only thought in Calvin's mind. He refused to think anything else.

The nurse walked over. "You all are going to have to leave."

Brian pulled out his badge. "Federal agent, ma'am, we're not leaving."

At Next Level Consulting office, the programming on television was interrupted with a special report regarding the shooting. Victoria was being interviewed on the accounts of the events.

"Ashley, you better see this," Monica suggested.

Ashley immediately picked up the phone and called Tracy. Magna answered the phone. "Who is this?" Ashley frantically asked.

"Agent Rivera. Who is this?"

"Ashley Harrison. Where are Tracy and JD?"

"Ashley, we are at MCV hospital. Call your mom and get here as soon as you can."

Ashley grabbed her keys and called her mom from her cell.

"I'm on my way. The hospital just called," Mama advised.

"Did they give you any information, Mama?"

"No, just that JD was in the trauma room."

"What about Tracy?"

"Just that she was there. I don't know if she was hurt."

"Mama!" Ashley cried.

"Baby, don't. Just pay attention to the road and get there safely."

People were gathering around the emergency entrance at the hospital as the news coverage went out. Cameras and reporters crowded the area trying to get information. The media frenzy had started. JD regained consciousness for a few minutes and asked for Tracy. Tracy wiped her face and bent over him, taking his hand.

"Hey," she said, gently smiling at him.

"You okay?" he asked.

"I'm fine." She smiled through tears. "It's you I'm worried about," she said. "You told me the other day you would never leave me; don't you go back on your word," she cried.

JD smiled. "Never," he replied, gazing at her. He closed his eyes; he lost consciousness again. She held on to his hand and kissed it as tears dropped from her eyes.

"We have to take him into X-ray now, Mrs. Harrison. I'll be right out to tell you my findings." Tracy stepped back as they took JD away. She watched until he was out of sight. Brian went with JD to X-ray.

Calvin hugged Tracy. "He'll be okay; this is not going to get him."

They walked out the trauma doors into chaos.

Officers began to push the media back to another area. Things were getting out of hand. The hospital administrator approached Gavin. Tracy and Calvin listened. "We are trying to get the area cleared for you. The governor's office called, and asked that we make sure the family gets through this ordeal immediately. Mr. Roberts, I understand you have federal agents on this man. One is in X-ray with him; could you point out the others?" Dan identified the others.

Martha came through the doors. "Tracy?"

"Mama, I'm so glad you are here."

Tracy reached out to her. She took her hands and tried to smile. "I talked to him for a brief moment." She inhaled and continued. "He was shot through the back, I think. They did not see an exit wound so they believe the bullet is still lodged in him. They took him to X-ray to determine where it is so they can go in and remove it."

Martha had been in Tracy's spot before, with her husband James. She was very proud of Tracy's composure, knowing that all Tracy wanted to do right now was break down and give in to the fear. But here Tracy was, very composed, explaining to her about her son's condition. This is the woman JD needs beside him; she smiled encouragingly. "He's going to be fine, baby, don't you worry."

"I'm so glad you are here." Tracy hugged her then composed herself again, but never let go of her hand.

Ashley came in. She hugged Tracy and kissed her mama.

"He's in X-ray," Tracy said to Ashley.

Ashley saw the look of fear in Tracy's eyes. That scared her to no end. She loved her brother and could not bear the though of losing him like she lost her father. Ashley looked to her mother for comfort.

Martha squeezed Ashley's hand. "It'll be okay," she said.

"Mrs. Harrison," the doctor called out. All three women looked up. He walked over to Tracy.

"This is his mother, Mrs. Harrison," Tracy explained.

Turning to Martha, the doctor continued, "The bullet entered through his back right below the left shoulder blade." Calvin, Gavin, Magna and Dan had gathered around. "The bullet is lodged against the back of the heart chamber. We have to remove it. We will need you to sign consent forms." The nurse came up and handed the papers to Tracy. Tracy gave them to Martha.

"How long will the surgery take?" Tracy asked the doctor.

"It's difficult to say, but I would estimate two hours at the most."

"Doctor, what is your prognosis?" Gavin asked.

Looking at the women, the doctor lowered his head. "It could go either way."

The administrator stopped the doctor and said something to him. The doctor looked up at the family, smiled, then disappeared behind the doors.

"I have a room ready for you all to wait in; that will be more comfortable," the administrator offered.

"I'll stay here," Tracy replied.

"I'll stay here, too," Ashley said. Martha didn't say anything. She went over to the wall and took a seat. Ashley sat beside her. Tracy couldn't sit; she walked the corridor.

Gavin, Calvin, Magna and Dan were going over the events in the courtroom. Two of the shooters were killed instantly; the other was at another hospital being treated. About an hour later, James came through one of the entrances. He went to Ashley and hugged her. "Are you okay?"

"He's in surgery," she cried as her arms went around him.

"Shh," James consoled. He brushed her hair away from her face. "JD's going to be fine. Look at me. You can't think anything else. He's going to be fine."

Ashley nodded her head and smiled. "I'm sorry. James, this is my mother, Martha Harrison." James extended his hand. "It's nice to meet you, Mrs. Harrison. I am truly sorry it's under these circumstances."

Martha smiled. "Thank you."

James walked over to Tracy. "Tracy, how are you holding up? Are you okay?"

"No," she smiled, "but I will be, just as soon as this is over." She took a seat next to Martha in an effort to draw strength from her.

Pastor Smith came in to talk to the family. "He is a strong young man who has God in his heart; he will be fine," Pastor Smith said. The pastor seemed so sure of his convictions that it actually put Tracy at ease. Tracy saw the doctor coming through the doors in his blue cap and coat. She stood up slowly; others joined her simultaneously.

"Who is Tracy?" the doctor asked.

"I am." She stepped forward. Tracy began a silent prayer as the doctor spoke.

"We were able to remove the bullet. He is resting comfortably in the recovery room. He is not completely out of danger, but his full recovery looks good. He may have some difficulty with the left arm. But with physical therapy he should make a full recovery."

Tracy breathed a sigh of relief. "Okay." She hugged the doctor. "Thank you."

"Can we see him?" Ashley asked.

"Well," the doctor answered, looking around at the many people in the waiting area, "not all at one time."

"Mama, you go first," Tracy suggested.

"Hold on," the doctor said, "my life was threatened in there. I was told by a very big man with a gun to get you in that room ASAP. So if you don't mind, would you come first and then Mrs. Harrison."

Tracy turned to Mama. "Go ahead, child, as long as I know he is alive I'm okay," Mama replied.

Tracy did not want to leave Mama there to wonder. She looked at the doctor with sad eyes. He exhaled. "Okay, both of you can come; but just for a few minutes."

The media's interest in this incident created a need for a news conference. The administrator set up a media center near the emergency entrance. Gavin handled the first press conference while JD was still in surgery. The crowd had grown to an uncontainable size. Every community in the city was represented. In one way or another, JD or his dad had helped them all. Extra officers were called in to handle the crowd. Most of the officers volunteered out of respect for JD and his father.

The little information that was available was slow in coming, and not satisfying the crowd that had gathered. They wanted to hear from a member of the family about JD's condition. Once his condition had stabilized, Ashley took over the press conference. She handled the crowd with tact and humor. Some of the crowd recognized who she was immediately. As she approached the Podium, one or two reporters called out: "How is your brother? Is he conscious?" "I will answer all of your questions in a moment. First, let me give you the latest medical information. Good evening," she started, "I'm Ashley Harrison, Jeffrey Harrison's sister."

The questions started coming. Ashley listened, but did not respond to any until the crowd had calmed down a bit. "It warms my heart to see how many of you are concerned about JD's well-being and I will be sure to relay your concerns to him. If you give me a moment I will try to answer all of your questions. JD is currently in the recovery room; he is not fully conscious; however, things are looking good for a full recovery. At this time, he is in guarded condition. Now, to answer one of your questions, JD is tough, always has been. It would take more than this to bring him down. Besides, he has to finish Mama's backyard or she will kill him." The crowd laughed a little. "Now I know you are all concerned about JD, and we thank you for that. But he lost a lot of blood. We are going to have to replenish the blood bank. If any of you could find the time and energy to donate a pint of blood, we would be eternally grateful. Now, I'm going back to my family and we will give another update as soon as we know more. Thank you." Ashley said a few words to Gavin and Dan, then left the podium.

James watched the news conference in the waiting room along with, Calvin and Magna. He was very impressed with Ashley's handling of the crowd. She calmed them, informed them and got them to donate blood, which made them feel helpful in some way. He was in awe.

Brian had been on his feet the whole time JD was in surgery. When Tracy and Martha came in to the recovery room, he went out to talk with his security staff to catch up on what had taken place in the interim. Brian had to debrief his superior on the events of the day. Everyone from the governor's office to the press had questions on the security of the courthouse. They all wanted to know how guns got into the courtroom. Brian questioned that himself. Was it possible that Juan's control reached that far? Was it an inside job? Shaking off the thought and confident that his friend was on the road to recovery, Brian could breathe and concentrate on taking steps to ensure this would never happen to JD again.

Chapter 24

Tracy sat beside JD's bed for what seemed like hours and talked about things they had discussed privately as Martha listened and waited. "I am still not agreeing to twelve babies; that's too many for me to handle while you are off in court somewhere. I think five children will be enough."

Martha laughed. "JD with children; I can't wait to see that day."

Tracy smiled. "Not just children, Mama, he's talking about twelve of them." Then she exhaled. "It's taking him so long to wake up."

"Be patient, child," Martha said, "God is doing His work."

JD squeezed Tracy's hand and she jumped up. "Jeffrey, do that again, please do that again."

Martha stood next to her son's bed just as JD opened his eyes. JD looked at his mom. "It's about time you opened your eyes." She smiled.

He turned and looked at Tracy; he squeezed her hand and firmly held it. She exhaled, with tears filling her eyes. "Hey," she cried out, smiling with relief. She pushed the button to get the doctor to the room. Tracy bent down, kissed his cheek, and whispered, "I love you." JD blinked, not able to respond.

The doctor came in. "Well, Mr. Harrison, it's good to see you awake. I am sure you are wondering where you are by now," the doctor continued while checking JD's vitals. "You are doing very well considering all you have been through today. Now, if you ladies would excuse us, I need to examine him a little closer."

Martha said, "Sure."

As Tracy started to leave, JD held on to her, and his heart rate started to increase when she tried to pull away.

"Okay, Mr. Harrison, she can stay, calm down," the doctor said.

Tracy held on to his hand tightly. "I'm not going anywhere," she said.

The doctor finished his examination and told Tracy things looked good. "He is going to be in and out for the rest of the night. But by mid-morning he will be more aware of his surroundings. We will move him into a room then."

"Doctor, thank you for everything," Tracy said.

He smiled and said, "You are very welcome. I am a fan of Mr. Harrison's. I like what he is trying to do with the city. He's a good man."

"Yes, he is."

"You get some rest now," the doctor said as he left the room.

Tracy took a moment to be alone with Jeffrey. "You scared me."

He whispered something, but she didn't hear him. She put her head down to his mouth.

"Twelve," he whispered, "football team."

She smiled, kissed his cheek. "Five—you have to settle for a basketball team." He smiled and went back to sleep.

Tracy said a small prayer and left the room. Ashley jumped right up. "Can I go in now?"

"Yeah," Tracy replied with a smile. "The doctor said he will be in and out for the rest of the night. He's fallen back to sleep, but he will wake up again soon." Ashley went into the room.

"Tracy, is there anything I can do for you?" James asked.

"I have a pretty bad headache. Some Tylenol would help."

"Well, this is a hospital; that should be easy," he smiled.

Tracy walked over to Brian, put her arms around his waist and laid her head against his chest. Brian hugged her and laid his chin on the top of her head. "Thank you for being there for him," she said.

"Always," Brian replied. "That's a promise."

He rubbed the back of her head. "There you go patting my head like I'm a dog again." They both laughed.

Gavin asked Tracy if she would do the next press conference since Ashley was in with JD.

"I'll try," Tracy agreed, "but I don't know how effective I would be."

"The doctor will be there to handle any medical questions. Any other questions you can't answer you can refer to me."

Victoria called out to Tracy as they entered the press area. "Tracy, how is JD?"

Tracy smiled at Victoria and stepped up to the microphone. There was a crowd out there and it took her a moment to compose herself. Tracy did not like crowds. She exhaled, and then began.

"Good evening; I'm sorry, morning," Tracy started, "my name is Tracy Washington. I am Jeffrey's fiancée. Jeffrey has regained consciousness and we did get a chance to speak with him. He is doing remarkably well, thanks to Dr. Canter and the staff here at MCV. He will remain in intensive care tonight, just as a precaution. Then they will move him to another room tomorrow, if all goes well tonight."

"Will Mr. Harrison continue on this case now?" a reporter yelled out.

Tracy looked down, then back up at the reporter with anger in her eyes. "Knowing Jeffrey like I do, I know this only pissed him off." She turned to Gavin and asked, "Can I say that?" The crowd laughed. Gavin nodded his head and smiled.

Tracy turned back. "Jeffrey gave his word to the Blackwell community that he would see this case to the very end. Those of you out there who know Jeffrey knows he is a man of his word. I am sure that the district attorney's office and the attorney general's office will continue in their efforts to assist Jeffrey and his staff with bringing this case to a successful conclusion."

Gavin smiled internally. *She is giving everyone their due.*

A number of reporters were yelling her name and a variety of questions at her. "Victoria," Tracy called.

"Tracy, that's a lot of blood on your blouse; are you okay?"

Tracy looked down. She hadn't changed clothes. It all began to hit her. As tears began to fall, she turned to Gavin. He could see she could not continue. Tracy looked at Victoria. "I'm fine, thank you," then stepped away from the podium. Gavin took over the press conference.

That scene was broadcast on every TV station across the state. The citizens' love affair with JD and Tracy began that moment.

Al saw the news report and was very proud of his little sister but was afraid this news would reach other people who would cause her more heartache. He asked to make a phone call.

Carolyn saw it, and knew any chance of breaking them up just ended. But she also saw a chance for Gavin to increase his number of supporters if he announced while the news was good for the DA's office.

Juan and his people saw the report and knew they had a more dangerous opponent in JD Harrison, now. They had to find a way to stop this man.

Chapter 25

A week later, JD was released from the hospital. Brian placed a 24-hour security detail on the house. One of the extra bedrooms was set up for Brian. For the first week, the house seemed to stay crowded all the time. Gavin came by to tell JD he was going to announce his bid for the governor's office and his engagement to Carolyn. Once JD returned to the office, he would take over as the DA. This was fine with Tracy. It meant he would be safe in the office, handling the administrative and advising part of the job. JD agreed, with a condition, that he conclude the Cortez case and Gavin not announce until he returned to the office. Gavin agreed, which pissed Carolyn off. Polls showed the DA's office had an 85 percent approval rating. Waiting could change that, but Gavin stuck to his agreement with JD.

Between Tracy, Ashley, Martha and Mrs. Langston, JD did not want for anything.

"If he wasn't spoiled as hell before, he sure is now," Ashley said one day when she was bringing a tray downstairs from JD's room.

Martha was in the kitchen cooking dinner. "Leave your brother alone," she said, "he's been through a terrible ordeal."

"I know that," Ashley replied, "but the ordeal is over now and he is still acting like he's dying."

"I see you are still over here every day catering to him."

"Well, that's 'cause I love his big head," Ashley said. Her cell rang. Recognizing the number, she responded, "Hey," with a smile.

"How's JD?" James asked.

"He's doing fine; upstairs eating up all the attention he's getting."

"Any way I could get some of your attention?" James asked.

"That could be arranged," she answered, smiling. "Where are you?"

"Heading to your place."

"I'll meet you there," she said, then hung up the phone. Martha stopped cooking and was watching her daughter. Ashley looked up. "What?"

"That's a very distinguished gentleman you are seeing."

Ashley blushed. "Yes, he is."

"Do you know what you are doing?"

Ashley sat on the stool. She exhaled. "I don't know, Mama, but I'm in too deep, now, to care."

"You are never in that deep. What are you expecting from this relationship, Ashley?"

"I don't expect anything, Mama."

"Why, is he married?"

"No, he's divorced."

"Does he have a family?"

Nodding, Ashley answered, "A son, James Jr."

"Ashley, you are a young woman, he's an older man. Are you sure you two want the same thing?"

"I don't know, Mama, we haven't really talked about it."

"Why not?"

"I don't want to rock the boat, you know what I mean?" Ashley replied.

Martha sat down beside her daughter. "I saw his concern for you at the hospital, Ashley. Don't sell yourself short here. I don't think asking an important question is considered rocking the boat. You might be surprised by the answer." Tracy walked down the steps hearing part of the conversation. She sat beside Ashley and waited.

"Okay, go ahead; what do you have to say?" Ashley asked Tracy.

Smiling, and shoving Ashley with her shoulder, Tracy answered, "I thought you would never ask. I think despite himself, James has fallen in love with you. He is probably gun shy from the first marriage, which did not go well. But I think you two can work through that." They sat there for a moment in silence. "Can James really, you know, do the do?" Tracy asked grinning at Ashley.

"Yes, he really can," Ashley answered, laughing at the question.

"I was just wondering. I mean James is a little older than us; can he hang all night?"

"Oh, honey, age doesn't matter with sex," Martha bragged. "My James was still going strong and I do mean strong until the day he died."

"Mama!" Ashley squealed, "You and daddy? Oh, that is so nasty."

"What's so nasty about it? How do you think you got here?"

The doorbell rang. "Saved by the bell." Tracy laughed as she went to the door.

Pastor Smith came by to visit with JD. The two discussed his future with Tracy. Pastor Smith suggested JD take this time to talk with Tracy about her family. It would be beneficial to know more about her family, but could be detrimental if he did not. If he had any intention of going into politics, her background would be looked into. Better to do it now than later.

That night as they lay in bed talking, JD asked Tracy about her family. He could feel her body tense at the question as she became apprehensive and edgy. "Tell me about your family," he said.

"What do you want to know about them?" Tracy asked.

"Anything you want to tell me," he replied. She hesitated, so he pulled her closer. "Whatever you tell me would not change my feelings for you. I know the person you are, now, and I love everything about that person." He kissed her forehead. "I just want to know how you became Tracy." JD rubbed her temple as her head rested against his chest.

Tracy exhaled. "I have a mother who doesn't like me very much; a sister who I believe loves me; a brother who's in prison, which you know about; and a sister who died when I was very young."

"What about your dad?"

She sat up. "Why are you asking me all these questions about my family?"

He pulled her back down to him, waited until she settled down, then said, "Because I love you and I need to know you trust me enough to tell me about your family. Besides, I need to know about my 12 children's grandmother and aunt, don't you think?" he said.

She smiled. "Five children."

"Okay, nine, a baseball team; now you can't argue with that," he said as he kissed her.

"Okay, I'll have five, you have number six, and then I'll have seven, eight and nine."

"Hmm, I will tentatively agree to that, but when the time comes for me to have number six I may need to renegotiate." Tracy laughed. JD waited.

"My dad used to drink a lot. When he did he always got loud and would argue with my mom. One day, something happened with my sister Joan, and she died. That's when Turk left and Valerie was sent to live with my aunt, leaving me, my mom and my dad, whenever he came home."

JD held her a little closer; he had questions, but did not want her to stop talking so he remained silent and listened.

"My dad came home angry one day." She shifted her weight as if preparing for a major blow. "He was arguing with my mom. His voice was so loud, almost booming. He and my mom were still yelling when he came into the room and grabbed me." JD could feel Tracy's body trembling as if she was reliving the moment. He rubbed her head as she continued. "My mom was fighting him, saying don't do this again. She hit him from behind, he hit her back and she fell backwards out of the room. He went to her. She sat up and yelled, 'Close the door, Tracy, and lock it!' I didn't know what was going on, so I ran to my mom. My dad grabbed me, yelled and threw me back into the room." Tracy hesitated as tears ran down her face. JD's heart was breaking from her hurt. "The next thing I remember was hearing Turk and another man's voice in the other room. Turk came in the room and took me over to the neighbor's apartment. When I came back home, my mom was different. She wouldn't talk to me and barely looked at me. The older I got the worse home became. She would always yell at me for no particular reason. She let me know that I ruined her life because my dad went away. It was like that until the day I left for college."

They lay there in silence for a moment. Her tears were dropping against his chest. He knew it was a difficult thing for her. "How old were you when this happened?" he asked in a comforting voice.

"Hmm, about eight, I guess."

"Do you all have the same father?"

"No," she replied.

"Do you remember who the man was with Turk?" She shook her head no. "Have you spoken to your mom or sister since you left home?" She shook her head again, no. "You were so young," JD said, "who raised you?"

She exhaled again. "Books, mostly. I would go to the library at school and take out books; sometimes 10 at a time. After dinner, I would go in my room and just read. When I was 10, we moved into this house Turk had found. Our next door neighbor would look out for me whenever my mom wasn't home, which was a lot. But I mostly stayed to myself."

JD understood things with her a little better now. Her reaction to Turk was so strong because he was her protector, the only one who showed her any love; actually, Turk showed her more love than she even realized. Carolyn talked about Tracy not having any social grace or guidance. Now he knew why. No one was around to teach her the proper decorum in certain situations. JD made a decision not to ask her about this again. When she was ready to tell him more he would listen, but not until she was ready. He kissed her, laid back and pulled her to him.

"Thank you for telling me."

Tracy lay there thinking about those days as JD's breathing became shallow. He had fallen asleep. She eventually fell asleep thinking it might be time to contact her mother.

The next week, JD went back into the office, only working half days. The first thing on the agenda was rescheduling a court date for Juan Cortez. JD wanted to convict him on manslaughter charges along with his friends, but for now he had to settle for the tax evasion case. He asked Mrs. Langston if she would be his private secretary after the case was done and he became DA. She accepted. He asked her to keep their conversation confidential until Gavin made his announcement at the news conference. She agreed. JD then spoke with Calvin about taking over his position as lead prosecutor; he accepted. JD had one more thing on his agenda before he left for the day.

"Brian," JD said into the phone, "will you be at the house tonight?"

"Yeah, I was planning on staying over. Why, what's up?" he asked.

"I need a favor. Could you meet me at Maxi's in about 30 minutes?"

"Alright, man. You okay?"

"Yeah, I'm straight."

JD walked into Maxi's. It was as if he had been gone for years and people were seeing him again for the first time. Everyone in the place came up to speak and shake his hand. They each wanted him to know they were glad he was doing well since the shooting. A few of the "street guys" offered to retaliate. "You know, we can take out the whole gang and be done with it," one offered. JD thanked them and said, "No, man, I got this one." Maxine actually came out of her office, which she rarely did. She looked him up and down, making sure there was no permanent damage on her childhood friend. JD assured Maxine he was fine, and when she asked about Tracy, he smiled and told her she would be invited to the wedding.

Brian arrived a few minutes later as JD requested. They sat in a booth and JD asked him to locate Tracy's family. He wanted to know if the door might be open for Tracy to reconnect with her family.

"How soon do you want it?"

"Yesterday," JD replied.

"Do I have time for a drink?" Brian asked.

A hand hit him on the head. "It's too early in the day to be drinking," Ashley said. She leaned over and kissed JD on the cheek, then sat beside him.

"Oh, look at this, he gets kisses and I get hits; oh, that's going to stop." Brian smirked.

"Thanks, Brian," JD said as Brian got up to leave.

"I'll be in touch," Brian replied.

"See you, Brian," Ashley said.

Ashley put her hand through JD's arm and put her head on his shoulder. "I need some advice."

JD looked at her; he knew this had to do with James before Ashley started. JD still was not sure about him. After all, it was not that long ago James was smiling at Tracy. "What's up?" JD asked.

Ashley hesitated. "About James." She put her elbow on the table, laid her head in her hand, then looked up at JD. "We are not officially together, together, but I'm in love with him. I don't know how he feels about me."

JD didn't say anything; he listened. It wasn't often these days that Ashley would come to him about her male friends. Before she went away to college, Ashley would share everything about boys with JD. At times it was too much for him to handle. Her talk about sex was not a conversation he looked forward to. But here she was looking to him for advice. JD had missed that.

Ashley continued, "Mama said I should ask where things are going, but I have this feeling if I ask that question I may not like the answer."
JD didn't know the story with James and Ashley, but Tracy mentioned the two together quite often. James appeared to be a very reserved man, not one to show emotions openly. He was a hard man to read, but JD did not take him for a player, by any means. He seemed to be the type to let only a few select people in to his inner circle. He wasn't sure if Ashley was one of the chosen. JD kept the thought. "You don't think he feels the same way about you?"

She hunched her shoulders, which made JD smile. That was her trademark when she was confused. "I don't know. Sometimes he makes me feel as if I am the only person in the world. But sometimes it seems as though he keeps a certain part of him shielded from me."

JD put his arms around her. "Why don't you give it some time? It hasn't been that long for you two. Be patient. If he is still around after a couple of months and you are still wondering, then," he hesitated, "you might want to let him go."

Ashley looked up at him with sad eyes; he knew that wasn't what she wanted to hear. JD kissed her forehead. "Sometimes feelings are not as easy for men to express as for women, especially if he's been burnt before. Don't rush him; just enjoy the time you two are together." In an attempt to make her feel better, JD said, "I haven't taken you shopping in a while. Let's take a ride."

Ashley jumped up. "You paying?"

JD smiled. "Sure, why not."

"Do you have your credit cards on you?"

JD raised an eyebrow as they were walking out the door. "Cards?"

Juan Cortez was still being held without bond. He got word that a new trial date had been set and Harrison was still directly handling his case. "What in the hell is it going to take to get this bitch off my back?" Juan asked his attorney.

"JD Harrison is not an easy man to shake. The simple fact is he does not ask for a trial date until he knows for certain that he has a conviction," she replied.

"You better find a way for this to go away or I will find a way for Harrison to go away."

"I'm not sure," she said, "but I believe you tried that and it did not work. But either way I don't want to know about it."

"Get to Hector," Juan ordered. "Tell him to go to the reserve plan; he will know what to do."

"I'm not going to tell him that," she said. "Anything you need Hector to know put it in writing, seal it and I will give him the note. In the meantime, I will file a motion to have Harrison removed from the case. It will not be granted, but at least it may give us grounds for appeal if you are convicted. I will strongly recommend that you make no further attempts to delay this trial by physical harm to Harrison."

Chapter 26

The news conference went just as Carolyn had planned. Making the two announcements simultaneously ensured JD being there with Gavin as he announced his candidacy for governor. The public would think JD was a supporter, whether he was or not. "Perception is the key," Carolyn said to Gavin.

The room was packed with dignitaries from the Democratic Party and all of Gavin's supporters. News reporters and television crews were there, including Victoria. All but a few from the DA's office were present and accounted for. There was a certain air of excitement in the room. "Senator Roth." JD extended his hand.

"JD," the senator greeted him as he shook his hand, "it's good to see you, my boy. How have you been?"

"I'm doing fine, sir, thank you for asking."

"Mrs. Harrison, it is wonderful to see you today." Senator Roth smiled.

"Thank you, Senator, it has been a while."

"Good morning, Tracy," the senator greeted.

"Good morning," she replied, surprised he remembered her name. "It's nice to see you again."

"It's good to see you, too. I don't think you are going to have any issues with Carolyn today," he said. "She is in her element here; in total control."

"Everyone is scared to death of her?" JD asked.

"You know it."

"Yes, that's when she works the best," JD replied.

The senator looked at JD and said, "That should be you up there, son."

JD looked at him with a questioning glance, as did Tracy. "Oh, I don't mean with Carolyn," the senator explained. "You should be the one making this announcement today."

"That's good of you to say, Senator, but I have enough on my plate right now," JD smiled, squeezing Tracy's hand.

"Well, whenever you are ready, son, you'll have my backing all the way," the senator said, patting JD on the back.

Carolyn walked up. "Good morning, one and all," she said. "Daddy, we are going to need you on stage; you too, JD."

Brian and JD's security detail walked up. "Mr. Harrison, this way please," one man said.

JD kissed Tracy on the forehead. "I'll see you when this is over."

Calvin, Jackie, Mrs. Langston, Magna and Dan came over as JD, Carolyn and the senator were leaving. Tracy hugged Calvin and Carolyn spotted the ring. She stopped walking and looked at JD with a frown. "So you decided to ruin your future anyway?" Carolyn said angrily.

JD looked at her. "What are you talking about, Carolyn?"

"That ring on Tracy's finger."

The senator grabbed Carolyn's upper arm. "You are about to announce your engagement to the next governor of this state," he said bitterly. "Let it go."

She pulled her arm away, put on a smile and stepped onto the stage. They took their seats and the news conference began.

After all the formal introductions had been made, Gavin made the announcement he was stepping down as district attorney. "The good news is that I will be leaving you in very capable hands. J.D. Harrison—" He could not finish the statement. The crowd began to clap and cheer as if they had just won the lottery. Gavin stepped back and looked at JD. JD held his head down and smiled; it was a humbling experience for him.

Mrs. Harrison said to Tracy, "His dad would be so proud of him." She stood and started clapping with the crowd. Everyone else that was supposed to remain neutral stood as well and began to clap. Gavin hushed the crowd.

After everyone settled back down, Gavin looked over at JD. "You are not planning on running for governor, are you?" The crowed cheered and laughed at the same time. JD smiled.

Gavin continued. "As I was saying, JD Harrison will be assuming the position of district attorney for the remaining two years of my term. It is the good people of the district attorney's office, such as JD, who afforded me the opportunity to step away from my position. I would like to serve the good citizens of the great Commonwealth of Virginia at a higher level. With your help and your blessing, I humbly submit my name as a candidate for the Democratic nomination for governor of the Commonwealth of Virginia."

The crowd applauded and cheered the announcement. The applause went on for a few minutes non-stop. Cameras started flashing. Television cameras moved in for a close-up.

Toward the end of his speech, Gavin announced his engagement to Carolyn Roth. She stood and joined him at the podium. Carolyn was raised for this role. She had all the right qualities a governor would need. She finally got what she always wanted—the spotlight. But it came with a price. Behind all the smiles and hand shaking, Carolyn Roth was fuming. And all her wrath was aimed toward Tracy. As she stood there at the podium kissing Gavin and waving her hand, she vowed to find a way to make Tracy Washington pay for taking away her full dream: public life, the mansion and JD Harrison.

Back at the office the new regime was settling in. JD held a staff meeting with all the employees. He wanted to let them know what he was expecting and what he planned to give in return. The staff was very receptive. They already knew JD, liked and respected him. No one was uncomfortable working for him. One or two would have to change their way of doing certain things. JD did things by the book. No cases would be assigned under-the-table. Most of JD's time was spent going over the managerial responsibilities that he had not been involved with previously. Getting acquainted with his new boss was easy; it was the current attorney general. JD had worked on several cases with him. The transition was smooth.

JD surrounded himself with good people who approached the law with the same enthusiasm as he. At the beginning he was going to have to pull some long hours to get caught up on the administrative end. After that he was sure things would slow down. Ironically, on his first day in the position, JD received a petition to appear in court before Judge Mathews. The defense was asking the judge to remove JD from the Cortez case to prevent the attempt at malicious prosecution. JD laughed at the petition, but called Calvin in for a strategy session just to make sure all bases were covered.

Tracy went back to the office after the news conference and jumped into the project she had left behind. It felt good to have things back to normal, at least for the moment. "Hey," Ashley said grinning, "I saw the news conference—looks like it went well. Carolyn seems to have everything on point with Gavin.

Did they set a date for the wedding?" Ashley looked at Tracy then smiled. "Have you set a date?"

Tracy smiled. "Not that I'm aware of. And as for me, no, not yet."

"I'm going to miss you so much, Tracy. You have been there for me through so much stuff," Ashley whined.

"Am I going somewhere?"

Ashley laughed. "No, but we will not be living together anymore. Do you realize we have lived together for more than six years?"

"I know this is a happy occasion, but it's sad, too," Tracy said. "You gave me the family I never had. Now we are really going to be sisters; isn't that something." They both laughed.

"I asked JD about a date and he said it's up to you," Ashley said. "So when is this going to happen?

"I don't know; we haven't talked about it," Tracy said.

"Okay, where are you going to live? You can't stay in JD's place, it's too small. Let's go house hunting," Ashley said eagerly. "We get to plan a wedding and shop for that, too."

"Wedding?. Ouch." The thought scared Tracy. "I hadn't thought about that."

"What the hell do you mean? That's the best part," Ashley asked, surprised.

"No, I can do without the wedding. Just let me have your brother for the rest of my life."

"One comes with the other." Ashley smiled. "With JD's career you have to have a wedding. There's no getting around that."

Tracy stretched out across her desk. "Do we have to?" she cried.

"Yes," Ashley replied.

Tracy sighed. "You are going to be there with me, right?"

"All the way."

"Maid of Honor?"

"With pleasure." Ashley smiled. They were silent for a moment. "Are you going to let Cynthia do the wedding?"

"I don't know about that, Ashley. How do I trust Cynthia to handle the most important day of my life?"

"It's a job; and Cynthia would not do anything to hurt her business. You know that, Tracy. This wedding is going to be a big event, one of the biggest in this city. She knows that."

"Ashley, even if I was willing to give Cynthia a chance, I don't think Jeffrey will."

"Tracy, Jeffrey will do anything you ask him to. Just think about it," Ashley replied.

"Okay."

Ashley hesitated. "Do you think James and I will ever make it to this point?"

Tracy smiled. "How are things going with you two?"

Ashley smiled. "Girl, I lie to you not, the man rocked me from one end of his bed to the other."

Tracy laughed. "That's good, but what else? Have you two talked?"

Ashley closed her eyes. "Yes, we talk all the time. But not the way you mean. I don't want to push him."

Tracy looked at her. "Are you okay with that?"

"For the moment," Ashley replied. They were quiet for a minute. "David's been quiet since the function. No notes or anything."

"Did James ever tell you what he said to him?"

"No, and I did not ask. And you would not have asked either, if you had seen the look on James's face when he came back into the room."

James was in his office when Karen Holt knocked on the door. "Do you have a moment, James?" Karen asked.

"Sure, have a seat," James replied. He sat back in his chair and placed his pen on the desk. He was wondering when Karen was going to stop avoiding him. She returned to work the week JD was in the hospital. During that time, James's attention was on Ashley. With all that was happening with JD, most of his free time was spent with her. He really did not have a chance to talk with Karen about David. James was sure David had put his own spin on what was happening. He was just as sure that whatever David told Karen, she believed. James had spent a lot of time with Ashley during the weeks following the confrontation with David. He did not trust David and did not want Ashley to be alone or vulnerable to him. He had seen David in action at several DNC functions. David knew how to put on a good front.

"James, we have not really had a chance to talk lately. I felt it was important that you and I talked before things went any further," Karen started.

Karen was a class act. James respected her and her abilities. He did not understand for the life of him why she was with David. "What is it you feel we need to discuss?" he asked.

"David tells me you have concerns about his past relationship with your friend Ashley."

James acknowledged, "Yes, that's true." Karen looked a little shocked, so James continued: "Did he tell you what those concerns were?"

"James, I know about the supposed attempted rape. I was there. If things had happened the way Ashley claimed, David would have been charged. There were no charges filed."

James knew women like Karen well enough to know they will protect and defend their man no matter how much evidence you put in front of them. "Karen, did David tell you what's happened recently?"

"Yes, he told me you insinuated my position here could be in jeopardy because of his past with your girlfriend," Karen exclaimed.

James smiled in disbelief. "And you believed him?"

"He's my husband; of course I believed him."

James stood up, put his hands in his pocket and looked directly at her. He had to take a minute. If he spoke too soon the anger he was feeling would be exposed. That would not be good. James never understood why some women were actually blinded by love.

"Karen," he said calmly, "you are a valued part of this administration. I have no intention, nor did I ever insinuate any intentions, of removing you. I have never and never will make business decisions based on personal issues. With that said, I believe you are in a difficult position. As long as I am commissioner, you are here with me."

Karen was speechless. She was ready for a fight with James. But he turned the tables on her.

"You must have said something, James. David would have no reason to lie."

James did not want to get into personal issues with Karen. Rather than telling her what actually happened, he chose to refer her to David. "Apparently he did have a reason. It's up to you to determine what that reason may be. Was there anything further we need to discuss?" James asked, in a tone that let Karen know the discussion was over.

Karen stood. "No, nothing else." She left the room.

James sat back down. "Oh, Mr. Holt, I did warn you," he said to himself. Too pissed to continue working, James called Ashley. "I really need to see you tonight."

"JD! Man, I'm glad I caught you," Brian said as he stepped into JD's new office. "I have some feedback on Tracy's family. You better sit down, JD." Brian exhaled. "I know what I found out is not all that there is, but I can tell you Tracy did not have a charmed life. And I have to agree with Al, she needs to stay away from her family."

"Tracy told me some of the story. What did you find?"

"Tracy's father had a thing for little girls. He had his way with the oldest sister—Valerie is her name—and the other sister, Joan. Word has it, Joan fought back, and ended up dead. The death report indicates she died during a rape; assailant unknown. Day moved out and took to the street life. The oldest girl was sent to live with an aunt. Tracy was young and his actual daughter, so she stayed with the mother. Rumors have it the father disappeared after a fight with Day, and never returned. After that, it was the mother and the little girl. The neighbors in their old neighborhood said that the daughter was left alone in the apartment regularly. The family eventually moved into a house that Day purchased in a different neighborhood, which is where the mother still resides. That neighbor said that the girl spent most of her time in the house or at school. Every now and then she would go to church with her family. When Tracy went away to school, she never came back. The mother is money hungry. Day was paying her a thousand a week, back in the day, to keep Tracy. Can you imagine that shit, man? Someone had to pay you to take care of your own child."

JD got up while Brian was talking. He was disappointed with the information he was getting. This was something he wanted for Tracy. JD wanted to give her a family. His idea of trying to reunite Tracy with her own family was not promising.

"JD, Lena Washington will do anything to get to Tracy's money."

"Damn, I was hoping Tracy would have a chance at reconnecting with her family." He hesitated. "Your people will keep a lid on this information?"

"Jones and I handled this one. It won't go anywhere."

"Thanks, B."

"You ready to roll?"

"Yeah, I need to hold Tracy for a while," JD replied.

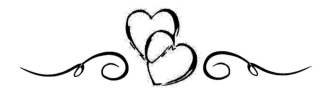

Chapter 27

That weekend began with a beautiful fall Saturday and JD was home alone. Physically, he wasn't able to resume certain activities, such as his Saturday pick-up games with Calvin and the guys. Tracy and Ashley were holding their regular tutoring sessions at the local high school. Then they were off to meet Cynthia and Rosaline.

While putting away papers from his briefcase, JD ran across the written report Brian had given him on Tracy's family. He wasn't ready to give up on Tracy and her family; although her mother might not be worth reconnecting with, her sister and extended family might be. JD overheard Tracy talking to Ashley about the wedding. She was concerned about having no one there to give her away. The only person right for the part was Turk, and that wasn't happening. JD thought she may have an uncle or male cousin who was not under the mother's influence.

JD opened the file, and then searched through the papers. There was an address for the mother and sister in Norfolk, which was less than a two-hour drive away. *Why not?* JD thought. He looked at his watch, then put the file away. When he grabbed his car keys, the telephone rang. "JD, this is James Brooks."

A little puzzled, JD asked, "Yeah, Brooks, what can I do for you?"

"I was wondering if you had some time today. There's something I need to discuss with you."

JD thought for a moment. He assumed Brooks wanted to talk about Ashley. JD was not sure if he was ready to have that conversation, calmly. But knew it would mean a lot to Ashley. "Where are you?" JD asked.

"I'm at the office."

"I was about to take a short trip; you are welcome to ride along."

"Yeah, I can do that. Should I come to you?"

"I'll drop by and pick you up in about 10 minutes."

"I'll meet you downstairs," James replied.

JD looked at the telephone as he hung up. He had to find a way to stop thinking of James as the enemy. Ashley liked the guy; there had to be something good about him. To be honest, the only reason he did not care for Brooks was that he tried to get with Tracy. Other than that, Brooks appeared to be a decent man.

James was standing outside the building when JD pulled up. James got in. "Nice ride." James looked around the BMW. JD pulled off. "What is this, a V-6 engine?"

JD shook his head. "V-8. All the horsepower a man needs." He beamed.

James smiled. "It's nice, man. But you do know, you will have to give this up when you run for office."

JD frowned. "Give up my ride, I'll be damned. Why would I do that?"

James looked out the window as JD hit Interstate 64 toward Norfolk. "You will have to go American, to satisfy the public."

JD laughed. "If need be I'll buy a Suburban like Brian's, but I'll keep my Beamer." JD laughed, then continued, "But, it's a moot point. I have no plans on running for any office."

James looked at him and laughed. "Everything you do says political-office bound. The DNC has been keeping an eye on you. You are an impressive young man, with a big future. If you don't at least consider it," James shook his head, "well, that will be an injustice to the citizens of the Commonwealth."

JD thought about it for a minute. "I believe that was a compliment."

James smiled. "You deal with the issues that everyday people need addressed: gang violence; making neighborhoods safe; the education system; making sure every child has access to quality education; the job market; setting up job fairs and adult retraining centers; family unity with special projects to get absent fathers connected with their children. If those aren't political issues, I don't know what is. Everything you do touches lives at the very core. You are what this state needs. Gavin is good people, but he is about the same old you-scratch-my-back-I-scratch-yours politics. People are craving something different. They need someone of substance; that's you." James laughed. "You may not be ready to acknowledge it, but that's where you are going."

JD shook his head. "I don't see it, for the precise reason you just said. I'm in those organizations you mentioned because I like working with people; I don't mix well with politicians. From what I see, most of them are not addressing the needs of their constituents, just their own desires." JD laughed. "Man, I can see me in the middle of a General Assembly session going off because of the senselessness."

James laughed. "Been there. Actually, on one occasion I saved them the trouble and put myself out of the chamber." They both laughed.

This is a good thing, JD thought. *Getting to know the man my little sister is in love with isn't so bad,* he said to himself. "So is this what you needed to talk with me about?"

James knew the mood would change now. "No, I need to talk to you about Ashley."

"What about her?"

"You realize we were having a pretty decent conversation there for a minute." James smirked.

"Is that about to change?"

"That will be up to you. I just need to say my piece."

"Alright, let's hear it."

"I'm sure you are aware I've been seeing your sister."

JD nodded his head acknowledging the fact. "Yeah."

"I usually try to keep a certain distance, but with Ashley, I've gotten more attached than I planned to." James looked out of the window. "Actually, I didn't plan it; it just happened. But before things progress any further, I need to know where you stand on it."

JD thought for a minute. "Brooks, when I first met you, I was under the impression you were interested in Tracy. Was I wrong?"

James shook his head. "No, you were right. Who wouldn't be? She is a very intelligent woman, with a mind that very few men can appreciate, sexy as hell and my guess was untouched until you." JD smiled. James laughed. "That's what I thought."

"But, since you can't have Tracy, you turn to Ashley. I have an issue with that."

James looked at JD. "I can understand that. Actually, Ashley caught me off guard and that is not something that happens to me often. I would have never approached a woman like Ashley. I always considered myself a conservative man. A free-spirited woman like Ashley would not have fit into my world, or so I thought." He smiled. "Apparently I was wrong. As I got to know her I found Ashley's outward persona was bogus. She is a very intelligent, confident woman who challenges me at every turn. And her mouth, I don't quite know what to expect from her sometimes." JD laughed, for he knew exactly what James meant.

"Some of the things she does drive me crazy, but then," James hesitated, "she would smile and I would feel it in my core."

JD pulled onto the exit for Norfolk. "Are you in love with Ashley?"

"No," James said quickly, "I'm not ready to concede that; no, no."

JD noticed James became uncomfortable. "James, Ashley hurts easily and loves hard. I don't want to see my sister hurt."

James exhaled. "It is not my intention hurt Ashley, but I've been through some things in my life that I have no intention of going through again. I don't know where we are going, but I will promise you this. I will take my time. Wherever it goes, it goes." James began looking around. "Where are we going?"

JD looked at the address on the paper. "We're here."

"Where?" James asked.

JD turned the engine off. "I believe this is where Tracy's mother lives."

James looked at the house. "I thought Tracy did not get along with her mother."

"She doesn't," JD said, "but I plan to marry Tracy. I have to do all I can to try to bridge that gap for Tracy and our future."

James warned, "You may be better off not doing this. Mothers-in-law can be a bitch."

JD laughed. "Coming from a man with experience."

Brooks laughed. "Unfortunately, yes."

JD stopped for a moment and looked around. "Well, no need putting this off. Are you coming?" James unbuckled his seat belt. "You might need some backup."

JD looked at the house Tracy grew up in. He smiled at the thought of her sitting on the front porch reading. From the outside the small, three-bedroom rancher seemed cozy. JD knocked on the door. He was having second thoughts, but he had come too far not to follow through.

JD knew who she was the moment the door opened. Lena Washington was an attractive woman who did not look her age. She had light brown eyes, just like Tracy's. Her hair was up in a ponytail, just like Tracy's had been when he first met her. She was shapely, maybe a size 12, and very stylish.

"Ms. Washington, my name is Jeffrey Harrison. This is James Brooks."

She looked from JD to Brooks. "Please come in." She opened the door wider.

As they entered the living room, JD looked around. He noticed pictures of children, a young woman and man—could be husband, wife—, and pictures of Lena; none of Tracy or Al. "Please have a seat," she said. "What can I do for you?"

James and JD sat down. JD began, "As I was saying, my name is JD Harrison."

"I know who you are, Mr. Harrison; I assume you are here about my daughter. What I don't know is why," Lena stated.

"Ms. Washington, Tracy and I are getting married." JD smiled. "We are planning the wedding. I thought it would be a good time to get to know her family."

Lena smiled. "Does Tracy know you are here?" she asked with a touch of humor.

JD smiled. "No, she doesn't, and I am not sure how she is going to react when I tell her."

"Mr. Harrison, I haven't talked with my daughter in years. Why would I change that now?"

"Because she is your daughter. She is about to go through a major change in her life. Wouldn't you want to be a part of that?"

Lena looked at James, then back to JD. "The question is, does she?"

JD smiled. "I don't know the answer to that, but I would like to explore the possibility of you two bridging this gap. Would you be open to that?"

Lena thought about it for a moment. "What would be in it for me?"

JD frowned. Lena saw his enthusiasm change. "I'm not sure what you mean," JD replied.

"My life is fine just the way it is. How would I benefit from connecting with a daughter who apparently does not want to connect with me?"

James was looking around observing their surroundings. Something about Lena reminded him of his ex-wife. Unfortunately, James was not a man to play word games. He generally went straight to the point. James sat forward. "Were you speaking of monetary benefits or moral benefits, Ms. Washington?" he asked, indifferently.

Lena smiled. "Why not examine both. Judging by her friends, Tracy seems to be doing well."

JD stood up. *Brian was right, this woman is about money.* "Tracy is doing well, but that had nothing to do with either of us."

James stood. "Just out of curiosity, what monetary amount would make it worth your while?"

Lena stood. "I would have to get back with you on that."

JD hung his head. "Ms. Washington, Tracy is a wonderful person. I believe you had a hand at her turning out that way. As much as I want to make this connection for Tracy, there is no way in hell I'm going to pay you to talk to your daughter." The frown on JD's face told James he needed to interject before more damage could be done. Lena smirked at JD, and then opened the door, ending the conversation.

"Ms. Washington," James began.

"Lena, please," she said as she turned to him.

"Lena." James smiled. "Thank you for your time, but we have to get back on the road now. If you ever find yourself in Richmond, please give me a call." He gave her his card. He touched JD's shoulder. "You have a good day."

Lena looked at his card. "I might do that, Mr. Brooks. Mr. Harrison, I'm sure we will talk again."

"Ms. Washington," JD replied as he walked away. Lena smiled, and then closed the door.

JD got in the car a little dejected. He didn't expect much, but this was over the top. "That woman is about money. I don't care if she never calls," JD said.

"Don't let your emotions control your response to this. Yes, she's a piece of work. But she can be handled. You just have to use a little finesse," James said with a smirk.

JD looked at James. "What do you have in mind?"

"Well, let me work on her," James said. He knew that what JD was trying to do was admirable, but his instincts told him they had just opened Pandora's Box. "Are you going to tell Tracy about this?" James asked.

JD put his head back on the headrest. "I have to. I don't keep things from her. I just hope she understands why I did it."

James smiled. "She will and she will love you more for trying." JD started the car and pulled off. James laughed. "Damn! I thought I had the mother-in-law from hell."

JD dropped James off at his office then called Tracy. "Where are you, babe?" he asked.

"I'm at my place talking with Cynthia and Rosaline about possibly handling the wedding. Can you come by?"

JD sighed. "I don't want to."

Tracy was quiet for a moment. "Will you come anyway?"

"What do I get if I do?" JD teased.

"A very grateful fiancée."

"I'm downstairs, let me up." Tracy smiled and buzzed the door open. JD kissed Tracy and whispered, "How grateful?"

She just smiled as JD spoke to everyone then took a seat. "So what are we talking about?"

Tracy looked at Ashley then at Jeffrey. "Jeffrey, I would like to hire Cynthia and Rosaline to coordinate the wedding. Would you be comfortable with that?"

"Will the end result make you Mrs. Jeffrey Harrison?"

Tracy smiled. "Yes."

"Then I don't care if Gandhi coordinates the wedding."

Tracy kissed him softly on the lips. "Thank you."

He frowned at Cynthia over Tracy's shoulder. "Cynthia, there will be a contract, right?" he asked.

Cynthia looked at him. "Of course."

JD looked back at her. "There may be one or two amendments to that contract. The final contract must be signed by Tracy and me. Do we understand each other?"

"What is it you think I'm going to do, JD?"

"What you always do, Cynthia, find some way to put Tracy down. This is her wedding; your place is going to be directing her wants, not yours. Now if you think you can do that, we are good."

Cynthia stood up. "I do not put Tracy down."

"Yes, you do."

Ashley and Rosaline both laughed.

Cynthia stopped mid-sentence then rolled her eyes at both of them. "I simply tell her what I think. I like to keep things real."

"Your keeping it real has been cruel. But Tracy considers you a friend. I'll be damned if I know why, but she does. If she wants you," he looked at Tracy, "I will not get in the way."

The doorbell rang. "Break!" Ashley smiled then buzzed the door open. "Ding; Round Two."

"Good evening," James said as he reached the top of the stairs.

"Hello," everyone responded.

"Am I interrupting something?" James asked, seeing the tense expression on Cynthia's face.

"No, just wedding plans," JD replied. "Have a seat."

James pouted. "I don't want to." Tracy laughed.

Brian thought he was dreaming when he heard the telephone ring. He reached to pick up the house phone, but the ringing continued. It was his cell; he jumped up, wondering who would call him this early on a Saturday morning. "Thompson, this is Tucker. I need to see you. Meet me at Maxi's in half an hour."

"Hey, Brian, can I get you something?" Frank greeted.

"Hey, Frank, do you ever go home?" Brian joked.

"Don't feel like it sometimes." He pointed to the table. "Your guest is here," he said looking over to the table.

Brian looked in the direction Frank pointed and saw Tucker eating. The feeling in the pit of his stomach made it obvious something was amiss. "Let me have a Hennessey on the rocks," Brian requested.

"It's a little early for that, ain't it?"

"Yeah, well I got a feeling I'm going to need it." Brian walked over and sat at the table. "Got to be important for you to be here of all places."

"Yeah, I feel like a damn virgin in the center of Sing Sing surrounded by death row inmates, with all these damn cops around," Tucker joked.

Brian chuckled. "Just wondering which one is going to screw you first."

"Yeah." Tucker laughed. "Juan is targeting Harrison again." Tucker stated.

"Tell me what I don't know," Brian said. Frank approached the table with the drink, the conversation stopped. "Thanks, man," Brian said, and then continued with his conversation. "He isn't crazy enough to make another attempt on a DA; especially this one. Hell, that would bring the whole force down on him, Fed, state and local."

"He's pissed. Harrison didn't take the out and is still gunning for him. People do stupid things when they don't think clearly and you can't think clearly when you're pissed. Besides, the plan was to slow Harrison's roll, not kill him," Tuck said.

"The kind of force they brought was to kill, not slow down," Brian said angrily. "But let's say you're right. How could they slow him down at this point?"

"Think about it: who's the one person in Harrison's life that would make him think twice if something was to happen to her?"

Brian thought for a moment. "Shit," Brian said, "love is a bitch."

"Yeah, tell me about it," Tucker said as he finished the last of the food on his plate.

"I can't officially put anybody on her."

"Well, you better do something. I was given direct orders. If anything happens to her, people will die." Tucker finished his coffee. "I'm out, man."

"Thanks for the heads up, man. You take care."

"Same for you, my man." Tucker left.

Frank came over to the table. "You good, Brian?"

"No, man, bring me another one. Make it a double."

Brian knew if it was in his power, nothing would happen to Tracy. He pulled out his cell, dialed a number. "I need you to cover JD's girl until further notice; anything goes down, shoot to kill, we'll get answers later." He disconnected and made another call. "Calvin. I'm at Maxi's. Can you get away?"

"Yeah, what's up?"

"I'll fill you in when you get here."

"Alright, you talked to JD?"

"No, I'm pretty sure he's with Tracy." Brian smirked. "You know he's done right?"

"Yeah, he's gone, but I ain't mad at him," Calvin replied. "He's got a good one."

"I don't know, man. I am not into that one-woman-for-the-rest-of-your-life shit. It doesn't even sound that effective, you know what I mean," Brian said laughing. "Think about it; women outnumber us. Now, if everybody goes to the one on one, like you and JD, what's going to happen to all the other women? Somebody's got to be available to help the lonely sisters."

"Oh and you are willing to make the sacrifice?"

"Hell, yeah!"

"You're a damn fool, B." Calvin laughed. "I'll be down in 10."

Frank came to the table with breakfast on a plate. "Maxine said you have to put something on your stomach if you gonna do all that drinking this early in the day. She said she gonna take care of you today, but you need a woman in your life."

Brian laughed and thought, *Has everybody lost their damn mind?*

Chapter 28

The first day back in open court for JD began with an uneasy feeling, but he was determined not to let it get the best of him. Today the security was tight; no one was allowed in the courtroom unless they were directly involved with the case. No media were allowed.

When JD left the house that morning, Tracy wasn't feeling well. She had been staying at JD's place for the past week. She did her work from home and would have it sent to the office by Ashley. It was easier to handle security that way. Brian and two other federal agents handled the detail rotation on both JD and Tracy. That was completely unofficial.

When Brian approached his superiors regarding the tip on Tracy, they informed him his responsibility was to protect Jeffrey Harrison only. The agency was not responsible for the family members' protection. That pissed Brian off, but he followed orders. Most evenings, Magna and Brian were at the house with them, therefore extra coverage was available.

Sometimes James and Ashley would stop by. James and JD were becoming close friends. The two would have what some might call arguments, but they referred to them as discussions about politics. Ashley would fill Tracy in on the happenings in the office and spend some time on the wedding. They had formed a very tight-knit little group.

JD was glad the trial day had finally arrived. Once this trial was over, he and Tracy could move on with their plans. Since his meeting with Lena, all he wanted to do was make her feel secure with their family.

The group from the DA's office arrived together. Brian drove JD and Magna. Calvin, Dan and two Federal agents rode in the other vehicle. If anything happened to the first group, the lead attorney in the second would take over the case. The media were on the front steps of the courthouse in full force. Before going into the courthouse, JD called Tracy. "Hey, babe, you feeling any better?" he asked.

"A little," she replied. "Is everything okay with you?"

"Yeah," he said, looking out of the window. "I have the full force of the city here with me today, don't worry."

"I'm going to worry until you come back through the door," she said with a sigh.

"Brian said there's nothing really wrong with you that will not be cleared up once this day is over."

"He may be right, but my head is killing me right now."

A little worried, he said, "Why don't you take a couple Tylenols and go back to bed? When you wake up this may be over."

"I may do that." She hesitated. "Jeffrey, please come home to me."

He closed his eyes and sighed. "That's my plan, babe. I love you."

"Me, too." JD hung up the phone then got out of the car.

Brian walked up beside him. "Don't worry if anything happens to you; I'll marry Tracy." JD froze in his tracks and gawked at Brian.

Calvin walked up behind JD and hit him on the shoulder. "I guess you better stay alive, partner," he laughed.

The trial took two days before it was turned over to the jury. On the second day, JD and his team knew they had a victory and so did the defense. Juan became irate in the courtroom when the mother of his child was called to testify against him. He looked at JD and yelled, "You will pay for this. You fucked with my family, I fuck with yours!" The judge had him removed from the court.

JD called Tracy on his way home just to check on things. She still was not feeling well, which was unusual. To his knowledge, Tracy had never been sick, not even a cold. "Everything is fine honey; I'm just taking it easy today," she told him.

"Things got ugly today. The case was given to the jury. Now, it's a wait and see."

"How do you feel about it?" she asked.

"We are on our way to Maxi's to celebrate."

She smiled. "Thank goodness, this is almost over. We can go back to our normal life."

"I kind of like the life we have," JD said. "I like having you at my place day and night."

"Yes, I like that, too, but I can do without so many people around all the time."

"I'm with you on that." He smiled. "Babe, we are at Maxi's; do you need me to come home?"

"No, enjoy yourself."

"Love you," he whispered.

"Me too," she replied.

Tracy went to the medicine cabinet to get the Tylenols, but they were out. Her headache was getting worse. She started to call Jeffrey to bring some home, but changed her mind. He had been so stressed about this trial; he needed this outing with the guys. She didn't want to disturb that. Tracy got in her car and drove to the drugstore.

When she pulled into the parking lot, there was a commotion behind her. A car had apparently cut off a white SUV. Tracy stepped out of the car and looked around. Before she closed the door, a young Hispanic man approached her from behind. "Ms. Tracy?"

"Yes," she answered.

"I have a message for Mr. Harrison."

Before Tracy realized what was happening, his fist hit her face with so much force that her head hit the top of her car. She was stunned. Blood started coming out of her nose. Another fist hit her face from the opposite direction. Tracy lost her balance and fell between the cars. A foot hit her side, like a sledgehammer, which continued to kick and pound her from what seemed like all directions. She tried to slide under the car, but someone grabbed her legs and pulled her back out. Tracy heard voices speaking in Spanish. She knew there were more than the one, but could not make out what they were saying. She tried to scream, but nothing came out. She tried to fight back, but could not. Someone stomped her hand and she cried out in pain. One of them picked her head up off the cement and said in Spanish, "You fuck with my family, I fuck with yours." The boy slammed her head on the cement. Everything seemed to go black then. Tracy put her arms over her head, and curled up into a fetal position. She prayed to lose consciousness, but it did not come fast enough. The impact of every kick kept her conscious. The kicking continued until her body became numb, but her mind was still aware. Then she heard what sounded like a gunshot, but she could not move. Her mind was closing and she hurt all over; she couldn't tell if the shot had hit her.

The kicking stopped; someone else was there. She heard a scrambling and then a car pulling away. "Tracy?" She heard a voice, but didn't recognize it. She tried to opened her eyes, but couldn't. Tracy tried to speak to the person talking to her, but she couldn't. She called out for Jeffrey; then she lost consciousness.

At Maxi's the celebration was in full force. This was a huge victory for the DA's office; it represented the end to the Latin Eagles reign on the Blackwell area. The tension turned into relaxed nerves for the moment, but the celebration was short lived. Brian's cell phone rang. "Thompson," he said with a drink in his hand. He dropped his drink and stood. "Where?" he asked, and looked around the room for JD. He hung up the phone, then dialed a number. "Protectee down," he said and gave the address. He looked directly at JD. All of a sudden other cell phones and pagers started to go off.

JD looked around, and then looked at Brian. "Is the jury back already?"

Brian had a blank stare on his face. "B, what is it?" Calvin asked.

Brian looked at JD. "It's Tracy."

"What about Tracy?" JD asked.

"She was attacked."

JD and Brian ran out of the bar and jumped into the Suburban. As Brian pulled away from the curve, JD frantically dialed Tracy's cell phone: no answer. Brian drove nonstop while he relayed the information he had to JD. As Brian talked, *I should have gone home* raced through JD's mind.

When they arrived at the scene, emergency vehicles were everywhere. JD spotted Tracy's car and jumped out before Brian came to a complete stop. JD ran towards the car, where an officer tried to stop him. JD pushed him away and went to her. Tracy was lying face down on the cement with an officer bending over her. At first sight JD felt as if a knife was being driven straight through his heart. She was covered in blood. Her face was badly beaten, and from what he could tell her body was badly bruised. JD could not believe this was happening. The woman he loved was lying on the ground, so still. For a moment, he was actually afraid she was dead. He removed his suit jacket and covered her. He knelt down beside her and began talking to her.

"Tracy," he called out. JD pushed Tracy's hair from her face. "Tracy, baby; I'm right here with you, baby. I'm right here with you." There was no reply.

"She's not conscious," the officer stated.

JD lifted Tracy's head from the cement and placed it on his lap. "Tracy," he whispered in her ear, and kissed her. "Baby, please," he said quietly, "stay with me."

The EMT bent down to check her vitals. He began talking into his walkie-talkie: "We have a female, age 20 to 25; she has bruises to the face; broken hand and ribs; possible internal bleeding."

JD assisted as the EMT put the brace beside her and gently turned her over. JD moaned; the other side of her face was so bloody you could not see where the injuries were. They picked her up off the ground, and placed her on the gurney, then continued working. Tracy remained motionless. JD stood over Tracy, talking to her the whole time. The action happening around him was a blur; his only thoughts were with her.

They put Tracy in the ambulance and JD jumped in. He prayed. He never asked why this was happening; only that God would give him the guidance to get through it. A calmness filled JD's heart. God would not take her from him, not now. There was so much they had to do together.

When they arrived at the hospital Tracy was taken directly into the trauma room. A nurse approached JD asking questions about Tracy. He answered and watched as they worked on her. She seemed so still, he thought. Two federal agents appeared by his side. JD looked at them. "Get away from me." He sneered though his teeth. They both stepped back, but did not leave his side. A doctor approached JD. "Mr. Washington?"

"Harrison," JD corrected, putting his hands in his pocket.

"Mr. Harrison, we have a couple of issues happening."

Magna and Calvin came into the area. JD did not turn; he remained focused on what the doctor was saying.

The doctor continued, "She has a broken hand, numerous facial bruises, broken ribs, and that's just on the surface. We are going to do X-rays to determine the extent of internal damage."

JD calmly replied, "Thank you, doctor." He watched as they took Tracy down the hallway.

Calvin knew not to press JD; he had seen JD this way when his father died. But JD needed to know some things. "JD," Calvin said, "they found a body at the scene, and he was shot. An Eagle tattoo was on his left shoulder; he was one of Juan's men."

"Get Brian, Calvin," JD said while walking into the waiting area. He pulled off his tie and sat on a bench against the wall. Calvin sat beside him, not saying anything, just sitting next to him to let him know he was with him. The two agents flanked them.

Magna came in. "They have a second man down; shot in the car that fled the scene about a mile away."

"Dead?" JD asked.

"No, they're bringing him in."

"Here?" JD asked too calmly. Calvin shook his head to Magna indicating not to answer.

"I'm not sure," she lied.

JD nodded as he laid his head back against the wall. He smiled. "Tracy wants Cynthia to handle the wedding," he said to Calvin. "Can you believe that?"

"Yeah, I can," Calvin responded. "Tracy's like that."

JD smiled then slowly a disheartening look emerged.

Brian walked in. JD stood as he approached. They both stepped to the side away from everyone. "How's Tracy?" Brian asked. JD took his hands and ran them over his face, then shook his head, but never responded. "It was definitely Juan's men," Brian continued. "At the moment questions are being asked about the shooter."

JD was standing with his back to the wall facing the door; Brian was facing JD with his back to the door. The door opened. EMTs walked in with a Hispanic man on a gurney. "Where's your weapon?" JD asked, as he began walking towards the young man. Brian stepped in front of him, but JD pushed him out the way. The two agents grabbed JD and pinned him against the wall. It took both of them to hold him down. Calvin and Brian stepped in.

"Let him go," Brian ordered. "Let him go!"

The agents released JD, then stood in front of the doors leading to the trauma center. "I can't let you in there," Brian told JD. "We know you're hurting; we want to kill him, too.

JD looked at them, as if they did not understand. "Did you see what they did to her?" he asked calmly. Ashley walked in and saw Brian and Calvin standing with JD. She ran between them, put her arms around her brother's waist and laid her head on his chest, just the way she did when their dad died. JD put his arms around her and began to console her.

"She will be alright," JD told her as he kissed the top of her head. JD was resting his chin on the top of Ashley's head as she cried. "It will be alright."

JD saw the doctor who had been working on Tracy coming down the hallway. JD went back into the trauma area as the doctor approached. Ashley, Calvin and Brian joined him. "Mr. Harrison, the good news first: in addition to the broken ribs, Ms. Washington has a punctured lung. We can go in and stabilize that situation. However, there is a complication."

"What complication?" JD asked.

"Ms. Washington was in her first trimester." Ashley was holding on to JD's arm and felt his body tense.

"She's pregnant?" JD asked.

"Unfortunately, the child did not survive the attack. However, I believe Ms. Washington will recover."

JD did not speak or move, his mind was racing. *Tracy was pregnant, with our first child, but the baby is gone.*

"Mr. Harrison, I know this may sound terrible, but she is a very lucky young woman. One more kick to her ribs and she would not be with us now. I need to go back in. I'll be back as soon as I have more to tell you."

"Is she awake?" JD asked.

"No." The doctor recognized the worry on JD's face; he had seen it time and time again. "Mr. Harrison, she is a strong young woman. She is going to make it through this and she will be able to have other children." The doctor turned and walked away.

This was too much for JD. He caused this. He was so intent on protecting everyone else; he let this happen to Tracy and their baby.

Ashley held JD and held him tight. It was her turn to comfort her brother. She looked up at him and could not read his expression. That scared her. Whenever JD was mad or hurt, she could always see it in his face, but at this moment she could not read her brother. Calvin, who usually was the voice of reason, could not contain the anger he was experiencing. As he looked at JD standing there motionless with Ashley, Calvin knew he had to walk away. He could not state his feelings at that moment, for it would only set JD off. Brian walked away; busting through the doors with so much force it broke the glass pane.

A crowd had gathered in the waiting area. Gavin and Carolyn were there along with James and JD's mother. Martha walked through the door as JD fell to his knees. James ran inside. Calvin came out the door.

"Is she dead?" Carolyn asked.

They all looked at her.

"Is that your prayer, Carolyn?" Calvin asked as he walked out the exit doors to get some air. James followed, taking Ashley out for some fresh air. JD grabbed his mother's hand as he stood. He towered over his mother as she looked up at him.

JD hung his head. "Mama, I can't do this," he said, shaking his head. "I can't."

"Hold your head up, son," she said. She smiled. "Tell me how she is."

He relayed what the doctor told him. Martha stood there looking up at her son. He was the spitting image of his father. Her heart was breaking for him. The guilt was all over his face. But now was not the time for self-pity; he had to be strong.

"Tracy stood in this very hospital not long ago, feeling just about the same way you are feeling right now. Not once did she say I can't do this. She was strong for you. Now you need to be strong for her. It's not easy being the person everyone turns to for strength—and having that one person you turn to out of commission. You want to just give up, give in. Well, you can't, because if you do: son, look at me." He looked down at her. "If you give up, who is going to be there for Tracy when she wakes up?"

"Mama, they savagely beat her and killed our child. I can't let that go." JD kissed her on her cheek, and then walked away. He heard what his mother said loud and clear. But he was not ready to let go of his anger; not yet.

JD walked to the waiting area; Carolyn started to say something. He put up his hand to stop her. Damn if he was in the mood for her. He walked out the door to where Calvin and Brian stood. He could see James in the distance consoling Ashley. For a moment, it was comforting to have someone else to help with his family. He smiled to himself; he was glad James was in business and not law. He prayed Ashley would not experience anything like this.

The three friends stood there in silence. Brian and Calvin were itching to voice their opinions.

Brian started. "Juan needs to be taken down."

"I knew you were going there. But we got to stick with the legal system," Calvin tried to reason.

"I'm all for the legal system. I pledged my life to it. But the legal system did not protect Tracy today. She is alive because of our bond," Brian argued.

"I admit, there are times when we must step out, but those times need to be limited and avoided at all cost. If it's not, we are simply another version of what we took an oath to stand against."

"Calvin," Brian hesitated, "what if that was Jackie in there instead of Tracy?"

"B, you can't make a decision like this based on emotions."

JD stood there with his hands in his pockets, looking at the ground as he always did when he was torn between right and wrong. His dad taught him not to do anything that would not allow you to look at yourself in a mirror the next day. But his father also taught him to protect your family at all costs. JD was truly torn here. "The propensity for violence" crept into his mind.

Gavin came out. "JD, the doctor is back." JD turned to go inside. He stopped, turned to his friends and said, "This case must come to an end. But it must be done according to the law."

Tracy was in intensive care. As JD sat next to her, he wondered why he had wasted so much time. He had allowed years to go by without her, when he knew from the very first time they met, he loved her. He kissed her hand. "Baby, I am so sorry it took me so long, but there will be no delays from this moment on," he said. She looked so helpless and weak lying there. But JD wasn't worried; he knew she was going to pull through. Tracy was strong. She has handled a lot in her life. This was just another hurdle for her to jump. And she would, he knew it.

Brian knocked on the window. JD went outside to see what he needed. "They need you for a press conference. There seems to be a small riot going on in Blackwell. Some of the residents there decided enough is enough. They have taken up arms against Juan's people. The media's coverage of the incident has caused the city to go a little crazy.

The mayor is asking you to speak directly to them through the media. Are you up for it?" Brian asked.

"I don't want to leave Tracy alone, man," JD said. "At some point I have to start putting her first. I just need her to know I'm here."

Gavin interjected. "JD, the residents over there trust you. If you could just take a moment to speak out to them from here, it could settle things down a little."

"It's getting ugly over there," Calvin stated. "You may be able to save a life here, JD."

JD thought about it for a minute. He looked through the window at Tracy.

He was exhausted. It had been a long day in court; then this. He was not sure he could conduct himself in the manner needed if the press pissed him off. This needs to end, once and for all; that he knew. "Alright, they get five minutes."

As JD stood at the podium, questions were coming from everywhere. JD remembered why he hated talking to the press. They never stop to listen. The crowd began to settle down, realizing he was not going to speak until they were quiet. "Good evening," he started. "This afternoon, a young woman I care deeply, no—" He shook his head. "A young woman I love with all my heart was brutally beaten. We believe the attack was related to a case I am prosecuting. At this time, we believe it may be the same individual who ordered the attack on me last month. It does not seem this individual will stop until I step down or I'm six feet under. As you can see, I'm still living and have no plans on stepping down." He hesitated before he continued. "I would love to do nothing more than to execute him with my bare hands. But I took an oath to uphold the law and I am a man of my word. I will not break that oath. To the residents of Blackwell, please, know I understand your anger and your need to do something. I am experiencing it myself. But I beg you to please stop the attacks. I gave you my word that I would help to clean out your neighborhoods of the gang activity, and I will continue to do that. If you continue with the actions you have taken, it makes us no different from the very people you are fighting against. There must be a clear separation of those of us that uphold the law and those who choose to break the law. If you choose to break the law, regardless of the reason, you will have to contend with me." He hesitated for a moment, then continued. "Please understand, my attention needs to be with Tracy right now. I cannot give her my full attention and be worried about what's happening with you all. Please give me the time I need to make sure my family is safe. Once that is done, I promise you my undivided attention."

"JD, in your position you are charged with the protection of the citizens of this city. What does it say to them when you can't protect your own fiancée?"

The vein in JD's neck got thick as he tried to swallow his anger. He cleared his throat. "It's because of my commitment to the residents of this city that we are here tonight. I could have walked away when the attempt was made on my life. Many said I should have. But I'm still here because I care about this city. Do you want this job, Charlie?" JD angrily asked. The reporter did not respond. "That's what I thought. Don't ever presume it's your place to tell me what my job is again."

"JD," Victoria called out. She knew JD was getting in trouble here. He needed to ease up a little. "Could you tell us how Tracy is doing? Have you been able to talk to her?"

JD took a moment. "I have been in the room with her most of the night; she has not regained consciousness."

"What was the extent of her injuries?" another reporter asked

"Abrasions to the face and upper torso; broken ribs and a punctured lung."

"What is the doctor's prognosis?" Victoria asked sadly.

"Barring certain complications, he believes she will have a full recovery."

"What about you, JD, you've taken some hits—will you be able to recover from this?"

"I can't answer that yet; I don't know."

"A report indicates there was a body on the scene of a Hispanic man. Is there any information you can give us on that?"

"I will have to refer that question to our chief of police. Thank you for your time," JD said and left the podium.

When JD returned to Tracy's room, the agent was not there. The nurse came, moving briskly towards them. She entered the room; JD followed behind her, then Brian behind him.

"What is it?" JD asked.

"Her heart rate is increasing," the nurse replied.

"What would cause that?" JD asked, very concerned.

"I don't know. She may be dreaming and something frightened her."

"Tracy." JD started talking to her and rubbing her forehead. "It's okay, babe. Whatever it is, I'm here. I'm not going to let anyone hurt you ever again; you don't have to be frightened. I'll stay here with you." He kissed her.

"She's settling down," the nurse smiled as she continued to check the monitor. "Keep talking to her, seems like she wants to come around. People, let's clear the room."

"Brian, get with Al," JD said calmly. "Let him know what's happening here. Tell Calvin to make sure things are in place at the office. Then try to get some rest." JD took off his jacket and shoes. He lay in the bed beside Tracy and began to talk to her. He wanted to assure her that she was not alone. The nurse came in to check Tracy's vitals. JD never stopped talking. He started speaking to her on their agreement about children. "You know, I've been thinking if you really want to show me how much you love me you would have child number six for me. You know, it would be difficult for me to carry a baby for nine months."

"What are you talking about?" The nurse smiled.

JD smiled. "We have an ongoing argument about the number of children we are going to have. I want 12."

"Wow!" the nurse responded.

JD laughed. "Yeah, that's what she said."

"How many did she say?"

"She agreed to five; but if I have number six, she'll have the rest."

"Now, that seems reasonable. If you have number six I will come and help raise all 12 for free," the nurse said as she laughed.

JD smiled at her; she had a very comforting way about her. "Don't laugh—I may have to hold you to that," he joked. Tracy squeezed his finger. "Tracy?" JD got up. "Tracy, babe, open your eyes," he pleaded. The nurse pushed the button to call the station as Tracy opened her eyes.

"Tracy, babe." JD smiled. "Hey." He kissed her face. "It's so good to see those eyes." Tracy was still groggy. She gave JD a faint smile.

The doctor came in. "Tracy, hi, I'm Dr. Shaw. It's good to see you awake." Tracy frowned then moaned as a tear ran down her swollen face. "I know you are in a lot of pain, but we are going to take care of that. We wanted you to wake up first. This is going to be a little uncomfortable," he said, removing the gauze from her face, "but only for a minute." They removed the ventilator and Tracy moaned from the pain. They gave her an oxygen tube to help with her breathing. The doctor gave an order, and the nurse left and closed the door. "Tracy, I need you to listen and try to concentrate on what I am about to say. I need you to tell me who you want to handle your affairs here. It is very important that we do this." JD stepped forward. "Stay back, Mr. Harrison, please, she has to say this. Tracy?" Dr. Shaw bent down to her ear.

"Jeffrey," she whispered.

"Okay," he said. "Is she left-handed or right-handed?" he asked JD.

"Right."

"Tracy, can you sign your name here for me?" He held the clipboard and gave her the pen. She signed then dropped her hand.

JD thanked the doctor.

"As her designee, you are the only one who can make decisions for her. For the next few days she will be in and out. Once she is not in as much pain, we will ease up on the pain medication. At that time, she will be more aware of her surroundings," the doctor advised.

"Thank you for taking this action. This had not crossed my mind and it should have."

JD completed the power of attorney form that Tracy had signed.

"Your mind was on other things, Mr. Harrison. She is going to sleep through the night once the nurse administers the medication. You might try to get some rest yourself. Good night, Mr. Harrison."

JD stepped back over to the bed. He looked at Tracy. Her face was clear of the blood now, but it was swollen and badly bruised. But she was still beautiful to him. "It is so good to see you awake." Tears ran down her face. JD kissed her. "I'm sorry babe, I'm so sorry."

The nurse came back into the room and administered the medication.

JD bent down to Tracy. He held her hand. "I love you more than I would ever be able to show you." He smiled and kissed her. "I need you with me, Squirt Two; I'm lost without you." JD waited until she fell asleep, then stepped out of the room.

Brian was talking with the agent, who was attempting to explain why he stepped away.

"A woman stopped by the room and indicated she was Tracy's mother," Brian advised JD.

"Where is she now?" JD asked.

"We don't know."

Gavin came down the hallway. "JD, the jury is back with a verdict. The verdict will be read in Judge Mathew's courtroom tomorrow at nine."

JD looked at Gavin, then back to Brian. Which should he deal with first: Juan or Tracy's mom? "I'll be in court in the morning. Just give me a minute here."

"It's been a hell of an emotional day, JD. You sure you want to be there in the morning?"

"Yes, I want to see Juan Cortez go down. But at the moment I want to know who was here

Ashley brought JD a change of clothes. They all tried to get him to go home to get some rest, but he refused. James came by during the night. He sat and talked with JD and Ashley into the wee hours of the morning. When Ashley and James left, JD did not sleep. He sat on the lounge chair in Tracy's room and watched her. It was killing him to see her like this and to know it all happened because of him. This happened to her because he loved her. He understood when the Eagles came after him, but he could not understand why they would go after Tracy. What made matters worse, even with the warning, they could not do much more than what was done to protect her. How many prosecutors have gone through something like this? He could not be the only one. What can he do to change this, to keep it from happening again?

JD stood up, walked over to the window, and put his hands in his pockets. He looked down, searching the very depths of his mind to come up with an answer. He could always resign his position with the district attorney's office. That would only hand a victory to people like Juan Cortez. JD knew this type of retaliation would not be eliminated no matter what he did, but there had to be a way to deter people from causing harm to a family member of an officer of the court. He stepped outside Tracy's room and called Calvin.

"How is Tracy doing?" Calvin asked.

"She is heavily sedated because of the pain. Calvin, they took my baby. How does a man deal with that?" JD cried into the phone.

Calvin could hear the hurt in JD's voice, but this was one time Calvin could not console his friend. "Do what you can to get these people off the street for good."

"That part I can do. But how do I get Tracy to forgive me for this?"

"Man, this is not on you; Tracy will be the first one to tell you that. Have you gotten any sleep?"

"No, just thinking," JD replied. "I need to know of any laws protecting officers of the court."

"I'll check into that, but I don't think any exist."

JD thought for a moment. "If there is no law covering this, we need to write one."

Calvin agreed. "We can start on it right away."

"Let's start with some research. Check with other DA offices across the state, past and present DAs. Let's see if there is a pattern that needs to be addressed."

"The problem with that is our number one research mind is out of commission."

JD smiled. "You're right. Then we go to the next best."

On his way to the correctional facility to talk to Al, Brian called Douglas to get information on the shooting. "I'm at your back door, can you get away?" Brian asked.

Douglas checked the lounge area of the club. "I'll be there in a minute."

As Douglas got into the car Brian asked, "What in the hell happened?"

"Cortez's people knew I was trailing her. They cut me off before I entered the parking lot. Apparently I wasn't the only one on her. Another car pulled up behind Juan's people. B, I'm telling you, the man came out shooting. He wasn't taking any prisoners; he was out to kill. Whoever he was, he saw me get out of the car. After he shot the first guy the other two jumped into the car and pulled off. I went over to Tracy; he nodded, got in his car and followed the other two. He meant for Juan's men to die."

Brian knew instantly it was Tuck. "They were warned; if anything happened to that girl, people would die," Brian replied. "The man was just keeping his word."

Douglas looked over at Brian. "Who in the hell are we dealing with here?" he asked. "Who is this girl JD is involved with?"

"He's not just involved with her, man. JD is going to marry this one."

Douglas shook his head. "Of all the damn women JD has had, why he want to pick the one with baggage?"

Brian shrugged his shoulder. "Tracy is worth any shit you have to endure to keep her." Brian did not mean to say that aloud.

Doug noticed Brian's sentiment. "You got a thing for JD's girl, B?"

"She's good people." He hesitated for a moment. "You know her brother."

Doug didn't miss it. "You did not answer my question, but who is her brother?"

Brian looked at Douglas. "Al Day."

Doug stared at Brian. "I didn't know Al had a sister." Douglas thought for a minute. "Are the others involved in this attack dead yet?"

"One in the hospital; one in jail. And, of course, there is Juan."

Doug sat back in the seat. "Well, knowing Al like I do, they will all be dead within the week."

Brian pulled into the correctional facility. He met with the warden for a minute then went in to talk to Al.

Chapter 29

That morning, some were surprised to see JD enter the courtroom.
Before the jury was brought in, Judge Mathews asked JD and the
defense attorney to approach the bench.

"How is she doing, JD?" Judge Mathews asked.

"She is still heavily sedated. But all indications are good," he replied.

"Ms. Vargas, if it is determined in any way that you had any inkling of
an idea this was taking place, I will personally have you disbarred."

"Your honor, this was never mentioned to me or before me," Ms.
Vargas replied.

"I pray that is true. Now step back," Judge Mathews replied.

"JD, I had no idea, and I am truly sorry," Ms. Vargas said as they
returned to their tables.

"Bring the jury in," Judge Mathews said to the bailiff.

The jurors took their seats. The foreman handed the verdict to the
judge. Judge Mathews read the verdict then handed it back. As the
foreman read the guilty verdict, JD stared at Juan. Once the verdict was
read, Juan turned to JD.

"Don't feel so good, do it?" Juan smirked. "Told you not to fuck with
my family."

JD smiled. "The thing about family: you never know where or when
they may show up." JD turned and walked out of the courtroom.

JD had thought that if he heard the verdict in person it would give
him some satisfaction, but it did not. He was pleased that Juan would be
going away for the rest of his life, but it was neither for the rape and
murder of Lisa Gonzalez, nor for the brutal beating of Tracy. Calvin,
Magna, Dan and Brian were all present for the verdict. But they knew it
was a hollow victory.

"Are you headed back to the hospital?" Dan asked.

"Yes, I'll be there until Tracy goes home."

"There is something I would like to arrange for her. Do you mind?" Dan asked JD.

"No, I don't mind. Dan, will you contact Senator Roth? Ask him to come by to see me at his earliest convenience?"

"There are reporters on the steps of the courthouse. How do you want to handle it?" Brian asked.

"Let's go out back. Calvin, will you handle the reporters?"

When JD returned to the hospital, Tracy had been moved to a suite. Nurse Gordon was in Tracy's room, talking to Tracy as if she was awake. "Yes, I tell you, that's a fine young man you got, girl. I don't know you, but I sure hope you recognize what you have."

"Good morning." JD smiled at the nurse.

"Well, good morning to you. Looks like you had a busy morning," she said, pointing to the TV. The news conference was taking place in front of the courthouse with Calvin and Gavin.

JD shrugged. "I'm just glad it's over with. What happened here? Why was Tracy moved?" JD asked as he walked over to the bed.

"The administrator received a call from the governor himself. He was told to put Ms. Washington in this suite and to make sure every convenience was given to you. Dr. Shaw approved it as long as I came along."

JD smiled. "I would have made the same request."

The nurse smiled. "You need to get some rest. You are not going to be any good to her in the shape you are in. Here, I made this couch up for you."

JD looked around the room. "This was very thoughtful of you. Maybe I will get some rest."

"Good, I will make sure you are not disturbed. Dr. Shaw ordered no visitors for the next 24 hours. What do you want to do with the flowers?"

JD looked around. "What flowers?" Nurse Gordon opened the door to the adjacent room. The room was filled with flowers, balloons and a box with cards in it. "Who in the hell is going to respond to all of those?" he laughed. Then it hit him. "I know just the person to handle that."

His laughter was contagious. Nurse Gordon began to laugh. "You are up to something devilish. I can see it in your eyes."

JD dialed his cell phone. "Ashley," he said, still laughing, "can you come up to the hospital and bring Cynthia with you. Oh, and I need to talk to James. Would you give me his number?"

JD hung up the telephone, still smiling to himself. He went over to the bed, kissed Tracy then removed his suit jacket and shoes. He lay down on the couch and went to sleep.

A few hours later, Nurse Gordon checked to see if JD was awake. "Mr. Harrison, there are some people here to see you. Are you up to it?"

JD stretched and looked over at Tracy. "Did she wake up at all?" he asked as he stood up.

"No, but she is still getting a pretty high dose of pain medicine," Nurse Gordon replied.

JD was a little worried that she was still asleep.

Nurse Gordon noticed his hesitation. "It is best for her to sleep right now. If she was awake, the pain would be unbearable."

"Alright, let them in."

When Cynthia walked in the room, JD turned his head so she would not see him laughing. Nurse Gordon looked on as he tried to make a serious face for the visitors. He walked over to Cynthia and hugged her. "Cynthia, I'm so glad you came. I need your help. Tracy has received several cards and flowers. As you can see, she cannot respond to them. Do you think you could possibly handle them for us? I wouldn't ask if there weren't so many things going on. You know they have to be done right. Tracy trusted the way you handle things like this, so I guess I have to trust you, too. Can you handle it?" JD asked with all the sincerity he could muster.

Cynthia looked at Tracy. "I will have to. Even if Tracy was up and about, I would have to do this for her. Don't you worry about it; I will have it done in no time. Where are the cards and flowers?" she asked, looking around.

"Well, it may take a little longer than that," JD said. "We set up this room for you to work from." He opened the door. The look on Cynthia's face was priceless. Ashley and James started laughing. JD stood there with an expression that pleaded for help.

Cynthia did not blink. "I will get my staff over here right away. This is going to cost, JD," she replied and then walked in the room.

JD closed the door behind her and laughed. "I could not resist that."

"Tracy is going to get you for doing that to Cynthia," Ashley said laughing.

"I think Tracy will forgive me this one time. James, thanks for coming over."

"No problem. What do you need?"

"Let's take a seat."

They sat in an area away from Tracy's bed. JD did not want her sleep disturbed. "James, Ashley tells me you are almost as good at research as Tracy is. If that is true, I need your help."

James did not hesitate. "What do you need looked into?"

"I need DA's offices across the state contacted. I need to know, how many DAs have experienced violence against their family or themselves due to a case they were prosecuting." JD advised.

James nodded his head. "We may also want to check how many past DAs left the job because of that violence, in addition to any that may have changed their strategy because of said violence." JD nodded, acknowledging his agreement in the direction James was going.

"Let's develop a line of questioning to submit to each office. They can respond anonymously. Some may be hesitant to answer certain questions," James stated.

"Can we assure them the information received in the survey will be kept confidential?" JD asked. JD and James continued with the details of the survey.

Ashley sat next to Tracy. She could not believe this happened to her friend. Tears came down Ashley's face. Just when things were coming together for her, this had to happen. Ashley had never seen Tracy so happy. She'd lived with Tracy for six years and never once did she ever see her smile from within. Lately, that's all she saw, an inner peace with Tracy. Even Cynthia had not been able to break Tracy's confidence these days. Now this.

"You are going to bounce back and be better than ever Tracy. You will see," Ashley said. "You know I need you to keep me straight. The office needs your guidance. Monica is acting like she is my boss these days. But I must say she is handling things in our absence. The office has not skipped a beat. If nothing else, we know Monica can handle the business. We might have to give her a raise or a really serious bonus." Ashley smiled.

JD and James walked over to the bed. "I have to go," James said to Ashley.

"I will talk to you later; I want to stay here for a little while," Ashley said. James left the room.

Ashley laid her head back against JD, who was standing directly behind her. "I don't understand why this happened, but I know she will be stronger because of it," Ashley said.

"It happened because of me, Ash. I will never forgive myself for this."

Ashley turned around to see if he was serious; he was. "Don't you take this on like you did with Daddy. Daddy's death was not on you and neither is this. You are not responsible for every detail in the life of people you love, JD. You know God is working his magic here. He is preparing you and Tracy for the things you will have to deal with in the future. There is no blame here, except for the people who did this terrible thing. Speaking of which, how is the investigation going?"

JD just looked at Ashley. She thoroughly dismissed his self-pity and moved on. He smiled at her, wondering if James had any idea what he had. "They got all three. One is dead, one in the hospital and one behind bars," JD replied.

"What kind of time will they get?"

"Not much, I'm afraid, unless we can get them on attempted murder."

"Then that's what we have to push for."

Nurse Gordon came in the room. "Mr. Harrison, there are a string of people here. They said they were called to this room."

JD went over to the door. He saw Rosaline and about five other people with her.

"Hello, Rosaline." JD smiled.

"Hey, JD. How is Tracy?"

"Still asleep."

"Well, we are here to work. Where do you need us?"

JD pointed to the room next door. "Thank you, Rosaline."

"Oh, JD, this is for Tracy, and there will be no charge for this."

JD smiled as Rosaline entered the room next door. "You two sure do have a lot of friends," Nurse Gordon commented.

"You haven't seen anything yet, wait till she wakes up. I got to go, big brother. I will talk to you later," Ashley said, kissing JD on the cheek.

It was getting late in the evening and Tracy had not been awake at all during the day. He understood her body needed the rest, but it had been 48 hours and Tracy still had not awakened. Later that night, Nurse Gordon came in the room. "We are going to start reducing her medication. We need her awake for a moment to check her responses."

JD gave her a sad smile.

"Keep talking to her, she can hear you," Nurse Gordon encouraged JD. He took her hand in his and began talking to Tracy. Eventually JD fell asleep on the side of the bed.

The sound from the television woke JD. As he lay beside Tracy, he wondered what was going through her mind. He wondered if she would still marry him after all of this. He remembered talking to Pastor Smith about this very thing happening. JD began to second-guess his actions. When he was shot, he should have gotten out then. But that would put the people in Blackwell back under Juan's control. Tracy's hand moved. JD didn't know if he was dreaming or if she really moved. "Tracy!" he called out.

Tracy slowly opened her eyes. She looked around as if she was trying to figure out where she was. She moaned; everything on her was hurting, from her head down to her toes. "Tracy?" JD called out again. She tried to focus on his voice. "Hey," JD smiled. Tracy tried to answer back but it felt as if a ball of cotton was in her throat. "Here, take a sip of water," JD said, as if he knew what she was feeling. He put the straw to Tracy's mouth, and then pushed the button for the nurse. Tracy took a sip; the water felt good on her throat.

Nurse Gordon was there in seconds. She brought some ice chips in with her, anticipating her waking up. The nurse put the ice chips to her lips. "This might help with the soreness."

Tracy tried to say thank you, but couldn't. Tracy looked at JD. A soft smile came to her face. She whispered, "Hi."

JD sighed with relief. "Hey, it's good to see you seeing me."
Tracy smiled then flinched.

"Tracy, I'm going to push this button to release some pain medication. It won't be much, just enough to take the edge off," the nurse said. Tracy nodded. JD kissed her.

"Yuck mouth," she whispered.

"You or me?" JD smiled.

"Me." She sighed.

"I don't care. I will take you, yuck mouth and all." He smiled. "I missed you these past few days," JD said. Tracy was trying to get her bearings.

"How long?" she asked.

"How long have you been here?" JD repeated. "Two nights," he told her.

"Why?"

"You don't remember what happened?" JD frown. Tracy thought for a moment. Then her heart rate began to increase. She was remembering the first hit. She moaned and squeezed JD's hand tight. Tears began to fill her eyes.

"Talk to her, Mr. Harrison. Try to calm her down," Nurse Gordon said.

"Tracy, it's okay. It's all over. You are here with me. I promise I will not let anything happen to you ever again." He kissed her face. He wanted to comfort her, make her feel safe. She began to settle down a little, but not enough to satisfy Nurse Gordon.

"Mr. Harrison, I'm going to have to put her back under if she doesn't calm down."

"Tracy, baby, please calm down. I can't take another night without you to talk to. Baby, please, please, calm down." Tracy tried to get the images out of her head. She closed her eyes, but that made them worse. She looked into JD's eyes and saw the worry in them. She began to take deep breaths to calm herself. JD continued to kiss her face. "Please stay with me tonight, Tracy, please," JD cried.

"It's getting better," Nurse Gordon said. "We are going to have to be careful with that. I don't want her to be in any distress."

"Okay," JD said, "I will keep her calm; just don't put her back under like that." A tear ran down Tracy's face. JD wiped the tear. "I wish I could take this pain away for you," he said. "I'm so sorry about all of this." He sighed, and then swallowed back his own tears. He crawled in the bed beside her, held her in his arms and talked to her until she fell asleep. Nurse Gordon closed the door to the room. She left instructions that no one was to disturb them tonight.

Tracy was having a rough night. She was very uncomfortable with the small dosage of medication. Nurse Gordon called the doctor and requested an increase in the medication, only to help her sleep through the night. As much as JD wanted Tracy to be awake, he did not like seeing her in pain. He waited until she dozed off to sleep before he left the room.

JD went into the adjacent room where Cynthia and her crew had been working earlier. He was really surprised and pleased at the number of responses they had been able to prepare. He smiled at the job the crew had done. He began to read some of the cards and the attached response. The memory of telling Tracy about the baby played in JD's mind. It was the hardest thing he ever had to do. He had no idea Tracy was pregnant and neither did she. When he mentioned the baby, Tracy's eyes lit up with excitement, even though she was in pain. When he told her she had lost the baby, Tracy lowered her eyes and said she was sorry for causing him pain. A tear fell from JD's eyes. He had caused all of this to happen and she was apologizing to him.

"JD," Senator Roth said, pulling JD away from his thoughts.

JD stood and extended his hand. "Hello, Senator, it's good to see you."

Senator Roth shook his hand. "I received your message from Daniel you need to see me. How is Tracy doing?"

The strain of trying to keep his emotions under control was beginning to show on JD's face. "She's in a lot of pain. They keep her medicated for comfort."

"JD, you know if there is anything I can do, all you have to do is ask."

JD pointed to the chairs. "Have a seat. I need your guidance on something. Senator, I want to have a bill put into law. I know the normal steps to presenting a bill, but I really want this bill to pass. Where do I start?"

"What is it about?"

JD sat back and let out everything he had been thinking since the attack on Tracy. Now that he had voiced his thoughts aloud, he was fearful of the reaction from others. He did not want people to think he was doing this just because his fiancée was attacked. The truth of the matter was that his research already showed that a number of good prosecutors switched to defense attorneys because of threats to their families or themselves. In addition, several prosecutors had been intimidated or killed because of their work. JD pushed the statistics in front of the senator.

"You will be dipping into my side of the law now, son," Senator Roth said. "You do realize to get a bill passed you will have to lobby politicians. You have always expressed a sincere interest in keeping a good distance between you and us," he said as he laughed.

JD sat forward. "I realize that. That's why I need your guidance on this. I am not a compromiser. You know that. Even with this, as important as it is to me, I will not compromise my beliefs or my word."

Senator Roth liked JD's stand on issues. *He always says what he believes, popular or not*, the senator thought. *We need more men like him out front in the party: someone not afraid to take a stand and mean it.* Senator Roth left the research on the table. "I'll read it later. Sell me on it." He was anxious to see exactly how JD would handle the pressure.

JD said, "Okay, this is the purpose behind the bill." JD proceeded to explain the statistics and their implications.

They talked for hours about the need for the bill. Senator Roth always knew JD had the ability to persuade people to his will. He never realized how intelligent and thorough JD was. During his argument for the bill he did not miss a beat. His arguments for and against the bill were both thorough and precise.

The next morning, Senator Roth dialed the governor's office. *If we handle this opportunity correctly*, he thought as he waited for the governor's assistant to put him through, *we may have our attorney general in this election, governor in the next election and possible president in 12 years.*

"We need to meet tonight with the leaders of both the Senate and the House," he told the governor. "I'll be there in 15."

Chapter 30

Two weeks later, Tracy was released from the hospital. The news media got wind of the release and was out in full force. Several reporters were outside the hospital exit when JD and Tracy came down. The questions started coming the minute the door opened. Cameras started going off.

"What are your plans now, Mr. Harrison? Are you going back into the office anytime soon?" a reporter asked.

"Don't take the bait, JD," Victoria said, who was standing next to the SUV with Brian. "You don't owe him or anyone any explanations." She kissed Tracy's cheek. "It's good to see you, Tracy." Victoria smiled.

"It's good to see you, too. What's going on?" Tracy asked.

"Nothing for you to worry about, babe," JD replied as he opened the door for Tracy to get in.

"Don't you think the people have the right to know when their DA will actually be in the office?" the reporter yelled.

Tracy looked at Jeffrey; she released his hand and walked over to the reporter. She extended her hand. "Hello, what's your name?" she politely asked. The look on JD's face as he stood behind Tracy let the reporter know there would be a price to pay for his actions.

"Charles," the reporter replied.

"Hello, Charles." She smiled. "My name is Tracy. I realize Jeffrey has spent most of his time at the hospital for the last week or so because of me. And I must apologize to the citizens of the city for that. I was being a little selfish with his time. But now that I will be home, Jeffrey will be able to give his undivided attention to doing what he does best, and that's protecting the citizens of the city from crime." Tracy was still holding the reporter's hand. "I will ask you to give us the remainder of this day and he will be all yours again. Can you do that, Charles?" Tracy asked.

Tracy had not noticed all the cameras and microphones surrounding them. But Charles did. He was not about to deny a woman with a cast on her arm and bruises on her face anything with all the cameras on them. "Yes, I can do that." He smiled.

Tracy kissed his cheek and said, "Thank you." She turned and was blocked by the crowd of reporters; she began to panic.

JD picked her up and handed her off to Brian. Brian put her in the car as JD turned back to Charles. He asked the other reporters to give them a moment. They did. He smirked at Charles. "Tracy is a very nice person; I'm not. Remember that the next time you try to provoke me."

JD got into the car just as Brian yelled, "Don't ever go into a crowd like that again, do you hear me?" Tracy flinched.

"The whole world heard you, Brian," JD said calmly.

He kissed Tracy. "Thank you, but you do not have to defend my actions. There will never be a time I will apologize for being by your side." JD smiled.

When they reached JD's condo, Martha had the family room set up for visitors. She had made the sofa up for Tracy to lie down and relax. Within an hour, Tracy was asleep on the sofa. JD, Calvin, James and Brian had gathered in the living room discussing the bill JD was trying to put before the General Assembly when Senator Roth rang the doorbell.

Earlier in the day, the senator had received a call from the governor during the news broadcast of Tracy's departure from the hospital. "That's the key," the governor said. "Get her and you will get JD, without question. The two of them together looks like the White House in eight to 12 years. Let me take a look at the bill," he said. "Get on the job, Roth. This couple could be the very lifeline the party needs. If you are able to get him, I'll back them."

"Senator Roth, hello," Martha said as she opened the door. "The men are in the living room." "Thank you, Martha. How have you been?"

"I'm doing just fine, John, thank you for asking. Are you trying to get my son into politics?"

"Yes, Martha, I am. I'm going to have that son of yours as my governor before I die."

"I'm glad someone is finally getting to him."

"Hello, Senator." JD extended his hand."

"JD." He shook his hand and smiled.

"Son, I'm going home now," Martha stated. "Make sure you get these people out of the house early; Tracy needs her rest."

JD kissed her on her cheek. "I will. Thank you for everything, Mama." JD watched as his mother got into her car. "Senator, everyone is in the living room reviewing the research received on the bill. Would you like to join us?"

"Yes," he replied. "I took several meetings regarding the bill. We may have some support."

About an hour later, JD was returning from seeing the senator to his car. He yawned and shook his head; he was exhausted. "You look tired, Mr. Harrison," Nurse Gordon said.

"A little," he replied. "Ms. Gordon, I can't tell you how much it means to me to have you here. I realize I am intruding on your down time. There was just no way I would have survived without your help. Thank you. Did you find everything okay?"

"I don't usually get close to my patients, but you two are special. I will be here as long as you need me. Yes, I found everything I needed," she replied. "I'm going to get her settled in bed before I leave."

"Don't worry about that. I'll take her upstairs. It's late, go home to your family."

"Okay, I'll see you in the morning. Good night, Mr. Harrison."

JD went into the kitchen. "You staying the night?" he asked Ashley, who was cleaning the kitchen.

"Wild horses could not drag me away tonight."

He smiled as he hugged her. "Thank you." He went into the family room. Brian was stretched out in the Lazy Boy. "Are you staying, too?" JD asked.

"Can Skippy have puppies?" Brian asked.

"No, Skippy is a boy dog."

"Yeah, well, I'm staying anyway," Brian replied as he settled in.

JD laughed, went over to the sofa and kissed Tracy. "Wake up, sleepyhead." He picked her up and carried her upstairs. She had lost weight while in the hospital. She was lighter than the barbells he lifted regularly at the gym. "We are going to have to fatten you back up. Mama's cooking ought to do the job."

Tracy kissed his neck. "Is everyone gone?"

"Brian and Ashley are still here, but everyone else is gone. I thought they would never leave," JD replied. "How about a nice, long bath?"

"Okay."

JD returned to the office the next day. His desk was loaded with cases that needed to be assigned. He did not want the success rate of the office to decline; therefore he wanted to assign the cases to the proper individuals.

Mrs. Langston came into the office. "Believe it or not, these are actually organized," she replied smiling.

JD sat in his chair. "Okay, do you have something for me?"

Mrs. Langston smiled. "As a matter of fact, I do." She pulled open one of his desk drawers. There was a container with oatmeal raisin cookies in it.

He smiled. "A cup of coffee, no interruptions for the day and I can get this completed."

Happy to see him back in the office, Mrs. Langston said, "A cup of coffee it is."

Within the hour, JD assigned the lower level crime cases. The rest of the morning was spent reviewing the evidence on each of the remaining cases. Before he assigned a case, he wanted to determine how much legwork would be needed for a conviction. He could allow the cases to be assigned randomly or based on political favors, as Gavin had in the past, but he believed this way would connect the right DA with the right case. He knew the ADAs very well, their strengths and weakness, likes and dislikes. He was going to assign the cases based on that information. By the end of the day, the assignments were put into the computer. JD was going to hold off on the assignments of the more difficult cases until he had the opportunity to meet with the head ADA in each department.

"Mr. Harrison." Mrs. Langston's voice came over the intercom. "Senator Roth is here to see you."

"Send him in, thank you." JD stood. "Hello, Senator. Come in, have a seat."

"JD, I need you to review the suggestions from your people and be ready to do a dry run before a select panel by day after tomorrow. Will you be ready?"

JD looked at his desk and laughed. "Sure, I could do that."

Senator Roth laughed. "Good. The result of that meeting will determine our next step. You do realize if you are successful with this, I will ride you until you become a part of the ticket for the upcoming election."

JD smiled. "I know you will continue to try. Hell, you've never stopped. But my number one priority at this point is Tracy and my home life. After that is settled, I will reconsider my position with the party."

Senator Roth stood. "That's all I ask. Just open the door. How is Tracy doing?"

"She's smiling again, that's good enough for me," JD replied.

Senator Roth smiled. "I'm glad to hear it. Well, you have a lot to do in a short period of time."

JD looked at the desk. "Yes, I do, but it will get done."

Senator Roth departed. JD called Tracy to let her know he would be late coming home.

"Mrs. Langston, would you call Calvin and then come in here for a moment?"

When she stepped into the office, JD asked, "Mrs. Langston, do you have any plans for dinner?" "No. What do you need?" she asked in a knowing tone.

JD gave an apologetic smile. "The case I originally planned to assign tomorrow will need to be done now. Once Calvin and I assign these cases, I will need them put in the system before we leave tonight. Could you give us a hand with that?"

"You got it." She smiled.

"Hey," Calvin said as he walked in.

JD laughed. "Call Jackie; we are going to be late tonight."

Calvin exhaled as he took off his jacket. "Already called her; what are we doing?"

JD pointed to the desk. "We are assigning cases."

It took them most of the evening, but the job was completed. All assignments were made and put into the database. JD knew some of his decisions would be questioned, but the assignments were made based on experience, not on promises. They were leaving the office, but JD and Calvin still had work to do. They agreed to meet at JD's place in an hour.

When JD got home, Tracy greeted him at the door with a kiss. "Hello."

JD was surprised to see her up and around, but was sure Nurse Gordon was encouraging Tracy to move around and get back to normalcy. JD smiled vibrantly. "That makes up for the entire day," he said. He kissed her again as they walked over to the sofa in the family room and took a seat. JD told her about all he accomplished during the day and about the visit from Senator Roth.

"Are you going to consider being a part of the ticket?" she asked.

JD shook his head. "I don't know. I am not sure I have the tolerance to deal with people making deals and compromises. Unless I see something different, I can stay where I stand."

Tracy looked at him. "Sometimes we have to step out on faith. Just follow the path of things put before us. It may not be what we planned for ourselves, but it very well may be the answer to your purpose in life."

JD looked down at her. "That was pretty deep. Do you believe that is my path?"

Tracy thought for a moment. "I believe you are destined to do great things. How that will come about, I don't know. I don't trust Carolyn Roth on a lot of things, but on this I do. She based her entire future on you and that belief. I see how people react to you and how you react to them. You actually care about people. Isn't that the very type of politician you say we need?"

"I think people go into politics like that, wanting to find a way to help people," JD said, "then something happens to them and they forget the reason they were there in the beginning."

"Well, if you decide to do this, don't make the same mistake others have made," Tracy said. "I promise, after you win and your head gets big, I will remind you of this conversation."

JD smiled. "You promise?" he asked as he leaned down to her.

"I promise."

"Excuse me," Mrs. Gordon said. "While you two were in here making out, Mr. Johnson came through the garage and is at the table eating your dinner."

They laughed. "Calvin is here already?" JD said as he got up.

"Hello, Calvin," Tracy said as she walked into the kitchen and kissed him on the cheek.

"Hey, Tracy," he replied, still eating.

"Is it good, man?" JD asked, teasing Calvin.

"Man, I love Jackie, but she can't cook; not in the kitchen anyway."

Mrs. Gordon smiled; she loved to see people eating and enjoying her food.

As Tracy sat down, she asked, "What do you think about Jeffrey running for office?"

Calvin stopped eating and looked up. "It's about time man; the party can really use you."

JD put his hand up. "We were just talking, playing around with it a little."

"JD, you need to seriously consider this. You could single-handedly rejuvenate the party. The party needs us, young, strong leaders with integrity. You know, we always sit around condemning the way the system is. Maybe it's time to try to do something to change it."

JD looked at Tracy then at Calvin—the two people he trusted the most in the world, besides his mom and sister. They both seemed to think he should enter politics.

"I will consider it. But that's a long way off."

"Okay if I put together an exploratory committee?" Calvin asked.

"Why?" JD asked.

"To determine how much support you would possibly have if you do decide to run," Tracy answered.

JD and Calvin turned to her. "What do you know about politics?" JD asked.

"Just what I read in books."

"What books?" Calvin asked.

JD said, "Don't; don't ask."

Tracy smiled. "What office are you considering?"

"Governor?" Calvin suggested enthusiastically.

"No," JD frowned, "that's Gavin's position."

"And you don't think you could beat Gavin?" Calvin laughed.

"I don't want to beat Gavin. Gavin has paid his dues. He deserves to be in the race," JD replied.

"See," Calvin said, shaking his head, "that is part of your problem, you don't have the killer instinct. When you run for office it's just like going to trial. You must know what the opponent knows. You have to be out to win, no matter what."

JD looked at Tracy. "This is exactly why I have never shown any interest in politics. Here we have a mild-mannered individual who has turned into 'Tony Soprano' just at the mention of politics."

Tracy smiled. "Let's say grace."

After grace the conversation continued.

"I don't think Calvin's statement was that bad," Mrs. Gordon said. "If Tony Soprano had been into politics, he would be looking to out his own mother to get more votes."

"Thank you, Mrs. Gordon," Calvin said with a grin.

"You are welcome, Mr. Johnson. Mr. Harrison, I have to go now. Will you need anything else tonight?

JD stood. "No, thank you. You have a good evening." JD walked her to the door.

"Is he serious about this?" Calvin asked Tracy.

She hunched her shoulders. "I don't know. It just came up."

"How would you feel about it if he did?"

"I would support anything that Jeffrey wanted to do without hesitation. But I will not influence him one way or another. Something like this has to be his decision."

Calvin looked at Tracy. "JD is a born leader. He always has been. If JD told people that a beer a day is good for them, the grocery store shelves would be empty by the morning. His leadership is sorely needed."

JD walked back in. "Mrs. Gordon's last day with us will be Friday. She feels you are doing very well and you can be on your own now.

The telephone rang. "I'll get it," Tracy said.

As she left the room, Calvin turned to JD. "Is this why Roth is taking on the bill with so much gusto?"

"I believe so."

"Are you ready to pay that price?"

JD looked into the family room where Tracy was on the telephone. He thought about her safety. "Yes."

"Jeffrey, it's the police," Tracy said as she handed the telephone to him.

JD took the call in the family room. When he returned to the kitchen he announced that the other assailant in Tracy's attack was killed.

Calvin looked at JD. "What are the odds on that happening without some assistance?"

JD looked at Calvin. "That's the exact question the police are asking."

That same evening, Gavin and Carolyn were in Northern Virginia campaigning. Senator Roth was with them, but on another mission. The leadership committee was working on completing the Democratic ticket for the state's top offices. All were willing to put their support behind Gavin as governor only if the remainder of the ticket was strong. Gavin was the only contender for governor and Daniel Graham for lieutenant governor. There were several candidates for attorney general. Senator Roth wanted to get a temperature rating on JD. Most of the leadership were very familiar with JD and his efforts in the city.

Senator Roth was pleased with the outcome of the meeting with key figures at the DNC. With their backing, he was certain JD would be the next attorney general, which, in turn, practically would assure Gavin as the next governor and Carolyn as the first lady.

"What are all the secret chats about, Dad?" Carolyn asked later in the evening.

"Just trying to get the ticket complete," he replied. There was no way in hell he was going to let Carolyn in on this. Her focus was in the wrong place. She was still doing things to interfere with JD and Tracy. Roth loved his daughter, but sometimes she did not know what was best for her, and at times, did stupid things. Carolyn was not looking at the big picture. She was too intent on her own little world. "How did Gavin do this evening?"

"We raised another million tonight," Carolyn replied.

"Good work, this early in. We will need every dime of it to get him elected."

"Are you worried, Daddy?"

"Unless we surround Gavin with the strongest ticket possible, he will not win."

"Then I guess we better get some strong people; who do you have in mind?"

"We are working on it," he replied as Gavin came in. "Gavin, how are you?" the senator asked.

"We are doing well tonight, from what Carolyn tells me," Gavin replied as they shook hands.

"Glad to hear it. Have you two set a date yet?" he asked.

"No, not yet. Your daughter is dragging her feet."

Senator Roth looked at Carolyn. He knew exactly what she was doing. He had warned her before she went down this path with Gavin. She was still holding out hope that something will happen with JD and Tracy.

"Well, I was hoping to be a part of two weddings before the year was out. But I guess I have to settle for the one."

"Which one is that, Daddy?"

"Oh, I was talking to JD the other night," he began.

"That's right," Gavin interrupted.

"He and Tracy set a date," the senator continued.

Gavin smiled. "That's one New Year's Eve party I am looking forward to."

"Same here," Senator Roth replied. "I hope I get invited to the bachelor party."

"I am putting in bids now to make sure I am invited." Gavin smiled.

Carolyn was appalled that the two of them were having this conversation in front of her, but more than that, she could not believe JD would actually go through with this. "I think both of you need to get a grip. I don't believe JD will ever get married."

"Why?" Gavin asked. "Because it's not you he is marrying?"

Carolyn knew she had to tread lightly here. Gavin had asked her several times to set a date. She just could not bring herself to do that until she knew he was going into the mansion. "JD never indicated we were heading in that direction. So, no, it's not because of that. I just think it all happened rather quickly."

"Well, since I have invoked such deep conversation, my job is done. I will bid you two good night." Senator Roth smiled, happy to have a reason to leave.

"Good night, Daddy, and thanks a lot."

"Good night, Senator," Gavin responded as he watched Carolyn. "So, now that JD has set a date, do you think we can?"

"Gavin, the only reason I have not set a date is because I would like our wedding to be held at the Executive Mansion." Carolyn put her arms around Gavin. "You know how much that would mean to me?"

Gavin was not a stupid man by any means. He knew Carolyn was holding out for the outcome of the election, but for now, he would play along with her. The votes and support her family could bring in were needed. "Are you going to show me how much it will mean to you?"

Carolyn smiled. "With every ounce of power I have left in me tonight."

A few days later, JD was in his office when Senator Roth stopped by. He arranged for JD to meet with other DAs across the state to get their backing and/or input on the Officer of the Court Protection Bill. The meetings would take him out of town for several nights. Tracy was doing better. Hell, she was itching to get back to the office. JD still was not comfortable leaving her this soon, but getting this bill passed was important and could affect so many people's lives. He agreed to the meetings, which Roth set up in each corner of the state, making Northern Virginia the last. That way, by time he met with the members of the General Assembly, all the kinks would be out of his presentation. Roth's mind was not just on the governor's race at this point. In his mind that was already in the bag. He wanted JD to get some national attention. Being that close to Washington D.C., Roth planned to have one or two of his fellow U.S. senators in attendance there. Roth arranged for Dan, from the attorney general's office, to join them. This would give others an opportunity to see the two working together.

JD smiled as he kissed Tracy that evening. He loved coming home to her and could not imagine his life any other way. "Guess what?" he said excitedly. "Senator Roth arranged for me to meet with DAs across the state to push my bill."

"That's wonderful, Jeffrey." She hugged him. "So they are taking it seriously?"

"It seems like it; at least Senator Roth is." They sat in the family room talking. "This means I will have to go away for a few days," Jeffrey told her.

"Can I go with you?"

"No, I checked with Dr. Shaw and he said it was a little soon. But you can go back into the office if you take it easy."

"Okay. How long will you be gone?"

"I'll leave tomorrow for Roanoke. I will probably stay overnight."

"The senator will be with you at all the meetings?"

"I think so, why?"

"I just want to make sure someone is there that will have your back."

He smiled. "What do you think will happen to me?"

"I don't know. But you are going to be around people who don't know you. That can always be uncomfortable."

"Well, Dan will be going with us on these trips. He'll be representing the AG's office on this."

"Does that mean the attorney general supports this bill?"

"I would think so," JD replied.

"Then I guess it's okay. What about Brian? Will he be going, too?"

JD shook his head. "No, Brian has a new detail. He is now protecting Gavin."

Tracy laughed. "You are not serious."

"I'm afraid so." JD laughed.

"Okay, who is protecting Gavin from Brian?"

"That's a good question."

Chapter 31

Tracy was always an early bird and today was no different. When she arrived at Next Level Consulting, no one was there. She went to her office first. Everything was exactly as she had left it two months ago. She put her purse away then logged on to her computer. There were a number of e-mails. Tracy pushed away from the desk. *They have waited this long; they can wait a little longer.* She walked around the office observing. The new people were set up well. New furniture had been strategically arranged to accommodate everyone. *We are going to have to look into getting another location or expanding this one,* she thought. When they first moved into this building they had only three employees. Now the staff had doubled and more space was needed.

Tracy walked into Ashley's old office, which she was now sharing with Monica. Monica really had done a wonderful job keeping things going while Tracy was out. She handled the day-to-day operations and Ashley handled executive decisions. It was nice to see things were able to continue without her. *Hmm, or maybe not.* Monica demonstrated her leadership ability at a time it was needed. Maybe it was time to move Monica forward in the organization; she certainly had proven her loyalty. Other than a few mishaps, things had gone very smoothly.

As Tracy sat at the receptionist desk, she logged on to the computer to review the files. First, she checked the client contact list. Response time was important in their business. Customer service was the key to retaining clients. The times were a little behind for Tracy's comfort. She made a mental note to contact clients herself today, just to get a feel for how they had been treated while she was out.

As the staff came into the office, they were happy to see her. She met one of the new employees, Heather, and liked her immediately. Before Tracy could really settle in, Monica beamed with excitement. "Okay, tell me about the wedding plans. I heard the date is set for December 31ˢᵗ, New Year's Eve. I'm game for that."

"I have to check with Cynthia on things," Tracy replied.

"What are you waiting for? It's only two months away."

"I know; I may have to change that date."

"Hmm, JD is not going to be happy with that."

"JD is not going to be happy with what?" Ashley asked, as she walked through the door.

"Ms. Tracy changing the wedding date," Monica replied.

"Hey, girl," Ashley smiled at Tracy as she walked into the office. "It is good to see you in here. What is this about changing the date?"

"With everything that happened I haven't had time to work on the wedding," Tracy answered.

"Have you talked to Cynthia about it yet?"

"No, I'll try to reach her today." Changing the subject, she asked, "What time will everyone be in?"

Ashley looked at her watch. "Now."

Tracy raised an eyebrow. "Do we have attendance issues?"

"Yes, people show up when they want to," Heather answered.

Ashley looked at her, and then back to Tracy. "Let's just say, I am glad you are back. Monica and I are not good at the discipline thing. Heather was getting tired of me saying things will get right when Tracy comes back. Now you are back. Make it right."

"Once everyone arrives, we will meet and discuss." Tracy exhaled.

"Well, I have calls to make," Monica said. "Let me know when you guys are ready."

Ashley went with Tracy into the office to give her a rundown on what had gone on during her absence, including personnel issues with one of the new account executives, Denise. They also discussed Monica and how they would show their appreciation for a job well done.

Later in the morning, Tracy was helping Alicia, the clerk, with filing. While Tracy was sorting through files Denise walked through the door. Tracy's hands were full of files. "Hello," Tracy said, "would you mind grabbing some of these, before they fall?"

Denise looked at her like she had lost her mind. "Yes, I do. I'm not paid to do manual labor; you are."

Alicia's mouth fell open. "I'll get those," she said as she took the files from Tracy.

"Thank you, Alicia," Tracy said then turned her attention to Denise, who was at her desk. "Let's try this again," Tracy said. "Hello, I'm Tracy Washington, the person who signs that paycheck you receive; and you are?"

Denise was a little embarrassed. "I'm so sorry. I'm Denise Jackson. I didn't know who you were."

"Apparently, but regardless of who I was, if someone in this office needs help with whatever, we help. There is no 'your job,' 'my job.' Everything in this office is everyone's job or responsibility. Is that understood?"

Denise took offense to the way Tracy spoke to her. "I said I did not know who you were. I'm not going to apologize again."

Tracy's voice rose a little. "I don't recall asking for an apology. Nor do I need one; however, I do have the need to make sure you understand that when someone is in need, you help!"

Ashley and Monica came to see why Tracy's voice was raised. "What's going on?" Ashley asked.

"I don't know what her problem is," Denise said, "but Ms. Whoever doesn't seem to appreciate the people who have been doing the work around here while she was out doing whatever."

Alicia and Monica sat on the desk. "This is going to be good," Monica whispered.

Heather looked at Ashley. "Ms. Washington asked Denise to help with some files."

Knowing how Tracy allows people like Denise to walk over her, Ashley interjected, "You do realize this is your boss you are addressing."

Tracy stood there for a moment, observing Denise.

"I was hired by you. Do things change now that she's back?"

Tracy smiled at Ashley. "No, things don't change, but personnel do. Do you have any personal possessions in that desk?" Denise looked at her dumbfounded. "Do you?" Tracy asked again.

"Yes," Denise said meekly, looking at Ashley. Ashley folded her arms across her chest. She knew Tracy was a fair person; there was no way she would fire Denise without giving her a chance. But Ashley wanted to see how far Tracy was going with this.

"I suggest you remove them immediately and take your ornery ass back out that door to where you came from. The rest of you, we have a staff meeting in my office," Tracy said with an unyielding look on her face.

"Wait a minute," Denise said as Tracy began to walk away. "You can't just fire me; I mean, Ashley, aren't you going to say something here?"

Tracy put her hands on her hips and looked at Ashley. "Well, don't look at me like that," Ashley said. "I like my job. I'm not getting fired on your first day back. I'll wait until tomorrow." Ashley laughed.

Tracy turned to Monica and Alicia. They both jumped up and went into Tracy's office.

Heather got up. "I'm going to be in there with them. I would like to keep my job, too."

Once the employees were out of the room, Tracy turned to Denise. "You see, Denise, I am the founder, co-owner and CEO of Next Level Consulting. I will be damned if I will allow someone whose paycheck I sign to speak to me and certainly not to our clients in the manner you just did. This business is my life's work. I did not develop it to work with people like you who have no respect for others. If you feel for some reason you are above anyone in this office, you are working in the wrong place. No one who works for me will ever look down on another human being." Tracy exhaled and looked at Ashley, trying to calm herself down. She turned back to Denise. "Now, if you feel you can be a part of Next Level Consulting with what I just said you are welcome to stay, for now. But don't ever presume you can speak to me in that manner again."

Tracy walked into her office and Ashley followed. The meeting began and a minute later Denise walked in and took a seat. Tracy never acknowledged the action; she just continued with the meeting.

After the meeting, Ashley stayed in the office. Ashley looked at Tracy; this was a different Tracy. She was more assertive and had a certain confidence about her now. Ashley smiled. "I am so very proud of you. Any other time you would have let someone like Denise ruin your day."

Tracy smiled. "She pissed me off!"

"No shit." Ashley laughed. "It's about time you got pissed off."

"Oh, speaking of people who piss me off, I have to call Cynthia."

"Don't change the date, Tracy, it will break JD's heart," Ashley pleaded.

"Ashley, this is the end of October. The wedding is supposed to be in December. That only gives us 60 days to put together 'the wedding of the year,' as Cynthia calls it."

"It can be done and will be done. If anyone can pull it off, you know Cynthia can.

Tracy sat back and exhaled. "If we keep it simple, I guess it could be done."

Ashley smiled. "Since JD is out of town, why don't we all meet at your place to get things started?"

"Okay, speaking of places, we have to find a house. Jeffrey's condo is too small for both of us. I mentioned coming back to our apartment to him and he had a tizzy."

Ashley laughed. "I know, he told me about it. He asked me what in the hell was wrong with you. Did you honestly think he would let you out of his sight after what happened?"

Tracy smiled. "I don't know what I was thinking. Well, call Cynthia and Rosaline; see if they can meet us at the house. Give me two hours to call clients and I'll join you."

"I'll call Mama to see if she could meet us there, too," Ashley said as she left the room.

Tracy looked at her e-mails. "Let's get these cleared up."

When Tracy arrived home, Martha was there and dinner was prepared. "Hello, Mrs. Harrison."

"Hey, Tracy, now what made you think you could change your wedding date? Come here, child, take a seat." Martha wiped her hands off. "Tracy, JD would be so hurt. The whole time you were in the hospital he was afraid you may not marry him."

Tracy stopped tasting the macaroni and cheese that was on the stove. "Why would he think that?"

"Honey, JD feels responsible for what happened to you. And he thinks you believe he's responsible for it, too."

"I don't."

"Then don't change this date. If you don't do anything else this year, you make sure you marry that man."

Ashley, Cynthia and Rosaline walked in. "Hey, hey, what's up home girl? We ready to plan this wedding?" Cynthia started.

"Hey, girl, hugs all around," Tracy said. "Mama has cooked dinner for us, but it's a working dinner. So grab a plate and take a seat. I'm getting married on December 31 if it kills me."

"Ha, you mean if it kills us." Cynthia smirked.

"You're right," Tracy replied, "because you got two roles to play; you too, Rosaline."

"Why two?" Cynthia asked as she took a seat at the table with her plate.

"Well, you have to handle the planning and be a bridesmaid," Tracy said.

Cynthia's fork of food stopped midway to her mouth. "What?"

Ashley turned from the stove. "What?"

"I want Ashley to be my maid of honor; Monica, Rosaline and you as bridesmaids. Now, all I have to do is find someone to give me away. I don't know how that is going to work out," Tracy said, ignoring the shocked look on Cynthia's face.

Ashley rubbed Cynthia on her shoulders. She knew Cynthia was touched by Tracy's gesture to have her in the wedding.

"Well, we were just going to have a nice wedding. With me in it—oh, it's on. It will be fabulous!" Cynthia said.

"Good," Martha said, "the church has been booked. JD called Pastor Smith the day after Labor Day. The pastor said whatever day was needed the church was all his."

Cynthia said, with a mouth full of food, "The problem will be the reception. Everything is booked for New Year's Eve."

Tracy smiled. "I have an idea for that." Tracy placed a call to JD, who in turn called Douglas. He offered the use of the Renaissance. Once the obstacle was removed, the planning of the wedding was moving forward. The women decided to order dresses from the Internet and have them altered; Tracy decided to use Monica's mother, Judith, who was a seamstress. Rosaline planned the menu; Cynthia developed the theme, and then arranged for music, flowers, decorators and invitations; before the women left that evening, the wedding plans were just about finalized. Tracy couldn't believe all they accomplished in one night.

Right before everyone was about to leave, the doorbell rang. Gavin and Brian stopped by looking for JD. "Hey, Brian, come in, please," Tracy said. "I'm sorry, but JD is not here."

"Do you have any idea where I could reach him?" Gavin asked.

"You could call his cell," Tracy suggested.

Brian was standing behind Gavin trying to cut Tracy off. Tracy was looking at him frowning. She did not understand what he was trying to tell her.

"I tried his number but I did not get an answer," Gavin replied.

"Tracy, we really need to wrap up; come on," Cynthia said as she came out of the family room. She stopped almost mid-sentence when she noticed Gavin and Brian in the hallway.

She smiled. "I'm sorry; I did not realize someone was here."

Tracy looked at Cynthia and noticed her flirt was on big time. "Oh, hmm, this is my friend Cynthia, who just happens to be our wedding coordinator. You know Jeffrey's friend, Brian." Tracy smiled. "This is—"
"Gavin Roberts." Cynthia cut her off. "How do you do?" Cynthia said while extending her hand to Gavin. Tracy raised an eyebrow and looked at Brian. "Much success to your bid for the governorship," she added with a smile.

"Tracy, may I speak with you for a moment," Brian asked.

"Sure, would you excuse us, Gavin?"

"Take your time, Tracy," he replied.

"Cynthia, would you keep Gavin company for a moment?" Tracy asked.

"It will be my pleasure."

Tracy took Brian into the kitchen. "What's going on, Brian?" Tracy asked.

"Gavin is looking for Carolyn. He thinks she is with JD."

Tracy raised an eyebrow. "Why would he think that?"

"I don't know, he always thinks that. He does not know where JD is and it needs to stay that way."

Tracy was a little bothered by the thought of Carolyn being anywhere near Jeffrey. Brian could read Tracy. "JD is not with Carolyn. Believe me, I know."

Tracy smiled at Brian. "Do you know where Carolyn is?"

"Yes."

"Well, just tell Gavin where she is and let that be that."

"I can't do that, Tracy."

Tracy frowned at Brian. "Why would you keep things from a person you are supposed to protect?"

Brian looked at Tracy. "Sometimes keeping things from them is protecting them." Brian exhaled. "I hate working for certain people."

"Then get off this case."

"I don't have a choice who I am assigned to protect," Brian said. "I don't work for myself like you do. I work for the government. You go where they tell you."

Tracy smiled. "Maybe you ought to think about doing that."

"Doing what?"

"Working for yourself. I would hire you. That way I could try to get you settled down."

Brian laughed. "No, thank you, I'll stay with the government—less dangerous."

When Tracy and Brian went back into the family room, Gavin and Cynthia were the only ones left. "I'm sorry that took so long, Gavin, but I did not reach Jeffrey. When I speak with him I will let him know you need to talk to him."

Gavin stood. "Don't worry about it, Tracy. I apologize for bothering you with this. Cynthia, thank you for your company. I enjoyed our visit. Brian, are you ready?"

"Whenever you are," Brian replied. "Tracy thanks for your advice."

"You should seriously think about it," Tracy replied. "Good night."

Tracy turned to Cynthia. "What are you doing? That man is engaged to Carolyn Roth."

Cynthia picked up her purse. "He's engaged, not married," she said, smiling. "I will talk to you tomorrow."

"I thought we had more to do tonight."

"It's going to have to wait. I have plans," Cynthia said as she left the house.

Later that night Jeffrey called Tracy. He told her about the meetings with the area's DA. He was excited about the outcome of this first meeting. "So how much did you guys get accomplished on my wedding?" he asked.

Tracy smiled. "Quite a bit. The ceremony will be at the church at 6:30 in the evening. The reception will be at the Renaissance immediately after pictures. Oh, sweetie, you did not say how much the Renaissance is going to cost." "No charge."

Tracy sat up in the bed. "Are you serious?"

"Yes."

"Jeffrey, that is so generous of your friend. Now we just have to get a list of guests from you. Can you put one together tonight?"

"Yeah, I'll do what I can and have Mrs. Langston fax you a list with names and addresses tomorrow. I may not be back until Friday, you know."

"Yeah, I know. I miss you already," Tracy said.

"Not as much as I miss you. I never once thought about being alone before. Being here without you makes me appreciate having you to come home to every day. Right now I miss watching you take your shower, brushing your teeth. I even miss that ugly ass purple scarf you put on your head at night."

Tracy laughed. "Oh no, you didn't go there."

"Oh, yes, I did."

"When you do come home, I'll make sure I wear that scarf just for you." She smiled. "You had a visitor tonight," she continued.

"Who?"

"Gavin came by with Brian."

"Gavin? For what?"

"Brian said he was looking for Carolyn. He thought she might be with you."

JD was a little blown by that. "Carolyn must be up to her games again," JD said. Tracy did not say anything. "Tracy?" JD called. "Please tell me you are not thinking Carolyn is with me."

"No, I don't think that. I was just wondering what kind of game Carolyn would be up to that makes him think she is with you."

JD tried to explain. "Carolyn has a way of manipulating people; you know that, Tracy. I'm sure she is doing everything she can to get Gavin elected. And I do mean everything."

"Jeffrey, I don't understand things like that. If you are going to marry someone you should not be with anyone else. Or even thinking about anyone else."

"I agree," JD replied.

"Then why are Carolyn and Gavin playing this game with each other?"

"Why do you say Carolyn and Gavin?"

"Because Gavin was here talking with Cynthia tonight and I got the impression that it was more than 'Hi, how you doing' conversation. You know what I mean?"

JD smiled at her through the telephone. "Tracy, some people don't love the same way you do. You give your all when you love someone.

You don't play games. You don't bring any drama. Carolyn is a drama queen. Everything centers on her, her needs and her wants. Nothing or no one else is important. Carolyn is not in love with Gavin. Gavin is just a means to an end for her."

"And Gavin?" Tracy asked. "Why is Gavin with her?"

JD exhaled. "Gavin is with Carolyn for just about the same reason. He wants to be governor. Carolyn is the daughter of a very popular senator. Her connections and money can get him where he wants to be."

Tracy cleared her throat. "Life is too short to play those kinds of games. Both of them will be very lonely people if they continue living life that way. And I know because I tried it, when you pushed away from me."

JD hung his head. "I know, it didn't work for me either. But it took me five years without you to learn that. I don't want to learn that lesson again."

"I don't want to either." They were quiet for a moment. "Jeffrey, does this mean I have to be concerned with Carolyn?"

After all they had been through, JD could not believe she asked that question. "Tracy I'm not going anywhere. You are stuck with me for the rest of your life, or mine, whichever comes first."

"Thank you for that, but you being with me is not my concern. If Carolyn is not happy, that means she will still be gunning for me. To date she has tried everything from humiliation to sexual enticement. I don't want any surprises at the wedding. Do we have to invite her?" Tracy asked.

JD laughed. "I think we do."

"Okay. When you come home Friday, we have to meet with the Realtor."

"Did you find a house?"

"Yes, two actually; you just have to pick one." Tracy hesitated. "Jeffrey, you know I will not have anyone from my family at the wedding. There is no one to give me away."

JD heard the sadness in her voice. "We can always walk down the aisle together," JD offered.

Tracy smiled. "No, I'll just give myself to you. I'm sure there is something that can be done."

JD did not know what to say to make her feel better about this. "We could always go to Jamaica to get married. Just you and me," he said with a touch of humor.

"You know, at one time I would have jumped at that offer. But now I'm kind of excited about the wedding."

JD smiled. "I'm excited about you becoming my wife, finally. I know it seems quick to some people, but it's not soon enough for me."

Tracy closed the laptop and lay back on the bed. "Mr. Harrison, why don't you tell me what you are wearing?"

"Hmm! Do you think you are able to handle that conversation, Ms. Washington?" JD replied as he lay across the bed.

"With you, I can handle anything. Try me."

"Well, Ms. Washington, at the moment I am completely unclothed, swinging in the wind."

Oh no, she blushed, *what had she gotten herself into?* "Okay, shall I join you?"

"Please do."

She removed her clothes. "I just removed your Redskins tee shirt; the only thing I have on is red nail polish on my toes."

JD smiled. "Describe you to me," he asked in his deep, sensuous voice.

Tracy's mouth fell open. "What!"

"Go to the mirror and describe you to me from head to toe," he asked seductively.

She smiled, and then pushed the bathroom door closed to reveal the mirror on the back, and returned to the bed.

"Okay," she said, "I'm lying on the bed on my stomach."

"Turn over," he said before she could continue.

"Now I'm lying on my back with my head hanging off of the bed because it's the only way I can see the mirror."

JD laughed. "You have no idea what you are doing to me right now, do you?"

"No, but it sounds like you are enjoying it."

"Do you miss me?" JD asked.

"Yes, I do."

"Close your eyes," he said.

"Think back to the very first time we made love." JD's voice became low and husky. "Do you remember?"

"Yes," she said in a seductive voice.

"Do you remember my hands on your body?"

"Yes," she replied again, and then asked, "I also remember my hands on your body. Do you remember that?"

She flipped the script on him; that he did not expect. He turned onto his stomach, "yes," he moaned. The conversation went on through the rest of the night. Neither of them got any sleep that night.

The next day was a long one for Tracy and JD. Tracy's day began in the office contacting clients. It was actually good to talk with some of them; it had been a while. Many expressed dismay about the attack; and others sent their congratulations on the wedding. Many insisted on an invitation to the ceremony. Tracy's guest list was growing. Later in the day, Tracy met with Cynthia to pick out invitations. Cynthia had narrowed the selection down to five. Tracy loved all of them, but was able to reduce the number to two. She would allow Jeffrey to make the final selection. Cynthia made it clear: the invitations must go to the post office Monday morning. While Cynthia was still in the office, Monica's mom, Judith, came in with pictures of wedding dresses. Ashley ran in. "No one gets a say on this but me. Everyone else, get out," she said.

Cynthia protested and Monica smiled. "My mom will tell me which one she picks anyway." Tracy, Ashley and Judith spent the rest of the afternoon locked in the office. When they came out, each one was smiling. "Okay, Mama; give," Monica said.

"No, baby," she said, "not this time." She smiled and left the office.

Tracy and Ashley laughed. "I'm getting married!" Tracy screamed. Ashley and Monica fell out laughing at her. They had never seen her so excited.

JD's day started with a meeting of district attorneys in Roanoke. The meeting went so well, it was suggested another be set for Friday afternoon. Senator Roth was happy with the notion of having more people hear JD's presentation. JD was more impressive than the senator anticipated. Not only was he able to hold his own with questions on the bill, but when the conversations went to politics, JD proved himself more than capable of expressing his opinions and ideas on issues. There were times when the group disagreed with his position. He broke down their points of contention until he had them wavering on their viewpoints.

One of the men JD and the senator met with was planning to put his hat in the ring for attorney general. He suggested if JD was to run he would drop out of the race and support him. JD was flattered but indicated he had not considered running at this time. The man encouraged him to consider it. "The party needs someone who has not been beaten into submission; we need you," he said. Senator Roth could relax a little now. Key people were beginning to see what he did in JD. In addition, JD had been asked to consult on the Melvin case.

The case involved six little girls who were abducted from their homes, molested and killed by Charles Melvin. However, the conviction was wavering. The evidence was not connecting to a point of more than a reasonable doubt. The AG's office was unrelenting about the outcome of this case. Unfortunately, the DA handling the case was at his wits' end.

He asked JD to review the files to see if fresh eyes could reveal anything to put a needle in this man's arm. Of course, anything having to do with children touched JD's heart, so he agreed.

That afternoon was the first moment he had to himself; he called Tracy. JD was smiling before she answered the telephone. He was remembering their conversation from last night; or, more accurately, this morning.

"Hello, you've been on my mind all day, Ms. Washington," he said.

"When will you be home?"

"Tomorrow morning, not a minute later. I miss you."

Tracy smiled. "You ever wonder if there was such a thing as being too happy?"

"Yes, the day I met you," he replied. "I'll talk to you later."

JD sat at the desk and began to read the case file.

Chapter 32

Carolyn had just hung up the telephone with her dad. He was still in Roanoke. She knew he was with JD, but was not sure what they were up to. The cover story was about some bill JD wanted to pass to protect his "precious" Tracy. Carolyn was getting real tired of that. Every time she turned around there was something in the paper about the "power couple," as they were called. That should be her and Gavin getting that publicity, not JD and Tracy.

Carolyn had to make some moves here. Maybe she could give Gavin a date. Have a formal engagement party. Invite all the right people. Who could handle that? TNT seemed to be the hot event planners at the moment. First Carolyn had to get Gavin to ask for a date again. She would have to play up to Gavin for the next week or so. By Thanksgiving the date should be set. They could have the engagement party on New Year's Eve. That was the date of JD and Tracy's wedding, but invitations had not gone out. With everything that had happened with them over the past few months, Carolyn was sure they would change their date. She smiled to herself: *maybe they will cancel altogether.*

Carolyn went into the bedroom; Gavin was still on calls with his advisors. She sat on the bed and began to lotion her legs. As she pampered, Gavin's attention was drawn away from his conversation. As he ended the call, Gavin wondered what she wanted. Any other time she would shower, pamper and change her clothes in the dressing room, unless she wanted something. "What is it this time?"

Carolyn never looked up; she bent over exposing her back to him. "Do you think you could lotion my back for me?" she invited.

Gavin put the telephone on the dresser; he took the lotion out of her hand as she lay on the bed. He straddled her and began to lotion her back.

"Do you think we could skip the function tonight and stay in, just the two of us?" she asked.

Gavin smiled. "We have a few people expecting us; we should not disappoint them."

She turned over and looked up at him. She rubbed his thighs. "Please, Gavin. We haven't had any real time alone in weeks. I'll call and make the apologies."

Gavin stretched out on top of her. "What reason will you give them?" She smiled. "I'll tell them the truth: Carolyn is a horny girl and she needs to get laid."

"I'm sure that will go over big with the congressman," Gavin laughed. He pulled her hands over her head. "Now, what is it that you really want?" He kissed her neck.

"I want to get married," she pouted.

He stopped, looked down at her. He'd been trying to get her to set a date for weeks. "Carolyn." He kissed her between her breasts. "Why now? I've been trying to get a date from you for weeks." He bit one of her nipples.

She moaned. "I wasn't sure, before," she replied as she wrapped her legs around him.

He held her hands above her head with one hand, while the other slowly caressed her body. "Sure of what, whether or not JD was truly going to marry Tracy?" She started to move but he stopped her. "That game is over, Carolyn," he calmly said as he looked down at her. He slipped his free hand under her and pulled her closer. She could feel his nature growing against her leg; she thought that gave her the advantage. But it wasn't to be: Gavin's patience with Carolyn's antics had run out. He was now taking control of their relationship. "I will not spend another day wondering where you are and what you are up to," he said in a very calm, cunning way. He ran his tongue from her navel, between her breasts, up to her chin. Staring down at her he said, "From this moment on, you will behave in a manner consistent with the first lady of this state in public and in private. You may not love me, but from now on, you damn well better act like it. If you don't, there will be no date needed."

She looked at him a little stunned. "You can't win this race without me," she said.

He kissed her feverishly, with every intention of getting her hot. She moaned. He broke the kiss. "Try me," he said as he got up.

Not sure what had just happened, Carolyn watched him grab his jacket and put it on. "Where are you going?" she asked with a frown on her face.

"Out."

She laughed, not believing he was going to leave her in a state of wanting. "You are going out"?

"Yes," he said coldly, "and I expect you to be here when I return. If you are not, I will assume you chose not to comply with my request. In which case the engagement is off."

Carolyn looked at him in total disbelief. "You can't be serious."

Gavin exhaled. "I plan on moving into the governor's mansion next January. The question you need to find the answer to is, will you?" He started to walk out, then turned and said, "Be sure to give the congressman our deepest regrets for this evening." He closed the door behind him.

Carolyn threw the pillow at the door. "Shit!" she screamed.

Carolyn knew, eventually, Gavin was going to rein her in. She thought it would not happen until they were married. She got up and dressed. She wondered if this was a bluff. Would he really break the engagement? She placed the call to the congressman's office making their excuses. Then she called her father. Carolyn told her father about Gavin.

"Carolyn, before you went down this path with Gavin, I told you he was not a fool. Nor was he a man to put up with your nonsense. He is right, you either commit fully to him and his mission or you need to step aside."

Carolyn frowned. "Daddy, would you still back Gavin if I did not marry him?"

"Yes." He went on to say, "This is about state government, not my daughter's love life. One has nothing to do with the other."

"Will there ever be a time when your daughter will come before the state?"

Senator Roth hesitated. "Yes, when my daughter stops playing games and takes her own life seriously. Carolyn, if for one minute I truly thought you loved JD, I would have fought tooth and nail for you. But you don't love JD or Gavin. It's about which one could give you the limelight you want. You seem to think that light is in the mansion. Well, okay—do what you need to do to get there. Then what? Do you think you are going to be happy, Carolyn? I don't."

Carolyn sat in the chair pouting. "I don't know what to do, Daddy," she cried.

"Well, you better figure it out soon. It doesn't seem like Gavin is playing your games any longer."

Hearing his daughter's anguish and feeling partially responsible, because he did spoil her rotten, he tried to give her some sound advice. "Baby girl, talk to Gavin when he gets home. Be straight with him. He knows you don't love him, but he wants you anyway. Just know, if this is the road you are going to take, don't expect your marriage to be anything more than a political arrangement. Can you live with that, baby girl?"

Gavin made a call from his cell phone. "Hello, do you think you may have a few moments for a new friend?"

They talked for what seemed like hours. It was the most relaxing time Gavin had had in a while. He liked Cynthia. She was easy to talk to. Every time he tried to put up a defense during the conversation, she would knock him down. The fact that he could possibly be the next governor of the Commonwealth did not ease her tongue at all. She was straight up with him and he liked that. When she thought he was being phony, she called him on it. After the first hour, he actually felt so comfortable around her that he took off his shoes and just laid back. Funny thing, he thought when he left Cynthia's place, when he had first met her she had reminded him of Carolyn. After talking with her tonight, he knew she was different from Carolyn. Cynthia was not about games; she told you exactly where she stood on things. Gavin enjoyed that.

Carolyn was sitting in the drawing room when Gavin returned home. She tried to be calm. "It's late. Where have you been?"

Gavin looked at her with a raised eyebrow. "That's funny, Carolyn; you are normally not concerned with where I am or what I am doing. Why are you concerned now?" Gavin asked as he took off his jacket.

Carolyn was more than a little frustrated at this point. He had been gone for hours. "You are supposed to be my husband soon. I am concerned," Carolyn replied. Gavin did not respond to her. He placed his jacket across the chair. Carolyn adjusted her attitude and tried again. "Gavin," she said calmly, "let's talk; I mean, really talk about where we are headed and why."

Gavin walked over to the bar and poured both of them a drink. "Okay." He handed her a glass. "I'm listening." He sat on the chair across from her.

Carolyn started, "Gavin, we both want the same thing. You have your reasons; I have mine. Neither of us is in love with the other, but we are good together and good for each other. And I do care what happens to us. I know you think that I am in love with JD." She nodded her head. "I thought so too, but now I'm not so sure of that. Maybe I was just in love with the idea of what we could have been together." She smiled. "I guess my pride got hurt when he dismissed me for Tracy. Hell, look at me." She spread her arms out. "I still don't understand it." Gavin sat back in his chair and smiled; Carolyn was a beautiful woman. As he smiled she laughed. "But, either way, I don't want that to happen to me again. I have played with you and I do apologize for that. I can only say I will never disrespect you in that way again."

Gavin set his glass down on the table, sat forward and folded his hands in front of him. "Carolyn, you are one of the most exasperating people I know. If I thought for one minute I could live without you in my life, I would have walked out that door long ago." He hung his head down and smiled. "We both have the same desires, and you are right about that. But you are wrong about one thing: I do love you. I love that crazy ass free spirit of yours that causes you to do stupid things. I love the confidence you have, the way you walk into a room and rule it. I love watching your mind work on the next scheme. I love that passion you show me when your guard is down. However, I don't love the way you try to manipulate others or me. And I hate it when we make love and you fake it."

Carolyn started to say something, but Gavin stopped her. He just wanted to get past this point. "I give up trying to wait on you to fall in love with me. Just tell me the date—and why?"

Now that she had her say Carolyn did not see any reason not to be straight with Gavin. "I was thinking next spring, right before the campaign appearances get heavy. I would like to have the engagement party on New Year's Eve," she said. Gavin looked at her, waiting for the why.

She rolled her eyes and said, "I know that JD and Tracy were supposed to get married that day. So I thought I would try to upstage them with our engagement party."

Gavin smiled. "Now, was that so hard?"

"That depends on your reaction."

He laughed. "Have you already made arrangements for the party?"

She looked at him as if he had insulted her with that question.

Gavin looked back at her. "Well, have you?"

She smiled. "Not yet, but I have plans in the works."

Gavin sat back. "I'm surprised you have not set things in motion. Go ahead with your plans. But I'm sure JD and Tracy are still getting married on New Year's Eve. Our engagement party will not upstage them. You really need to let the anger you have towards Tracy go. She didn't take JD from you; you never had him. Nevertheless, I will support whatever you choose to do, as long as it does not hurt anyone I care about. JD is someone I care about and a colleague. You don't want me in a position to make a choice between the two of you. As for Tracy, JD will be the least of your worries if you hurt her."

Carolyn stood. "Okay," she said, not sure what he meant by that. "Are we good here?"

"As far as the marriage goes, I know where you stand. Make the plans for your wedding. Just let me know where and when. I'll be there."

Carolyn never had anyone to profess their love to her. It wasn't such a bad feeling, but she didn't know how to respond. She never had been in the position to have to consider someone's feelings before, but there was something in the way Gavin spoke that made Carolyn feel not as sure about her hold on him.

"I'm going to bed now," she said. "Are you coming?"

Gavin looked at her. He knew he could have her tonight if he wanted to; and he did. But at this point he was tired of trying to get her to care about him. He was thankful she was finally honest about her feelings. That was more than he had from her before. The marriage would be one of political convenience to him from this point on. "No, I have some things I need to do, but you go ahead."

Carolyn was bothered with that answer. She knew when he left Gavin was as ready as she was. *Could there be someone else?* She thought for a minute. *No,* she answered herself, and dismissed the thought. "Okay, good night."

"Good night," he replied. Carolyn hesitantly went upstairs. Gavin pulled out his cell and dialed Cynthia's number. "Thank you for this evening," he said.

"Anytime," Cynthia replied. "Good night." They ended the call.

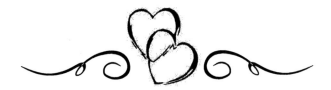

Chapter 33

Senator Roth and JD's plane landed on time. The senator's car was waiting for them at the airport. JD called Tracy from the car to let her know he was on his way home. Senator Roth listened and watched JD. "You are in love with that woman, aren't you son?" he asked when JD hung up.

JD hung his head as he put his cell phone away. "Yes, sir, I am."

"Did Carolyn ever have a chance?"

JD thought for a minute. "No," he said honestly. "But it wasn't on her, it was on me. I fell in love with Tracy years ago, but I was into advancing my career and would not admit it. No one who came along after that had a real chance with me."

Senator Roth admired the way JD accepted this love into his life with no doubts or hesitations. "So the wedding is definite?"

JD smiled. "New Year's Eve."

"You're going to have one hell of a coming year, JD. I hope you are ready."

JD looked at the senator then out the window, then back at the senator. "Are you referring to the marriage or are you referring to your plans for me?"

The senator laughed; he was wondering when JD was going to broach the subject. "Both, son," he said as they pulled into JD's driveway.

"Thank you for everything, Senator," JD said as he shook his hand.

"I'll be in touch, JD. Tell Tracy hello for me."

"I'll do that." JD watched as the car pulled away. He wondered if he was ready for the New Year himself.

JD opened the front door to find Tracy sitting at the top of the staircase waiting for him in nothing but his Redskins tee shirt. "Welcome home." She smiled. JD closed the distance between them while removing his suit jacket and tie. He gathered her into his arms as she wrapped her legs around his waist. No words were needed as the two ascended into the bedroom unable to think or speak of anything other than the degree of desire the absence created between them. Neither of them really cared about the outside world or its issues. All they wanted was to hold each other until they were both satisfied.

They made love for hours, trying to make up for the days they were apart. Just as round three was about to start, the telephone rang. On the third ring, JD knocked the telephone to the floor. Tracy laughed, then pulled him back down to her.

JD laughed. "Help," he cried weakly as Tracy straddled him. JD eased her hips down and moaned as he entered her again. He placed kisses from her throat down between her breasts and inhaled the scent he had longed for while he was away. He held her tight as she moved her hips in a slow rhythm that created a fire within him that literally took his breath away. JD couldn't tell you who was in control at this point. All he knew was he could not get enough of Tracy.

Tracy's cell phone rang, but she did not have the strength or desire to answer. Her movement was slow and easy, just as their explosion that followed. They sat there in the center of the bed, her head on his shoulder and JD caressing her back, as they waited for their bodies and minds to settle. The cell phone continued to ring. Tracy reached over and answered, still resting in JD's embrace.

Cynthia's voice came through loud and clear. "I don't give a damn how many babies you are trying to make. I have a wedding to plan and invitations to get out by Monday. Get your asses down here now."

Tracy hung up the phone. "We have to go," she said while kissing the side of his neck. JD eased her body up then back down onto him.

"Jeffrey," Tracy whispered, "the wedding."

"Hmm, hmm," JD moaned as he repeated the action while kissing her neck.

Tracy arched her back to allow him deeper entry. She tried to ignore the feeling building in her body. "We are trying to get a wedding off in two months; we have to go," she said unconvincingly as JD ran his hands down her body. JD lifted her body and entered her again. Tracy sighed. "Umm, okay, one more time."

When they arrived at the Renaissance, Cynthia was fuming. "Do you know what kind of time restraints I have on this wedding? You and JD," Cynthia said looking at him, "can get your jollies off on your time, not mine."

"I'm sorry," Tracy said with a smile.

JD came up behind Tracy and kissed her neck. "I'm not," he said as he walked by.

"Mr. Harrison," a waiter called out, "Mr. Hilton had to leave but will return shortly. He said take your time, whatever you need is at your disposal."

"Thank you," JD replied.

"Okay, Cynthia, what do you need?"

"I'm not talking to you, JD. I need you to sit here and select from these two invitations. Tracy, you come with me."

JD read the invitation, which was fine, but the unspoken was loud and clear. Tracy did not have any family to take part in this service. The thought disturbed JD and he frowned.

"Do you see your life coming to an end?" Douglas laughed.

JD stood and smiled. "Doug." He shook his hand. "No, man, just the opposite."

"I don't know, man, you looked a little down a minute ago."

"Yeah, well it definitely wasn't about marrying Tracy." JD beamed.

"Good, I'm glad to hear that. You two have been through enough. By the way, where is she?"

"Somewhere in the building with Cynthia."

Douglas laughed. "Man, I hope you have your checkbook protected with that one."

JD laughed. "With Cynthia, you don't have to tell me."

"Did I hear my name?" Cynthia asked.

"Yeah, in the same sentence with money," JD snickered.

"Oh, good, I like that combination."

JD grabbed Tracy by the waist. "Babe, you remember my friend Douglas."

"Sure, hi, Douglas." Tracy extended her hand.

"Tracy," Douglas replied. Tracy froze. She had heard that voice before, but she couldn't quite place where.

"Did you find everything you needed?" Douglas asked.

Tracy dropped her hand. That was the voice that talked to her the day of the attack.

"Tracy?" JD called out. "Tracy, are you okay?"

Tracy looked at JD: did he know it was his friend who was with her that day? "Tracy, what's wrong?" JD asked again very concerned.

Tracy looked at Douglas—the expression on his face told her all she needed to know. "I'm sorry," she said shaking her head, "I'm fine."

Douglas realized she recognized him, but he didn't know how she could. She was unconscious when he was there. "Are you sure you're okay?" Douglas asked in a low, calm voice.

"Yes," she said as she stepped up and hugged him. She kissed him on his cheek. "Thank you, Douglas, for everything."

An unspoken bond formed between them at that moment. Douglas knew she would never tell anyone he was at the location of the attack. Douglas smiled. "You are more than welcome."

JD watched the exchange between them and wondered what they were not saying. "Okay, you two. It's not that big of a deal; just a building."

Tracy smiled up at him but did not look him in the eye. "You're right. I'm just a little emotional about all of this," she said as she put her arms around JD's waist.

"Hold on to those emotions. We have more of this building to look at," Cynthia said as she pulled Tracy away. Tracy looked back at Douglas and smiled.

JD looked at Tracy, then Douglas. "Doug, man, I think you are blushing."

Doug smiled. "You hold on to her; she's a good one."

JD knew what the answer would be, but he asked anyway. "Do you want to tell me what that was all about?"

Doug looked at JD. He did not need to be put in the position of prosecuting his friend for defending his girl. "Naw, I don't think so. You ready for this marriage shit, man?"

JD looked at Tracy then back at Douglas. "If you had that, you would be too."

Douglas raised an eyebrow. "Yeah, you right."

They both laughed. "You ready to get into a tux, man?

Douglas's smile widened. Although he and JD had been friends since high school, he did not exactly fit into JD's world. JD was a big-time district attorney and Doug ran a nightclub. Douglas was touched when he asked him to be a part of the wedding party. "It would be an honor. Thank you, man."

JD smirked. "That's what you say now. Wait until you have to deal with Cynthia and this wedding."

Tracy came back into the room. "Jeffrey, we have to go. We have an appointment with the realtor."

"Okay, babe. Listen, Douglas agreed to be a part of the wedding."

Tracy smiled. "Welcome aboard; I wouldn't have it any other way." She looked up at JD. "You ready?"

JD got in the car. "Do you want to tell me what that was all about with Douglas?"

Tracy did not want to get Douglas in trouble by identifying him as the man on the scene of the attack. The timing couldn't be better, since the case had just been closed by the detectives. "I'm just really happy he is around," Tracy replied. She pulled out the package on the houses and gave   JD   the   first   address.

Chapter 34

The trip with Senator Roth had been very successful. JD received a lot of support for the bill and was able to meet some colleagues across the state. But JD was glad to be back in the office. He had left instructions with Calvin on how he wanted case assignments handled. The high profile cases were assigned based on who could bring in a conviction, not on office politics. JD expected the controversy and anticipated the heated debates that would take place during the staff meeting. Well, he would deal with that during the meeting. In the meantime, JD placed a call to the DA in Roanoke handling the Charles Melvin case. There were two pieces missing to the puzzle that should have been addressed prior to the case going to court. The DA advised him that the political pressure forced his hand to take Melvin to trial expeditiously. JD suggested he request a recess until the issues were addressed. He advised the DA to call the AG's office and inform them, based on the current evidence; the case would result in an acquittal. The attorney general called JD and reviewed the case file with him directly. They agreed: it was best to request a continuance until the key issues were addressed.

The judge in the case, however, refused to grant a continuance because the case had been in trial for three months. He felt the issues should have been addressed prior to the charges being made. The attorney general and the DA asked JD to take over the case. With a new DA on the case, the court would have to grant the continuance and give them the opportunity to tie up loose ends. The current attorney general was planning to run for a senate seat in November. A loss on this case, so close to the campaign, would certainly play against him. The AG knew JD very well and knew if he tried the case he could and would bring in a win for him. They may have different political affiliations, but both the AG and JD did not like to lose, especially when the case had to do with children. JD agreed to take the case if the current DA would co-chair. The AG agreed. Now the problem for JD was trying the case in Roanoke County with the wedding only six weeks away and the house closing weeks away.

As JD tried to sort through timeframes, Calvin knocked on the door. "You need to see me?"

"Yeah, come on in. Have you been keeping up with the Melvin case?"

Calvin nodded. "Yeah, the six little girls," he replied as he took a seat.

"That's the one. The AG has asked me to take it over. With the evidence they have, he is going to get off. I sent the investigators back out to do some more legwork. There was a witness who saw him in an area of the county. No follow-up on the witness was conducted, or a search of the area in question. I will lay odds, that's where the girl's clothes are going to be found. The witness, if reliable, will be able to put Melvin in the area around the time of the girl's disappearance."

Calvin asked, "Why wasn't this witness checked out before? You know that will be the first question the defense is going to ask. Then they will insinuate a frame, because of the delay."

JD acknowledged Calvin's observation. "That's why the AG is requesting a change in DA. Our contention will be a more experienced DA should have been assigned to the case originally. However, due to the budget restraints it was impossible at the time."

"That might fly, especially since everyone, even the judge in this case, wants to see this bastard behind bars," Calvin added. "But, JD, how are you going to handle the case with the wedding coming up?"

JD exhaled. "I will request a continuance tomorrow, which the judge indicated he will grant with the change. I'll give the investigators a week to follow up with the witness. If they do not turn anything up, I'll see if we can pull Brian from Gavin's detail and send him out there. If all goes well, we can have this case wrapped up within 30 days. The AG's office will provide the chopper for transportation until the case is a done deal."

Calvin looked at JD. It was time for him to make the next move. He closed the door. JD waited. He knew what Calvin wanted to discuss. The same thing people had been talking to him about for the past few months. "What's holding you back?" Calvin asked.

JD stood and walked over to the window. He put his hands in his pockets and looked down at the floor, the way he always did when he was searching for answers. He exhaled, then looked up. "If I decide to do this, it will change our lives. Are you in with me if I decide to run?"

"I'm with you whether you run or not. But you and I both know it's time to make that move, one way or another."

JD sat back down. "Alright, there are things I need looked at before I make a final decision. Let's get Brian and Douglas in on this. We can meet at the Renaissance tonight and talk things through."

Mrs. Langston came through on the intercom. "Mr. Harrison, the staff has assembled in the conference room for the meeting."

"We will be right out," JD replied. "Okay, let's go calm the natives."

JD had several messages waiting for him after the meeting. Brian and Douglas both were free to get together tonight. Tracy called and his mom called. Tracy was trying to get things set for the new house. JD knew he was leaving a lot on Tracy, but it couldn't be helped. The Melvin case was important for so many reasons. The case was being watched nationally, because of the nature of the crimes. It was also important to bring closure for the parents of those six little girls. No use putting it off any longer—he had to let Tracy know about the case. He asked Mrs. Langston to call Tracy first, and then he would talk to his mom.

"Hey, babe," he started. "I have good news and bad news. Which do you want first?"

Tracy closed her eyes. "Give me the bad first."

"I have to go back to Roanoke tomorrow. The AG asked me to take over a case they are having a little trouble with."

Tracy was disappointed. She had a number of clients she wanted to connect with at the office. On top of that, a thousand and one things had to be done before the wedding and the closing on the house. Tracy understood his work was important, so she did not comment on the wedding or the house. "How long will you be gone?"

"Just for the day. I'll be back tomorrow night," JD replied, then added, "I also have a meeting tonight after work. Did you have anything you needed me to do?"

Tracy thought about the long list of things that needed to be done. "No, I guess it could wait a day or two."

"I'm sorry, babe."

"It's okay. What's the good news?" Tracy asked, really in need of it now.

"I was able to clear the calendar for the dates you gave me. So tell me, where do you want to go for our honeymoon?"

Tracy smiled. "Anywhere you are would be just fine for me."

JD smiled. "Hey, let's tell everyone we are going out of town and spend our honeymoon at the new house; uninterrupted, just you and me, for two whole weeks. We could actually start working on our first baby."

Tracy smiled at the thought. "It would technically be our second," she said.

They were both silent for a moment. JD was still feeling responsible for the attack that caused Tracy to lose the baby. He remembered how she took the news in the hospital. Tracy had no idea she was pregnant. Telling her she was and then telling her she had lost the baby was the hardest thing he ever had to do in his life. He would have given anything not to have to tell her about it at all. "Tracy, if there was any way I could make that hurt disappear, I would."

Tracy did not hold Jeffrey responsible for the loss of their first child. "I'm not asking you to, but I will ask you to let it go, Jeffrey. You will not be able to help me heal from that loss until you heal. The guilt you carry around is going to eat you up alive if you don't let it go. You can't let it be an unspoken part of our life. We need to be able to talk about it without it causing either of us to feel any guilt about what happened. Every time I mention it, you go into this apology mode. I don't need an apology from you; you didn't cause me to lose our baby. It just was not meant to be. But don't worry; you still will get five children."

JD smiled. "Twelve, a football team."

"Okay, but number six is on you." Tracy laughed.

JD knew he was a lucky man to have Tracy. "I love you, Tracy," he said sincerely.

"I love you, too, Jeffrey."

"I'll see you tonight when I get home," JD said as he hung up the telephone.

All the guys were in the house, Douglas, Brian, Calvin and JD. JD was fully prepared for the onslaught of ribbing he was going to get from his friends. "JD, man, I would have never picked you to be the first one to bite the dust," Douglas said.

"Me either," Brian added. "I thought it would be Calvin. Women were always able to control him."

"What the hell do you mean by that, B?" Calvin asked.

"Oh, come on, Calvin, you know women used to whip your ass for fun," Douglas teased. JD just smiled, knowing they were going to hit him next. "Speaking of whipped, JD, my man," Douglas said in a joking tone.

"I knew it was coming." JD smiled. "Here we go."

"You're breaking up the karma here."

"Shit," Brian laughed, "you got my blessing, man. 'Cause if I had that phat ass, the hell with the karma."

"Karma be damned," Calvin said as he laughed.

"You got that right."

"You really are going to do this?" Douglas asked.

"You're damn right, I'm going do it. I should have done it a long time ago," JD replied.

"No, man, you weren't ready then and neither was she. It's happening when it is supposed to happen," Calvin said as he took a drink.

"I just want to make sure it happens," JD said. "So much has hopped off in the last six months. I don't want to take a chance on losing her."

"I hear that, man," Brian said, "you two have been through hell and back in a short period of time. But it's made you stronger."

Douglas nodded his head, agreeing with Brian. "At some point in every man's life you have to take stock. You have to determine what you want from this world. If you know you have met that one to take to the next level, then go for it."

"Here, here," Calvin said, "to the next level."

They all picked up their glasses and took a drink. JD was a blessed man to have these three friends. He trusted each of them with his life. He knew if anything were to happen to him, each of them would step up to take care of Tracy and any children they may have.

JD leaned forward. "Let's look at the next level," he said seriously. "How do you guys feel about me running for attorney general?"

Brian and Douglas looked at each other, then at Calvin. Brian ran his hand around his mouth and down his chin. Douglas sat back in deep thought. "Have you talked to Tracy about this?" Brian asked.

"It's been mentioned," JD replied.

"She gets first say. That's how it is should be." Douglas sat forward. "You know that political game ain't a joke. They are worse than the shit we deal with on the streets. They will go after your family, dead or alive." Douglas cautioned.

"Yeah," Brian added, "then come after your firstborn."

"They will dig up every woman you have ever thought about being with, and you know you have a record, JD. It will not be just about you either; there's Tracy. Anything that may be in her past will be looked at and scrutinized," Doug added.

"Al is going to come out. You do realize that," Brian added, "maybe Tracy's family situation."

JD hung his head; the last thing he wanted was for Tracy to have to go through anything because of his decision. He stood, put his hands in his pocket, then walked over to the door and looked down. Brian looked at Douglas.

Douglas went over to JD. "Man, you are one of the best at what you do. It doesn't matter if it's in a courtroom or on the house floor; you know your shit. You have always been a leader. This state could use you; there is no doubt about that. I want you to think long and hard about this before you decide. You don't owe your father your life." JD looked up. "Hear me out," Douglas said before JD had a chance to respond. "Your dad was a damn good man—we all know that. We also know you've been living your life based on his wishes for you. Now you have to take what he instilled in you and move forward. It has to be what you want, not your dad, mom or Tracy. That political life doesn't stop when you go home at night. It's 24/7."

Brian got up and stood on the other side of JD. "You could have an effect on a lot of people's lives, man. It would be good to have an honest-to-goodness good man in office. But you may be the only one. You will have to surround yourself with people you know and trust and even that may not be enough to protect you. Now with all that being said, don't stop at the AG spot; go for the gusto."

"Hell, run for president," Calvin said.

Douglas looked up; JD looked around; and Brian said, "Here, here."

JD looked at each of them as if they had lost their minds. "President of what?"

Brian shrugged his shoulders then sat back down. Douglas shook his head then sat back down.

JD stood there with his hands in his pocket looking at his three friends. It was humbling to think they thought that much of him. "Each of you has lost your damn minds." He chuckled as he sat back down. Calvin smiled; he knew at that moment JD began to take running for AG seriously. Before, JD was asking questions just to satisfy Senator Roth's curiosity; now that he knew his boys were behind him, it was a go.

"This is what I need from you. I want each of you to take a part of my life and run it through the mill. Between the three of you, there should be no stone left unturned. I need to know what's out there and who has it. I'll get James Brooks to do the same on Tracy."

"Why Brooks?" Brian asked.

"If there's anything out there I need to know, Tracy should be the one to tell me. If Brooks finds anything, he will be discreet and he will protect Tracy at all costs; even against me."

"Alright, it's a go. How much time you giving us?" Douglas asked.

"I'm not going to make any decisions until after the wedding. So you have until the first of the year," JD advised.

Douglas looked at JD. "Man, I am proud as hell of you. You lead the straight life and it's going to pay off for you. May God's blessings be upon you, my brother."

They all drank to that.

"I have one question," Brian said.

"What's that, B?" JD asked.

"Why Calvin got to be the best man?"

That night when JD got home, Tracy was lying across the bed asleep. He pulled his shoes off and lay beside her. He put his arms around her and pulled her to him. She kissed his cheek and lay on his chest. JD believed in his heart this was what he was meant to do with his life. His only concern was what effect all of this may have on Tracy. He rubbed her back and considered how his decision would affect their marriage, their children or their future. He made a mental note to set up a meeting with Pastor Smith and to call James Brooks to get the ball rolling. "President." He laughed.

"Of what?" Tracy asked sleepily.

"Nothing, babe." He kissed her forehead. "Nothing at all."

Chapter 35

Tracy arrived at the office around 9:30, which was late for her. She had taken Jeffrey to the airport to catch the chopper to Roanoke. He had seemed so deep in thought this morning. Tracy attributed his quietness to the case.

"Good morning, people," she said.

"Good morning, Ms. Washington," Heather replied.

"Hey, Tracy," Monica said. "Did you see the dresses? They came in last night."

Tracy smiled. "No, not yet."

Alicia handed Tracy her messages. "Your Realtor called. She said it was important."

"Thank you," Tracy said as she headed to her office.

"Excuse me, Ms. Washington," Denise called out.

Tracy stopped. "Yes, Denise?"

"I was wondering, are you going to be looking for a larger place for us? You know it's getting a little cramped in here."

Tracy raised an eyebrow. "It's on my list to do."

"Well, when you call your Realtor back you may want to mention you need a larger building with windows and offices."

Tracy looked at Denise rather amused. She knew Denise was right, but it never ceased to amaze her how forward Denise was about things. "Is there anything else?"

"No, I think that will do it for now."

Tracy laughed. "Okay."

Tracy went into her office and sat down. It was only 10 in the morning and she was exhausted. Between planning the wedding and arranging for the new house, she was worn out. After all, she only been out of the hospital for a few weeks and had been going non-stop ever since.

"Hey," Ashley said from the doorway, "you look beat."

"Well, thank you and good morning to you."

Ashley sat on the sofa in Tracy's office with her cup of coffee. "I talked to Cynthia this morning. Carolyn Roth is having a Christmas party to announce her engagement."

Tracy yawned. "Okay, it's not tonight, is it?"

Ashley laughed. "No."

"Good," Tracy replied.

"What can I do to help, 'cause you're about to fall out of your chair," Ashley said, half laughing.

Tracy smiled as she laid her head on the desk. "I don't know. I'm too tired to think."

"I'll tell you what, I'll get with Cynthia and take over the wedding stuff while you handle the house stuff."

Tracy yawned. "Okay."

Ashley laughed. "What on earth did you and JD do last night?"

"Nothing," Tracy said. "I was packing and fell asleep before he came home, I think."

Ashley raised an eyebrow. "He did come in last night?"

"Yeah, it was late, but he came in."

"Where was he?" Ashley asked.

"I don't know, I didn't ask," Tracy said as she sat up.

Alicia came to the door. "Ms. Cynthia is on line one for you, Ms. Washington."

Tracy made a face. "Don't ever let Cynthia do your wedding; she will run you to death. Let this be a warning." Alicia laughed.

Ashley picked up the telephone. "What you need, whoreletta?" Ashley asked laughing.

"Did you see the dresses?" Cynthia inquired.

"Yeah, mine came in last night."

"Well, mine needs to be adjusted. We all should meet up and try the dresses on together."

"Okay, but tonight is not good for me or Tracy. Let's meet tomorrow," Ashley suggested.

"That will work. Where's Tracy?"

"Lying on her desk asleep."

"Call on line two, Ms. Washington."

Tracy looked up at Alicia and exhaled. "Thank you, Alicia." Alicia smiled and walked out of the office.

"Look, I got to go," Ashley told Cynthia, then hung up the telephone.

Tracy picked up the phone. It was the Realtor. The house closing was set for next Friday. If all went well they could move into the house the first of December. Tracy hung up the telephone; she wanted to cry. "What is it now?" Ashley asked.

"We close on the house next week."

"Next week is Thanksgiving."

Tracy frowned. "That gives me 10 days to pack up Jeffrey's place and my stuff at the condo, buy furniture and plan a wedding." Tracy started whimpering.

"Okay, okay, don't panic. I'm the maid of honor with superpowers. First things first." Ashley picked up the telephone. She called James. "I know we had plans tonight, but Tracy's in a little bit of trouble and needs my help, so I have to cancel."

"That's fine. I've just been handed a project from your brother that I need to get started on. I'll call you later," James replied.

Then Ashley called her mom. "Hi, mom. We need your help at JD's place. Can you meet us over there in about an hour?"

"Sure I can," Martha replied.

"Thanks, Mom, see you there," Ashley said as she hung up the telephone. "Okay, now for the best part." Ashley walked over to the doorway. "Ladies, would you all step in here for a minute?" Everyone came into Tracy's office. Ashley began. "This is the mission, should you choose to accept it." Everyone laughed. "I need you guys to hit the Web sites; we have to do some serious shopping. We have a four-bedroom house we need to buy furniture for. Any questions?"

"Yeah," Denise said, "what's the limit?"

Tracy looked at Ashley. "No limit"

Denise smiled. "Oh, I like this game."

"Any help you can give me on this will be appreciated." Ashley smiled as everyone left the office. "Now, the next call we can make from the car. Let's go." While they were in the car, Ashley called Clair, James's housekeeper. Ashley did not know Clair very well, but she really liked her. Since James had this woman in his home, Ashley knew she had to be trustworthy. "Clair, this is James's friend, Ashley"

"Hello, Ms. Ashley. Mr. Brooks is not in," she stated.

"Oh, I know, I called for you." Ashley told Clair the situation and asked if she knew anyone who could handle setting up the house. Not only did Clair have someone to help with the house, but she also gave Ashley someone to help with the moving.

When Ashley and Tracy reached JD's place, Martha was just pulling up. "Hey, Mom," Ashley greeted her. Upon entering the house Ashley instructed Tracy to go to bed.

"You've got to be kidding—there is too much to be done," Tracy argued.

"Yes, there is, and we don't have time for you to have a relapse. Now go take a nap."

Tracy looked at Ashley, then at Martha. She was too tired to argue with either of them. "Alright, I will take a short nap. Then I will come down to help." She went upstairs.

"What's going on?" Martha asked.

"Tracy is wearing herself out trying to handle the wedding and the house. And JD is not helping. He's handling some case in Roanoke, Tracy said. I arranged for the big things to be packed and moved. Tracy did not want to intrude on JD's personal stuff so I thought you and I could do it."

Martha looked around; boxes were packed and labeled already. "Looks like Tracy got a good start, but we are going to need more boxes. Who is going to pack up Tracy's stuff?"

"Mom, Tracy is so organized; her stuff is going to be a breeze. We'll get JD done, then I'll start on her."

Martha and Ashley each took a room. While she was packing up the family room, Martha came across the box of pictures she had given JD that belonged to his father. She smiled as she went through looking at some of them. Martha looked at one picture of her husband James, another man who looked familiar, but she could not place him, and a woman sitting between them. She wondered about the picture for a minute, and then set it aside. She would ask JD about it when he got home.

By the time Tracy woke up from her nap, Ashley had gone back to the office and Martha was in the kitchen cooking dinner. The majority of the rooms downstairs were boxed up, with the exception of the furniture.

"Did you have a good nap?" Martha asked.

Tracy smiled. "Yes, thank you. Boy, you guys really got a lot done. Thank you so much."

Martha pointed to a chair. "Sit down, Tracy. Let me talk to you for a minute." Tracy did as she was told. "Baby, listen to me. You are now a part of a huge family. You don't have to do everything by yourself. Part of being a family is helping each other. There was no way you could have handled packing this house and your place by yourself. Pick up the telephone whenever you need help, that's what family is for. Okay?"

Tracy smiled. "Yes, ma'am."

"Good, now eat. When do you expect JD home?"

"Some time tonight. Where's Ashley?" Tracy asked.

"She went back to the office. She said she had to check on furniture or something."

Tracy looked at the clock. "I better head back over there."

About an hour later JD got home. "Hey, Mom." He kissed her on the cheek. "What are you doing here?" he asked as he lay his briefcase down.

"Hi, son. I came over to help Tracy with some packing." Martha put her hand on her hip and hit JD with the spatula. "Why is she trying to pack this place up by herself?"

JD jumped back. "Ouch, Mama, I planned on helping, but I got called away on a case."

"That is no excuse—don't you put things before your home. You understand me?"

"Yes, ma'am," JD replied as he took a seat at the counter. "What's all of this?"

Martha turned around. "Oh! Those are some pictures I came across of your father."

JD picked up some of the pictures. "Man, look at this." He smiled.

"I was looking at that one; I don't know the people in there with your dad."

"Yes, you do, Mom. I don't know the woman, but that's Senator Roth right there."

Martha came out of the kitchen and looked at the picture. "It sure is. Well, I'll be." She laughed.

JD looked at the picture again. "The woman looks familiar, too, but I don't know from where."

Martha looked at it. "I don't think I know her."

JD smiled. "I'm going to show this picture to the senator, and I'll bet he will get a kick out of it." JD put the picture in his briefcase.

When Tracy got home, JD met her at the bottom of the stairs. "I had to find a quick way to say I'm sorry for leaving all of this on you. So I ran you a hot bath."

Tracy looked at him. "It's going to take a lot more than a tub of hot water to get you off my list tonight."

"I thought it might." He walked past her to lock the door. He turned off the lights, took her hand and led her upstairs. The table in the sitting room was set up with candles and the dinner Martha had cooked. Tracy looked up at him and smiled. "That's for later," he said and continued into the bathroom. Candles were placed around the tub with rose petals in the water. He had a magnum of champagne with two glasses and a bowl of strawberries on the side. Tracy hung her head down and smiled. She began taking her clothes off. JD joined in. They settled into the bath facing each other. JD poured a glass of champagne for each of them. He handed a glass to her. "This is to our wedding, our new home and our new life together as one." He smiled.

They both took a drink.

Tracy set her glass on the side of the tub and then settled down into the water. "I think I might forgive you."

The next morning, JD stopped by James's office. "I appreciate you taking on this task for me, James. I need someone who is going to have Tracy's best interest at heart."

James shook JD's hand. "I'm happy to do this. Are you going to need opposition to anything we might find?"

JD nodded. "Yes, we will." He placed his briefcase on James's desk and pulled out the folder Brian had given him on Tracy's family. "This was just a quick glance, but we need to go deeper into her family history."

James saw a picture lying in the briefcase. "You missed this," James said as he picked up the picture.

"That doesn't go with the file," JD said. "That's a picture my mother found of my dad and Senator Roth. I thought the senator would get a kick out of seeing it."

James looked at the picture and then at JD. "What is your father doing in a picture with Lena Washington?"

JD frowned and took the picture out of James's hand. "What?"

James raised both eyebrows. "That's a young Lena Washington, but Lena Washington nonetheless."

JD looked at James with a puzzled stare. "Are you sure that's her?"

James shrugged his shoulders "Look at it closely, man. Isn't that the woman we met a few months ago?"

Looking at the picture closer, it did look like her. "Why would she be in a picture with my dad?" JD asked aloud.

"I could be wrong, you know," James offered. "Why don't you let me ask some questions, since I have to go see her anyway?" James took the picture from JD. "I'll let you know what I find."

James sensed JD was reluctant to let the picture out of his possession. "I will not let anything happen to it. I'm sure there is a very simple explanation."

"Alright," JD agreed as he closed his briefcase. As he started to leave, he stopped and looked at James. "My instincts are not usually wrong. This is not going to turn out good."

"Let's not jump here, JD. Let's ask questions; then react to the findings; not before."

JD nodded. "Thanks, James. Let me know what you find out."

"I will, JD. Don't worry about this," James said as JD walked out. James didn't want to let on, but he had a bad feeling about the picture too.

James put in a call to his investigators. He advised them of the confidential aspects of the case. James did not turn the picture over to the investigators. He felt that this part of the investigation needed to be handled very discreetly. He took down the address for Lena Washington—that visit he would have to make in person.

James searched his calendar for a free day. His schedule was tight. This weekend he had promised Ashley his undivided attention. They were having difficulty getting together since the planning of the wedding had gotten intense. Next week was the week of Thanksgiving. James Jr. was supposed to arrive on Wednesday and stay until Sunday. That definitely meant no time with Ashley. James was not ready to introduce the two of them yet. He never liked the idea of James Jr. getting involved with any of his woman friends. Not only was it confusing to the boy, but it would cause issues with his mother. James definitely did not want to deal with baby mama drama right now. The first weekend in December, tuxedo fittings were scheduled for the wedding. James was surprised JD asked him to be a part of the wedding party. But he accepted with honor. James sat back and shook his head. He hit the intercom. "Karen, would you step into my office for a moment?" James did not want to put this on hold for days. This question needed to be put away with urgency. The wedding was only a month away; neither JD nor Tracy needed the question of this picture hanging over their heads.

James arranged for Karen to handle the office while he was out. He called Clair from the car and asked her to pack an overnight bag for him. James left instructions with his secretary to contact the organizers of the meetings to let them know Karen would be sitting in for him. He asked her to make reservations at a hotel near the address on the paper he gave her and to call him with the details. He also advised her he would be out for the remainder of the week.

Afterwards, he called Ashley. "What are you up to today?" he asked.

"We are trying to get Tracy's house furnished by next Friday."

James frowned. "Shouldn't Tracy and JD be doing that?"

"Yeah, but JD is working on a case in Roanoke and handling the DA's office here. His time is very limited."

"Is his credit card limited, too?" James laughed.

"Excuse you!"

"Hey, I have experienced your shopping. I think I better call JD and warn him."

Ashley laughed. "Don't you dare. Where are you? You sound like you are in traffic."

"I am," James replied, "that's why I'm calling. I'm on my way out of town for a day or two. Something I need to work on. If all goes well I should be back by Friday."

Ashley sighed. "You are not going to miss our weekend, are you?"

"No, I will be back in time for our rendezvous."

Ashley smiled. "Well I hope so. It's been a week or so and I'm feeling a little horny here."

James laughed. "I promise to return soon, just to take care of that situation for you."

"Thank you, Mr. Brooks; I truly look forward to you doing just that."

James smiled. "I'll call you later tonight." He hung up the phone.

He missed being with Ashley this week. James smiled to himself. *When did she get under my skin?* This was supposed to be an uncommitted relationship, but he found it difficult to go days without speaking with her. He thought about the recent argument regarding James Jr.

He told Ashley that James Jr. would be with him during Thanksgiving, so she automatically invited them to dinner with her family. James declined the invitation and told her why. She was not very receptive to his reasoning.

"Okay, I get that we are not really in a relationship here. But, you are talking about Thanksgiving. What are you guys going to do, stay here and twiddle your thumbs?"

"Actually, we plan to spend some quality time together."

"Just you and him; no family, no turkey, no football!" Ashley exclaimed.

James walked away from Ashley. She followed him. "James, what could the harm be? We don't have to touch each other. Or do anything to make him think something is happening with us. Hell, that's going to be easy right now."

"Ashley," James yelled, "this is not up for discussion. I don't remember asking for your approval on my plans with my son."

That statement hit Ashley hard. She picked up her things and headed to the door. Ashley turned back to him. "You know I have a good family; a huge family with lots of kids. I thought you both would enjoy a good meal, nice people and some kids for James Jr. to play with. I had no intentions of infringing on your time with your son." She slammed the door as she left.

James didn't bother to call Ashley for a day or so, because he felt she had crossed the line. He alone made decisions for his son. When he did call, Ashley wasn't ready to talk to him.

"James, I understand your position. I will not interfere again. But right now I need to step back and get myself in check. So give me a day or two to do that." She hung up the telephone.

James remembered how he missed Ashley during those days. At this point, he was not ready to concede he was in love with her, but damn if she was not making him think twice about things.

James was formulating a plan in his head on how to get the information he needed out of Lena Washington without raising suspicion or causing any further problems for Tracy. As he entered the highway to Norfolk, he thought about the meeting with Lena and JD. The first thing he noticed was that Lena's first priority was to herself. She recognized JD the moment she came to the door. Lena took a moment to read JD to see just how into Tracy he was. Then she took time to determine if he could be played and how. Once she realized JD truly loved Tracy, she knew when and how to approach JD's pocket. James had sat back and observed the entire process. He knew 10 minutes into the visit how it was going to end. JD was very experienced with women; however, he was not experienced with vultures, and James was.

James placed a call to his bank, and asked them to make $10,000.00 available to him for immediate withdrawal if needed, at a local bank in Norfolk. James wanted to be sure there would be no limitations on his efforts to extract information from Lena. He checked into the hotel, and then placed a call to his secretary thanking her, as the accommodations were perfect. He had access to the Internet, which meant he did not have to go out to do any research. The investigator who his secretary had contacted had already left information on Tracy's family. The hotel concierge had made reservations at the most exclusive restaurant in the area. He also requested that a car and driver be available as needed. James had more than his share of experience on how to get the attention of women like Lena Washington. He had been married to one for five years.

As he settled in his room, James pulled out the two reports, one from Brian's investigation and one from his investigator, and began to compare notes. After he reviewed the information and had dinner he made his move and called Lena. "Ms. Washington, this is James Brooks. We met a few weeks ago."

Lena was surprised to receive the call. She had been wondering how she would go about opening that door. When JD and James left her house that day, Lena made some inquiries. She knew what Tracy's company was worth and she had a good idea where Tracy and JD were heading. "Mr. Brooks, I remember you. What can I do for you?"

"I am in town for a day or two on business. I was wondering if you were free for dinner at Rhonda's tomorrow."

That caught Lena's attention—Rhonda's was *the* restaurant in town, and you could easily drop $500 before you hit the main course. Knowing she didn't have plans, she still said, "I'm afraid I have plans tomorrow evening."

James knew the game. "Maybe another time," he said.

Lena was not going to let this opportunity slip away. "How long will you be in town, Mr. Brooks?"

"I'll be pulling out Friday."

Lena knew that did not allow a lot of time for her to play. "Since your time seems to be limited, I may be able to adjust my appointments for tomorrow. What time did you have in mind?"

James expected that response. "I'll have a car to pick you up around 6:30."

Lena was impressed; he was sending a car. "That is very generous of you, Mr. Brooks. Thank you."

"You'll find me to be a very generous man, Ms. Washington. I look forward to seeing you tomorrow," James said as he disconnected the call.

Now that he had set things in motion, James decided it was time to handle some of his own business. First he called James Jr. He missed being with his son. At one time, James considered staying with his son's mother just to be a daily part of James Jr.'s life. But the constant arguing was not good for their child. But as much as they fought, the one thing that was consistent was their love for their son. Talking with James Jr. always left James in a good mood. Tonight was no different. James took his shower and lay across the bed. He missed Ashley. He closed his eyes; if he could only find a way to have Ashley and James Jr. in his life.

The next day, James spent the morning meeting with the investigators. He learned Tracy had a good-size family. There was her sister Valerie, who had three children, two girls and a boy. Tracy's brother Al had two daughters. James also found out that Tracy sent gifts to all of her nieces and nephews every birthday and Christmas. For some reason, that information did not surprise James. Tracy was a very generous person. She may not have a relationship with them, but she would never ignore them. For the most part, Tracy's family was doing okay. There were, of course, as in every family, one or two who were struggling. James read the information surrounding the death of Tracy's sister. The most interesting information came from the interview with Tracy's aunt on her father's side.

The aunt indicated there was a possibility that her brother, Billy, was not really Tracy's father. According to the aunt, that was what caused her brother to start drinking. Lena had not, as far as she knew, admitted it to anyone. But she was sure her brother knew he was not Tracy's father. When Billy disappeared, Lena blamed the little girl. Lena did not want to have the child, but when her brother found out Lena was pregnant he was thrilled and convinced her to have the baby. He had loved that little girl and Lena for giving her to him. When he found out Tracy was not his, it cut him deeply and he was never the same after that. He started drinking and no longer had any respect for Lena. He could never look at

Tracy the same either. The aunt felt bad about the way the little girl was caught up in the middle of things. From what the aunt remembered, Tracy was a sweet little girl with a quiet demeanor about her. After her brother disappeared, Lena treated the little girl as if she did not exist. Lena believed if she never had Tracy her life would have been different. Lena was never the type to take responsibility for her own actions. She always had to blame someone else. There was no one else around, so Lena blamed Tracy.

James closed the report. He looked at the picture of Senator Roth, James Harrison and Lena Washington. Wondering when and where the picture was taken, he turned it over and looked at the date. The picture was taken in the month of January, 25 years ago. It looked like they were at some type of party. All three were seated at a table with several drinks on it. James thought, *It may not be a party; it could be a nightclub.* James looked at the date again. Then he pulled the file apart looking for Tracy's information. It wasn't in there.

"Shit." James was getting a little flustered as he looked for something on Tracy. He went over to the computer and pulled up Next Level Consulting firm's Web site. He pulled up Tracy's bio.

When James saw the information he was searching for he was furious. He could not believe what was happening here. He leaned against the table, trying to catch his breath.

"Damn!" he exclaimed aloud. He picked up the glass on the table and started to throw it against the wall he was so frustrated. James stopped himself. "You are jumping to conclusions here. Just calm down: get the facts; all the facts," he said to himself. He set the glass back down on the table. He picked up the telephone to dial a number, but changed his mind. What if he was wrong? He did not want to discuss it with anyone yet, not until he was sure of what the truth really was. James went to the bar and poured a drink. He swallowed the first one straight down. He poured the second, and held it.

"Lord, I don't come to you often. I promise to change if you would grant this one prayer. Please Lord, don't let this be. Make me wrong on this, Lord. Please, make me wrong on this." James looked at the date on the picture: January 25 years ago; and then Tracy's birthday, September 16, 25 years ago; exactly nine months later.

Chapter 36

James was at the restaurant when Lena Washington walked in. James stood as she was escorted to the table. "Ms. Washington, you look stunning tonight," James said. And she did, but he could not care less. What they had to discuss could affect not only JD's and Tracy's lives, but his and Ashley's as well.

Lena smiled. "Thank you, Mr. Brooks," she responded as she took a seat. "I must say I was a little surprised to receive your call. To what do I owe the pleasure?" She smiled.

Damn if Tracy didn't have Lena's smile and her eyes. James smiled. "Your daughter has your smile. It's one of my favorite things about Tracy."

"I'll take that as a compliment, Mr. Brooks. Is that the reason we're here tonight, to talk about Tracy?"

James motioned the waiter over and ordered drinks and dinner. "Yes, it is. I believe it would be in everyone's best interest for you and I to have this conversation alone." The waiter brought the drinks to the table. "Thank you," James acknowledged.

"You don't appear to be the type to play second fiddle to any man, Mr. Brooks. Exactly what part do you play in this scenario?" Lena asked.

"Concerned party." James smiled as he took a sip of his drink. It was taking every ounce of patience in him to not ask the question that was burning in him. "The question I have for you is what part of the scenario you want to play. The mother who wants an opportunity to build a meaningful relationship with her distanced daughter; or the mother who will not be allowed to be a part of her daughter's life regardless of where JD and Tracy end up?"

Lena sat back. "What role do you see me playing, Mr. Brooks?"

"I see you as a mother who wants to make an honest attempt to redeem herself in her daughter's eyes."

Lena smirked. "What makes you think I need to be redeemed?"

James put his hands up, stopping her from going any further, and sat forward. "Please, Ms. Washington, don't insult my intelligence or waste my time. You know, before I placed the call I did my background work. Let's not play games here. What type of relationship are you willing to have with your daughter and what will it cost?"

Lena smiled. "A man that gets straight to the point. Then I will do the same. I like to live well, Mr. Brooks, without questions or restraints. I took a trip to Richmond. You could sit my house inside the condo Tracy lives in. The mini-mansion JD and Tracy are about to move into is worth what, close to a million on the market? Now, I don't have to live at that level, but something comparable will do."

Damn! She did her homework; James did not know the price on the house JD and Tracy were buying himself. "So to have you in Tracy's life it will cost a house and a generous monthly allowance."

Lena wondered if she had reached too high, too deep. She noticed Brooks did not flinch when she put the terms on the table. She took a sip of her drink. "Yes," she replied.

The waiter delivered the meals to the table. When he left, James said, "Before we go any further into details of this arrangement, I have one or two questions. Now, Lena, before you answer, please know, I am not a man of patience. I want answers and will not tolerate being lied to at this point."

"Am I to assume we have an agreement here?"

"No. You can assume we are negotiating and nothing is being thrown off the table, yet. Are you ready to answer my questions?"

Lena sat back. "Sure, what do you need to know?"

James pulled the picture out and laid it on the table. "Is it possible that either of those two men could be Tracy's father?"

Lena smiled. "Where in the hell did you get that picture? Damn, I looked good."

James raised an eyebrow. "Yes, you did. Now, answer the question."

Lena said, "William Washington is Tracy's father."

James looked at her. "Are you sure of that? You should know, the conversation ends with the incorrect answer," James said in a tone to let Lena know he wanted the truth.

Lena licked her lips. "I'm not sure."

James accepted that. "Do you know who either of those men are?"

Lena shook her head. "That was a long time ago. I think this one was a police officer or something and the other was some politician. Why?"

"The date on the back of the picture is January 25 years ago. Tracy's birth date is September, 25 years ago. I ask the question again, is it possible that either of those two gentlemen could be Tracy's father?"

Lena honestly never thought about it. She put her fork down and looked at the picture. "That night was wild. We were at the Sahara Club all night drinking. I remembered one only because he was some rising politician. His friend was there to try to keep him out of trouble. We all left together and I woke up the next day in a hotel room. The politician was not there, but the friend was. He made sure I got home okay the next day."

That did not help James. "Do you remember being intimate with either of them?"

Lena shook her head. "No, I don't." She thought for a moment. "It was a few months after that I found out I was pregnant with Tracy."

Since Lena did not know who the other man was in the picture, James was not going to offer the information.

"I truly believed that Willy was Tracy's father when I married him," she said. "It wasn't until we were in a car accident that I found out Willy was not her father."

James had to ask, "Why do you hold Tracy responsible for your indiscretion?"

Lena exhaled. "I did not want that baby. Willy promised he would take care of me and the baby. He begged me to have it. So I did. When he found out she was not his, he went back on his promise. I was stuck with raising a child I never wanted."

"But she was just a child. She did not ask to come into this world. Why blame the child?"

Lena looked at him as if he had lost his mind. "Who else would I have blamed?"

James shook his head; he motioned the waiter to bring the check. Lena had managed to redeem herself a little, but not much. James wasn't convinced Tracy would benefit from having this woman in her life. He left the table believing she would be better off just the way things were.

"Lena, I will be in touch. In the meantime, here is an incentive for you to continue your path of honesty. The car is waiting to take you home."

Lena stood. "When can I anticipate hearing from you?"

James had lost interest in making Tracy's family whole again. Now he just wanted to make sure Tracy's future stayed intact. "When I get all the answers I need to complete my investigation. Good night, Ms. Washington," James said and walked away.

James stepped outside into the fresh air. He exhaled several times. He had a sinking feeling in his gut, this was not going to be simple. However, James knew, if he came to this conclusion, someone else could come to it also. James could not get the thought out of his head. Could James Harrison be Tracy's father? Is it possible JD may be marrying his half sister? James did not know where to turn now. He went back to the hotel. He took a shower trying to relax, but it did not work.

With no further reason to be there, James packed his bags, checked out of the hotel and headed back to Richmond.

On the drive home James felt trapped. If he kept this information to himself, JD and Tracy would get married and be happy; no one would be the wiser. But he would know they could be brother and sister. Is that why Ashley and Tracy had that instant connection in college? They have been closer than some sisters.

"Ohhh, Ashley." James could not stand the idea of rocking her world with something like this. He pulled over when he reached Williamsburg; he had to think. Okay, there are three people in that picture; one is dead and one doesn't know what happened that night.

"Let's talk to the one person left," James said to himself then called JD.

"James, what have you found out?"

He did not want to lie to JD, but he knew the information was premature. "I did get some information, but I'm not ready to release it yet."

JD did not like that answer. "What the hell does that mean, James?"

James understood his frustration, but he wouldn't cause JD or Tracy any undue stress or worry. "JD, you asked me to handle this part of the process for you. Trust me and let me do this my way."

When it came to Tracy, he did trust James. JD knew James was the one friend outside of his family that Tracy could depend on. "You are right, James. I put it in your hands; I have to trust your judgment on this. What do you need?"

James exhaled. "I need an audience with Senator Roth, tonight."

JD was taken aback by the request. He looked at his watch; it was getting late. "Can this wait until tomorrow?"

"No," James replied, "this needs to be dealt with tonight."

"Alright, let me give him a call; I'll get back with you."

James hung up the telephone then pulled off again. Before he reached Richmond, JD called and indicated Senator Roth was at his estate and could see them tonight. James knew JD would want to know what was up; but he was not going to tell JD anything until he had to.

James stopped by to pick up JD. Boxes were everywhere. James could see Tracy's touch. The boxes were labeled by rooms. Each had a detailed itemization of what the contents were, then a label indicating which box should be unpacked first. James laughed and shook his head. JD laughed with him. "I don't know how you deal with it."

"Tracy makes it easy, man. Only Tracy would take the time to put that much detail into packing a box. And every box is like that. I can find shit I haven't been able to find in years."

James needed a laugh. Seeing this put everything into perspective for him. He was going to get an answer to this question if it killed him. JD and Tracy are preparing to move into their new life together and he was going to do all he could to make sure that happened.

"It makes me wonder, now, how I ever got anything done before she came into my life," JD said.

"Well, you don't have to be concerned with that now. You two are on your way." James smiled. "You ready to roll?"

JD grabbed his keys. "Let's go." As they got into the car, JD called Tracy. "Hey, babe, I just left the house with James. He's kidnapping me for the night."

Tracy laughed. "Will he have you back by December 31ˢᵗ?"

"Only if you pay the ransom." JD smiled.

"How long will you be gone?"

"I'm not sure. Will you wait up for me?"

"Only if you promise to make it worth my while."

JD smiled. "Oh, I promise," he said with a tone of certainty.

James enjoyed the personal banter between the two. He sent up a small prayer: *You know what I need here, Lord.*

JD finished his call with Tracy then looked over at James. "You ready to give me something?"

James looked out of his side window, then back to the front. "I met with Lena Washington tonight."

JD raised an eyebrow. "Was it any better than before?"

James smiled. "Actually, it was. I now know, the woman shouldn't be in Tracy's life. Not even to give her away at the wedding. You probably couldn't afford her."

JD smiled. "That much?"

James nodded. "A house, comparable to the one you are about to move into."

JD laughed. "Hell, I'm not sure we can afford that one. Tracy keeps telling me we can, but I don't see it. Anything else?"

James nodded. "Yeah, a monthly stipend."

JD looked out of the side window of the car. "What kind of mother demands payment to be a part of her own daughter's life?"

"The kind that didn't want the child. According to Lena, she was promised certain things if she carried the child to term. Of course, as time went on her husband was not able to fulfill that promise. She was left with a small child who she never wanted. If nothing else, Lena Washington is an honest woman. She tells it as it is."

"I guess Tracy got that trait honestly," JD said.

"She got her smile, too. If Lena is any indication, Tracy is going to age very gracefully." James smiled.

JD looked at James. "Should Ashley be concerned here?"

James shook his head. "Oh, hell no! I was married to a Lena Washington for five years. That was enough for me."

JD pointed. "The entrance is on the right." James turned in.

As they got out of the car James turned to JD. "I will need to talk to Roth alone. If he chooses to share the information with you, then I will tell you everything I know. But it has to be his choice. Understood?"

JD stood with his hands in his pockets, looking down at the ground. Something deep in him told him things were not right and James knew why. If this was Brian or Calvin asking him to trust them, he would without question. But this was Brooks, a man he knew was more dedicated to Tracy than to him. He was putting Tracy's future in this man's hands.

"Understood," JD replied.

Senator Roth opened the door. "JD, come on in."

JD made the introductions. "Mr. Brooks needs to speak to you alone, Senator."

Senator Roth shook James's hand. "What is this about, Mr. Brooks?"

James responded, "I give you my word it is best discussed in private." Senator Roth trusted JD without question. If he brought this man to him this late in the evening it had to be important. "Come into my study, Mr. Brooks. JD, make yourself comfortable." JD watched the door close. "Senator, I need you to look at this picture." James handed the picture to him.

Roth looked at the picture. He laughed. "Where did you get this from?"

"JD's mother found it among some old pictures when they were packing up the house. Do you remember the night that picture was taken?"

Senator Roth shook his head. "Not really, but I do remember the woman. She had a smile that lit up the room."

James smiled. "She still has it. Senator, we may have a situation. The woman in the picture is Lena Washington. Lena Washington is Tracy's mother."

Roth looked at the picture again. He did see the resemblance. "Why is that an issue?"

James didn't have the patience to be tactful. "On the day that picture was taken, were you intimate with Lena Washington?"

Senator Roth laughed. "Did you really look at this picture? Hell, if I remember correctly, we may have gone into the next day."

James cleared his throat. "Was James Harrison physically involved in that evening?"

Roth wasn't quite sure what James was trying to ask. "Was James with Lena that night?"

"Yes," James replied.

"James wasn't that type of man. To be honest, more than not, James was trying to clean up my mess back then." Roth laughed. "I was really

IRIS BOLLING

out there back in the day. That's why I never remarried—too busy running the streets after my divorce. James was married, had JD, and I believe Ashley was on the way." Roth laughed. "James messing around on Martha was like JD messing around on Tracy; it's not going to happen."

"Senator," James said, "look at the date on the picture."

Roth turned the picture over. "Okay." Roth shrugged his shoulder.

"That picture was taken 25 years ago in January. Tracy was born nine months later. Lena's husband left because he found out the child wasn't his. When this first surfaced, I was afraid James Harrison may be Tracy's father. I was concerned about JD and Tracy getting married and I am grateful for that relief. However, we now have a new concern."

Roth stood. "You can't be serious about this." Roth walked behind his desk. "You're thinking I may be Tracy's father?"

James shook his head. "Senator, to be honest, my concern was with JD and Tracy. If you are telling me James Harrison never slept with Lena Washington, then I'm done with this."

Roth exhaled. "To be honest, I don't believe he did. But I don't remember the whole night. Have you talked with Lena Washington?"

"Yes, while Lena doesn't remember your names, she states you two were pretty intoxicated that night and she only remembers waking up with Harrison in the room, who made sure she got home okay."

Roth nodded. "That sounds like him."

James didn't like loose ends. "Senator, we need to know for sure. JD is marrying Tracy in less than 30 days."

Roth sat down. "That can't be. Have you shared this with JD?"

James shook his head. "No. I know we will need to tell him something tonight. I was hoping you were a little clearer on what took place that night."

Roth paced the floor. "Do you know how many lives this could affect?" James knew Roth didn't expect an answer. "We have to tell JD," Roth said. "There is no way we can let him go into this marriage not knowing."

James shook his head. "I'm not so sure that would be the best thing to do. We are not just talking about JD and Tracy. We are talking about the entire Harrison family. If James Harrison didn't sleep with Lena, there is no need for anyone to ever think it may have happened. My problem now is how do we find out for sure?"

"Blood tests," Roth suggested.

"How do you propose we do a blood test without raising suspicion?" James asked.

Roth thought. "We will need a sample from Tracy—the hospital should have that—and a sample from me, which I will give willingly."

James was surprised with Roth's reaction. "Aren't you concerned this information may get into the wrong hands?"

"If it's something that will cause a problem for JD, we need to get it cleared up now. JD's future is too important to the party. There are ways this can be done discreetly. I've learned a long time ago, secrets only hurt a political career and a marriage," Roth cautioned. He walked over to the door and called JD in. "You better take a seat, son," Roth said. "Go ahead, Brooks; you have my permission to relay the information to JD." James explained the situation while Roth fixed him a drink.

Once James was finished, JD began to laugh. "You cannot be serious about this." JD looked at James then to Roth. "You can't be serious, James."

Neither James nor Roth changed their stance. A stunned look came to JD's face. James sat; he knew it was just hitting JD.

"Tracy is not my half sister. I don't know what the answer could be here, but, it's not that," JD said. "So where do we go from here?"

"JD," Roth said, "we have to look at this from all directions, son."

"I don't give a damn how many directions you look at this. My father is not Tracy's father. He would have never done that to my mother," JD said angrily.

"I agree," Roth said calmly, "but we need to make sure. I am willing to do whatever needs to be done to get this cleared up."

JD looked at Roth; he respected the man, but he was trying to deface his father's memory and take away the one person who makes his life work.

James could feel the anger radiating from JD and he understood—he was blind-sided with this information. "Now is not the time to lose our heads. We have a journey to take and no time to waste. JD, is it possible to get a copy of Tracy's medical records from the hospital?"

JD looked at James. "I'm sure we could."

"Good," James continued before anyone could say anything. "Senator, we will need a sample of your blood. You indicated you knew someone who could handle this discreetly. Would you mind placing that call now?"

Roth walked out the door. "I'll make the call in the other room."

James looked at JD. "You have to keep your cool about this. From all accounts, Roth is probably Tracy's father. However, I cannot close this investigation without Roth's cooperation. Now I know this is coming at you from nowhere, but work with me on this."

JD was losing it. He always prided himself on handling situations with tact and control. That went out the window with this. JD finished his drink and threw the glass with full force against the wall. James exhaled; glad JD had released some of the tension. "Feel better now?"

JD looked at James. "I am marrying Tracy next month. I don't give a damn whose child she might be!"

James smiled. "Just so you know, I'm committed to getting you down that aisle next month."

JD hung his head, put his hands in his pocket and begin to pace. "I don't believe my father would have cheated on my mother, and then brought the picture home with him."

James responded, "I don't believe he would have either. I do believe he brought the picture home to protect Roth. A picture like that could have been used against him in so many ways."

JD looked at James. "This has to be played out in a way that my mother will never, and I mean never, get wind of it."

James turned to JD. "We need to ensure not only that your mother never knows, but Ashley as well. I cannot allow something like this to hurt her."

JD had not considered how this would affect Ashley or her relationship with James. He was only thinking about how it affected him and Tracy.

"James, man, I'm sorry. I didn't take you into consideration on this. I appreciate the way you are trying to handle this."

Roth came back into the room. "I heard a bomb go off earlier. Is the deck all clear now?"

JD smiled. "Senator, I apologize. This is all coming at me a little fast. You knew my father, Senator; the suggestion of something like this would have sent him through the roof."

"Like you," James said.

JD chuckled. "Yeah."

"JD, I'm as certain James did not sleep with Lena as I am that I did. Now I don't know if I am Tracy's father or not. The test results will answer that. My concern is Carolyn. My daughter has been through a lot this year. I don't want her hurt by this. I honestly believe she has a chance at happiness with Gavin. This may cause her to lose focus again. At all costs, this must stay between the three of us here."

James cleared his throat. "Four—Lena is not a stupid woman. She is aware of this picture and its possible meaning. If she thinks it's worth her while, she will dig further."

Roth looked at JD. "Okay, what do we need to keep her quiet until we can sort this out?"

James started laughing. JD joined him and took a seat. They both sat there laughing and looking at Roth. "A house and a monthly stipend should do it," James laughed.

"How soon can all of this be resolved?" JD asked.

"If we have the child and potential father together, it can be determined in days." James looked at JD. "If the results are not clear, we may have to get Tracy and Lena together."

JD shook his head. "After what you reported to me, James, I'm not sure I want that woman anywhere near Tracy at this point."

"JD, look at it as keeping the enemy close." James pulled out his cell and dialed Lena's number. "Lena, James Brooks here. It seems I need your assistance here in Richmond. Would you be available tomorrow? Of course, all your financial needs associated with this venture would be covered."

Lena agreed to the short trip. Senator Roth set up the testing with his associate for Friday. Once all the arrangements were made, JD and James left the senator's home.

"James," JD asked, "if we have to, how will I get Tracy to this testing?"

James exhaled. "You can take the hard way, which is to tell her the truth. Or you can take the easy way." JD looked at James. "Take a q-tip, stick it in her mouth and tell her it's foreplay."

JD laughed. "In other words, lie."

James nodded. "Exactly."

Chapter 37

Lena arrived at the hotel as scheduled. JD made it clear he wanted to meet with Lena personally before any agreements were made regarding Tracy. He did not intend to allow this woman the opportunity to hurt Tracy again. That morning, JD caught the chopper to Roanoke to review evidence found in the Melvin case and called the hospital to have Tracy's records released to Senator Roth's physician. This was a true test for JD. The case was breaking wide open and the situation at home was just as complex. Both needed his immediate attention. JD left Roanoke and returned to Richmond to meet with Lena that afternoon.

James met Lena at the hotel lobby early that morning. He wanted to make sure Lena did not run into Roth or Tracy during her time in Richmond. Lena was advised the meeting between her and JD was to discuss Tracy and the role she would have in her life. In actuality, James wanted to make sure Lena was under control just in case she connected his questions to the picture. To keep Lena occupied he arranged for them to have lunch.

While standing in front of the hotel waiting for the car to arrive, they were seen by Cynthia and Ashley. "Ashley, girl, ain't that your man standing over there with a woman that's not you?"

Ashley turned as the car pulled up. The driver opened the door and James and Lena got into the car. Ashley watched mortified as the car passed them. Cynthia looked at Ashley. "Why are you not calling him on your cell?"

Ashley was too stunned to do anything. "I'll have to deal with that later," she said and walked away. There was no way she was going to lose her cool in front of Cynthia.

When Cynthia drove off, Ashley called Tracy, who attempted to calm her down. "There has got to be a perfectly innocent explanation to this,

Ashley. You know James is not a man to play games. Where are you anyway?" Tracy asked.

"I'm at the hotel bar," Ashley replied.

"Have they returned yet?"

"I don't think so," Ashley said. "I just don't believe this shit."

"Ashley, calm down. You don't know what is going on. Is it possible the woman is James Jr.'s mother? She could be just dropping James Jr. off with James."

Ashley thought. "That could be," she said, a little calmer.

Tracy exhaled. "Don't you think you should leave now, before they do come back?"

Ashley was still not quite sure. "No, I have to know."

"Okay, stay where you are. I'll be there in a minute. Don't do anything before I get there. Promise me," Tracy insisted.

"I make no promises," Ashley replied angrily.

Tracy got into her car and drove to the hotel. When she arrived, it took her a minute to find her friend, but when she did, Ashley was well on her way to being drunk. "My goodness Ashley, what are you doing?" Tracy took the drink out of her hand. "Would you give us some black coffee, please," she said to the bartender. "I can't believe you are doing this. It is two o'clock in the afternoon and you are drinking like a whale." Ashley sat straight up. "There they are," she said. James and Lena headed to the hotel lounge. As she followed their movement, she frowned. "What the hell is JD doing here?"

Tracy turned just as JD stood to greet James and the woman. "I thought he was in Roanoke today."

"Hum...hmm, and James was supposed to be out of town, too," Ashley slurred. They looked at each other. "I may be drunk, but I know something is up, Ashley slurred. Let's go, Tracy."

"Ms. Washington," JD spoke as he took a seat at the table.

"Hello, Mr. Harrison," Lena responded, "it's nice to see you again."

JD smiled. "We can dispense with the niceties, Ms. Washington. I'm here only to make sure you clearly understand the conditions of any arrangement made here today. Under no circumstances is Tracy ever to know you are here for any reason other than your sincere desire to establish a relationship with her. If Tracy even suspects something different, previous agreements will be null and void. Do I make myself clear?"

Lena looked at JD. *He is a handsome man,* she thought. "Tracy has good taste, Mr. Harrison." Lena smiled.

JD asked the question again. "Do you understand the terms of this agreement?"

"Yes, I do," Lena replied as she sat forward. "What I am not clear on is exactly what it is you want me to do."

James pitched in. "We haven't come to a complete agreement on the particulars. We asked you here today to determine how to proceed. Any direction we go must not be harmful in anyway to—" James stopped mid-sentence. "Damn!" He spotted Ashley and Tracy walking towards them. "We better make a decision quick."

JD turned just as Ashley, who was walking in front of Tracy, reached the table. "Hello, big brother," she said while trying to hold her temper in. She turned to James, who was now standing. "James," she said with fire in her eyes.

Tracy walked up to JD, her back to Lena. She raised her eyebrows. "I'm sorry, honey," Tracy kissed JD. He held her by the waist; not wanting her to turn. "I tried to stop her," Tracy whispered to Jeffrey.

JD looked at Tracy, not sure how to get out of this situation. He smiled. "Tracy."

Ashley stumbled over to James. "Are you enjoying your day out of town?"

James noticed Ashley was a little intoxicated. "It seems you have," he said with a smile.

Lena sat there watching these two supposedly controlling men squirming with these two women. She didn't have to ask who wore the pants in these relationships. It was actually kind of nice seeing JD out of sorts. He seemed to be at a loss for words. *What the hell, I'll help him out.* "Hello, Tracy," Lena said.

Tracy tensed immediately; JD could see it in her eyes. Tracy turned and could not believe her eyes.

"You know this woman?" Ashley asked with attitude.

Tracy could not respond; she was shell-shocked. She leaned into JD.

"Tracy," JD began.

"JD, let me," Lena said. JD wasn't sure if he should; he didn't trust Lena at all. He held his breath, as did James.

Ashley was a little too drunk to get the whole picture, but whatever was going on she knew was not kosher. "James, what's happening?" Ashley asked.

"Tracy, you have grown up to be a beautiful woman," Lena said as she stood. "I wondered when I first met JD how you were able to get such a handsome man. Now I see."

Tracy was trying to be polite, but all the memories of her life with her mother came to the forefront. She always tried to be professional in public, especially around JD. She did not like being rude. The last thing she wanted to do was embarrass him in any way.

"Hello," Tracy said. "Would you excuse me?" Tracy walked away.

Ashley looked at James, then JD. "What have you two done?"

JD went after Tracy.

"James?" Ashley questioned.

"Ashley, this is Lena Washington, Tracy's mother."

Ashley was a little taken aback. "Hello," Ashley forced out.

James pulled his wallet out and paid the check. "I think we better go."

"I'll be upstairs in the room," Lena said. "It seems you have some explaining to do."

Lena turned to Ashley. "It's nice to meet you, Ashley. Don't be too hard on him. He was actually trying to do a good thing." Lena left the restaurant.

Ashley sat down, one because she was getting dizzy and two because she could not believe Tracy's mother was here. "Is this something good, James?" Ashley asked.

James shook his head. "I don't know, Ash. I just don't know." He looked at her with a questioning smile. "Why are you drunk at three o'clock in the afternoon?"

Ashley laid her head on the table. "Because I saw you with that beautiful woman at one o'clock in the afternoon."

James smiled. "You are the only beautiful green woman I see."

Ashley looked up and smiled, then threw up at James's feet.

"Why did I not see that coming?" James said as he pulled the napkin from the table to clean Ashley up.

JD caught Tracy outside the hotel entrance. "Tracy, wait babe," he called out.

Tracy turned, a little confused about the direction she needed to go. Her heart was racing and she felt tears coming to her eyes. "I have to go," Tracy responded.

Lena came out of the door and walked over to them. She smiled. "Tracy, would you mind coming up to my room to talk? It will only take a minute." Lena saw the confusion in Tracy's eyes. She had an opportunity here to take control of the situation and possibly write her own ticket. "Please, Tracy, give me five minutes and if you want to leave after that I won't stop you."

JD didn't know what Lena was up to and he didn't like it, but there was no way he was going to leave Tracy alone with her. He did know they needed to take this inside, out of public view. A number of people spoke as they walked by. "Let's go inside, Tracy," JD encouraged.

Tracy looked at him. Why was Jeffrey with her mother? When did they meet and why did he not tell her about it?

"Yes, let's do that," she replied, looking at Jeffrey angrily. The look did not escape JD.

As they entered the lobby, James and Ashley were coming from the restaurant. Lena shook her head and smiled. "Let's take her up to the room before she throws up."

"Too late for that," James said. They all rode the elevator in silence. JD was thinking he did not like the idea of not being straight with Tracy.

That would only give Lena the upper hand in this situation. But right now they needed Lena to cooperate with them. Tracy was wondering how JD could have kept this from her and why. Lena was honestly a little torn. It was good to see Tracy all grown up, with a man who apparently really loves her. But she had to keep focused on the reason for the trip: money. James was praying that JD kept his cool long enough to get what they needed from Lena and Roth. Ashley was just praying that the damn elevator would stop soon.

As they entered the room, James took Ashley into the bathroom as Lena walked over to the desk and put her purse down. Tracy stood close to the door.

"Tracy," JD put his hand out to her. She looked at him, feeling a little betrayed. JD put his hand down and walked back to her, took her hand and walked over to the sitting area. He was ready to defend every action he had taken regarding Tracy's mother.

"Tracy," Lena said, walking towards her, "please sit for a minute." Tracy was not used to her mother talking to her in such a calm manner. Tracy sat down on the couch and JD sat beside her. She grabbed his hand and held on.

"I know this seems a little strange to you," Lena said, "but I would like to try to explain it. A few months ago JD and James came by to see me. JD thought it was time for you and me to try to have a relationship." Lena smiled. "His concern was the 12 grandchildren he says I'm going to have. JD felt it was important for your side of the family to be a part of any children you two may have together. When he first approached me about this I was reluctant. You and I never had a mother/daughter relationship. You were always your father's child, not mine. When your father left, I held you responsible for some bad decisions I made. JD had no idea just how bad our relationship was, but I did. Frankly, I didn't think there was any way you would be able to forgive me for the way I treated you back then. So, needless to say, I rejected his request."

Lena sat on the chair in front of Tracy and continued. "Then a few weeks later, I saw what happened to you on the news. I decided to see for myself just how you were doing. I came to the hospital and there was a guard at the door. I told him who I was and he let me in to see you. You were badly beaten and on a ventilator at the time. I spoke with your doctor and he told me you would recover. I stayed the night and watched JD and those two in there, at the hospital with you. I knew you were okay. So I went home.

"The other day, I received a call from James, who is apparently doing some research for JD on your family. I thought it would be a good time to reconsider my original decision. James decided this was an issue JD needed to be in on. So he asked me to come to Richmond. JD was explaining his opposition to all of this being kept from you when you and

Ashley walked in. JD's position in all of this was one of protecting you from being hurt or disappointed."

Damn, she was good, JD thought. With the exception of one or two embellished moments, Lena technically told the truth. Tracy did not show any expression as Lena was talking. With all that had happened between them, Lena had never lied to her. The story Lena lay before Tracy was believable, but Tracy did not trust Lena. She was a selfish person and did nothing unless something was in it for her; usually money. "How much did it cost them, Mommy? You see, I would like to pay them back for all expenses that were accrued on my account. So how much did it cost them to get you here to talk to me?"

Lena smiled; her daughter was not a dummy. *You're not going to get too much past her, and that's good,* Lena thought. "To date, just expenses, but James put out a pretty penny for dinner the other night." Tracy smiled. "At least you keep it real, Mommy. You never did fake anything with me. I always knew where I stood," Tracy said.

It hit JD why Cynthia had such an effect on Tracy. He could never understand it before, but now he knew. Lena was always brutally straight with Tracy. So was Cynthia. It was how Tracy was raised; it was the only way she knew.

JD squeezed Tracy's hand and she turned to him. "You should have come to me with this. I could have saved you some time and money." She turned to Lena. "Mommy, thank you for taking the time to explain." Tracy stood. "Here's my card, please have the hotel to contact me regarding the bill. Have a safe trip home." Tracy turned to JD. "Are you ready to go?"

JD stood, not sure if he should intervene. Lena had made an honest attempt to open the door with Tracy and it seemed Tracy was closing the door. "Are you sure you don't want to stay and talk a little longer?" JD asked.

Lena interjected. "JD, it's getting late. I'm sure Tracy needs time to adjust." Lena stood.

Tracy walked towards the door. "Mommy, you take care," Tracy said without emotion.

Lena walked out of the room. "You do the same, Tracy," she said with a bland tone to match Tracy's.

Seeing the two of them together at that moment gave JD a little hope. Maybe somewhere down the road, Lena and Tracy would be able to accept each other.

Tracy had a few choice words for JD, as soon as they got home. JD pulled in first and waited for her to park and get out of her car. As soon as she was out, he pulled her to him and kissed her. When she tried to pull away he would not let up. He continued to kiss her overpoweringly. Tracy eventually wrapped her arms around his waist; it was the only thing to keep her knees from buckling under her. JD eased up on the kiss a little as it became more loving. "Hmm." JD ended the kiss. He looked down at Tracy. "Sister, my ass," he said.

Tracy opened her eyes with a frown. "What?"

JD smiled. "I'll tell you one day when we are old and gray."

Chapter 38

Saturday morning, Ashley woke up at James's house with a headache and questions. James gave Clair time off. He planned to spend the weekend with Ashley before James Jr. came into town. James was in the kitchen attempting to cook breakfast when Ashley ventured down. James started laughing as soon as she entered the room. Her hair was everywhere and she looked a little pale.

"Well, good morning, would you like some scrambled eggs?" James laughed.

Ashley took a seat at the table. "You are not funny," she grumbled as she slumped into a seat.

James put a cup of coffee in front of her and smiled. "You look good in my shirt."

"You look good without your shirt." Ashley replied as she sipped her coffee. "You are enjoying this too much."

"Would you care to explain yesterday to me?" James asked as he took a seat.

Ashley held her head up. "Would you?"

James sat up. "After you. What exactly caused you to drink yourself into a stupor? I believe you mentioned jealousy."

Ashley protested. "I am sure I did not say that, drunk or not. I may have said something to the effect of seeing you with another woman, but at no time did I indicate I was jealous. Now, that's my story and I'm sticking to it," Ashley said as she got up a little too quickly. Her head was still spinning. "Damn," she exclaimed, "Hennessey straight is nothing to play with." She sat back down.

James didn't like seeing Ashley like this and he felt responsible for her discomfort. "I'm having a hard time trying to ascertain why seeing me with another woman would cause you to react in the manner that you did. I am around women all the time. If I were interested in being with any one of them, it would not be difficult for me to do. You causing this type of harm to yourself would not change that."

"I hate it when you are logical." Ashley grinned.

He got up, walked around the table, and picked her up in his arms. "I chose to spend my time suffering through the humiliation of you throwing up on me in public because you are so damn fine. Especially when you are green and jealous." He kissed her feverishly.

Ashley put her arms around James's neck and seized the moment. As the kiss ended, she smiled. "I'm glad I brushed my teeth before I came downstairs."

James smiled. "Not as glad as I am." He placed her on the table, positioning himself on top of her. He looked admiringly into her eyes and wondered when she stole his heart. He knew she stole it, because he'd had no intentions of giving it away.

Ashley wrapped her legs around his waist and thought, *Damn, I love this man.* "Since we are on the table, would you like some breakfast?"

"Hmm," James replied, "shall I start with the cherries or go straight for the bread pudding?"

Ashley laughed. "You can start wherever you want."

Lena was preparing to check out of the hotel when an envelope was pushed under her door. She opened the envelope and smiled. It was an invitation to Tracy's wedding with a note attached. "If you are free, you are welcome." Surprisingly, Lena was happy to receive the invitation. At this point, she had no idea how everything was going to turn out, but at the very least she was able to redeem herself a little with JD, and hopefully Tracy.

Senator Roth was in his kitchen reading the paper when Carolyn came in. "Hey, Daddy," she said as she kissed his forehead.

"Hey, baby girl," he replied with a smile.

Carolyn blushed; she loved the endearment. "Gavin and I set a date for the wedding—June 16. The engagement party will be two weeks from Saturday, here."

The senator smiled at his daughter. "Are you sure this is what you want to do? A marriage without love can be hell. I know; I went through it with your mother."

Carolyn laughed. "I remember." Carolyn was silent for a minute. "Daddy I'm not so sure it will be a marriage without love. Whatever it turns out to be, I'm now committed to making it work."

Senator Roth pulled his daughter onto his lap and hugged her. "Baby girl, I loved you from the moment you entered the world. I spoiled you rotten." He laughed as she hit him. "Well, I did and don't regret one moment of it." He hesitated for a moment. "Would you do your old man a favor?"

Carolyn looked at him. "Anything, Daddy, what is it?"

"Would you mind not inviting your mother to the wedding?"

Carolyn laughed and so did Roth. Carolyn kissed and hugged her daddy. She knew if she did not have anything else, she had his love all to herself. Roth's heart was breaking for his little girl. If what he suspected was true, Carolyn would be the one to lose the most.

Gavin knocked on Cynthia's door. "Would it be egotistical of me to ask you to remain my friend in light of my pending marriage?"

Cynthia stepped back into her apartment. "You better come inside before someone recognizes you," she said glumly. "I was a bit surprised to hear the wedding date was set after our conversation the other night," Cynthia stated.

Gavin loosened his tie and sat on the sofa. "I'm sure you were," he replied. He took Cynthia's hand and pulled her down to the sofa beside him. "When you and I spoke the date had not been set. That happened when I returned home. Carolyn made it very clear: she is not in love with me. However, we do have the same objective. We both want to move into the mansion. Our marriage all but guarantees that for both of us. I am going to be the next governor, and I will marry Carolyn." He held Cynthia's hand in his. "What you have to decide is if you can be my rock in private, because I am going to need one. I will be in the spotlight and there will be certain appearances I will have to keep up. We will have to be discreet. But I will never disrespect you or take you for granted."

Cynthia was disappointed. She had made a connection with Gavin that she had not had with any other man. Cynthia leaned in and kissed Gavin. Gavin pulled her body next to his. "I'll be here until it no longer feels right for me," she replied. "All I ask is that you be honest with me. Can you handle that?"

Gavin smiled "I believe I can do that."

While packing boxes for the move, JD tried several times to approach the topic of Lena with Tracy, but she was not receptive. Tracy felt it was better to leave well enough alone. At this point in her life she didn't need or want any explanations from her mother. The biggest problem she had right now was dealing with JD keeping all of this from her for months. He never once mentioned meeting her mother.

"Why would you keep something like that from me?" Tracy asked.

"I wasn't sure what the outcome would be. When James and I met with Lena the first time, she was not what I was expecting. After the meeting I believed it was best to leave things as they were."

"What changed your mind?"

JD could not tell her what truly forced him to reconsider his position with Lena. If he did that, he would have to reveal the whole paternity test situation. If he revealed that information, his mom, Ashley, Tracy and Carolyn could be hurt. He was not going to chance that. And JD did not want to lie to Tracy so he decided to take another route.

"I met with Brian, Calvin and Douglas the other night. We discussed the possibility of me running for attorney general. Before I make a major decision like that I want to know what is out there on me. Since we are getting married, I decided to have your background checked out also. I didn't want any of my friends to conduct the investigation, because I wanted your privacy protected, even from me. Anything I learn about you, I want to come from you. So I asked James to handle your background check. I know he is your friend and would only reveal pertinent information that may have an effect on a campaign."

"We already know what the downfall will be: I'm the sister to a kingpin you convicted. What could hurt a campaign for someone running for attorney general more than that?" Tracy asked.

JD put down the box he was working with and sat beside Tracy. "If I decide to run, the first thing I will do is disclose the connection with you, me and Al. The only problem with that disclosure is that we will have to hire security. The disclosure of the connection will cause more problems for you than it will for me."

Tracy wasn't sure she understood that. "You know, if you decide to do this, our lives will change. You will truly belong to the community then. Right now everything you do with the church and community organizations is voluntary. If you run and win, and you will win, then it's your responsibility to keep the citizens of the state safe; there will be no options. When reporters like Charles approach you, you will have to address the issues. Your life will no longer be your own."

JD thought for a moment. "That would mean your life would no longer be your own either. Would that be a problem for you?"

Tracy leaned back against the box she was labeling and sighed. "Jeffrey, I want to be your wife. Whatever comes along with that I'm willing to take. No questions asked."

It didn't matter how many times things happened to them, Tracy never ceased to amaze JD with her support of him. He pulled her leg until she was face to face with him. "Sometimes I look at you and wonder why God blessed me with your love."

Tracy smiled. "Have you made a decision yet?"

JD shook his head. "No, I want to wait until the reports are in. Then I'll talk with Pastor Smith."

"Will you make me a promise?"

JD smiled. "Anything."

"Will you not make a decision until after the wedding? Or at least not tell anyone your decision until then. I really need to get through the wedding without any further distractions."

JD agreed; they both needed a little less drama. He would really enjoy their honeymoon without outside distractions. "I'll do one better; no major announcements on anything until after our honeymoon."

Tracy's smiled broadened. "Now you may kiss me, Mr. Attorney General." JD complied. "Hmm," Tracy said, "I wonder if being the third most powerful man in the state would alter your lovemaking abilities in any way."

JD pulled her onto his lap. "Shall we start sharpening those skills?" he asked as he kissed her between her breasts.

"Okay, commander-in-chief." She giggled.

"That's the president." JD laughed.

"I'm thinking towards the future," Tracy said as she eagerly kissed him.

Chapter 39

The next few weeks went like a whirlwind for JD and Tracy. Thanksgiving dinner was held at Mama Harrison's house with the whole Harrison clan in attendance. James and James Jr. did come for dinner. By all appearances James Jr. fit right in with all the other children who were there. Ashley kept a respectable distance from James, at least as much as she could.

The pending wedding was the buzz. Tracy was a little overwhelmed with all the people talking to her about the wedding. The family was going to take some getting used to for Tracy.

"You sure you want to marry into all of this?" James joked with Tracy.

Tracy gave James a questioning glance. "Are you?"

James blushed. "I have not committed to anyone; you have."

Tracy laughed. "That's what you think."

The closing on the house took place the next day. JD was impressed with the way Tracy handled business. She reviewed every document, made requests for adjustments and arranged for all the financing. He never realized before how respected Tracy was in the financial community. The vice-president of one of the local banks came to the closing to assist personally. The man greeted Tracy with eagerness to please. JD sat back and observed the man's reaction to every request Tracy made. At one point he was sure he heard the man ask which account she wanted the $500,000.00 taken from. Now JD did not pay a lot of attention to their accounts, but he did not think for a minute they had that kind of money in one account, much less multiple accounts. Tracy never flinched; she advised the man to have half the funds transferred from his account and the other half from hers. JD looked at the banker, knowing he was going to laugh at the request. The banker went into his laptop; keyed information in and indicated the transfer had been made. JD made a mental note to himself to check his account to see just how much money he had. JD acknowledged he was in uncharted territory here. Tracy, on the other hand, seemed to be in her element.

JD stepped away when his cell phone rang. It was a call from Senator Roth. The test results were in. Senator Roth knew what this meant to JD, so he did not question the results. He was indeed Tracy's father. JD didn't realize it, but he had been holding his breath until the moment Roth spoke the words. Roth's only request was that this information remains confidential. JD easily agreed. As he disconnected from the call, he worried about the position all of this left Senator Roth in. Well, JD thought, Senator Roth always did want him as a son-in-law.

JD and Tracy walked out of the office with the keys to their new home. On the way to the house JD asked about the transfer of money. Tracy told him neither account was devastated by the transfer. JD laughed; when Tracy did not join in he just looked at her. He was going to have to take a moment one day and check his bank account.

JD and Tracy entered the house through the front double doors. They both stood there in the foyer looking around. You could see into the sunroom, the family room, a portion of the dining room and the living room. To the left was a doorway that led to what would be JD's home office. To the right in the center of the foyer was the staircase that led to the second level; at the top of the stairs to the right was the master suite and to the left were three bedrooms the two hoped to fill with children. JD turned and closed the doors behind them. Tracy walked over to the staircase and sat.

JD looked at her. She was his life, the sun in the morning and his moon at night. And now this was their home. He smiled. "Do you promise to greet me from there every day?"

"I do," Tracy said.

JD smiled. "This is the beginning of our life together. Are you ready?"

Tracy walked over to him, put her arms around his waist, and looked up at him. "Yes, I am ready."

JD looked into her eyes. "Which room do you want to start our family in?"

"Right here is good for me," Tracy replied.

As JD kissed her, he ran his hands under her butt and slowly lifted her up. Tracy's legs automatically went around JD's waist. Just then the door opened behind them.

"Oh, please, that has to wait!" Ashley proclaimed. "We got too much to do." She pulled Tracy literally out of JD's arms. "Come on, Ms. Organizer, start directing."

Tracy looked back at JD and smiled.

JD smiled back. The unspoken understanding was there: this would be finished later.

Thanks to Clair's connections, the house had been cleaned inside and out. As the furniture arrived, the deliverymen were directed to the appropriate rooms. By nightfall, the house was pretty straight. Everyone who helped with the move was so worn out, most of them crashed at the house. They sat around and talked until they started dozing off one by one.

Eventually, JD and Tracy went upstairs and finally had a moment to be alone. All of their clothes were not at the house yet, so Tracy changed into one of JD's tee shirts. When she came out of the bathroom JD was in the sitting room at the far end of the bedroom. He sat there with the bottom of his pajamas on; his long legs stretched out and his head lying back on the lounge chair. *Damn, that man looks good with half his clothes off,* she thought. Tracy walked over to him, straddled his lap and laid her head on his chest. He rubbed her back as they both sighed with relief. One of the reasons Tracy decided on their new home in East End of Richmond was because of the view. They could see the outline of the city from the window in the sitting room of their bedroom. "Do you remember the first time you kissed me? We were looking at that same skyline," Tracy reminisced.

JD ran his hand under her shirt and down her back. "You don't have no drawers on." JD smirked.

Tracy giggled. "No, I don't." JD could feel her body laughing against his chest. "It was not intentional," she said as she playfully bit his nipple. That sent a ripple through his body as every tired muscle came alive. They relaxed comfortably without speaking, JD caressing Tracy's back, she caressing his chest. He kissed the top of Tracy's head. Tracy reached up and kissed the side of his neck. JD could feel the very essence of Tracy beginning to become moist against his stomach. Tracy could feel JD growing firmly against her thigh. Tracy adjusted to allow JD to spring freely through the opening of his pajamas. JD slowly slid Tracy's body down his body until the tip of him was at her entrance. Tracy moaned at the slight touch. She ran her hands up his chest, caressing his nipples. JD ran his hands up her back then down to her waist.

His jerking motion let her know he needed to enter her. He pressed her hips down onto his shaft. She widened her legs and he slipped right in. He filled every inch of space within her. Tracy savored the feel of him, not wanting to leave any portion untouched. JD's hands followed the movement of Tracy's hips. As her pace increased, so did his. Her breathing began to intensify; as did his. JD held her tighter as he felt her body tensing for her release. The rhythm of their bodies raced together, both reaching for the very highest echelon of ecstasy. At the point of true bliss, Tracy inhaled with a small scream escaping from her lips. JD moaned as he released his expression of love within her.

They both lay there, hearts pounding with lovemaking juices escaping down their thighs, neither of them able to move. They fell asleep in that position in each other's arms.

When Tracy woke the next morning in bed with comforters piled on top of her, she had no recollection of when she got there, how she got there, or why she had so many comforters on her. As Tracy pushed them aside, there was a note lying on the floor. "I wanted to make sure you stayed warm. I'll see you downstairs." It was signed, "Me."

Tracy smiled, jumped in the shower and dressed quickly. As she came downstairs she could identify all the voices that were penetrating the house.

"Good morning," Tracy greeted everyone as she walked over to Jeffrey. She threw her arms around his neck, pulled his head down to her and kissed him as if no one was in the room but the two of them. JD dropped the fork that he was holding, put his arms around her waist and pulled her in. Brian got off the stool, walked around and stood beside them observing.

"What in the hell are you doing, Brian?" Calvin asked.

"Don't disturb me right now, man, I'm taking notes."

Tracy broke away from JD.

"Don't mind us," Ashley said, "we just sitting here."

Tracy inhaled. "Coffee?" JD handed her his cup. "Thank you," she said. "What's on the agenda today, people?" Tracy asked as she sat at the table.

"We have to do tuxedoes today," JD replied.

"We have to meet with Cynthia for final touches," Ashley said as the doorbell rang.

Tracy looked at JD and started laughing. "That's our doorbell."

JD looked at her. "Yeah, you want to answer it?" Tracy smacked him on the shoulder. JD smiled and shook his head. He watched her walk across the room. *Damn that woman turns me on,* JD thought.

"You want to stop looking at that woman like you are ready to undress her?" Brian said laughing.

"Hell no," JD replied.

"Damn, girl," Cynthia said as she entered the kitchen. "With everything in, this house is off the chain. Tracy, you have to show me around. But first I have something for you guys." She put her bag on the table and pulled out invitations. "Since I was coming over, I decided to deliver this in person." JD took the envelope from Cynthia's hand.

"What is it?" Tracy asked.

JD smiled. "It's an invitation to Gavin and Carolyn's engagement party."

The next week as Tracy worked in the house, JD worked vigorously to bring the Melvin case to a close. The news of additional bodies being found prompted national news coverage. Requests from the media for interviews with JD intensified. With the wedding and the move into the house, JD was being pulled in several directions. JD agreed to every interview that was held in Virginia. The first and main interview was given to Victoria. The coverage of the one-on-one interview went national, just as they expected. JD executed the interview with tact and finesse. He appeared to be diplomatic with the issue of him taking over the case. Anyone watching the interview had to be captivated with JD's depiction of the case. It was methodical the way he laid out every step of the evidence found, without revealing any information that could hinder the prosecution of Melvin.

Once the interview went nationwide, the publicity surrounding the case became fanatical. The morning shows on the major networks invited JD to discuss the case with them. Each of those interviews was handled via satellite from the attorney general's office with the AG, JD and the original prosecutor. Most of the questions were directed to the attorney general. When asked what prompted the second investigation into the area where the additional bodies were found, the AG deferred the question to JD. JD handled the national media with the same composure as he did the state level. At no point did he ever take credit for the second investigation; he indicated it was a collaborative effort between the Roanoke DA's office and the Richmond DA's office. JD's performance was impressive, to say the least, and it did not go unnoticed.

The head of the Democratic Governors Association called. He wanted a bio on this charismatic young man handling the national press with such ease. The next call went to Senator Roth from the Senate Majority Leader, Chris Neshak; his question was simply, is this man one of ours? Roth was pleased to receive the call and was ready to give the full rundown on JD Harrison. Senator Neshak decided to give Roth a little help with his plan to get JD into office. He called the local networks in Virginia and asked for all footage on JD Harrison. Once the information was received, Senator Neshak gave the footage to a head reporter at one of the major national networks. They edited different footage and began to air editorials pertaining to JD's professional career. That footage included the gang reduction efforts, the attack on Tracy and the murder attempt on JD. The public wanted to know more about the young man who would bring Melvin to justice.

With urging from the DNC, Senator Roth called JD and set up a meeting to revisit the question of him running for office. Roth had to get a commitment from JD, now.

Senator Roth arrived at JD's office precisely at 5:30. He knocked on the door while JD was on the telephone with Tracy. JD motioned for Roth to come in. "Babe, I'm not sure what time I'll get home. Hopefully it will not be too late; wait up for me. I'll talk to you later."

Roth smiled at the conversation. "I used to talk like that, you know," Roth said laughingly when JD hung up the telephone.

JD smiled. "I don't know how she puts up with me, but I thank God every day that she does."

Roth took a seat. "JD, the result of the test puts us in a bit of a situation. I will technically be your father in-law."

JD thought for a moment. What he was about to say to Roth had to be done tactfully.

"Senator, I can't begin to imagine how many emotions you must be dealing with since the results came out. If they had come back inconclusive, I'm not sure I would be marrying Tracy at the end of the month. I never thought once about the situation all this has put you in. I don't know if you have had a chance to work through all of this."

"It has caused me a sleepless night or two," Roth replied, "but we both agree, neither Tracy nor Carolyn needs to know about this. It will only cause problems for everyone involved."

JD sat back in his chair. "You do realize Lena Washington is going to be a problem if she ever puts two and two together. How are you going to handle that?"

Roth's plan was to have the report altered. Roth knew JD would not like the plan he had to keep Lena Washington off him, but it was the only way he knew to keep her from using the situation to her advantage. Roth sat up.

"JD, there are a lot of things I am willing to be accountable for without hesitation. This situation, however, can be detrimental to Carolyn and Tracy. According to you, Lena will use whatever she has at her disposal to get whatever she wants. I am not willing to allow that type of person to have any information that can harm Carolyn. If I have to suppress information to protect her, I will."

"So you are keeping the report from Lena."

"Yes, and if she happens to come across it, it will reveal nothing."

JD understood where Roth was coming from, but it disturbed him that Roth could alter the report. It all seemed dishonest to him. "Are there any documents I have received from you that were altered in any way?" JD asked curiously.

Roth was a little offended by the question. But he had to remember, JD dealt with issues head on then suffered the consequences.

"Let me ask you a question, JD. Have you told Tracy about the results of the test?"

"No."

"Why not?" Roth asked.

"Tracy didn't have a good childhood. There are a number of issues she is still trying to sort through concerning her mother. To give Tracy another issue with her mom would be cruel."

Roth sat back. "What is the difference between you withholding the information and what I am doing?"

James Brooks walked through the door and addressed both Roth and JD. "You will be altering a legal document because you love your daughter. JD is withholding information because he loves your other daughter. If both of you continue down this path, it will backfire. It always does."

JD looked at his watch. He did set the meeting with James, Brian, Calvin and Douglas for 6:30. "Anyone else out there?" JD frowned, concerned someone else may have overheard.

"No. If you plan to keep this information under wraps I suggest this be the last conversation you two have on the matter. The two of you must agree to let this go. Or at the very least be careful where you hold these conversations," James advised.

JD and Roth nodded in agreement. "Making this information public knowledge would not benefit anyone. Do we agree this conversation ends here?" Roth asked. JD nodded in agreement. James took a seat.

"Are we making a decision tonight on the race?" James asked JD.

"We are gathering information."

"No, son, we are making a decision tonight," Roth corrected. "JD, you need to be aware of the interest that has surfaced since you took over the Melvin case. I have received calls from the national level concerning you. The question may not need to be publicized, but a decision must be made before we leave here tonight."

JD did not intend to go back on his word to Tracy. He promised a decision would not be made before the wedding. "I have a beautiful woman at home who I have to keep happy. She has moved us into a home without my assistance, completed the furnishing of that home without my assistance, and is now planning a wedding without my assistance. I am not going to do anything to upset her before she says 'I do.'"

Brian and Douglas walked through the door. Everyone spoke. JD buzzed Calvin, who was still in his office working. As Calvin came into the room he began the roundtable. The information on JD's professional career was spotless. Calvin did a review on every case JD had ever handled. There was no indication of misconduct, no indication of racial bias, no indication of favoritism until the Day case.

"What happened with the Day case?" Roth asked.

Calvin looked at JD. "Al Day is Tracy's brother. I handled the plea bargain with the AG's office directly," JD explained.

"Was this before or after you became involved with Tracy?" Roth asked.

JD shrugged. "That depends."

"On what?" Roth asked.

"On what you consider involved," JD replied.

"Now is not the time to mince words," Roth said.

"I met Tracy when she was a sophomore in college. At the time I was an ADA. It did not seem proper for me to see someone that young, so I kept my distance. When I was assigned the Day case, we reconnected after the conviction and sentencing."

Roth thought about it. "Did you do anything in that case you would not have done in any other case?"

"No."

"Then let's move on."

Brian gave his findings. He did a thorough search into JD's scholastic records and family. "I was able to pull records from the fifth grade through law school. He ranked second in the graduation class behind one Calvin Johnson." Brian smiled as he turned to Calvin. "Man, I did not know you had it in you." Calvin looked at JD. "His family is solid with the exception of one or two cousins and Uncle Joe. They have each had an infraction or two with the law." Brian smiled.

JD laughed, "What did you get, Doug?" JD asked.

"The sports career of JD Harrison was honorable. The records are intact, but I did come across a police report at Harmon with the Harrison name connected, but it was sealed. Nothing else. Everyone I spoke with sung your praises on the court and field."

"It appears the only issue we will have to address will be Tracy." James spoke up quickly. "The issue with her family and especially her brother will have to be addressed. From all accounts, this will be the area the opposition will find to be the most vulnerable." James stood. "Knowing how you feel about Tracy, when anyone tries to attack her, you will react. However, this situation can be handled effectively if you are proactive with it."

"How do you mean?" Roth asked.

"You take it to the media. You put it out front when you announce. Any questions that come up about it, you answer, without hesitation. Remember, you have nothing to hide here. Make a full disclosure of the case with her brother. And remember, in the end you did prosecute the brother of the woman you are marrying."

Roth agreed with the assessment James made. They discussed the different scenarios on how the information could be handled with the media.

Next, they discussed the financial aspects of a campaign. "It could take serious money to run this campaign if you are opposed," Calvin said.

"I don't think money or the opposition will be an issue if you decide to run," Roth said. "The only thing missing at this point is your commitment."

JD stood, put his hands in his pockets and look downward, searching his mind. Making this move would change his life and Tracy's as well. JD had no doubt Tracy would support him if he decided to run for attorney general. This move would definitely keep his family from harms' way.

The events of the past year had made JD keenly aware of his vulnerability. Under no circumstances did he want to take a chance on another shooting or attack on Tracy. They planned to start a family soon. Now he had to take the protection of his future children into consideration. After the loss of the baby, the reality of what he did for a living hit home. If JD continued in the role of district attorney, he would be just as involved in cases as before, which would place potential danger on his family. If he ran for AG and won, he would be working in the area he loved, which is the law. It might even afford him the opportunity to help a few people along the way. The two community groups he had started could certainly benefit from his being in office. This might give him a chance to help other localities with gang reduction. He might be able to bring the same level of success he had with the Richmond metro area to other parts of the state.

JD looked around the room. The men in the room were looking to him as their leader. Senator Roth was there to support him in the political arena, in which he himself would be like a fish on land, completely out of his element. Then there were Brian and Douglas, the two men he knew would protect him and his loved ones against any foe, personal or professional. Then there was Calvin, JD's childhood friend, now his confidant and most trusted advisor. And James Brooks, one of the most intelligent men he had come in contact with in years. James was someone who had proven to be a good advisor and friend to him and Tracy. With this group of men behind him, JD was sure the advice and support would always be there for him. No one said anything as JD walked the room contemplating his next move.

"James," JD asked, "how bad can this get for Tracy?"

James quietly advised JD, "Tracy is a very private person. Dealing with large groups of people is something she will be the first to tell you she is not good at. I have a different opinion. I believe Tracy has a certain effect on people. She has a way of making someone feel as if he is the most important person in the world when she talks to you. I honestly believe Tracy is your strongest asset. Now Tracy is not a Carolyn Roth, no offense meant, Senator, but Tracy will not play the political wife game. Tracy is going to be who she is, and as things come out about her past, it is going to hurt her."

Douglas added, "Tracy is a tough little lady, and she is smart on the street level and professional level. She will be able to handle the press."

Brian laughed. "Hell, she will have them eating out of her hands."

JD looked at his watch; it was after 10. He called home and put the call on speakerphone. "Hey, babe," JD said.

Tracy sounded asleep. "Hey, sweetie, when you coming home?" she yawned into the phone.

"In a little bit," JD replied. You sound tired."

"I am. If you keep leaving me alone at night I'm going to call Brian to take care of me."

Brian cleared his throat. "Hey, Tracy, babe I'm right here. Whatever you need I will be there in 10 minutes."

The guys in the room laughed at the expression on JD's face. "Babe, you are going to get Brian's ass whipped if you keep that up."

"Jeffrey, why do you have me on speaker phone?"

"We were having a conversation I felt you should be a part of. Before you say anything, let me tell you who is here. Senator Roth, James, Douglas, Calvin and, of course, Brian, who I am about to put out."

Tracy was silent for a minute as everyone said hello. "Jeffrey, pick up the telephone for a moment, please."

JD complied. The guys in the room watched JD's facial expression go from pure amusement to unrequited lust. He put the phone back on speaker.

"What can I do for you gentlemen?" Tracy asked in the sweetest voice one can imagine.

JD cleared his throat. "Babe, the question is on the floor, are we running for attorney general?"

"Hmm," Tracy sighed, "Jeffrey, you have five very intelligent, honest men in that room with you. I believe each of them has your best interest at heart. Whatever they advise should take precedence over my opinion. I take it your hesitation in committing is because of me. You are concerned that I may not be able to handle a political campaign. That cannot be your deciding factor. Your factor should be do you believe you can do something to help the people of Virginia. If you tell me you believe that, I will be with you at every stop across the state, shaking hands and kissing babies."

Roth smiled at the response. "Tracy," James said, "you do realize that information regarding your family will surface and questions will be asked?"

"Yeah, then we answer the questions. Jeffrey is the one people will need to be able to accept in this position, not me. Now when he runs for president, then we will have to be concerned with my background."

Roth laughed. "I like that girl."

"I don't know how much exploring you guys have done, but you do realize you will have to collect thousands of signatures to get Jeffrey on the ballot before June and you have to talk to Gavin about all of this. To help you along, Mrs. Gonzalez has collected two thousand signatures; Pastor Smith has another three thousand. Magna hit several places in Northern Virginia last week and collected a little over a thousand. Dan collected two thousand in Roanoke. So you have an additional two thousand to collect."

JD was stunned. "When did you get all of that done?"

Tracy sucked her teeth. "We got that started the first time you and I discussed the possibility of you running for office. It didn't make sense to discuss it without knowing if there was any interest from the public. If we went through any political committee, there was a chance of you thinking about running getting out. So I turned to some friends who I knew would get the job done without leaks. All the data on the regional breakdown of the state is on your computer. As soon as you get your political action committee set up, you have several people ready to send in contributions and Mrs. Gonzalez is putting together a team of volunteers." Tracy yawned. "Now, with all of that said, gentlemen, for the next few weeks each one of you belongs to me. And Mr. Harrison, I want uninterrupted time for the next month. We have to get through the holidays and the wedding. Senator?"

Roth laughed. "Okay, Tracy, I understand. Nothing will take place before the wedding."

"Good. Babe, I'm going to sleep now. Wake me when you get home."

JD shook his head. Tracy never ceased to amaze him.

"I'll be home in 10 minutes." JD disconnected the call.

"Maybe I was wrong," James smiled, "she may actually be better than Carolyn. No offense, Senator."

"None taken."

Douglas stood. "I think we have been talking to the wrong Harrison. From this point on, let's get Tracy in on these conversations a little earlier."

Chapter 40

During the week that followed, JD decided to talk with Gavin personally to get his honest feelings on him joining the ticket. Gavin invited JD to his house for the discussion. "JD, you have always been opposed to the political machine. What's changed?" Gavin asked.

"Tracy," JD replied. "For some reason she believes I can help people. Tracy knows I love the law, everything about it. Protecting those laws and making them work the way they were meant to is important to me. Always has been. If I stay in the DA position, you know me, Gavin, I will be just as involved with cases as I was under you." JD exhaled. "Being that involved in cases could put Tracy and our future family at risk, just as it did in September. I don't want to go through that again."

Gavin had wondered how JD dealt with the shooting and the attack on Tracy. Other than the first night Tracy was in the hospital, JD showed no emotions about the incident. Now he could tell how deeply it all affected him. "It's only natural to want to protect someone you love, but you are entering into a lifestyle with politics, JD. It's not just a change of career path. It's just as you always said. There is a lot of compromise and still not getting shit done. There will be times when you will have to be around people you know are dirty, but you have to keep face. You can never let them know what you are really thinking." Gavin laughed. "You have never been able to keep your mouth shut when someone is not on point with you."

JD laughed. "I guess they will have to get used to me."

Gavin smiled. "How are you going to handle the situation with Al Day?"

"I'm still working on that one. I hate the thought of taking Tracy through all that publicity."

"Well, that she is going to have to deal with. This will not be the last time controversy will be coming your way. Understand that up front, and you will be okay."

"How is Carolyn going to handle all of this?" JD asked.

Gavin walked across the room and fixed a drink. Gavin and JD had always been able to talk to each other about personal issues. Most times, it was JD listening to Gavin's advice on staying unattached. When JD started with Tracy, there was an understandable barrier. JD wanted to protect Tracy from Gavin or anyone else that may want to do her harm. Then there was Carolyn. Gavin had known Carolyn was seeing JD, but he also knew JD was not serious about her. Unfortunately for Gavin, he fell in love with Carolyn almost the moment he met her. Carolyn only began to show attention to him when it appeared he was going after the governor's seat. Even with that, Carolyn did not commit to Gavin until she knew for sure JD was going to marry Tracy. At that point, Carolyn did not completely become his. She began to play around with his political analyst behind his back. Gavin had reached his point of patience with Carolyn.

"I'm not sure, nor am I concerned with how Carolyn is going to handle this. The truth of the matter is, JD, you and I have always made an invincible force as a team. We had a hell of a winning streak going. Why not take that to the highest state level."

JD walked over to the bar, poured a drink and sat next to Gavin. "What's happened with Carolyn?"

Gavin smiled. "You know Carolyn; she likes to play games."

JD knew that very well. "Yes, she does, and plays them well. But you two are good together. I can see the two of you in the mansion. The thing Carolyn has not realized is eventually one gets frustrated with the game and wants something real."

Gavin nodded. "You're right, and I have reached that point."

JD frowned. "Gavin, don't give up on her."

Gavin put his drink down. "I'm not giving up completely. Carolyn and I will be in the mansion as husband and wife, but it will be in name only. At some point every man has to go into self-preservation mode. I'm there. I can't allow her to cause any more damage."

"That's going to lead to a pretty lonely life," JD said.

"Not for me; I have moved on in that department."

JD shook his head. "Do you think that is wise with the campaign coming up?"

Gavin smiled. *JD is finally on board and that winning attitude is in check*, he thought. "It won't be a problem."

Carolyn walked into the kitchen from the garage. Surprised to see JD and Gavin at the bar in the family room, she took a moment to gather herself. Carolyn smiled and walked into the room.

"Well, good evening," she said as she kissed Gavin.

"Hello, Carolyn," JD said. Carolyn stood there beside Gavin with her arms around his shoulders. She tensed for a moment, not knowing how Gavin was going to respond. Gavin had not touched or attempted to be with her since the night they set the wedding date. The gesture did not go unnoticed by JD or Gavin. Not wanting Carolyn to lose face, Gavin put his arm around her waist.

"How have you been, JD?" Carolyn asked, relieved.

"I'm good. I can see you are doing well," he replied.

"Gavin makes sure I'm happy." She smiled.

"As it should be."

"JD is here to discuss joining the ticket as the candidate for the AG spot," Gavin said to Carolyn.

Carolyn looked at Gavin, then back to JD. "Well, isn't that just wonderful." She hesitated for a moment, and then smiled. "I always told you politics was your destiny. What made you come to that conclusion now?"

JD swallowed his drink. "It's a long story, for another time," he said as he got up to leave. "Gavin, I will not be making any announcements until after the wedding."

"JD, when you announce is not important. The fact that you are joining me is. I'm glad to have you on board."

JD shook Gavin's hand. "Thanks, man. I'll talk to you later."

JD looked at Carolyn; he could tell she was fuming inside. "Carolyn, I'm happy for you and Gavin. I believe the two of you are going to make a formidable force in the mansion."

After JD left, Carolyn turned to Gavin. "Are you comfortable with this?"

Gavin grabbed his coat. "Why wouldn't I be? I've worked with JD for years. I know he's a winner. With him on the ticket, the mansion is a guarantee," Gavin said as he kissed her forehead.

"Where are you going?" Carolyn asked.

Gavin turned and raised an eyebrow. "Out."

Carolyn did not like the game Gavin was playing. "You asked me to play the role of the loving spouse?" she asked while folding her arms across her chest.

Gavin stepped back into the room. "It's strange that a month ago you were eager for me to go; you never wanted me around unless there was a function we had to attend in public. Now you are concerned with where I'm going." He laughed as he put his coat on. "I'm getting a little confused here, Carolyn. You made it clear you did not love me. Your words; not mine. What difference does it make where I'm going, as long as I am not interrupting anything you want to do?"

"I'm not trying to keep tabs on you or anything like that. It's just that the party is Saturday and we should be seen as the happy couple, don't you think?" Carolyn answered with a tad bit of sarcasm.

"That's just for the public, isn't it?" Gavin looked around. "I don't see anyone here; we don't have to pretend when we are alone, Carolyn."

Carolyn exhaled. "That's just it, Gavin; I seem to be here alone quite frequently, while you are out doing whatever you do," she said as she poured a drink.

Gavin made a sad face. "Aw, is little Carolyn lonely? Don't you have some party details to attend to, or where's Jackie?"

Carolyn swallowed; at least she had his attention for a moment. "Jackie's out with Calvin, doing Christmas stuff."

Gavin nodded his head up and down. "The normal things real couples do this time of the year."

Carolyn closed her eyes and bit her lip. She did not want to lose her cool with Gavin right now, but she was tired of going to bed alone every night. "Maybe we should be doing those things," she said.

"Let me get this straight. You want to go Christmas shopping with me?"

Carolyn looked up with a smile. "If that's where you are going." She looked sideways at him. "Are you shopping for me?"

Gavin put his gloves on. "No," he said.

Carolyn threw her hands up in the air. "I give up, Gavin. I just give up. I don't know what you want from me. I'm doing everything in my power to make sure you get into the mansion. You ask me to change, to adapt to what a first lady should be; I did. You ask me to stop my indiscretions; okay, I did. Now you don't want to spend any time with me. What more is it you want from me?" Carolyn asked, forcefully putting her hands on her hips.

Gavin stood there looking at Carolyn. *Is she really that clueless?* All he wanted from her was love. He shook his head. "You know, JD never thought about doing the one thing he was born to do until he found Tracy. She gave him the one thing that completed him. You could learn a lot from her," Gavin said and walked out the door.

Carolyn threw the glass at the wall as Gavin closed the door.

Gavin and Carolyn's engagement party was the last thing Tracy wanted to attend. However, she was there for JD; at least that's what she kept repeating to herself. *This is important for Jeffrey.* Gavin was now a partner, of sorts, to Jeffrey. There were going to be many occasions the four of them would have to be at together.

While at the party, Tracy and Ashley were exploring the house and just happened to walk up on Cynthia and Gavin. "This is a formality. You know what I am dealing with here," Gavin said to Cynthia.

Cynthia straightened Gavin's bow tie and smiled. "You have a good night. I'm a big girl. I can handle this. You do what you have to do to make this work." Gavin kissed Cynthia gently on the lips, then walked out of a door on the other side of the room.

That night Ashley wanted to approach Cynthia, but Tracy stopped her. "Now is not the time," she said, "Gavin and Carolyn are about to make their entrance."

The entrance was nothing short of majestic. Between Carolyn and Cynthia, the engagement party was what dreams were made of. After the introduction, Gavin bent on one knee and presented Carolyn with a ring made of emeralds (her birthstone) and diamonds that seemed to light up the room. If any of that was planned, it did not show on Carolyn's face. She seemed to be as overwhelmed as everyone else in the room. Tears actually filled her eyes. Cameras went off in every direction. As they walked down the staircase, the dance floor cleared. As soon as their feet touched the floor the music started playing. As they began to dance, people gathered around, admiring the couple. They were breathtaking together dancing. Yes, it was easy to imagine this gentle giant Gavin and the stunning Carolyn taking this dance into the mansion.

At this point one would think that the parents of the couple would join them on the dance floor. Not at a Carolyn Roth function. Anything and everything Carolyn did, including her engagement party, was geared towards winning the mansion next November. Carolyn instructed the hostesses to ask JD and Tracy to join them on the dance floor on the second song. Tracy was taken back a little as JD led her to the dance floor. He pulled Tracy close and whispered, "Don't worry about the people. I'm here with you." He smiled down at her. Tracy smiled back, closed her eyes and danced with her soon-to-be husband. The audience applause and cheers were so loud, it brought a huge smile to Carolyn's and Gavin's faces.

The political crowd was seeing a preview of the year to come. A year from now, most of the guests were praying the two couples on the dance floor would be dancing at the next inauguration. Some of the guests— Republicans—were taking notes; they would have to find a way to prevent this from becoming a reality. The political power base in the room this night alone would be undefeatable. As the song ended, an upbeat tune began to play. Carolyn had selected the music well. It was important to make sure people understood: this was a young, vibrant ticket in the upcoming election. From experience, Carolyn knew neither JD nor Tracy would shy away from good music. They did not disappoint her;

they began dancing and so did Gavin and Carolyn. Others began to join the couples on the dance floor. Soon the party was in full swing.

As expected, the engagement party was on the front page in the Flair section of the Sunday paper. Gavin and Carolyn were center stage, with a quarter-page spread, as it should be. Smaller pictures on the same page showed well-known politicians from across the state that had attended the celebration. Further down was a picture of JD and Tracy, with a reminder of the wedding scheduled for New Year's Eve. A larger picture at the bottom of the page showed Gavin and Carolyn, along with JD and Tracy, dancing. The caption read, "The Future of Virginia." Tracy gave the page to JD, who was reading the sports section.

"We look good, babe," JD said.

Tracy relaxed on the sofa and put her legs across JD's lap. "I saw something last night I'm sure we should not have seen."

JD looked at her from the paper. "What?"

Tracy studied JD for a moment, not sure for so many reasons if this should be spoken of or not. Cynthia was her friend and Gavin was running for governor and marrying JD's ex-girlfriend, but her first priority was to Jeffrey. JD sensed her hesitation. He kissed the top of her foot. "Tell me your secret or I'm coming up your leg."

Tracy made a sound with her lips. "That's easy—come on up my leg." She laughed. JD pulled her down the sofa to him. Tracy laughed. "Okay, okay, okay, I'll tell you."

JD ran his hands under her boxers. "Too late. I don't want to know now." He kissed her navel. "What gives?"

Tracy's smile faded a little. "I saw Gavin and Cynthia in one of the rooms last night. They were a little close."

JD raised his head from her stomach. "What?" he said in a surprised voice. Then he asked, "How close?"

Tracy frowned. "Kissing close."

"Get out," JD said. "Did they see you?"

Tracy shook her head. "No. We stepped back so they would not see us."

"We who?"

"Ashley and I." Tracy watched JD intensely. "What do you think of that?"

JD rubbed Tracy's calf. "I don't know, babe. What do you think? You witnessed it. Do you think there's something going on there?"

"Yeah, I do." JD wondered if that was what Gavin meant the other day when he said he had moved on. "What are you thinking?" Tracy asked.

"Gavin had alluded to something not being right with him and Carolyn the other day when we talked. But I didn't know what he was referring to then. This could cause a problem if Gavin does not handle it right."

"Are you referring to the campaign or the error of being with another person when you are committed to someone?"

JD closed his eyes; he heard the robot in *Lost in Space* warning, "*Danger, Will Rogers, danger.*" He gave Tracy a devilish smile. "Babe, commitment means different things to different people. You and I are fully committed to one another because we love each other and we want to grow old together regardless of where our paths lead. Gavin and Carolyn are only partially committed to each other. They both want the same thing and need each other to accomplish the agenda. If that agenda did not exist they would probably not be together."

The telephone rang. "Saved by the bell," Tracy said as she answered the telephone.

Chapter 41

Before Tracy knew it, it was the day before Christmas Eve; the wedding events were in full swing. JD and the boys were having final fittings for tuxedos. Rosaline was making final arrangements on the food. Cynthia was finalizing everything else. The final fitting of the gowns was attended by Tracy, Ashley, Mrs. Harrison and Mrs. Langston, at Tracy's request. Tracy wanted an outside opinion. Ashley and Martha would not say anything that they thought would hurt Tracy's feelings. It seem like everyone was walking on eggshells around her lately. When Tracy stepped in front of the center mirror in Judith's dress shop, tears came to Ashley's eyes. Mrs. Langston walked over to Tracy and spread the train of the gown completely out. Martha just sat there and smiled. "I don't think I have ever seen a dress so befitting anyone in my life."

Judith smiled. "Did it turn out the way you wanted it, Tracy?"

Tracy looked at herself in the mirror. All week people treated her like a helpless child; she could not understand why. Her nerves were fine and she had no question about the steps she was about to take. She loved Jeffrey. There was no one in the world she would ever want to be with other than him. Nothing had shaken her resolve until now. Looking at herself in this dress broke her. She stepped back from the mirror as a vision of her brother in the field the last time she saw him came to mind. Then Jeffrey was standing in front of her covered in blood saying he loved her. Her mind flicked and she was lying in her own blood. Then there was the baby, the one she would never see. Then Vanessa and Carolyn were sneering at her with the entire Harrison family in her house. The house, the holidays, the wedding, her mother, Jeffrey's campaign, all of it was going in circles in her head. Her whole world was spinning out of control. She began to shake her head, "I can't do this," she whispered. Ashley ran to her just before her knees buckled.

"Tracy!" Ashley called out as she broke Tracy's fall. "Tracy," she called out again.

Mrs. Langston got a cup of water. Tracy was lying on the floor with the dress spread out beneath her. Ashley removed the veil from Tracy's head. Mrs. Langston flicked small drops of water on Tracy's face. Judith went into another room. When she returned she handed a cup to Martha. Martha put the cup under Tracy's nose. Tracy flinched.

As Tracy opened her eyes, tears were streaming down her face. "Ashley, I'm so tired. I need to go home."

"Baby, you are going to be alright," Martha said. "Come on; let's get you out of that dress."

Tracy nodded her head. "Okay," she said softly.

Martha stood in front of the mirror so Tracy could not see her reflection. Ashley and Mrs. Langston helped Tracy up. Ashley went with her into the dressing room, and slowly began to help Tracy undress. Ashley was quiet; she knew Tracy very well. Tracy needed a moment to breathe and think.

"When was the last time you slept?" Ashley asked tenderly.

"The first night we moved into the house," Tracy replied demurely.

With a touch of concern, Ashley asked, "You've been keeping it from JD?" Tracy nodded. "What is it—the wedding, the campaign or your mom?"

Tracy looked at Ashley as she stepped into her jeans. She slowly buttoned her jeans and pulled her sweater over her head. "Yeah," was all Tracy said as she sat on the bench in the dressing room.

Ashley hung the dress on the door then sat beside Tracy. "The dress is exactly what you talked about. It is beautiful. No one can wear that dress but you." Ashley smiled. Tears were coming down Tracy's face. Ashley took Tracy's hand and held it. "A lot has happened in the last year. Let us review," Ashley said as she looked at Tracy.

"Professor Wood." Tracy smiled.

Ashley laughed. "You know it." She hesitated for a moment, and then continued. "First you stole my brother's mind." Tracy laughed a little. "Well, you did. The poor man was walking around looking for his brains for weeks." Ashley smiled. "Then you stole his heart; and now you are trying to steal his life from him." Tracy wiped the tears from her face and frowned at Ashley.

Ashley squeezed Tracy's hand. "If you back out of this wedding, and I know that is what you are thinking, it will kill JD. He is so in love with you, Tracy. JD is able to finally do what he was born to do because he has found his better half. Do you know how many people go through life never finding that one true love, that God-made person who was meant for only them?"

Tracy inhaled. "I'm so tired, Ashley. I can't do what Jeffrey needs from me. I thought I could do this, all of this; but I can't." She cried. She shook her head back and forth, then put her face in her hands and cried. "Jeffrey is going to be so disappointed in me, Ashley. I am so afraid when I walk down that aisle that Jeffrey will not be there."

Ashley hugged her friend until she calmed down. Mama Harrison stepped into the room and removed the dress and veil. Martha handed a cool washcloth to Ashley. Ashley looked at her mom. "You better call JD."

Tracy looked up. "No, no, please don't let Jeffrey know about this, please," she begged.

Ashley wiped Tracy's face, and then hugged her tightly. Ashley began to cry. "Tracy, please calm down. You are scaring me." Ashley cried as she continued to rock her. Mrs. Langston stepped into the room. Martha pulled Ashley and Mrs. Langston pulled Tracy. Mrs. Langston took the washcloth from Ashley's hand. Martha and Ashley left the room.

"Hold your head up, Tracy," Mrs. Langston said calmly. She folded the cloth and placed it on Tracy's forehead. Then she reached into her purse and pulled out a sandwich bag with oatmeal raisin cookies. Mrs. Langston handed one to Tracy, then bit into one herself.

"I remember the first day you walked into the office looking for JD," Mrs. Langston said, as she sat beside Tracy. "You had this incredible smile that you thought was hiding the sadness you felt that day. You were scared, just like you are now." Mrs. Langston smiled. "What you don't know is, JD was scared, too."

Tracy frowned. "Nothing scares Jeffrey."

Mrs. Langston laughed. "You do. You scare the hell out of JD. You should have seen him straightening his tie and checking his hair before he came down the hallway to meet you." She hesitated, remembering the day. "When you two went into his office, both of you were scared. But when you came out, both of you were at ease. You went into the office as two very scared individuals; but you came out as one. You two draw strength from each other and that's what marriage is all about. The next time you put that gown on, you will be walking to your strength. Don't let your fears hold you back."

Tracy removed the washcloth. She lowered her head, and then bit into her cookie. "I'm not sure I can make it down that aisle alone," she said as she chewed the cookie.

"Just keep your eye on the prize. He will be at the other end keeping his eyes on you."

Tracy exhaled. "How do you know he will be there?"

Mrs. Langston bit into the cookie again. "Because he said he would and JD Harrison is a man of his word."

Tracy looked at Mrs. Langston; she was much calmer now. "Do you always carry cookies around with you?"

"Yeah, you never know when you might need them."

Tracy bit into her cookie again. She looked at the remainder of the cookie then back at Mrs. Langston. "Do you think you could walk with me down the aisle and bring some of these cookies with you?"

Mrs. Langston smiled. "If that is what it will take to get you down the aisle, I will be happy to."

Tracy relaxed. "I guess we should let people go home, now that I have come back to my senses," Tracy said, feeling a little embarrassed. "May I have another cookie?"

Mrs. Langston stood. "Come on, you can have the whole bag."

As they left the dressing room Ashley and Martha were waiting with the dress.

Judith thanked Tracy for letting her be a part of the wedding. "Don't you worry, girl, all brides go through this at some point. You have a happy holiday."

Tracy smiled. "The dress is beautiful. Thank you so much for making it."

Ashley had the dress. "I believe this belongs to you," she said to Tracy.

"You hold on to it, Ashley, and whatever you do, don't let Jeffrey see it," Tracy ordered.

"Yes, ma'am." Ashley smiled. She put the dress on the backseat of her car, still concerned about her friend. "Let's get you home and to bed; you need to get some sleep."

Tracy shook her head. "We have to go to the office and give out Christmas bonuses."

As they got into the car Ashley suggested, "I can give out the checks this year. You need to get some rest, Tracy."

"I'll go home afterwards and try to get in a nap before Jeffrey gets home."

"Okay," Ashley agreed hesitantly. "You are out of the office by noon, no questions asked. Pinky swear?"

"Okay," Tracy agreed as she gave the pinky swear.

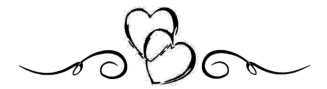

Chapter 42

Tracy was exhausted. As always, whenever she was stressed her body would shut down on her. With Jeffrey's possible campaign, the wedding, all the holiday parties and visits, she was wearing thin. Even she was at a point to admit that. JD was a little concerned about Tracy after talking with Ashley. The Harrison family had a tradition of putting up the Christmas tree on Christmas Eve. In the past Tracy spent holidays alone so JD took it upon himself to get the house ready for the holidays. Not to interfere with his mom's tradition, he made plans to put up their tree and decorate the house the day before Christmas Eve. He invited a few friends over to help. Now he was wondering if that was a good idea. When he arrived home, JD went upstairs to find Tracy in her study. With his finger he motioned to her, "Come with me."

She walked over to him. "I have no energy, so if we are about to make love, it's all on you."

JD took her hand. "Not even married yet and you are closing down on me," he joked.

"I'm sorry." She smiled as she took his hand and followed as he led her to the bedroom. Upon entering the room he pulled her top over her head and dropped it on the floor. Turing her around, he pulled her hair off her shoulder, and used a hairpin to hold it up. "What are you doing?" she asked.

Without a reply, he reached around her waist, unbuttoned her jeans, and pushed them to the floor. She stepped out of the jeans, and then turned towards him. He kissed her as he released the hook on her bra. Thinking they were about to make love, Tracy pulled his sweater upwards.

He pushed her hands away, "Nope, you can't have any right now."

Tracy stepped back and raised an eyebrow. "Excuse you!"

She gasped as he picked her naked body up and carried her to the bathroom. He placed her in the warm bathwater. Candles were lit strategically throughout the room and the music system was playing smooth holiday jazz. He laid her head back on the pillow that he placed on the headrest of the tub, and then stared down at her.

"I need you to lie here and relax for a while. When I think you have released some of that tension in your shoulders, I will come back, dry you off and put you in the bed. Then I want you to sleep—not play sleep, but sleep."

Tracy was really enjoying the lavender scents and the pulsating water against her body. "How did you know this was exactly what I needed?"

JD smiled. "The same way you know what I need." He kissed her, dimmed the lights, and then closed the door. Tracy relaxed down into the water to enjoy the tranquil surroundings.

The last thing JD wanted was for Tracy to be tense this week. As he walked down the stairs to get Tracy a glass of wine, he saw Ashley and Cynthia coming up the walkway. Opening the door he whispered, "I just put her in the tub. Then I'm going to make sure to goes to sleep. Are you two going to be able to get this done quietly?" JD asked as they walked into the kitchen.

"Do you have a bottle of Hennessey in the house?" Cynthia asked.

"Plenty," he replied.

"Then we are straight." Ashley laughed.

"I'll be down as soon as Tracy's asleep," JD said as he took the bottle of wine and two glasses upstairs.

Cynthia shook her head. "How in the hell did Tracy get to be the lucky one?"

"She earned it," Ashley replied as she opened the back door for Brian and Douglas. "Shh, Tracy is not asleep yet; she might hear you."

Brian smirked at Douglas. "Damn, I feel like Santa Claus sneaking in so the children won't see."

Douglas growled, "I'm Santa Claus; you're Rudolph."

Cynthia laughed as she handed each of them a shot of Hennessey on the rocks. Brian swallowed his in one gulp, and handed the glass back to her. "No ice next time. Where do you want this monster?" he asked, looking at the Christmas tree he was hauling in.

"Over there, Rudolph," Cynthia replied pointing to the corner.

The house was decorated inside and out. There was no denying Cynthia was good at what she did. Rosaline had the house smelling like grandmother's kitchen on Christmas Day. Ashley and Monica wrapped the gifts Tracy and JD had in the family room. Brian, Douglas, Calvin and James were all in the family room sitting in front of the fire talking and drinking. Cynthia had released them of their duties 30 minutes earlier. Prior to that, the men were up to their necks in lights, balls and bows. Ashley really got a kick out of James trying to hang lights on the house. "It's a good thing the bedroom is on the other side of the house. All that noise you were making could wake up the dead." Ashley laughed.

"This is the quiet evening before the fire you promised?" James teased her.

"I was promised a home-cooked meal. How did they get you, Doug?" Brian asked.

"Actually, I volunteered. JD called, said Tracy needed a little Christmas cheer. I was there."

Cynthia walked over with a plate of food. "See, that's what you call a real man." She sat on Doug's lap and started feeding him with her fingers.

Brian looked at Calvin. "Ain't that some shit." Calvin laughed.

"Dinner is ready, gentlemen," Rosaline said as she continued to place food on the table.

"For a little lady, you can sure spread a table," Brian eagerly commented.

They all sat at the table. "Don't you think we need to wait for JD and Tracy?" Rosaline asked.

"No," Ashley replied and then said grace. Everyone said amen, and she continued, "I hope JD can get Tracy to sleep through the night. She really needs the rest. She has been going non-stop for months now."

"So has JD, with the Melvin trial that they threw at him," Calvin added.

"Let's be real, people, both of them have had a hell of a year. Our job as their friends is to get them through this wedding and on with their lives without any more incidents," Brian replied with food in his mouth.

"Well, the job may be a little more than that," James stated. "I have a series of questions to pose. You three are Tracy's closest friends; and you three are JD's closest friends. Is there any doubt in your mind that the two of them are capable of being a powerful political force?"

They all looked around. "I don't have any doubt that JD really could be president," Calvin offered. When he did not hear laughter, he continued, "If they mesh the way I think they will, we really may be sitting in the White House for Christmas dinner one day. I think Tracy is the strength JD needs to accomplish that."

"I agree," Cynthia said. "I have known JD just about all my life, and Tracy as long as any of us. I have been around them together and apart. I have to say: together they are a force to be reckoned with. Look at the total picture. JD is the legal mind, the mouthpiece. He is a natural born leader of people."

Douglas sat up. "Tracy is a person who cares deeply for people. She has a knack for getting to people when they least expect it."

"JD can, too. I've seen him negotiate with people from all walks of life. He is able to get people to do things for him, without question. And I'm talking about people from thugs to governors." Calvin smirked.

"Let's not forget Tracy's business mind," Rosaline pitched in. "Next Level is a company that has been in existence for less then five years and they are close to being a million dollar organization. Not just clients fuel that, it's the company's portfolio, too. It's Tracy's investment mind that has the company ratings so high."

"Yeah, look at what she did with JD," Ashley laughed. "I mean, he was doing okay, but with Tracy handling the finances, he can have anything he wants now, and so can I."

"Maybe I should get her to handle my finances; I could use some help." Brian smirked.

"Then you should. She started our business and took over our finances. Now six months later I got a serious bank account," Rosaline said, smiling with pride.

Brian pulled his chair closer to Rosaline. "How serious is that bank account?" He smiled.

Rosaline smacked him on the shoulder.

"Maybe Tracy should be running for governor?" James laughed.

"No, it should be JD. Tracy is the quiet, logical mind who works best behind the scenes. JD is the charismatic personality who helps people to believe and hope for a better life," Cynthia stated.

"I believe JD and Tracy could accomplish anything as long as they are together. They feed off each other," Douglas added.

"Do you think with guidance and time they could capture the White House?" James asked.

"What white house?" Ashley curiously asked.

"The one in Washington," Calvin answered.

James sat back and watched the idea of it all going through the minds of JD and Tracy's friends. If the people at this table did not believe, there was no need going to the public for anything more than the run for attorney general. As he surveyed the room he did not see any doubt in the faces of the people at the table. No one questioned the idea of JD and Tracy being in politics.

"It's no secret that some pressure is being put on JD to run for office," James acknowledged. "If he decides to run, they will need the undying support of all of us at this table to succeed. Tracy is going to need each one of you ladies in her corner when news starts to hit the fan from JD's past relationships. JD is going to need you guys behind him a hundred percent when questions come up about Tracy's family," James continued. "If any of you have the slightest doubt, now is the time to let them know. Once they get into it, there is no turning back."

"What about you, James; what's your position on this?" Brian asked.

"If JD decides to run, I will resign my position and put all my effort into getting him elected. That's how much I believe in him."

"I can't quit my job, but I will support Tracy on anything," Rosaline added.

"You definitely have me," Cynthia responded.

"I'm in for the long haul," Douglas stated.

"Brian and I will follow JD to the end," Calvin replied.

James looked at Ashley. "Anything that you or JD is a part of, I'm in," she answered.

Brian stared at James. "Brooks, let me ask you another question."

"What's the question, Brian?"

"I have been trying to hit that since high school," he said pointing to Ashley. How in the hell did you slide up in there?"

James smiled and looked at Ashley. "I was waiting for a real man, not a little boy," Ashley responded.

Doug and Calvin started laughing. "I have told you about asking questions you don't want the answers to," Cynthia stated, laughing along.

"You all seem to be enjoying yourselves." Everyone turned to see JD and Tracy standing there.

"'Bout time you two got up," Brian said.

"Hey." Ashley smiled. "Oh, you look much better now," she said to Tracy.

Tracy smiled. "Did you guys do this?"

"We didn't have anything else to do, so we came over here to hang out." Doug smiled.

"Cynthia, if you don't get that huge Santa out of my front yard, I will cause you serious bodily harm," Tracy ordered.

"Can I watch?" Brian laughed.

Cynthia smiled. "I knew you would just love that. And it blows up automatically when the lights come on. Now, how can you not love that?"

"Have a seat; I'll fix you a plate." Rosaline laughed.

Tracy inhaled. "Look at the tree! Cynthia, that is wonderful. How did you do that?"

Cynthia was beaming with pride. "Don't worry about it. Just remember to call me to do the White House tree when you get there."

Tracy frowned. "What?"

JD handed a plate of food to Tracy then sat next to her. "You guys did a great job. Thank you."

"That's what good friends do; support you when you're standing and pick you up when you are down," James offered.

JD looked around the table. "Seems like you all have been picking us up a lot this year."

Tracy nodded. "It has been quite a year. I'm not sure how we would have made it through without each of you beside us. My prayer for the next year is to see each of you back here sitting in this exact spot." Tracy was beginning to feel emotional again. So to break the mood she added, "Even you, Cynthia."

Everyone around the table laughed. "Oh, shut up and eat," Cynthia said as she walked around the table to Tracy. Cynthia hugged her from behind. "I love you, too, Squirt Two."

Ashley and Tracy looked at each other stunned, and then started laughing.

Chapter 43
The Wedding

Saturday, December 31ˢᵗ, was a beautiful day. The only true drama was the threat of snow by early evening, which just happened to be the time the wedding was scheduled. Everything else had fallen right into place. Cynthia made sure the smallest of details were addressed prior to her going to sleep the night before. Even the last minute change to the program was complete. Cynthia left nothing to chance. Looking back on the day, some would say Cynthia had a conversation with God as to what time to let the snow begin. The day was just that perfect for JD and Tracy.

The bridal party started early with Penne, the hairstylist, and his team of beauticians handling the hair, nails and makeup. The women in this party were naturally beautiful; Penne just took each of them to the next level. Martha and Mrs. Langston were included in the package. To keep everyone relaxed Penne had a caterer prepare breakfast in the lobby of the salon. There were no other appointments set for the day. Only the Harrison-Washington wedding party was allowed. Once Penne was satisfied with each woman's appearance, they were all allowed to leave.

The women were stationed at Ashley's condo; the men were at the house. Cynthia arranged for a full body massage to be given to each of the bridal party members. She didn't want anyone tense, especially Tracy. Cynthia noticed all morning that Tracy was unexplainably calm, not showing any of the emotions a normal bride would have. There was no nervousness, or edginess. Tracy was just as pleasant and sedate as they come. That concerned Cynthia, but she was ready. Cynthia put a few valiums in her purse before she left home, just in case Tracy began to freak out at the last minute. What Cynthia did not know was that Tracy was the last person she had to be concerned with.

After the rehearsal dinner the night before, JD and Tracy were forced to go in separate directions. Tracy was sent to Ashley's condo with the ladies, JD back to the house with the guys. "We are not going to tempt fate," Cynthia demanded. The men had the bachelor party and the ladies had a talk-a-thon. Both events went on into the wee hours of the morning. All the guys at the house were well over the legal limit for intoxication or just fell asleep. The women were all asleep, with the exception of Tracy and Ashley. Ashley could see Tracy was not going to get any sleep; she seemed to be losing her grip again. Ashley suggested she call JD just to talk for a minute, but before Tracy could dial the number, her cell phone rang.

"Hey babe. Can you get out?" JD asked.

Tracy looked around. "I think so. Where are you?" she asked, anxious to see him.

"Downstairs."

Tracy smiled. "I'll be down."

Ashley gave Tracy a robe. "It's cold outside," she said as she turned over to go to sleep.

"Thanks."

"Yeah, yeah, I'm going to tell Cynthia."

As soon as Tracy opened the door, JD grabbed her hand and ran to the car. "Cynthia is going to get you," she said laughing.

"She's going to have to find us first."

"Where are we going?"

"Somewhere they will never think to look for us." He smiled as he kissed the back of her hand. JD parked the car in his mother's driveway, then opened the trunk and pulled out a sleeping bag. He took Tracy by the hand and walked to the back of the house. JD unzipped the sleeping bag, stepped inside, then sat in the lounge chair on the patio. Tracy sat between his legs and lay back against his chest. He wrapped the rest of the bag around his shoulders and Tracy's body.

"Did they really think they were going to be able to keep us apart tonight?" JD asked.

"They sure were trying." Tracy smiled. He kissed the top of her head. They sat there silent for a few minutes. "Jeffrey," Tracy said, "I'm so scared."

JD hugged her tight. "I know, that's why I kidnapped you tonight."

Tracy exhaled, releasing tears. JD could feel the tension in her.

"Tomorrow is just a formality, Trace. The people there will be there to wish us well."

She shook her head. "I'm not scared of the people. As long as you are at the other end of the walkway, I can ignore the people." Tracy hesitated then continued. "I'm afraid I will disappoint you somewhere down the line."

He kissed the side of her face. "I've lived my entire life trying not to disappoint anyone. It doesn't work. So I have learned to take it one day at a time, do the best I can then pray for another day to try again if I fail." JD looked over the yard he used to watch his father working in and prayed his father was watching over him and Tracy tonight. "Are you concerned about me going into politics?"

Tracy nodded her head. "I'm not sure I'm made for it, Jeffrey. I watched Carolyn at the engagement party. She is awesome. I know Gavin is the person out front, but Carolyn is steering that vessel."

JD laughed. "You're right, and that's what you do for me." His tone changed to a serious one. He spoke calmly and thoughtfully. "I have grown in ways that I can't explain since you came into my life, Trace. I truly believe I can do anything as long as you are with me. You make me better at everything I do."

Tracy smiled. "I don't think there is anything you can't do, Jeffrey. If you wanted to become governor of the state or president of the good old USA, I truly believe you could do it. And it doesn't have anything to do with me. It's just who you are."

"I know politics is not something you signed up for, but I would like to try it." He hesitated and squeezed her tighter. "If you think it would interfere in our life together, I won't do it. The only thing I will allow to interfere with you and me is our 12 children."

"Five, man." She elbowed him in the stomach. "Five."

He laughed. "Alright, but we get to start now."

Tracy shook her head. "No buddy, you not getting any until tomorrow." She laughed.

"You are acting like a wife already. A man can't get any." JD looked around the yard and thought about his dad. "My dad told me once if I was patient I would find a girl who would fulfill all my dreams. I hope he can see us here and know that I found that girl. I can't wait to marry you, Tracy." Her body relaxed against his. "This time tomorrow you will be Mrs. Jeffrey Harrison."

"I think I would like to go by Mrs. JD." She smiled.

JD laughed. "That's the first time you ever called me JD."

Tracy pulled his arms tighter around her. "The first day I met you at the apartment, you introduced yourself as Jeffrey. You'll always be Jeffrey to me." She yawned.

JD pushed Tracy's head back against his shoulders and settled down in the blanket. "Go to sleep. You have to get up in two hours." Tracy closed her eyes. Surprisingly, within minutes she was asleep.

JD lay there having a one-sided conversation with God. His first request was to make sure his father knew he had found the girl of his dreams. Then he asked God to guide him in his life with Tracy. "Please give me the wisdom to make her feel loved every day of our life together.

Bless us with healthy children, five or 12, your choice. Most importantly, Lord, please let tomorrow be a perfect day for her. If it's in your power, have Tracy's mother there. I think she would like that." JD closed his eyes and fell asleep.

Cynthia received a call from Brian. Since a number of senators, congressmen and the governor were attending the wedding, federal agents wanted to do a once-over of the church and reception hall within the hour, a matter of national security. Within another hour, Cynthia had received requests from the national networks to allow cameras in the church. Cynthia knew that would freak Tracy out, so she went to JD. "No, this is a private event. Don't you think five hundred guests are enough?" he replied.

Cynthia huffed; a part of her job was making sure the best decisions were made with all aspects taken into consideration. "JD, listen, before you give a flat-out no, national coverage of this event could do a world of good for the campaign. Both you and Gavin could benefit from the exposure."

JD stopped what he was doing. "Let me think about that for a moment; okay." He put his finger to his chin and looked upward. "Hell to the no!"

Cynthia huffed again. "Okay, what about outside of the church across the street. Now think, JD; that is public property. They don't have to have our permission to be there. They could just catch you two coming out of the church," Cynthia said, raising an eyebrow to a very reasonable compromise.

JD thought for a moment. "Across the street from the church. I don't want any cameras in Tracy's face."

Cynthia smiled. "You got it. Oh, by the way, if Tracy so much as sneezes in the church today, I will kill you with my bare hands."

Innocently he replied, "I don't know what you are talking about."

"You damn well do know what I'm talking about. What were you thinking, sleeping out in the cold the night before the wedding? I swear you men just don't think."

He smiled. "Neither one of us was cold."

Cynthia threw him a look of disgust. "I'm out. Make sure the guys are at the church by five."

Brian and Cynthia met the agents at the church at 2 p.m. Due to the nature of the event and the status of some of the guests, special arrangements had to be made to seat certain dignitaries early, Gavin and

Carolyn being two of them. Carolyn called to get a precise time and place they should arrive. Cynthia gave Carolyn the information, and then stared at her cell phone when the call was complete. Brian watched her reaction to the call. "Gavin could not place that call to you. It would be too suspicious."

She glared at him. "Excuse you!"

Brian snickered. "No excuse needed. You were wondering why Gavin didn't call to get the information." He walked over to her. "Carolyn always handles social events. If Gavin popped up with the information you just gave her, she would wonder why, thus raising suspicions. Gavin is not a dumb man; he knows what he is doing. The question is, do you?"

Cynthia put her phone away. "As security, aren't you supposed to keep everything you hear or see confidential?"

Brian nodded. "Yeah, why—are you telling anyone?" he asked, raising an eyebrow. When she didn't respond, he continued. "I didn't think so. The question is still on the table; do you know what you are doing?"

"Why do you care?"

"Because I hate to see an intelligent woman, like you, get caught up in a no-win situation."

Cynthia started to say something, but he cut her off. "Gavin is not just marrying Carolyn, he is marrying the state. Neither of them is going to give up that goal. Carolyn didn't give it up for JD and Gavin is not going to give it up for you. How long do you think it will be before someone gets wind of you and Gavin? Do you think he would jeopardize the campaign for you?"

Cynthia went into her sister girl bag. "Thank you for your unsolicited account of my life. Now mind your own damn business."

"Every time he uses me to contact you, it puts me in a position to have to cover for his ass. That makes it my business. Oh, but, my bad, I thought you deserved better than an hour on Christmas Eve and a five-minute phone call on Christmas Day. But you made yourself clear. I will not speak about it with you again," Brian shouted as he walked away. The agents walked through the door and Brian went to greet them.

Cynthia knew he was right; she should not be second to anyone in a man's eyes. Brian approached with the agents. Cynthia shook the conversation off then got back in business mood. "If you so much as disturb one rose petal, you will not have to be concerned with a terrorist attack—you will have to deal with me."

Brian looked at the agent. "Man, you will have better luck with a terrorist, so don't mess up the damn church."

They did a once-over on the church and strategically placed agents around the grounds. The same was done at the Renaissance.

By the time Cynthia returned to the house it was time for the wedding party to leave for the church. She wanted all the women at the church by 4 p.m., since they were dressing there. Penne agreed to come in around 5 to do any last minute touch-ups to the hair. Photographers were scheduled for 4:30 to get the before pictures.

TNT had all employees on this event. Each was equipped with an electronic communication device to have instant access to Cynthia. There were hostesses to handle the VIPs and hostesses assigned to the other guests. No one was going to walk away from this event feeling anything but pleasure at being a part of this couple's special day.

"It's 3:30; the limo is out front, ladies. I need everyone front and center for inspection," Cynthia yelled through the house.

"What is she going to do, tag us as she completes her inspection?" Ashley laughed.

Tracy was sitting in a lounge chair reading a book. "Let's see what she needs," she suggested.

Ashley and Tracy went into the living room where the women were standing at attention in front of Cynthia. Cynthia, with her Bluetooth in her ear, looking like something from *Star Trek*, was walking the line checking the hair, makeup and nails of Rosaline, Monica, Martha and even Mrs. Langston.

Tracy laughed. "She has them all standing at attention like soldiers or something."

Cynthia scowled at her. "Don't you defy me, Tracy Washington, soon to be Harrison."

"Aye, right, Captain Kirk," Tracy replied as she tripped while trying to stand at attention.

Ashley was standing next to Tracy trying not to laugh, but it didn't work for any of them. All the women began to laugh at the look Cynthia gave Tracy.

Cynthia joined in. "Alright, make sure you have your bags. Let's get to the car."

Tracy hugged her. "Are you okay? You seem a little down."

Cynthia was feeling a little sorry for herself. As the others went down the stairs, she turned to Tracy, "I want what you have—the fairy tale. But I don't think it will ever come for me."

Tracy took her hand. "I didn't think it would come for me either. I still can't say that it has. It's a one day at a time issue for me. But I know I love Jeffrey enough to go for it."

Cynthia had a questioning look on her face. "How did you know JD was the one?"

"My heart told me six years ago when I first saw him." Tracy smiled.

"It doesn't work that way for everyone, Tracy," Cynthia sadly replied.

"Once someone touches your heart; you'll know it and it will work, just that way."

Martha and Mrs. Langston rode in the first limo with the flower girl. Monica, Rosaline, Cynthia, Ashley and Tracy rode in the second limo with champagne in hand. During the ride JD called. "Hey, babe, where are you?"

"On the way to the church." Where are you?"

"We're still at the house. Cynthia won't let us in the church before 5. Are you nervous?" He asked.

Tracy shook her head. "Not at all. What about you?"

JD looked down at the floor, then back up. "I'm good. I have something for you."

Tracy smiled. "What is it?"

"Hold on for a second."

Tracy heard a few clicks in the phone, then, "Hey Sugie," the voice boomed into the phone. Tracy tried to stand up in the limo, but hit her head on the ceiling of the car. The glass of champagne fell on Cynthia. "Turk! It is so good to hear your voice. Oh, Turk, I wish you were here." The women in the car looked at Tracy, wondering who in the hell she was getting so excited about.

"I wish I was there too, little sis. But you got JD. You are in good hands. What was that you told me that day in the field? Your friend said he was out of your league."

Tracy smiled. "You remember that. That was Cynthia."

"Yeah, where is she now?" Turk laughed.

Tracy laughed back. "She's my wedding director and one of my bridesmaids."

"All I want to know, is she eating crow?"

"No, I think she is kind of happy for me. It's hard to tell with her."

"Well, if she ain't, I am. I really don't have to worry about you now, Sugie. Harrison is a good man, through and through. I know you gonna be straight now; he will not allow anyone to hurt you. He loves you almost as much as I do."

"I know he does. I love him and you, too."

Turk was a little touched by his little sister's words as he realized he was no longer the main person in her life. "Sugie, my time is about to run out for this call. I just want to tell you I love you and I will always be here for you whenever you need me."

Tracy's eyes began to tear up. "I love you, Turk. I wish you could be here for this. I will take lots of pictures and send some to you, okay?"

Turk smiled. "Give them to JD. He'll make sure I get them. Smile pretty, alright? I love you, Sugie."

"I love you, too, Turk. Bye."

JD came back on the line. "I'll see you at the other end of the aisle."

Tracy blushed. "I'll be there," she said, then hung up the phone. She turned to Ashley. "I'm getting married today."

Ashley smiled at her. "I know." They hugged each other.

"Oh, cut that shit out before somebody starts crying." Cynthia sighed.

The photographers arrived while Cynthia was doing a final check on the women. Everyone in the large dressing room was ready, so she sent one photographer in that room to begin with candid pictures. She went into the smaller dressing room with Tracy and Ashley. Ashley was standing with her back to the door and Tracy was standing in front of her. When Cynthia opened the door, Ashley turned to see who it was. Tracy stepped back to look past Ashley and came into full view. Cynthia was simply amazed at the vision that stood before her. For the first time that day, she was brought to tears.

"Tracy," she said, almost in a whisper, then shook her head and smiled, "I take back every word I have ever said about you not being right for JD. Looking at you this moment, I couldn't imagine another person being at his side."

Tracy smiled, then walked over and hugged her. "I could never imagine another person making this day happen for me." Cynthia exhaled. Ashley wiped a tear from her eye.

Cynthia touched her earpiece. "Okay, thank you," she spoke into it. "JD and the guys just arrived."

Tracy's smile widened. "Well, that's a good thing."

The photographer knocked on the door. "Are we ready for pictures in here?"

Cynthia looked at Tracy. "Yes, she is ready."

The photographer stepped inside and began taking shots. Cynthia turned to leave.

"Cynthia, would you take one with me?" Tracy asked. "And call Rosaline in here for a minute. I just want a picture of the four of us together, looking good." They laughed.

It was a good thing JD had a large family. Between the males in his family and the employees hired by TNT for this event, they had enough groomsmen to place two at each of the five aisles in the church. To assist with security issues, dignitaries were ushered in and seated together in the center. Party affiliations were ignored at this event per JD's request. Family members were seated to the left and right aisles. Concerned that Tracy's side would be empty, Cynthia placed friends and some of JD's many relatives in that area. When a couple walked up, Cynthia overheard them saying they were family of the bride, it took her by surprise. She went to the hostess handling the announcements and asked who was here on behalf of the bride. The host pointed out a woman and a couple. Cynthia approached them. "Hello, I'm the wedding coordinator. I was told you are relatives of Tracy." She smiled. "I would like to make sure we announce you properly. May I have your names?"

Lena smiled. "My name is Lena Washington, and I'm Tracy's mother. This is Valerie, Tracy's sister, and her husband, Ben Chavis."

Cynthia wrote the names down, praying she did not have a look of surprise on her face.

"Is it Ben or Benjamin," she asked, trying to be polite.

"Will it be possible for me to see Tracy before the ceremony?" Lena asked.

Cynthia did not want to offend the woman by saying "Hell no, you haven't seen her in all these years, you don't need to see her now," so instead she replied, "I will check on that for you."

Lena stood. "I'll go with you."

She smiled and hesitantly spoke, "Alright, just follow me."

Tracy and Mrs. Langston were in the dressing room talking when Cynthia came through the door. "We have an issue," she exclaimed.

"What is it?" Tracy anxiously asked.

"There's someone here stating she's your mother and would like to speak with you," Cynthia explained.

Tracy inhaled. "Okay."

Cynthia was not sure if this was the right thing to do. "Tracy, we are minutes away from the ceremony, are you sure you want to talk to her right now?"

Mrs. Langston went to the door and opened it. Lena stepped in, looked at Tracy in her gown and for the first time in a while she saw her little girl. Lena didn't say anything for a minute and neither did Tracy.

"Cynthia, let's step outside and give them a moment," Mrs. Langston suggested.

Cynthia hesitated. "Tracy," she said as she took her hand, "you going to be okay?"

Tracy smiled. "Sure, you go ahead. This will only take a minute." Cynthia walked pass Lena and closed the door behind her.

Lena slowly walked over to Tracy and smiled. "You are a beautiful bride," she said proudly. "Thank you for the invitation. I hope you don't mind, but I brought Valerie and her husband."

Tracy smiled. "No, I don't mind."

Lena was uncertain where she wanted to go from here. Her intent had been to get with JD or Brooks to question them further about the picture. She wasn't certain, but it seemed there may be an opportunity to increase her personal cash flow if her suspicions were correct. When she arrived at the church something made her want to talk to Tracy. "I'm sure mothers are supposed to say something wise and meaningful to their daughters at this moment. I have no idea what that would be." She smiled. "I take it you've had sex with this man?" she said in a questioning tone.

Tracy simply raised her eyebrows and smiled. "Have you seen Jeffrey, I mean really looked at him?"

Lena laughed. "Yes, I have; that's a fine ass man. I know I would not be able to keep my hands off of him."

Tracy smiled. "Alright now." A moment passed. "Why did you come today?" Tracy asked.

Lena took in a deep breath. "Do you want me to be honest or tell you what you want to hear?"

Tracy thought. "Honesty always works well with me."

Lena nodded her head. "Alright, I came here to talk to James Brooks about something that took place the last time I saw you," Lena confessed, "but when I got here and saw all the people I was kind of wondering how you were going to handle it. You always were a loner. Maybe I finally got hit with the mother bug for you. I don't know. Something made me feel like you needed me. Isn't that funny?" Lena snickered.

"No, it's not funny at all," Tracy replied. "I think every daughter needs their mother on a day like this. So much uncertainty and nervousness naturally comes along with the happiness of a wedding day."

Lena looked at Tracy. "Do you need me, Tracy?" Lena walked over to Tracy and took her hand. "I haven't done a lot for you in the past; I can't change that now. But I would consider it an honor to walk you down the aisle to marry that fine man."

Tracy stepped back and pulled her hand away. "Hmm, I'm not sure we can do that," Tracy stuttered out.

James knocked on the door and walked in. Cynthia had not felt comfortable with the scene in Tracy's dressing room, so when she left Tracy, she went directly to the room JD was in with the minister and the groomsmen.

"JD, Tracy's mother is in her dressing room. Now I don't know if that is an issue or not, but I thought you should know."

JD stood up immediately and walked towards the door. "Son, wait," Pastor Smith said.

"Pastor Smith, you don't understand, I have to go. There is no telling what that woman is saying to Tracy," JD explained.

"I'll go," James offered. Now James was standing in the room with Tracy and she was a vision.

"Tracy, is everything okay?" James asked. Lena stepped aside and James took in a full vision of Tracy. His breath caught as he exclaimed, "You are beautiful!"

Lena smiled and responded, "Thank you." Tracy laughed and so did Lena.

James relaxed a little. "Mrs. Washington, how are you?" he asked, wondering why in the hell she showed up.

Lena exhaled. "I'm fine, and no I haven't said or done anything to upset Tracy. So you can go back and tell JD to relax."

Tracy looked at James. "Tell Jeffrey I love him and will see him in 10 minutes or so," she said.

James looked at Lena then back at Tracy. "You're sure?"

Tracy nodded. "Yes, I'm sure."

James hesitated for a moment, and then left the room. Lena looked at Tracy. "Baby girl, I've been around the block a time or two and a have sense for these things. It seems like that man is very protective of you. Are you sure you are marrying the right man?"

Tracy exhaled. "I'm not sure of many things in my life, but one thing I know is you brought me into this world to marry Jeffrey."

Lena was certain of that fact, too. "Well then, I guess you better get this show on the road. Do you mind if I stay here with you until it's time?"

Tracy exhaled nervously. "No, I need the company."

Lena smiled. "Are you nervous?" she asked with a little excitement.

Tracy giggled. "No, now that's crazy."

Mrs. Langston and Cynthia came back into the room. "Okay, Tracy, JD is waiting and the ladies are lined up. It's show time, girl!"

Ashley stepped in the room. "Veil has to come down now." Ashley smiled, and then hugged Tracy. "I have been waiting for this moment for six years. Welcome to the family."

Tracy smiled. "Let's go get that man." Ashley laughed.

The only people in the vestibule were members of the wedding party. Cynthia had everyone standing at attention. The music was playing as the processional had begun. "Tracy, step back, no one can see you until those doors open," Cynthia whispered loudly.

"Okay," Tracy replied. "Are you going to take the *Star Trek* thingy off your head before you go in?"

Cynthia reached up and pulled the phone off while Ashley and Tracy laughed at her. "That's not funny, stop that."

Lena smiled and stood to the side, watching Tracy.

"See you inside." Ashley smiled as she released Tracy's hand and walked through the doors.

The double doors to the sanctuary closed after the flower girls entered. Tracy and Mrs. Langston were led to the doorway as Lena stood in the background.

JD and Tracy opted not to play the traditional wedding song for her entrance. Instead JD's cousin Alexis Harrison was asked to sing a song made popular by Celine Dion, *"Because You Loved Me."* At the rehearsal the night before, the soloist was instructed not to start the song until Tracy stepped into the sanctuary; only the piano introduction would start once the doors were opened. Tracy was ready, or so she thought. The doors opened simultaneously. As the congregation stood, Tracy froze. The church was filled with people; too many people for her. Mrs. Langston felt Tracy tense immediately. "Tracy?" Mrs. Langston whispered, trying to coast her forward.

Tracy did not budge. "I don't see Jeffrey," she said. "I can't see him," she repeated quietly, but with fear.

"Relax, Tracy, he's down there," Mrs. Langston replied, but Tracy wasn't moving.

Mrs. Langston looked over at Lena. "She is not moving."

Lena stepped up and took Tracy's hand. Mrs. Langston put her shawl around Lena and stepped to the side. "Tracy, breathe, hold your head up and smile." When Tracy did not respond, Lena squeezed her hand and said, "Tracy look at me!" When she did, Lena smiled. "Now breathe, breathe."

"I can't see Jeffrey," Tracy cried.

"Oh, he's down there, believe me, but you have to take the first step. Take a step with me," Lena said softly. "Let's go marry that man." Tracy looked at Lena and smiled back at her. "Let's go, baby girl," Lena coaxed.

Tracy stepped forward; JD took a step towards the aisle, put his hands behind his back and smiled. Now Tracy could see him standing there in his white tails. "My goodness that man looks good in a tux," Tracy exclaimed.

"He looks damned good," Lena replied.

Tracy laughed and stepped forward. All the people in the church disappeared to Tracy. The only person she saw was Jeffrey. Alexis began singing.

For all the times you stood by me, for all the truth that you made me see; for all the joy you brought to my life; for all the wrong that you made right; for every dream you made come true; for all the love I found in you; I'll be forever thankful; you're the one who held me up; never let me fall; you're the one who saw me through it all.

JD watched as the love of his life walked towards him. Words could not describe the vision approaching him. Tracy was dressed in an A-line satin and lace gown with long lace sleeves and a Chinese collar with a diamond-shaped opening above the breast line, where a single teardrop pearl hung from the collar. The dress accentuated every curve in her body. Her hair was up in a ball with a veil that fell right beneath her chin. As she walked past the crowd of people, the back of the dress revealed the same diamond-shaped opening leading down to a delicate bow right above her hips. A satin train with lace overlays flowed behind her.

As hard as he tried, JD could not contain himself. His eyes filled with tears and his heart was filled with love for this woman. His heart was beating so loudly he was sure people around him could hear it, but he couldn't take his eyes off of Tracy long enough to check. JD smiled and wondered why God had blessed him in this way. He wanted to step out and grab her; it was taking too long for her to reach him. As Tracy and Lena got closer to him, he could see Tracy's smile and his heart settled.

You were my strength when I was weak; you were my voice when I couldn't speak. You were my eyes when I couldn't see; you saw the best there was in me; lifted me up when I couldn't reach; you gave me faith 'cause you believed; I'm everything I am because you love me.

Alexis stopped just as Tracy reached JD. JD took Tracy's hand in his and kissed the back of it. "I'm glad you could make it," he whispered.

Tracy smiled. "I'm glad to see you, too."

JD could not resist. He bent and kissed her gently on the lips. Pastor Smith cleared his throat; the congregation exclaimed "Aw!" as if in chorus, laughed, and then took their seats. Lena took a step backwards, as JD and Tracy took a step forward. When they reached the podium, Pastor Smith said, "Son, don't you kiss that woman again until after you say 'I do.'"

JD and Tracy laughed.

"Before we begin with the ceremony, I have a personal statement for JD. I have known you just about all your life, from the time you broke Mrs. Carey's window and hid behind the church." The congregation laughed, and he continued, "To the time you and a young girl were caught in a compromising position at the high school."

JD cleared his throat and leaned forward. "Pastor Smith, could we not go there?"

"I have a point, son," he continued. "To the time you, Calvin, Brian and Douglas ran the car through Mrs. Carey's front yard and ruined all her rose bushes." The congregation continued to laugh. Pastor Smith began to get serious. "To the hurt you experienced at your father's untimely death. But none of those occasions, as memorable as they may have been, will ever erase the memory of the first night you spoke with me about Tracy, just about six years ago. You woke me up about two in the morning. Now I know I said you could call me anytime; I didn't mean it literally." JD laughed. "You simply said, 'Pastor Smith I met this girl. Every fiber in my body tells me she was sent here by God just to be with me. But she is young and I don't think I am ready for her.' That's because you were a wild boy." Pastor Smith laughed, then continued. "I told you to wait; be patient and let God reveal his plan to you. Today that plan is revealed. For we stand here in the presence of God, family and friends this evening. I could not be any prouder of you, for the man you have become and the decisions you have made for your life, if you were my own son. I am confident your father is looking down upon you at this moment smiling with pride."

JD swallowed, trying to hold back the tear that was threatening to escape. He looked down at Tracy. Tracy stepped closer, then reached up to wipe the tear from his face. JD put his hand on top of hers and kissed it. Tracy had no idea how grateful JD was for that touch. He composed himself. Mama Harrison wiped a tear away, as did most of the congregation.

Pastor Smith continued, "We stand here in the presence of God, family and friends on this beautiful winter evening to join together this man, Jeffrey Daniel Harrison, and this woman, Tracy Alexandria Washington, in holy matrimony. Who presents this woman to this man?"

"Her mother," Lena replied, and then took a seat next to the family. A few of the people in the congregation leaned forward to see her.

John Roth was one. He did not know she would be at the wedding. The senator's mind began to whirl with what-ifs.

"Daddy, are you okay?" Carolyn asked, noticing his discomfort.

He patted her on her hand. "I'm fine, baby," he said.

On the other side of Carolyn, Gavin flinched. It never dawned on him that she would be at the wedding. Lena Washington knew him as a police officer. She suspected he helped Al kill her husband. Gavin went through a lot to keep that past under wraps.

"Gavin, are you okay?" Carolyn asked.

He just patted her other hand. Carolyn looked from Gavin to her father; she knew something was up, but had no idea what. In the back of the church was Tuck, Al's lieutenant. He was wondering why Lena was there and how Al was going to take the news.

JD and Tracy stepped forward. Ashley spread Tracy's train out as they stepped up. JD and Tracy faced each other throughout the ceremony, never looking at Pastor Smith or their friends, just each other. They exchanged vows, smiling through each word as if it was their own secret, just between them. After the vows, the choir, led by JD's cousin, Alexis, sang, "Jesus is Love," by the Commodores during which time JD, Tracy, Martha and a surprised Lena Washington took center stage and lit unity candles. Each mother was presented with a single rose. They had not planned for Lena, so Tracy gave her rose to her mother. The mothers were seated again. JD and Tracy stood before Pastor Smith as he said one last prayer to ask for guidance for this young couple.

"You may salute your bride," Pastor Smith said to JD.

Jeffrey and Tracy kissed for the first time as husband and wife. It was not the quick kiss on the lips. Jeffrey pulled Tracy close to him, as they seemed to have literally merged into one. They exchanged what was a tongue-wagging, jaw-locking kiss that every person in the sanctuary and beyond could feel to the very depths of their souls. When it appeared JD was not going to stop anytime soon, Pastor Smith touched him on the shoulder. "Son, we have to bring this to an end."

JD reluctantly complied, then smiled down at Tracy and whispered, "I love you."

Tracy smiled back, "Me, too."

As the couple faced the congregation, Pastor Smith announced, "I proudly present to you Mr. and Mrs. Jeffrey Daniel Harrison. The sound of applause and cheers combined with the ring of church bells signified the end of the ceremony as JD, Tracy and the wedding party marched out of the sanctuary.

Chapter 44

JD and Tracy were immediately taken to a room away from the people streaming from the sanctuary to catch a moment with the happy couple. The directress, Cynthia, assigned for the wedding closed the door to the room then placed a guard there. JD grabbed Tracy and finished the kiss that was interrupted by Pastor Smith for dignity's sake. He understood; after all they were in a church with hundreds of people watching. Tracy held on to JD. Her mind was spiraling. Could this be real? Did she just marry Jeffrey? She pulled back to see for herself that all of this was real. He just watched the expression on her face with wonder. "What is it?"

Tracy was a little bewildered. "Did we do it? Did we really do it, Jeffrey?"

JD was just as hyped. "Yes," he said as he cupped her face in his hands. Tracy reached up and put her hands on top of his. Tears ran down her face as she exhaled. It seemed she had been holding her breath for days waiting for something to happen.

Outside the door, the wedding party members were all just as excited as the couple inside the room. They were eager to get to the couple. "Give them a moment. If you guys feel like whatever you are feeling, think about what they are feeling right now. Give them a minute," the directress instructed.

Cynthia walked up to the girl. "Get the hell out of my way." The girl stepped out of the way. Cynthia opened the door and everyone piled in.

Standing in the vestibule of the church were the dignitaries and their guests. For security reasons, they were all together talking and waiting for clearance to leave. Pastor Smith asked all family members to remain for pictures. Lena, Valerie and her husband Ben were still inside the sanctuary with Martha and other family members. Lena stepped out for a minute and looked around at all the top-ranking members of the political elite of Virginia. Why would all these very powerful people be at this wedding? Lena wondered. As she looked around recognizing face after face as newsworthy figures, one person out of the crowd caught her attention. Lena waited; eventually he would have to turn around again. After all, it had been a long time since the last time Lena saw him. She could be wrong.

A bit of excitement was taking place to the left of where Lena was standing. JD and Tracy were heading back into the sanctuary to take pictures. People were congratulating them. Tracy was clinging to JD around these people. Lena could tell Tracy was not completely at home with this crowd. JD, on the other hand, fit right in. It was as if the crowd of political giants was admiring this young man. Tracy spotted Lena. She smiled, not so much at her mother, but just relieved to see someone other than those surrounding her and JD. The rest of the wedding party, with the exception of James, went into the sanctuary.

Lena was watching the synergy between JD and Tracy around these people. Anyone who did not know Tracy would think she was right at home with this group. But Lena knew better. Tracy would prefer to be around books or computers, not around people she did not know well. Lena frowned. *What has Tracy gotten into?*

"Good evening," James spoke. "I'm surprised you are still here."

"Mr. Brooks. I decided to hang around and observe," Lena responded.

"We all appreciate you being here for Tracy. I think it was actually what she needed." James stepped closer, looked down at Lena. "If your plan is to stay around to cause any issues for anyone connected to JD or Tracy, you will end up dealing with me."

Lena did not exactly fear James, but she did have a certain amount of respect for his ability to intimidate. Lena looked around. "Look at her, James; I'm glad she is happy with JD. But is she happy with the people around him?"

James knew Lena had a point. He could see Tracy was not comfortable with all the people around.

"Do you think you could help her out here?" Lena stepped back inside the sanctuary.

A few minutes later JD, Tracy and James were coming through the door. The traditional wedding picture session began. This was tiresome to JD and Tracy equally, but they complied with the tradition. When they walked out of the church, crowds of people were still outside waiting to get a glimpse of them. News cameras began flashing as they stepped onto the steps of the church. JD waved as people yelled their congratulations to them. Tracy smiled as she saw the snow beginning to fall lightly. "What a perfect way to end the ceremony." She beamed. JD looked into her eyes and kissed his bride; the crowd cheered.

As guests arrived at the Renaissance, waiters were about with glasses of champagne and trays of hors d'oeuvres to taste until dinner was served. Those that wanted spirits of a stronger nature were directed to the open bar. Gavin was about talking with party members while Carolyn and Jackie had taken a seat at the bar. Carolyn ordered a pitcher of martinis, while Jackie was having white wine. Jackie could tell Carolyn was in rare form tonight and was not happy.

"It was a very touching wedding," Jackie said. "I think those two are the real thing."

"Yeah, yeah, and all that's holy!" Carolyn said sarcastically.

Jackie couldn't sympathize with Carolyn on this issue any longer. "You know, Carolyn; you always said you wanted to be first lady of Virginia. Well you are marrying Gavin and he is a shoo-in for governor. You got what you asked for. Why can't you be happy for JD even if you are not happy for Tracy?"

Carolyn stared at her friend. "Why in the hell would I be happy for either one of them? JD is about to do the one thing I always said he would do: run for office. Tracy is at his side, not me."

"JD made that decision, not Tracy. So why do you hate her so much?"

Someone else answered Jackie's question before Carolyn had a chance to. "Because she's a damn goody-two-shoe," said David, "that everyone thinks is so sweet and innocent, but I know different."

"Here, here." Carolyn raised her glass to him, and then took a drink.

Jackie turned to see David Holt standing behind her. Jackie gazed at Carolyn. Jackie could not believe he was there. She knew Gavin had warned Carolyn to stop her indiscretions. Jackie wasn't sure if Gavin knew, but she knew David was the man Carolyn had been stepping out on Gavin with. It was stupid to have him at this event. "Have you lost your mind, Carolyn?"

Carolyn took a drink. "I don't have the slightest idea what you are talking about."

Jackie looked around for Gavin. "Well, you better figure something out quickly."

Gavin walked up behind Carolyn. "Hello, David. Is Karen with you tonight?"

David frowned. "No, I'm afraid she's a little under the weather tonight, sir."

"I'm sorry to hear that. Please give her our regards. Carolyn, Governor Bolling wants to take pictures with us," Gavin said. "Excuse us, David."

"Sure, honey," Carolyn replied with a smile so sweet no one could tell it was phony.

The hosts began to seat people at the very elegantly set tables. The wedding party was gathered in the lobby of the Renaissance waiting for the announcements to begin. The music was pumping through the speakers. Penne was there touching up makeup and making sure hair was in place. Tracy started singing, then moving, to "Purify Me," by India Irie. JD joined in behind her. Monica started, Brian behind her and the rest just joined in. They were having their own little party in the lobby. It was good to have this relief session. It had been a long evening and everyone was ready to celebrate. They were anxious to get inside. Then Luther's "Love Won't Let Me Wait" began; that was their cue. The directress began the introductions. After Ashley and James were introduced, the doors closed.

JD kissed Tracy. "Are you nervous?"

Tracy smiled and held JD's hand. "No, I'm not."

The doors opened as the directress introduced JD and Tracy. They entered with an air of decorum and elegance that befit royalty. The crowd cheered, clapped and showed every sign of approval available to them. JD acknowledged people as they walked through the crowd of well-wishers. Tracy's stomach was doing that flip-flop thing, but you could not see it in her presence. She was the picture of perfection; Penne made sure of that.

Cynthia had figured it would be late by time they arrived at the reception since the wedding was at 6:30; people would be ready for dinner. The reception program was short and sweet. Once JD and Tracy were seated, Pastor Smith said a grace. Then Calvin and Ashley made the toast to the bride and groom together.

Ashley began: "When people look back to speak of JD and Tracy, some will say this all started just about one year ago. If Calvin and I are a part of the conversation, we will say it started six years ago. I was there the moment they met, and Calvin shortly thereafter. I would dare to take it a step further. If you believe the old adage that God made one person for each of us, as I do, then I would say that at the age of six God looked at JD and said, 'That boy is going to need some help in his life.'" The crowd laughed. "And he was right. So he sent down an angel or two to take a rib from JD and made Tracy. For Tracy completes JD. Those of us, even the skeptics like Brian," Ashley laughed, "who did not believe in love, now believe. JD and Tracy have taught us that if you wait, love will come."

Calvin laughed. "Now we all know JD did not wait. Or should we say he had fun while he was waiting." Those who knew JD laughed. "But when JD met his little sister's roommate from college, he was in love. However, his commitment to his career prevented him from pursuing the then-19-year-old girl. As fate would have it, six years later they were reunited. This time JD did not allow his career or anything else to interfere. It was evident to all that the two of them would be here on this day. I'm sure that JD and Tracy are meant to do great things. But the most impressive of all is teaching each of us to believe in love." He raised his glass; the crowd followed. "To Jeffrey and Tracy. May your life together be blessed and guided by the love reflected in your eyes today."

The crowd responded, "To Jeffrey and Tracy."

The whole time Ashley and Calvin were talking, anyone observing the couple could see they were silently caressing each other with every touch or look they shared. Not even Carolyn could insinuate it was anything other than love between the two. As Ashley and Calvin completed their toast, a tear dropped from Tracy's eyes. JD simply kissed it away. This man had no problem showing his love for his wife in public or in private.

The evening was being enjoyed by all. Normally after dinner and the traditional events of a reception, people began to leave. No one left this reception. Cynthia had planned on a smaller crowd for the New Year's Eve party planned immediately after the reception. Even the snow falling outside did not entice people to leave. They were enjoying the festivities.

Now, just like with any event, there were one or two issues happening on the down low. The leadership committee from the Democratic Party wanted a moment to talk with JD. Senator Roth asked JD if there was a place they could talk privately. JD carried the men into the Chambers. They took a seat in JD's room. None of them had been privy to the special rooms in the Chambers. They were impressed with the privacy of the rooms and several asked about membership.

Present in the meeting were Governor Bolling, Senator Roth, Senator Costen, Delegate Franklin, Daniel Graham, Gavin, JD and the head of the DNC, Stanley Covington.

"JD," Governor Bolling started, "thank you for giving us a minute of your time. I realize you probably have other things on your mind right about now. However, we would like you to consider becoming a part of the Democratic ticket in November. Each of us in this room has discussed this at great length and we believe that a Gavin, Graham, Harrison ticket would guarantee us an across-the-board win in November. We have put together numbers in all four regions of the state. The results for you were off the chart. People are very pleased with the job you have done and want to see you do more."

Stanley Covington introduced himself to JD. "I understand you have reservations about entering the political world. From what I'm told, you are a man of conviction and do not like compromising on principles.

That is exactly what our party needs to rejuvenate our constituents. We have taken a good look at you and at your career. I can give you my word; if you decide to join us I will be available to you to handle any situation you are not comfortable with throughout the campaign. I'm not going to try to snow you here. There are going to be issues you and some party members may not agree on. Nevertheless, under my reign, I want to be open to change. We need young, innovative minds like yours to take us to the next level. The DNC is looking beyond this election as far as you are concerned. We want you to be a major part of the future of the Democratic Party. What would it take to make you a part of the ticket?"

JD was standing near the door with his hands in his pockets, eyes on the floor while they were talking. He looked up at Daniel Graham. "Are you a part of the ticket?"

Daniel glanced at him. "I'm waiting on you. If you declare, I'm there."

JD knew Senator Roth was holding his breath for his response and he did not want to disappoint him. "Senator Roth will be my advisor for the party. I chose my staff with some guidance from the DNC. For me to be a part of this ticket, it must be understood up front: my wife is my number one priority at this point in my life. If you believe you can accept that, then I would consider it an honor to be a part of the ticket."

Gavin chuckled and Dan nodded with approval as Governor Bolling shook JD's hand. "Welcome aboard."

JD smiled. "Thank you."

Stanley Covington hit JD on the back and laughed. "Gentlemen, hold your glasses high. I believe the Democratic Party has just been reborn."

Tracy was mingling with guests in the main ballroom. As she talked with Magna and Victoria, she noticed David at the bar. Tracy looked around for James and Ashley, but did not see them.

Recognizing the look on Tracy's face, Magna asked, "What's wrong, Tracy?"

Tracy exhaled. "I don't believe he is here." She walked over to the bar. She smiled at Doug, then looked at David. "He is good," she said to the bartender, who was about to pour another drink for David. "How did you get in here?" she politely asked him.

David gawked at Tracy with a cynical smile. "Why, I was invited, darling."

Tracy shook her head. "I don't think so."

Magna did not like the vibe she was getting from David. "Maybe you should consider leaving," she suggested.

"Where's your friend?" David asked, ignoring Magna.

Carolyn walked over. "It appears you two are about to have a serious confrontation; what's the problem, Tracy?"

Magna could not believe this woman was still playing games with Tracy. "After all this time, two murder attempts and a wedding, you are still up to no good?"

Carolyn rolled her eyes at Magna. "I ask again, what is the problem?"

"Why is David Holt here?" Tracy asked.

Carolyn looked at David and said, "I invited him; he's my guest."

Tracy looked at Carolyn. "I'm sorry, Carolyn, but your guest is not welcome here."

David aggressively stepped towards Tracy. Douglas immediately came from behind the bar and Brian appeared out of nowhere. "Man, we had this discussion before. Do you really want to try me?"

David looked from Brian to Douglas. Brian stepped to Carolyn and whispered in her ear so no one could hear. "Your boy toy can leave on his own, or I will kick his ass and you will be left with explaining it all to Gavin. What's it going to be?"

Not pleased with the turn of events, she rolled her eyes. "David, you better go."

David looked around, then finished his drink. When he turned to leave, he saw James and Ashley approaching. David smiled and winked at her and said, "You look so tempting, Ashley." James stepped in front of her as David walked by. "It's not over, Ashley, remember that." David looked at James with disgust. "We will meet again," he stated as he left the building.

James turned to Ashley. "You okay?" he asked, understanding the threat from David.

"I'm fine, and so are you," she said flirtingly.

"Are you flirting with me, Ms. Harrison?" James asked, smiling.

"I believe I am, Mr. Brooks." She smiled.

James hugged Ashley and felt her shiver. Her words and her body language told two different stories. David Holt's words frightened her and James knew it.

"I will never allow that man to hurt you in any way," James whispered as he kissed Ashley's temple.

Tracy turned from James and Ashley and glanced at Carolyn. "I don't know your connection to David and I don't care. But if you ever invite him to another function I give, you will be leaving out the door with him, I don't care who you are married to." Tracy walked away.

Brian stood there and stared at Carolyn. "You're a piece of work; you had your boy toy here with the man you are supposed to marry." He chuckled. "You a bold bitch, that's all I can say. I'm glad JD got you the hell out of his life."

"They won't live happily ever after; she is not half the woman JD needs."

"That shit is getting old, Carolyn. The man made his choice; let it go." Someone handed Brian a note. Brian read the note and turned to Douglas. "Where is JD?"

"He was in the Chambers," Douglas replied.

Brian looked at Carolyn. "You're a bad loser, Carolyn, but a loser nonetheless," he said, then walked away.

Jackie, who had missed the confrontation, ran over to Carolyn excited. "Carolyn!" She exhaled. "Calvin just asked me to marry him!" She beamed and presented a beautiful engagement ring.

Carolyn's jealousy overruled her tongue. Why was everyone getting the fairytale and not her? "Who gives a shit?" Carolyn said and walked away.

Jackie's excitement faded as she watched someone she considered a friend storm away. Calvin held Jackie. "She did not mean that, honey."

Jackie exhaled. "Yes, Calvin, she did."

Gavin and Roth were standing outside the Chambers discussing the events that just took place when Lena walked towards them. Gavin's back was to Lena, but Roth could see her approaching. She was too close for him to make a retreat. He had prayed he would be able to get through the night without running into her. No such luck. The proverbial shit was about to hit the fan. Gavin noticed Roth's attention had wavered; he turned to see Lena at his side. Before she was able to say anything to either Gavin or Roth, Carolyn approached and seemed to be upset.

"Gavin, I need you," she said then glared towards Lena. "Alone."

Gavin was a little concerned, as Carolyn seldom lost her composure, but he was happy for the escape. Her timing could not have been more perfect. Simultaneously, Stanley Covington approached Senator Roth. "Senator, may I have a moment of your time?"

Roth looked from Lena to Covington and excused himself.

Lena looked from Gavin to Roth and then back. *You may escape me tonight, but we will have our moment,* she said to herself.

Gavin held Carolyn at arm's length, as they stepped to the side. "What is it, Carolyn, what's wrong?" Tears came down Carolyn's face. Gavin had never seen Carolyn in distress, much less with tears streaming, especially not in public. He pulled her close. "Carolyn, what is it?" he asked. She put her arms around his neck and cried. "Carolyn, it will be alright, whatever it is. It will be alright," he consoled as he kissed her cheek. "Shh," he said as he rubbed her back trying to calm her. He pushed her hair back from her face and looked into her eyes. "I'm not sure what it is, but it will be alright." He smiled and kissed her lips lightly. To his surprise, Carolyn kissed him back, and it did not feel forced. Hesitant to hope, he kissed her again and she responded. Gavin ran his tongue across her lips. She parted her lips to allow him entry and he complied. Cynthia stood in the doorway watching the scene as long as she could, then she turned and walked away.

Brian found JD as he walked into the Chambers. JD would want to know this bit of news. "JD, I need to see you for a minute."

"B, man, I really need to find Tracy right now. Can it wait?"

"No," Brian said. "Juan Cortez was transferred to the same correctional facility as Al Day today. They found him beaten to death in his cell at 6:30 this evening. There are no witnesses and no clear suspects."

JD hung his head and smiled. "You never knew where family is going to show up."

He looked at Brian and smiled. "Looks like the year is ending as it should."

Tracy peeked in the door. "Is it okay to come in?"

JD smiled. "Yeah, babe, I was just coming to look for you."

Tracy walked over to him. "It's almost midnight. I don't want to miss this celebration."

Brian smiled at the sight of his friends. It had him wondering, *what if.*

"I'm out, JD," Brian said.

"Alright, man," JD replied, not looking back.

"See you, Brian." Tracy kissed him on the cheek.

Chapter 45
The Beginning

JD and Tracy sat in the Jeffrey Harrison room of the Chambers in the same spot they began nine months earlier. Both were content to sit there alone as they listened to their guests count down to the New Year. JD smiled as he looked at his wife of about six hours. "Can you believe the year we had," he said, massaging the back of her neck.

"I remember sitting in this very spot the first night we really talked and wondered if I was dreaming the whole thing up. I was so scared that if we walked out of this room I would wake up and none of it would have happened." She smiled.

JD laughed. "My memory was a little different. I was trying to figure out how I was going to keep you in my life. I knew about all the women in my past and did not want it to interfere with our future. But I never doubted that we would have a future together from that night on. Well, maybe once."

Tracy gazed at him. "When?"

"When you left me."

Tracy frowned. "I never left you."

JD nodded. "Yes, you did, when you walked in on Vanessa."

Tracy sucked her teeth. "That was one, maybe two nights."

"Whatever it was, it was too long," JD remembered.

Tracy laughed. "I'm sorry."

JD kissed the side of her face. "That's alright, as long as you never do it again."

Tracy inhaled. "I thought you were talking about the attack."

JD shook his head. "I never thought I was going to lose you then, not once. I knew God had plans for us. Even when I was shot, I knew I would pull through. This day was written long before you and I met. I truly believe that," JD said as he kissed Tracy's neck.

Tracy held her head up and marveled at the love she saw in his eyes. "Jeffrey, we had a wonderful wedding. My prayer is to be able to see that look you have in your eyes every day for the next 50 years."

JD kissed her lips lightly. "For the next 50 years, you're not getting off that easy, Mrs. Harrison. It's going to take you that long to raise our 12 babies." JD said as he parted her lips to kiss her for the first time in the New Year.

"Five babies; five," Tracy said. They laughed and kissed as they began the next chapter in their life together.

Read on for a sneak peek into the continuing
saga of the Harrison family and friends.

The Heart of Him

Iris Bolling

2008

The Heart of Him
Prologue

Ocho Rios, Jamaica was a beautiful seventy-six degrees in February. Ashley stood on the balcony in a shirt that belonged to the man lying in the bedroom. Naked as a jaybird under his shirt, a gentle breeze tickled the lower part of her back. She appreciatively looked at her surroundings and smiled at the way her life had turned out.

During her senior year of high school, her father, a police officer, was shot and killed by a 14-year old gang member. At the end of that year, she entered Harmon University, where she met her business partner, best friend and now sister-in-law Tracy Washington. That was the beginning of the changes in her life as well as that of her brother Jeffrey, better known as JD.

Ashley smiled as she sat on the lounge chair and crossed her legs. She held her head back to allow the cool breeze to swim over her face. Here she was, Ashley Renee Harrison, a partner in a million dollar consulting firm; the sister to the candidate for Attorney General of Virginia, and the woman James Avery Brooks allowed into his very guarded life.

Ashley turned to look at James, who was still asleep on the bed and chuckled to herself. The best thing to ever happen to her was snoring loudly from the inside of the room. She made a mental note to call Tracy, and thank her for the all expense paid trip to sunny Jamaica and to tease her about the weather. Virginia, which was home, was under three feet of snow, with more on the way. She smiled, while drinking a glass of champagne, thinking of JD and Tracy finally happily married.

Wishfully, Ashley wondered if she would have the fairytale wedding like JD and Tracy. The two were married on New Year's Eve in a wedding ceremony reminiscent of Princess Diana's and continued to be the topic of conversation two months later. Ashley really did not need all of that. A simple ceremony with family and friends would suit her just fine.

She stood and leaned against the balcony railing with her back to the beautiful landscape that was below and set her eyes on the muscular body of James Brooks. A slow frown creased her forehead as it dawned on her; James never talked about his family. As she thought about it, his friends appeared to be those acquired through JD. At different events they attended, she met several business associates who all seemed very impressed, if not in awe of him, but no one was introduced as "a friend."

There were women she met who let her know instantly, usually in a "checking a sister out from head to toe" sort of way, that there was more than a business relationship between them and James. However, James's actions sent a clear message that he was no longer available to anyone but her.

Her eyes traveled up the long muscular leg that laid half covered by the sheet, over the hump that was his impressively firm butt, which was hidden by the sheet, up to his strong back and wide shoulders that were exposed. Ashley inhaled and smiled, for just the sight of him turned her on.

"Ashley?" James called out lifting his head from the pillow. Ashley smiled and thought; *it's a shame that the sound of her name coming through his lips could make her moist in hidden areas.* His voice was a rich deep baritone and whenever he called her name, it sounded like a song coming from the smooth sound of a saxophone. It was his voice and that ever so manly smile of his that captured her heart the first time they met.

The moment Ashley saw James; she knew he was the man her mother told her about all her life. Martha Harrison, her mother would say, "Never settle for someone that is less of a man than your father." Of course, at the time there was no one who could match the man her father was, or so she thought. Then one day, while standing at the receptionist desk in a state office building, there he stood. She estimated him to be at least 6 foot, 4 inches tall. She was 5 foot, 8 inches with three-inch heels and she had to look up at him. Even in his tailored suit, she could see he had a well-built body. Not exaggeratedly like the men with muscles screaming to get out, but certainly well defined. The funny thing was she was not supposed to be there, or maybe as fate would have it, it's exactly where she was suppose to be.

Tracy, her partner, prepared a bid for Next Level Consulting Firm, to be considered for an organizational efficiency project. The deadline for the submission was 5 o'clock that day. This was a State contract and Tracy wanted to make sure the proposal was in the proper hands. Instead of using a carrier, Ashley volunteered to deliver it to the name listed on the advertisement in person. When she entered the building, there were groups of people standing at the receptionist desk in the midst of a conversation. Ashley could not help but notice the handsome brother that stood out from the rest. He smiled and continued with his conversation. Unfortunately, she did not have time to get her "game" on. Tracy had entrusted her to deliver the package that could kick the company into another level of success and she was not going to let her down. Ashley politely smiled and turned to the receptionist. She explained she was there to submit the proposal to a Mr. James Brooks and asked if she could deliver it personally. The receptionist began to response when the gentleman she noticed a moment before stepped over and introduced himself, "Hello, I'm James Brooks; how may I help you?" Ashley thought she was going to die the moment she heard the deep rich voice. From that moment on she began imagining waking up every morning to that voice. Ashley smiled as she remembered the way she pondered over that man for weeks.

"Are you going to join me or just stand there watching?" James asked, breaking into the memories flowing through her mind. James sat up on the edge of the bed with the sheet still partially covering his body. She stepped back inside the room and slowly walked over to the bed and his outstretched hand, "I think I'll join you," she smiled as she knelt between his legs and kissed his chest. "I can't believe we have been inside this room for two days."

"Since this is our last day here, I say let's go for three" he growled kissing the side of her neck.

She moaned as his kisses moved from her neck to the opening of his shirt, she was wearing. She held her neck back to allow him access to the center of her throat. He pulled her upwards until he was able to capture her nipple between his lips. Ashley held his head to her breast, increasing the pleasure of his lips. She stretched her back as he pulled her onto the bed allowing her to sit straddling him. He removed the sheet that covered his nakedness. Ashley looked downward then back up to his face smiling at the arousal she had ignited in him. "Well hello Mr. Brooks" she moaned as the tip of his desire slid easily into her moist fold.

She began to move slowly allowing her body to embrace all of him inside her, inch by inch, by inch. She eased down his shaft, loving the way he filled her. The two moved in a rhythmic pattern, slow and easy. Entering a place, which no other person could take either of them.

James lay back on the bed, carrying her with him. Ashley slowly rose bracing herself with her hands against his chest. Sitting straight up, she moved her body in a slow circular motion allow him to hit that spot; the one that could only be reached when he wa   ly embedded within her. Her nails dug into his chest as the tension   gan to soar closer to the fire that needed to be quenched.

He held her hips tightly as her movement began to intensify. The feel of her thighs pulsating against his, and experience of her surrounding him so completely, was sending indescribable pleasure through his entire body. However, he refused to surrender to it. His reward for his patience was the expression on her face as she climbed closer to her release. Feeling the end coming near, James sat up to close the space between them. One hand held her hips merged with his, while the other moved up her back to her shoulders pulling their bodies together so close it was as if they were one. Ashley's arms circled his neck holding on. Her head fell backwards as their bodies moved as one traveling towards the destination of ecstasy.

There it was! Her explosion so deep it reached the core of him causing a chain reaction. He lifted her body up and slammed her back down again. James lips went to the base of Ashley's throat as a scream escaped them simultaneously, each calling out the other's name.

They sat there holding each other, his arms wrapped around her body and her legs wrapped around his. Ashley placed her head on his shoulders and he held her protectively as perspiration from their bodies dripped down his chest and between her breasts and the juices from their mating flowed between their legs. Minutes ticked away on the clock before either of them could safely speak.

Once her mind cleared and her heart stopped racing, Ashley exhaled, "I think we better leave this room before one of us dies of exhaustion."

James caressed her back and kissed the top of her shoulders, "If it's my time to go, this is exactly the way I would want my life to end" he smiled still nestled inside of her.

Ashley's hand absent-mindedly traced the muscles of his arms, "I love the feel of your hands on my body," she said almost in a whisper. "I love the feel of you inside of me. And I love you James Brooks." When James did not respond, her hand stopped tracing his arm. She raised her head from his shoulder and began to pull away. "I'll go take a shower now," she said, hurt by his lack of a response.

James held her in place with one hand and turned her face to him with the other. He looked into her eyes and she could see the love there. He leaned his forehead against hers and gently kissed her, "Ashley," he whispered as he closed his eyes.

Ashley waited for the words, but they never came. She cupped his face in her hands and kissed his forehead. He wasn't ready, she thought to herself, but, one day she will hear those words she longed for from him. "Would you like to join me?" she smiled.

"I'll be there in a minute," he replied. He watched as Ashley walked into the bathroom and closed the door. He lay back on the bed and closed his eyes. The disappointed look in her eyes tugged at the heart of him. But he had to protect his heart. He survived the damage his ex-wife caused, but swore he would never allow another woman to have that much power over his heart again.

James stood, and walked over to the bathroom door. He slowly pushed it open and watched Ashley as she showered. Exhaling, he acknowledged the fact he could not imagine a day of his life without her in it. She crept into his life unexpectedly with her zest for true love and happiness. Reflecting on the last year, he began to feel alive the moment he met her.

Standing in the lobby of the Department of Special Service, an agency he was commissioned by the Governor to lead, he overheard his name from the woman with the gorgeous legs that seemed to go on forever. He stepped over to the receptionist's desk and introduced himself. The woman was young, attractive and feisty as hell, not at all the type of woman for his conservative taste, but certainly one that was hard not to notice. He accepted the proposal and took it home with him that night to review.

The proposal for change was nothing short of ingenious, and captured his attention immediately. He pulled up the web site listed on the document and reviewed the bio of the two owners. The first thing he noticed was both women were very attractive and very young. Ashley was clearly the most noticeable and the oldest at twenty-five. The other, Tracy Washington, was twenty-four and was the founder of the company that was started during their junior year in college. He looked at the proposal on his desk, then back at the computer screen. He decided someone else had to have prepared the proposal. It was too in-depth to have come from either of the two young women on the screen.

The next morning he asked his secretary to set up a meeting with the representative from Next Level Consulting. The only time he was free was after business hours; therefore a dinner meeting was set.

When Ashley strolled into the restaurant wearing a black cocktail dress that revealed a very trim, shapely body and those beautifully shaped long legs, James immediately regretted the dinner meeting. His mind wondered to her body, rather than the business at hand. Fortunately, James learned the hard way that physical attraction fades. It was better to concentrate on the mind.

They discussed the proposal and the details of the contract. During which time James discovered Ashley was not the mastermind that designed the proposal. She presented it well and in a smooth manner that let him know she was more then capable of handling herself in the professional world. Experience had taught him that beauty was not the most important asset to a woman. Ashley certainly stimulated his body, but he needed someone who could stimulate his mind as well. He ordered his body to ignore the attraction.

James later realized Ashley was not going to be ignored. Repeatedly they found themselves present at several public functions. Ashley did not have a problem expressing her interest in him. Soon she began inviting herself along to events they would both be attending. "We are both going to be there, so we might as well be there together," she would say. The professional relationship turned into a personal one before he realized it was happening. He began to enjoy the attention from her and found he missed it once it stopped.

He found there was a lot more to Ashley Harrison than just her apparent beauty; she was sassy as hell. She had no problem speaking her mind. At times, he never knew what might come out of her mouth. She had a way with people that made them feel like they were somebody special to her all the time. She made him smile inside and out. Ashley had a love for life and family that he had lost, thanks to his ex-wife. Being around her made him look forward to the next day and definitely nights. However, it also made him long for the family life he had exiled himself from years ago.

"Are you going to stand there gawking or are you going to join me?" Ashley asked from the shower door. James smiled as he closed out the memories and joined her in the shower. He conceded, he cared deeply for her, but that was as far as he would let it go.